N. C. SCRII

CW00351953

SEA OF SOULS

Contents

Selkie (noun): A mythological creature that takes the form of a seal in the water but is capable of shedding its pelt to resemble a human on land

SILVECKAN

The Drift

Cape Dromair

The Wilds

Blackwood Estate

Kinraith

Caolaig

Tarmouth

The Teeth

Pencairn

Corran Narrows

Isle of Corran

Arburgh

Mairburn

Twaloch

Pronunciation Guide and Glossary

Persons of note

Isla Blackwood [EYE-lah]

Catriona Blackwood [kat-REE-nah]

Cormick Blackwood [CORR-mick]

Darce Galbraith [DARSS gahl-BRAYTHE]

Eimhir [AE-veer – 'ae' rhymes with 'stay']

Finlay [FINN-lay]

Lachlan Blackwood [LOCH-linn – soft 'ch' sound, known as a voiceless velar fricative]

Nathair Quinn [NAH-hir]

Nishi [NIH-shee]

Locations of note

Adrenian Sea [add-REEN-ee-inn]

Arburgh [ARR-bruh]

Breçhon [BRAY-shon]

Caolaig [CULL-aeg - 'ae' rhymes with 'stay']

Kinraith [kin-RAYTHE]

Silveckan [sill-VECK-an]

Vesnia [VEZ-nee-ah]

Animals and creatures

Brollachan [BROLLA-chan – soft 'ch'] – a shapeless, malevolent spirit that haunts the Wilds seeking unsuspecting bodies to possess

Cirein-cròin [KEE-rin CROW-inn] – a legendary sea monster once rumoured to roam the Silvish coast

Cù-sìth [coo-SHEE] – a dark, demonic hound found in the Wilds. Legend says those who hear its howl thrice will become paralysed with terror

Gun-anam [GOON-ann-AHM] – soulless spirits of slain selkies

Kelpie [KELL-pay] – an undead water horse made from salt and spray

Selkie [SELL-kay] – a seal shapeshifter which can shed its pelt and take the form of a human

General terms

Auld [AWL-d] – old

Bairn [bay-rne] – a young child

Burl [burrl] – to spin around

Burr [burr] – common Silvish accent, with rolled 'r' sounds

Caraid [CARR-itch] – friend

Close [cloa-ss] – a small alley or street

Dreich [DREE-ch – soft 'ch'] – dreary, grey weather

Firth [firth] – an inlet or estuary leading to the sea

Laird [LAY-rd] – lord

Loch [soft 'ch'] – lake or sea inlet

Machair [MACH-irr – soft 'ch'] – a grassy plain

Scunnered [SCUNN-nirrd] – irritated, annoyed

Samhain [SAH-win] – autumn harvest festival

Skerry – [SKERR-ee] – a small, rocky island

Sgian dubh [SKEE-an DOO] – a small ceremonial blade or knife

Wee [wee] – small

Wynd [wine-d] – a small alley or street

PROLOGUE

Dark be the water, and darker still the creatures that lurk within.

No matter how many times the old seadog pushed away from port, he never forgot the truth of those words. Ask any sailor worth their salt and they'd say the same: the open water with all its swells and storms wasn't half as dangerous as what was beneath it. He'd learned to live with the fear, but it never went away. It remained a cold whisper at the back of his skull, reminding him what dwelt out there.

Tonight, the late-summer sea lay flat and still, and the stars glinted bright and clear. The seadog knew better than to trust favourable weather and a sturdy hull to keep him safe. He knew how quickly the fickle wind could turn. But for now, the crossing was smooth, and he allowed himself to dream of home.

By the time he realised his mistake, it was already too late.

It was a sailor's superstition, and an old one at that, but it had stuck with him. He should have known better than to think of home before Silveckan's shoreline was in sight. It was too much like tempting fate, daring the terrors in the depths to stop him reaching port.

Dark be the water, and darker still the creatures that lurk within. He knew those creatures well. They left nothing in their wake but a ship's carcass and the bloated bodies of those lucky enough not to be dragged to the depths.

Aye, the old seadog should have known better than to believe nothing more than waves would come knocking at the hull.

The first sign was the change in the wind. It was too quick, too deliberate. It sent a troubling chill through his bones, cold enough to make his remaining teeth chatter. The flag thumped in protest at the top of the mast, billowing in on itself before unfurling in the opposite direction. In the moment it took him to regret his fleeting thoughts of home, everything changed.

His eyes were weary, but he could still make out the shift on the horizon. A curtain of rain crawled towards the ship, blocking out the stars. As he watched, it grew, stretching across the hazy line between sky and sea.

The roar of thousands of droplets thundered across the water, bouncing off the waves until all at once they hit the deck. The seadog's ears rang with the pattering as the crew screamed orders back and forth, their cries devoured by the howling of the wind.

Running would not save them. His folly had made certain of that.

He peered into the water. The waves leapt angrily, throwing themselves into the hull as if the ship had somehow scorned them. The water was black under the pall of storm clouds, the tips of the waves frothing like the jaws of a rabid animal. They had no port to make berth in, no weapons to defend against what was coming. Not even a sentinel could save them now, even if they'd been so lucky to have one aboard.

Beneath him, the hull creaked and groaned. It had begun.

The seadog stood on the deck, the biting wind reddening his face and freezing the coarse grey whiskers on his cheeks. He looked out at the water on which he'd spent so much of his life. The water he'd known could claim him any time it wanted. It might have been a comfort to him, like being reunited with an old friend, were it not for what lurked underneath.

The ship had already begun to surrender to the storm's fury. The crunch of timber filled his ears as the deck splintered and pools of dark water seeped in around his ankles. Long, lithe shadows shot past beneath the waves, circling the drifting carcass of the ship.

The water was at his waist. It wouldn't be long now.

If there were screams amongst the wind, he couldn't hear them. Nobody could hear them, not here, so far from the haven of dry land.

The shadows slunk closer. Their prize was within reach. The seadog looked around, the icy water lapping at his chin, and saw the last of his crew disappearing one by one beneath the waves.

The creatures would show no mercy. It was not in a selkie's nature to show mercy.

At long last, a strong pair of jaws closed around his ankle, crunching through flesh and bone. The old seadog drew a final breath and filled his head with thoughts of the shoreline he'd recklessly yearned for, the shoreline he'd never see again.

The surface vanished. Salty water filled his lungs. He thrashed, then fell still, and the black depths swallowed him whole.

CHAPTER ONE

Seven years ago, the sea called to Isla Blackwood, and she answered.

It shamed her to admit it, but leaving Silveckan's shores was the easiest decision she'd ever made. She'd gulped down the breeze, filling her lungs with salty air, relishing the sharpness of it. She'd tasted the spray on her lips and swallowed it along with the promise of the horizon. The promise of something out of reach, waiting for her to claim it.

On any other day, the memory might have made her smile. The way she'd cast off adolescence like a set of old furs she no longer needed. The way she'd swept up the gangway onto the deck as if whisked there by the bitter, burlin' wind that came in from the east that morning. The way she'd looked out over the waves to the edge of the world and thought to herself, *Aye, this is where I'm meant to be.*

But Isla couldn't smile. Not today. She held a crumpled letter in her fist, its words burning like a brand against her palm. The ink had long since smudged; her compulsive opening and scrunching of the parchment had left it a tattered, wretched thing. Each time she peeled back the folds, she hoped the letters might have changed, as if by some impossible magic they'd rewritten themselves into sentences free from the pain they held. Each time, Isla was left disappointed. Even with the ink bleeding and blotched, she knew the words contained within. She'd committed them to memory, every hopeless scribble.

The sickness has taken root again, her mother had written. *I'm afraid this time it is entrenched too deep for the doctors to dig out. My only wish, dear Isla, is for you to return. I won't ask you to remain forever; that is an anchor I will never burden you with again. All I want is to see you one last time before this affliction takes me. There is something I must tell you, something I should have told you long ago, and it requires words a quill cannot do justice to. Come home, my child. Allow me to give you the gift I have kept from you for too long, before it is too late for us both.*

The letter had been waiting for her the last time the *Ondasta* docked. Isla didn't know how long the dispatch lad had been carrying it, waiting for the winds to bring them back to port so he might pass it on for a handful of copper coins. All she knew was by the time it reached her hands, it was already too late.

"You look troubled, my friend." Lucrezia joined her on the quarter-deck, a pewter tankard in her hand. "Is it the weather? I never knew the air could get so cold while staying so damp. Here, take this. It will warm you up, if nothing else."

Isla brought the tankard to her lips, bracing herself for the stale tang of whatever ale Lucrezia had dug up. She took a sip, surprised to find the liquid oaked and pleasantly smooth, a far cry from the swill the bosun usually brought her. "Is this *wine*? Cap'n will have your head if you pinched this from the stores, Luc."

"Not just any wine." A gleam of mischief brightened Lucrezia's eyes. "A vintage from Bréçhon, no less. Oh, wipe that horror off your face, will you? It was the captain's idea. Call it a parting gift."

The gesture was a kind one, not to mention expensive. Isla should have been able to muster some semblance of gratitude for it. But Lucrezia's casual uttering of *parting gift* sent a pang of resentment through her, as sharp and swift as a blade between the ribs. For the first time in seven years, the tides were carrying her towards Silveckan. Towards home, whatever that meant now. All because of the ink-stained piece of parchment enclosed in her fist. A summoning Isla would never—*could*

5

never—have ignored.

A summoning she was already too late for.

Lucrezia must have noticed the look cross her face, for her expression quickly sobered. "We're making good time. As long as the winds stay with us, I'm sure we'll—"

"No," Isla said. "We won't."

The night was clear, with no mists or clouds to obscure the constellations mapping the skies above. But the stars were not the only lights in the darkness. Isla had spotted something in the distance—a faint glow above the choppy waters, sending shattered reflections dancing across the waves. An orb of light hovered there, flickering and ethereal, bobbing like the sea beneath it.

Lucrezia followed her gaze, her brows knitting together. "What *is* that?"

"A spirit," Isla replied, her voice scratching. "There are many names for it, but in common Silvish, it's known as a will-o'-the-wisp."

"Is it dangerous?"

"Depends who you ask. Some say it lures unsuspecting travellers to untimely deaths, that it pulls captains off their course and dashes their ships against the rocks. Others say they're an omen. The light from a soul extinguished in the mortal world."

"You don't think..." Lucrezia paled. "Isla, you can't believe this has anything to do with your mother."

Isla took another long sip of wine, relishing the warmth spreading through her chest and the light haze clouding her head. The will-o'-the-wisp drifted in the breeze, its ghostly light so faint Isla thought it might disappear the next time she blinked. Perhaps she could fool herself into believing it was a trick of the light, an unnatural reflection of the moon bouncing off the waves. Perhaps she would sail into Caolaig in the morning and find her mother as she remembered her from all those years ago—rosy-cheeked and high-spirited, whirling from room to room as if carried by a wild wind.

Still, the will-o'-the-wisp lingered, its pale light fading and brightening like the rhythm of a harbour torch. She couldn't deny what it was, or the message it brought her. Silveckan was an old land filled with old magic. If this was how her island saw fit to welcome her home, she would be foolish to ignore it.

Isla glanced at Lucrezia. The bosun's eyes were full of pity. Isla didn't need pity. She needed the winds to unfurl and whisk them back to a time before the dispatch lad pressed that wretched parchment into her hand. She needed the *Ondasta* to skip over the waves and arrive in port yesterday. She needed the impossible.

"My mother is dead," Isla said, and dumped the rest of her tankard into the churning waters below.

The next morning, Isla woke to the sound of rain. It pattered off the deck above her cabin, rousing her from sleep with the steady rhythm. By the time she pulled on her boots and climbed the ladder leading up from the crew quarters, the deck had become slick and slippery underfoot. She worked her way towards the bow, steadying herself with a hand on the gunwale. If this was to be her last day on the *Ondasta*, she wouldn't tarnish it with a careless fall.

A drizzly veil hung from the clouds, obscuring Silveckan's coast in the distance. If the will-o'-the-wisp hadn't been enough of a sign she was home, the weather had made certain of it. Damp and dreich, with a chill in the air that seeped through her skin. A cold reminder of what she was coming back to.

"So *this* is Silveckan." Lucrezia appeared beside her with a look of bemusement. "I certainly see why you've never been tempted to return before now."

"You should see it in the winter."

7

"I'd rather not." Lucrezia shuddered. "The sooner we're back in the Adrenian Sea, the better. There's something in the air here that makes me wonder if I'll ever feel warm again."

Isla didn't say anything. She'd already felt the change as the island loomed ever nearer. The golden colouring that Vesnia's sun had kissed her with had long since faded during the crossing; her skin had turned bone-pale once more, so leached of colour she could see the blue-green webbing of her veins underneath. The wind had bitten her lips dry, leaving them sore and starting to crack. She hadn't even stepped ashore and already Silveckan was laying claim to her, leaving its mark across her skin.

"We should head to the aft deck," Lucrezia said. "Captain says your village port is too small for the *Ondasta* to dock in, so she's sending us over in the tender."

"You're coming too?"

Lucrezia shrugged, a small smile spreading across her lips. "Someone has to take the tender back, don't they? I suppose you'll have to bear my company a little longer."

A bittersweet swell of emotion rose in Isla's chest as she said her farewells to the captain and crew. The *Ondasta* had been her home these last few years. The ship had taken her to ports across the breadth of the Adrenian coast, to places she'd never imagined. She'd slept in the wooden belly of its hull, climbed its proud rigging, examined navigational charts under the moonlight on deck. It had promised her more than the still, unchanging stone of her family's coastal estate ever could. It had carried her towards the piece of herself that had always been missing, lingering just out of reach. The piece of herself that, after seven years at sea, she'd still been unable to find.

Now, it carried her back to Silveckan. As much as she loved the *Ondasta*, Isla couldn't help but resent it a little for that.

The tender skimmed easily across the waves towards Caolaig's main jetty. The rain thinned into a light drizzle, misting Isla's face and clinging to the loose strands of her braid. She could see the cliffs now; they rose from the water in pillars of grey, speckled by scores of seabirds nesting in their crooks and crevices. Snow-white gannets and bright-beaked puffins cawed and chattered across the breeze, heralding them to shore. Below them, the waves dashed against the surrounding sea stacks in a gentle roar, the sound sending a shiver skittering down Isla's spine.

That was when she saw it. The selkie.

Isla instinctively signed a ward of protection. An old habit, one steeped more in superstition than any practical use. She was no sentinel. The tides-gifted magic didn't run through her blood, no matter how many years she'd spent wishing it did. She couldn't cast an enchantment to stop the creature in its tracks or summon the waves to take them to safety. If the selkie attacked the tender, only a blade or a well-placed shot would stop it.

But the beast didn't move. It lay on a rock, its dappled grey-and-black fur damp from the spray, its flippers splayed out beneath the curve of its belly. It stared at her with beady eyes, its long whiskers flicking as it bared the pink of its mouth in a wide yawn.

Isla released a breath and allowed her shoulders to loosen. It was a common harbour seal, nothing more. The animal basked on the rock in plain sight, too brazen to be one of the skinchangers. Selkies hunted in packs, lurking in the cloak of mists or the chaos of a storm. On land, they shed their pelts and struck from the darkness, never revealing themselves until it was too late. They were too cautious—too cunning—to risk themselves in the open like the creatures they masqueraded as.

Still, Isla couldn't help the touch of dread wrapping its fingers around her heart. She was no stranger to monsters. The *Ondasta* was the pride of the Vesnian Tidesguard, protecting the Adrenian coastline from the dangers of the deep—storm harpies, sea serpents, a nasty infestation of sirens one summer. But nothing chilled her skin like the things that lurked in the waters of home. It was easy to forget the prickle of fear out in the warmth of the Adrenian Sea. Now, she no longer had that luxury.

9

"Approaching our mooring," Lucrezia called, picking up a thick length of rope and positioning herself at the edge of the tender. She slung a loop towards the dock, coiling it around the iron cleat and pulling them in close. As soon as the hull brushed against the jetty, Lucrezia hopped out, grunting as she worked the rope back and forth to secure a well-formed knot.

Isla followed, accepting her hand as the bosun helped her onto the slippery wooden surface of the jetty. "I'll miss you, Luc."

"Of course you will." Lucrezia snorted and pushed her hair from her eyes. "You've never worked with a better bosun, nor are you likely to."

"Ever the braggart."

"Ever honest is what I say." Lucrezia flashed a wide grin. "For what it's worth, I'll miss you too. You've been a good navigator, but an even better friend. Replacing one of those things is considerably easier to do than the other. Speaking of which..." She jumped into the tender, rummaging for a small lockbox stowed under the bench. "I have something for you. Seemed only right you had one of your own after all we've been through."

Isla took the wooden box in her hands and snapped open the clasps on the side. The lid slid back with a push of her thumbs. Inside, nestled in a simple white cloth, was the most beautiful pistol Isla had ever seen. The curved stock was a deep mahogany set with mother-of-pearl plating, and the silver metal of the barrel was etched with an intricate, swirling pattern, glinting in the dull light.

Isla brushed her fingers over it. "Luc, I can't accept this. This is the pistol the cap'n gave you when she made you bosun."

"And now I'm giving it to you." Lucrezia folded her arms. "I'd feel better knowing you had it. If you don't have your crew to protect you anymore, this will do the job instead. Or do you want all those lessons to go to waste?"

Isla lifted the pistol from the box. It smelled faintly of black powder, and the stock felt warm despite the dampness in the air, as if Lucrezia's grip still lingered around it. The curve fit Isla's hand like it was meant to be there as she brushed her thumb over the smooth, polished wood.

"Thank you," she said, fixing Lucrezia with a solemn gaze. "For everything."

Lucrezia pulled her into a fierce hug and pressed a kiss against her cheek. "Use it well, though I pray you'll never need to." She let go of Isla's arms, her smile painfully wide across her face. "Goodbye, my friend. What is it you say in Silvish? If tides be kind, we'll see each other again."

"If tides be kind," Isla echoed. She stowed the pistol and lockbox in her pack and watched from the jetty as the tender slipped away. The rain picked up again, pockmarking the waves with ripples. She could barely make out the *Ondasta's* dark silhouette through the downpour. She wouldn't see it weigh anchor and fill its sails. She wouldn't see the retreating stern as it diminished in the distance.

Though if the wrench of pain in her chest was anything to go by, perhaps that was for the best.

After a while, Isla tore her eyes from the end of the jetty and walked towards the harbourfront. Caolaig hadn't changed much in the years she'd been gone. The small fishing village bustled with activity, awash with sounds so painfully familiar that Isla almost forgot how long she'd gone without hearing them. The scraping of wooden langoustine creels being piled up and emptied, water dripping from the rope netting. The frantic Silvish spoken back and forth between the fishers and the market merchants, the language soft and rhotic compared to the Vesnian dialects Isla had grown accustomed to. The mewling cries from the seabirds circling overhead, waiting to swoop down on any scraps that had carelessly fallen.

Nobody recognised her as she traipsed through the centre of the village, her pack heavy on her shoulder. Not that Isla was particularly disappointed—or surprised. She'd been a lassie of only eighteen when she'd left, and life on the open water had changed her as much as the passing years. The scorching sun left her with smattered freckles across her forehead and the bridge of her nose, lingering as her skin paled. Her cheeks were thinner than they used to be, her limbs lean and wiry after seven years of hard work and modest ship rations. If her less-than-refined appearance made it easier to avoid questions from well-meaning locals, all the better.

Isla lifted her gaze to the steep green-and-grey face of the surrounding crags. The rough-cut steps carved into the cliffside led to a winding coastal path that would take her to the summit. To Blackwood Estate.

She began the climb. The trail wound up the cliffs, the grass soon giving way to rocks and stones, as if the green skin were peeling back to reveal ancient bones beneath. The memory of the wisp seemed distant now, like a dream fading with the light of dawn. Maybe it hadn't been an omen after all. Maybe it was by unhappy chance that a ghost-light had found itself blown out to sea. It didn't mean her mother was dead. It didn't mean...

"Isla? Is that you?"

She looked up at the voice. The man in front of her could have been a stranger. Long gone were the scrawny shoulders and awkward posture of the fifteen-year-old brother she'd left behind. Lachlan Blackwood had sprouted tall and grown into the chiselled edge of his jawline, the sharp ridge of his nose. When he saw her, his tawny eyes brightened, and Isla caught a glimpse of the boy she'd chased and scrapped with and tormented with forbidden bedtime stories of howling cù-sìth and shadowy brollachan.

Then grief twisted his expression, and it was all she needed to know.

"I came as soon as I saw the sails," Lachlan said, his voice tight. "I've never seen a ship that size this far north. I expected you'd make berth in Arburgh and charter a fishing boat to bring you home."

"The cap'n is a kind sort. I've worked hard for her over these last few years, and she granted me a favour." Isla broke off, her throat thickening. "When I received the letter, she... I mean, I tried to..."

Lachlan dropped his head, his eyes glittering, and Isla's heart shattered.

"I'm sorry," she whispered. "I was too late."

Lachlan hesitated, then stepped forward, wrapping his arms around her and pulling her into the shelter of his chest. It was a gesture neither of them knew how to lean into, one missing years of practice, and Isla couldn't help but hate herself a little for it. Everything about her brother was new and unfamiliar. The short, pushed-back crop of golden hair, no longer sleek and braided. The faded white scar down the side of his chin. Her memories of him scattered with the next gust of wind, and all she was left with was a man she'd missed the chance to know.

"Are you staying?" Lachlan pulled back, fixing her with a pointed look she remembered all too well.

It was the worst thing he could have asked. A thousand excuses and explanations dried up on Isla's tongue, leaving her with no words to offer. She didn't know the answer. All she had was a scrunched piece of parchment that had called her back when nothing else could.

The worst part wasn't that she only had herself to blame; it was that she'd do it all over again. Nothing could have stopped her getting on that ship seven years ago. It was only now she was back that she realised how much of a betrayal that might have been to the brother she'd left behind.

Lachlan looked away. The corner of his mouth pulled into a strained smile, and he placed a gentle kiss on the top of her forehead. "Forget I asked. It doesn't matter. I'm just glad you're home, Isla."

"Me too," she managed, the lie burning her throat on the way out.

After all, if this was home, why had it always felt so wrong to be here?

CHAPTER TWO

Lady Catriona Blackwood looked regal even in death. Something in the lines and creases of her pale skin, in the proud stiffness of her jaw, made her seem like she'd been carved from stone. Isla half wondered if it was truly her mother in the coffin and not some monument they'd chosen to bury in her place. It was difficult to reconcile the wide smile and sparkling eyes of the woman she remembered with the cold, unyielding features of the one before her now. Nothing—not even her mother's face, it seemed—was as she'd left it.

The rain eased off when the time came for the casket to be lowered into the ground. The clouds still hung dense and grey like a shroud over the estate, but if Isla squinted, she could make out patches of blue. It wasn't quite sunlight, but perhaps that was beyond what any of them could have hoped for.

Laird Cormick buried his hand in a crumbling mound of soil and scattered it over the casket, his lips moving in a murmured litany. Lachlan stood beside him, almost his father's height, and carefully gathered his own handful of wet earth with trembling hands.

Isla's stomach lurched at the sight of them. Her looks favoured her mother; she had the same tangle of sable-toned hair, the same sea-green eyes. Watching her father and brother with their fair features and golden hair was like staring into a painting that didn't include her, a place she didn't belong. An anxious flutter rose in her chest. She wanted to run.

She wanted to board another ship and never look back. Tides take her, what was she *doing* here? What right did she have to pretend she was part of this after being away for so long?

Her father beckoned her over. "It's your turn," he said, squeezing her shoulder.

Isla nodded, throat too tight to reply. She pressed her hand into the soil, the clumps sliding under her fingernails. Her other hand was deep in the folds of her cloak, clenched around the remains of Lady Catriona's letter.

There is something I must tell you, something I should have told you long ago, and it requires words a quill cannot do justice to. Come home, my child. Allow me to give you the gift I have kept from you for too long, before it is too late for us both.

The coffin blurred in front of Isla's eyes. She was too late. In every way that mattered, she was too late. She'd never again see her mother's eyes brighten at the first bluebells sprouting in the woods each spring. Never again hear the smooth, measured timbre of her voice as she settled an argument. Never again hold her close and smell the fragrance from the gardens clinging to her skin—peppermint and lavender and wild garlic.

And she'd never get the chance to ask her what she'd meant by the words in her letter.

Isla squeezed the parchment, its tattered edges digging into her palm, and cast the soil from her other hand across the coffin. It hit the lid with a dull thud, laden with a terrible finality.

"Goodbye, Mother," she whispered. "May the tides carry you to fairer seas."

The skirl of bagpipes carried across the breeze as the rest of the gathered mourners said their farewells. Isla recognised a few of them: the estate's blacksmith, the innkeeper from Caolaig's tavern, some of the older fishers, their beards grizzled and skin weathered. Lady Catriona had been loved and respected. The village folk knew her well—better, perhaps, than Isla did these past few years.

After a time, only she, Lachlan and their father remained. The three of them stood at the grave, their shared grief thick in the air between them. Isla looked down at the hole in the ground that had swallowed the coffin, and with it, the last traces of her mother.

"She'd have been glad you were here for this." Cormick turned his head towards her, his eyes understanding even in their sorrow. "The sickness... It spread quickly. Truth be told, I feared my letter wouldn't reach you in time."

Isla startled. "It didn't. The only letter I received was from Mother herself. You didn't know she'd written to me?"

Her father's face paled. "No, I didn't. I suppose she must have sensed what was coming and slipped a missive out with one of her attendants. Whatever her reasons were, I'm glad she did. I'm glad her words brought you back to us in time to say goodbye."

Isla tightened her grip on the crumpled letter in her cloak. "Her words...were not what I expected. She spoke of a matter she had to tell me in person, something a quill and parchment were not enough to convey."

"She made no mention of anything like that to me." Cormick furrowed his brow. "Perhaps she wanted the chance to set things right between you both. I know she regretted trying to keep you from leaving. She spoke often of it, of the way you parted."

"It wasn't about that." Isla expected the old bitterness to rise in her throat, but all she tasted on her tongue was guilt and regret. "I had the feeling it was something about me. She spoke of a gift."

"A gift?" A thoughtful look passed across her father's face. "Well, of course. As firstborn, Blackwood Estate is your birthright. I imagine she wanted to prepare you for the duties that would fall to you, the responsibilities that running the estate entails."

"But I don't..." Isla glanced at Lachlan. Her brother stared off into the distance, his expression wooden. "She knew how I felt about the estate. This was something else, I know it."

Cormick put his arm around her shoulder and pulled her close, ruffling her hair with one hand. "Allow me to reflect on it, and perhaps something will come to me. Right now, my mind is besieged by sorrow. It's difficult to think of much else but your mother and the hole she leaves behind in all of us."

"Of course." Shame rushed to Isla's cheeks. "I shouldn't have said... I didn't mean—"

"You and your brother should head back to the manor and get ready for this evening," Cormick said, his smile strained. "This feast is in your mother's honour, and I know she would want you both in your finest attire. Let's make her proud, shall we?"

Isla pressed her lips together and nodded tightly, falling into step beside Lachlan as he started across the grounds. The wail of bagpipes faded into the distance, leaving them in an uneasy silence neither of them dared to break.

She opened her mouth, then pinched it shut again. Tides, it never used to be this difficult. There was a time she'd have known what to say to scatter this tension between them. How was it she could navigate the Adrenian Sea with nothing but the stars to guide her, but was unable to find her way across this uncharted ground she and her brother stood on? How had everything changed so much?

Lachlan cast her a sideways glance. "I hadn't considered that as you returned, so would your shadow. I'd forgotten what its shade felt like."

Isla flinched. Maybe things hadn't changed at all. "If this is about the estate, I assure you, my feelings on the matter remain the same as they were seven years ago. Birthright or not, I've no intention of claiming it. That burden is all yours, wee brother."

"It's not about the estate." Lachlan shook his head. "This letter, the one Mother sent you in secret... That's the real reason you came back, isn't it? Don't deny it," he added, when Isla tried to protest. "It might have been seven years, but I still know you well enough to catch you in a lie."

"I came back because she asked me to. As for the rest, I..." Isla snapped her mouth shut. "You wouldn't understand."

"I was fifteen when you left, not a wee lad who didn't know what was going on. I understood better than you think." His smile tightened. "Our home, our family, were never enough for you. There was always something missing, wasn't there? That's what you went searching for, and that's why you returned."

"I..." The words dried up in Isla's throat. "I didn't realise you saw so much."

Lachlan lowered his head. "I don't blame you for leaving. I know you needed to get out from under the weight of this place. But your absence left a wake in our family, a wake that took me years to pull myself free of. Now you're back, I fear I'll only be caught in its current once again."

"Lachlan—"

"I don't want to fight." He let out a long breath. "Truly, Isla. I'm glad you're here. I just didn't think it would change so much, so soon."

Me neither, Isla thought. Lachlan's words cut deep, paring down to the bone. How could he see into the heart of her so easily after so much time apart? It was like he knew exactly where to slide the blade to pierce at the truth she never wanted to admit, even to herself. There *was* something missing. There always had been. It was why she'd left. It was why she'd spent seven years out in the open waters searching for it.

It was why she'd returned to Silveckan.

Fresh shame welled in Isla's throat. She mourned her mother, of *course* she did. But more than that, she mourned the part of herself that might have died along with Lady Catriona. The part of herself that might now be forever beyond her reach.

Isla lifted her eyes towards the walled estate, taking in all the places she'd once called home. The lone windswept sentry tower, the thatched roof of the stables, the stone gargoyles along the length of the Auld Hall. They'd all belonged to her once. Why was it so difficult to believe they could again? Why was it so difficult to imagine rebuilding a life here?

"Home," she said to herself, and tried with all her heart to believe it.

Of all the things Isla found herself learning to navigate again, swapping her breeches and tunic for an elaborate gown was far from the most challenging. There was something rather nostalgic about slipping into the silky skin of the underdress and pulling it tight at the waist. She smoothed the skirts into place and whistled to herself as she fastened the delicate gauze overlay that swept across her shoulders and down the exposed skin of her arms.

When she caught her reflection in the mirror, she stilled. Staring back at her was the woman she'd left behind when she walked up that gangplank and sailed from shore. The woman she might have been, if only she'd stayed. Not a stranger, but someone who no longer existed.

Until now, at least.

Isla tore her eyes away and gathered her dress as she made her way towards the staircase leading to the Auld Hall. Her head spun with a thousand thoughts, each more dizzying than the last. She'd barely had time to breathe since returning—barely had time to *think*. All she wanted was for the night to be over so she might sink into the soft sheets of a proper bed and let the embrace of sleep wipe everything from her mind. In the morning, she could start anew. In the morning, she could decide her next steps. In the morning, she could—

"So, the guest of honour finally arrives. I see your timekeeping hasn't improved any since you've been away."

Isla snapped her head up. Standing at the entrance of the Auld Hall, his arm resting casually on the hilt of his rapier, was Darce Galbraith. He looked exactly how Isla remembered him—tall and lean, with pale skin and sharp features that gave him an unsettling air of intensity. He was clad in dark leather armour embossed with the Blackwood family sigil and wore a prickly expression Isla recalled only too well.

She stifled a groan. Of all the members of the Blackwood Watch she could have run into, of course it had to be him. Her father's personal swordmaster and loyal bodyguard. But before that, he'd been the young squire once tasked with the impossible duty of keeping an eye on her, thereby becoming the single greatest irritation of Isla's childhood.

And if she recalled correctly, the feeling was mutual.

Isla fought the urge to scowl, instead lowering her head into a stiff nod. "Sergeant Galbraith, it's been too long. I hope the years have been kind to you."

"Kind enough, aye."

As taciturn as ever, Isla thought. Darce had always been cold and grim, a glare from his dark brown eyes capable of turning her to stone. On more than one occasion, she'd overheard her mother's young attendants giggling behind their hands and calling him handsome, but Isla couldn't see it, not when he was so stern-faced all the time.

Then again, maybe that was only with her.

She cleared her throat. "If I'm late, what does that make you? Shouldn't you be inside watching over my father and brother in that hawklike manner of yours?"

"Your brother is exactly the reason I'm out here," Darce said flatly. "He's conspicuously absent, and I've been sent to make sure he's not got himself into some trouble I have to pull him out of."

Isla couldn't help but snort. "Such a fine use of your talents, Sergeant. I see now why my father keeps you around. Whatever would we do without someone to track down Lachlan when he's off chasing skirts?"

"Oh, he's well past chasing, and it's not just skirts anymore either," Darce said, the corner of his mouth twitching. "But the little laird is my problem to deal with. You'd best get in there before they send someone searching for you as well."

Before she could reply, Darce set off down the corridor, as menacing as a cù-sìth on the prowl. Isla spared a thought of pity for her unsuspecting brother, then pushed through the doors into the Auld Hall.

Laird Cormick sat at the top table, clad in mourning vestments, a chair empty on either side of him. Isla's heart lurched. Her father cut a lonely figure without Lady Catriona by his side. He seemed older, vulnerable in a way that made her chest seize.

When he saw her, he broke into a smile and waved her over, eyes shining. "At least one of my children made it this evening," he said, giving a good-natured chuckle. "You're a bonnie sight, Isla. Cat—your mother—she'd have been..." He trailed off, the words disappearing into the chatter of the hall.

Isla slid into the empty seat beside him and squeezed his hand. "She always did like an excuse to put on her finery and empty the kitchens. We'll do her proud, like you said."

"Aye." Her father nodded, his smile trembling. "That we will."

The evening passed in a blur of food and wine, leaving Isla so full she feared the stitches of her dress might pop loose. Back on the *Ondasta*, a good meal meant a hearty serving of dried beans and salted beef, washed down with mead or grog or whatever swill Lucrezia had scrounged from their last port. Isla couldn't remember the last time she'd eaten like this. Fresh langoustines dripping with hot butter. Roasted grouse, tender and rich on a bed of sweet blackberries. Oysters too, not garnished with lemon and vinegar like in Vesnia, but fresh out of the shell, soft and slimy as she slurped them down with the briny juice. The Breçhon wine slipped down her throat too easily, filling her with comfort. It was almost enough to make her forget the whisper in the back of her head warning her that this was not enough, that it would *never* be enough.

Neither Lachlan nor Darce reappeared, and as Isla scanned the lengths of the tables, she noticed another prominent absence from the gathered nobles and village folk. "Our wayward uncle didn't make it up from Arburgh then?"

Cormick barked out a scornful laugh. "Muir? He'd have to haul himself out the bottom of a bottle first. The old sot hasn't left the capital in years, and if the death of his own sister isn't enough for him to pull his head out of his arse, I don't know that anything will be." He closed his eyes for a moment, then turned back to her, his face sombre. "Isla, I know you don't want to talk about it, but at some point we must discuss you taking over your mother's duties. Blackwood Estate will be yours one day, whether you like the idea or not. It's what Cat wished for you. *That's* the gift she wanted to give you, not some riddle in a letter. You have to understand..."

Isla pursed her lips as he trailed off, his eyes glazed and distant. Her father was drunk. She could smell the smoke and peat of whisky on his breath. If there was ever a time to have this conversation—and Isla wished there never would be—it certainly wasn't now. Not when their grief was still so raw. Not when slurred words might cut and sting and leave wounds they couldn't take back.

She pushed her chair out from the table, steadying herself against a rush of light-headedness from the wine. "Excuse me, but I need some air. I think a stroll around the gardens will do me some good, if I have your blessing to leave."

Cormick looked like he'd barely heard her. He waved his hand, releasing her with a dejected nod before returning to his glass. Isla stole one last look at him, her heart tight with shame and sorrow, then gathered her dress and hurried from the table as quickly as her unsteady legs would carry her.

She didn't stop at the gardens. She didn't stop at the estate's iron-wrought gates, either. She kept walking until the grounds were far behind, lost to the night.

The old coastal trail was a path Isla knew well, winding across the clifftops overlooking Caolaig. The village was quiet tonight. No laughter or music spilled out from the tavern below. No boats slipped in or out of the harbour. All Isla could hear were the sounds of the coast: the soft yawn of the waves lapping against the sea stacks, the whistle of the wind as it skimmed across the jagged rocks and steep green slopes, the night-time chatter of the storm petrels as they left their burrows to flit across the cliffside. It was peaceful. It was exactly what she needed.

She tucked her dress underneath her and sat in the damp grass, staring out across the glittering waves. The fresh air chased away her dizziness as she sucked in a deep breath, filling her lungs with cold relief. Somewhere across the water, far out of reach, the *Ondasta* was sailing back to Vesnia. Back to the land of crystal waters and beaches of black volcanic sand, of lemons and olives growing ripe on the vine. Its warmth was a distant memory. Silveckan's late-summer wind already had a bite to it, sinking its fangs into her skin with no promise of ever letting go. Now she was home, she feared no knowledge of stars or sextants or sea charts would ever be enough to escape again.

"Well, you're easier to track down than your brother, make no mistake."

Isla whirled around, heart racing. Darce Galbraith had slunk up on her without a sound. He towered over her with a dark frown, the faint glow of moonlight accentuating the angles of his jaw.

So much for peace.

"What are you doing here?" Isla asked stiffly. "Did my father send you?"

"Laird Cormick retired to his quarters some time ago, as you should have done," Darce replied. "I'm only here to make sure they don't find you washed up with the tides when the dawn comes."

"How considerate of you. Could it be you've actually grown fond of me after all these years?"

Darce grunted. "Fond of the coin your father pays me for keeping you out of trouble, more likely."

"And you do it with such charm and grace." Isla glanced up at him. The last time she'd seen the sergeant, he'd been only a little younger than she was now. Though seven years had passed, she couldn't deny he wore them well. His cheeks had lost some of their boyish youth with the coarse stubble shadowing them, and there were more creases around his eyes than she remembered, but the maturity suited him.

Darce caught her eye and smirked. "And you accuse me of having a hawklike manner. Something you want to say?"

Isla flushed, grateful for the darkness leaching the colour from their surroundings. "Just thinking how nice it was not to have your constant presence at my heels these last few years."

"You'll get used to it again, I'm sure. Tides know I'll have to."

Heat rose in Isla's chest. "I'd almost forgotten how much of an insufferable, arrogant—"

Darce chuckled. "Now there's the wolf cub I remember. Best I take my leave now, before your bark turns into a bite."

"A handful of insults is all it takes to get rid of you these days?" Isla arched an eyebrow, trying to hide her annoyance at the old childhood nickname. "If I'd known that, I'd have started much earlier."

Darce shrugged. "It seems I've found you clearheaded enough not to stumble off the edge of a cliff. I'll let you make your own way back this time." He adjusted the fur-lined cloak around his shoulders and turned towards the trail, the wind ruffling his tousled crop of black hair. "Though I'll remind you not to stay out too long. Dawn is only a few hours away."

Isla frowned. "What does dawn have to do with anything?"

"How many years has it been since you last drilled blades with someone who wasn't a sailor?" Darce tilted his head, fixing her with an appraising look. "As your father's swordmaster, it's my duty to ensure you haven't gone sloppy over the years. Now you're back, it only makes sense we resume your morning lessons."

Isla squirmed, the evening's indulgence of food and wine still resting heavily in her belly. "You can't possibly expect me to—"

"Dawn, Isla. Don't make me come looking for you."

He disappeared beneath the ridge of the winding trail, leaving her with nothing for company but the nip of the wind and the crashing of waves against the shore. The gloom seemed more ominous in the wake of Darce's words. She knew why they drilled blades. She hadn't forgotten the seal in the harbour. The creature might have been harmless on this occasion, but that wouldn't always be the case. Any bairn brought up along the coast heard stories of the horrors that emerged from the churning water. Horrors capable of shedding their sealskins and walking on two legs like any human.

Skinchangers. Seawalkers. Selkies. The Silvish tongue had many names for them, but none did justice to the sense of dread that accompanied every storm, every foul change in the weather. Even after seven years on the Adrenian Sea, Isla hadn't been able to shake the pinch of fear that came with rising winds and a darkening sky.

She sighed. Her solitude was of little comfort now. Whatever peace she'd come out here to find had fled with Darce's retreating footsteps. No matter where she turned, there was another reminder of the life she'd left behind. Another anchor intent on shackling her to shore.

For now, Isla thought, staring out over the black horizon. *Only for now.*

CHAPTER THREE

D ustings of pale pink and orange already streaked the sky by the
time Isla forced herself out of bed and into the crumpled, stale
clothes that had served her for the past few months on the *Ondasta*.
Tight-fitting breeches, a loose linen shirt and a sturdy pair of tanned
leather boots pulled up to her knees. Vestments she could move around
in. Vestments she could swing a sword in.

Or attempt to, at least.

She raced down the stairs two at a time and tore across the cobbled
courtyard. It was already past dawn. The unfamiliar softness of a proper
bed and the weighted comfort of cotton and furs had held her in a deep,
contented slumber far longer than she'd intended. Not even the intrusive
warbling of the starlings nesting in the eaves had been enough to rouse
her. She was late. And if Darce was in as stern a mood as he normally was,
Isla would pay for that mistake.

The dull, hollow clacking of whalebone sparring swords reached her
ears long before she rounded the archway leading into the training
grounds. The echo bounced off the inside of her skull like a hammer,
sharpening the throbbing pain in her temples. Tides, she was *not* ready
for this. Part of her wondered whether to risk turning around and retreating to the snug sanctuary of her bed. Then she remembered Darce's
warning.

Isla took a breath and squared her shoulders before marching determinedly into the enclosed yard that housed the training grounds. Darce was already there, of course. He stalked the yard, each step slow and purposeful. The decorative rapier he'd brandished on his belt the night before was nowhere to be seen; instead, he cut an impressive figure with the long, bone-edged blade of a claymore. He gripped the training sword easily in two hands as he circled his opponent, coiled and ready to strike.

It wasn't until then that Isla noticed Lachlan. The sight of him knocked her off balance at first—her brother had been more averse to Darce's morning drills than she was. On more than one occasion he'd been dragged out of hiding by Laird Cormick and flung into the yard, surly and disinterested as he threw half-hearted swings in an attempt to satisfy their father. Watching him now as he matched Darce's footsteps was another reminder of how much had changed.

Darce leapt forward, swinging with a speed that didn't seem possible. Lachlan blocked the blow and swiped with his sword, but Darce was too quick for him. He sidestepped, spinning on the balls of his feet and bringing his claymore to bear at Lachlan's back.

"Nice try," he said gruffly. "Might have worked better if your footwork didn't give you away with every step." He turned towards Isla, surveying her with narrowed eyes and pursed lips. "You're late."

Isla bristled. "Does it matter? It looks like you have enough to occupy your attention."

"I can make room for one more." The edge of his mouth twitched. "Unless last night's liquor has left you too delicate to pick up a sword?"

The chill of the morning breeze wasn't enough to temper the flush that rushed to Isla's cheeks. Her stomach was already churning, half from nerves, half from her overindulgence the previous evening. The pounding in her temples spread to the nape of her neck, swelling inside her skull like it was ready to burst. The last thing she wanted to do was pick up a sword, but worse would be to admit defeat.

She walked over to the weapons rack, selecting a lightweight wooden cutlass. The training sword was familiar enough in her grip, but she could count on one hand the number of times she'd swung a blade over the last seven years. "Surely it's too early in the morning for insults," she said. "Even for you."

Lachlan snorted. "Oh, he's already well warmed up when it comes to insults, believe me. What was it you said earlier, Galbraith? Something about having seen wilting thistles with more posture?"

"And more of a prick," Darce added. "But it was a fair assessment, little laird. You can't expect to survive a raid if you don't land a strike on the enemy, after all."

A shiver that had nothing to do with the crisp bite of the morning air raced down Isla's spine. The mention of raids brought back too many unwelcome memories. Retreating behind barred doors. Huddling in the lamplight with her mother, Lachlan sniffling between them. Never knowing when the door would open, and whether it would be the Blackwood Watch bringing news of safety or a selkie bearing down on them with bloodlust and death.

"What do you mean?" she asked, fighting to keep her voice steady. "Have the attacks grown worse?"

"Aye." Darce's eyes darkened. "They hit Caolaig last summer, but we took a force and drove them off before they spilled too much blood. Some of the smaller settlements haven't been so lucky. There aren't as many sentinels around these parts as there used to be."

A familiar tug of longing pulled tight in Isla's chest. Not for the first time, she imagined how it might feel to have the old magic sing in her blood, to be able to summon the waves and cast wards against the creatures that came from the water to kill them. The thought had been a comfort against a darkening sky and churning sea, no matter how fanciful and childish it seemed. No matter how many times it left her disappointed.

Lachlan shot Darce a stony look. "I still haven't forgiven you for not letting me join you that day. I may not be a sentinel or a swordmaster, but I could have helped."

"You're going to be a laird one day, and it's not a laird's job to fight off selkies," Darce said, giving him a friendly punch on the shoulder. "That's what your father pays expendable bastards like me for." He turned back to Isla. "Enough distractions. It's your turn. Time to see whether you remember anything I taught you."

Isla wrapped her fingers around the padded hilt of her cutlass. She fought to keep her breaths steady as her lungs begged for more air. It wasn't fear, not quite. She had no reason to fear Darce. But that didn't mean she was looking forward to this.

Darce lowered himself into a deep bow. Isla returned the motion with a stiff spine and wheeled around, ready to strike.

The next thing she knew, she was on the ground, her shoulder stinging from an invisible blow and her chest aching from where Darce had winded her with a kick too fast to avoid. She lay in the mud, dazed and disbelieving. Darce had closed the distance between them in the time it had taken her to draw breath. She hadn't the chance to raise her sword in defence.

She rolled over and pushed herself to her feet, the damp fabric of her shirt clinging to her skin. "I see we're skipping the basics this morning," she said, resetting her stance. "You couldn't have done me the courtesy of a warning, Sergeant?"

"Consider yourself warned." There was no humour in Darce's voice, only steel. "Now, let's try again."

He rushed towards her, but Isla was ready for him. She fended off the heavy blow with a snarl, her arms throbbing as the rattle of whalebone on wood jolted through her muscles. Before she had time to steady herself, Darce unleashed a sweeping strike that would have taken her legs out had she not leapt back in time.

"You're not as quick as you used to be," he remarked, eyeing her coolly. "I left myself open there—you should have pressed the advantage instead of scrambling away."

Isla scowled. "Are we here to talk, or are we here to fight? I didn't come here to listen to your endless disapproval."

"I don't think you've ever listened to my disapproval, no matter how warranted it was." A wry smile tugged at the corner of his mouth. "But if it's a fight you're after, I can oblige."

He pressed forward again, giving no quarter as he threw his weight behind another ferocious blow. It was all Isla could do to keep herself upright as she parried his sword. Darce wielded the two-handed claymore like it was a feather, bringing it down on her again and again with a speed and grace that should have been impossible for the size of the thing.

She let out a yelp as the whalebone blade clattered her knuckles, bursting the skin open and leaving her hands raw and bloodied. Her cutlass fell to the ground, and she stooped to pick it up without thinking, only to be met with the blunted edge of Darce's blade against the back of her neck.

"Careless," he said, his voice tight with displeasure. "Taking your eye off the enemy will get you killed."

Isla swatted his sword away, her cheeks burning as she forced herself to her feet for a second time. She felt Lachlan's eyes on her, though she didn't dare meet his gaze for fear of what she might find there. Satisfaction would sting enough, but pity would be worse.

She straightened her spine, readying her cutlass at her side, but Darce shook his head. "It's best we leave it there for today."

The resignation in his voice only stoked Isla's anger. "That's it? What happened to the feared swordmaster I remembered? Don't tell me the years have turned you soft."

"There's only so much disappointment I can take," Darce replied evenly. "As for turning soft, you might want to reflect on your own character before casting aspersions on mine. It seems all those years at sea have amounted to little more than a sloppy sword arm."

Isla charged at him, feinting one way then slashing towards his forearm. Darce stepped neatly out of reach, punishing her clumsy attempt with a swift, brutal blade between her shoulders. Even with a blunted edge, the impact sent a searing pain down her back, drawing a guttural cry from her throat. She whirled around just in time to block the next blow, staggering under the weight of it.

Droplets of sweat beaded across her forehead, catching loose strands of her hair as she twisted one way and then the other to scramble clear of Darce's advance. Each parried blow tore at her aching muscles, leadening them with fatigue. The pain in her temples pulsed more insistently than ever, and her mouth tasted dry and foul. She couldn't go on much longer. She didn't *want* to go on much longer. But neither could she submit, not when it would mean proving Darce right. Not when it would mean failing in front of Lachlan, letting him believe she'd become weak over these past years. She was more than she'd been before she left. She had to be.

She ducked under Darce's next blow and thrust forward, only to be met with a blunt elbow under her chin. The impact snapped her head back and sent her sprawling to the ground, mud splattering her face as she landed.

"Galbraith." Lachlan's voice rang out across the courtyard, carrying a sharp warning.

If Darce replied, Isla didn't hear it. Her ears were muffled with the strain of her breathing. Something tightened in her stomach and she retched, bringing up bile. It burned her throat as she coughed and spluttered, her face hot with shame.

Shit. This was a mistake. She was in no state to be swinging a sword, even in training. Being horribly out of practice was bad enough, but to have had the pride and arrogance to come down here with a headache and churning stomach... It was little wonder Darce was enjoying this.

Isla staggered to her feet, forehead clammy and palm slick around her cutlass. She wiped her mouth with her mud-stained sleeve and forced her spine upright, taking in ragged breaths.

Darce met her eyes with a questioning gaze. "Had enough?"

31

"Tides take you, Galbraith."

He grabbed her arm and pulled her close, lowering his voice until it was little more than a growl against her ear. "Don't make this look worse than it already is. Walk away while at least some of your dignity remains intact."

Isla pushed him off, heart hammering furiously. She rolled her wrist and slashed forward, crying out as Darce rapped his claymore against her already-bloodied knuckles, knocking the sword from her grip. In a swift motion, he dropped one hand from the hilt of his blade and grabbed her by the collar of her shirt.

His brown eyes glinted dangerously as he pushed her up against the stone wall. "If you don't know when to give up, then perhaps a sword isn't for you."

Isla whipped her hand to her belt and drew the weapon Lucrezia had gifted her upon their parting, pressing the barrel under Darce's stubble-coated chin. The pearlescent casing shone in the grey light, and when Isla pulled the hammer back with her thumb, the staccato click of the gun cocking sent a pleasant shiver down her spine.

"That's all right, Sergeant," she said. "I prefer pistols."

The only sound between them was that of their laboured breaths. Even the circling gulls above hushed their cawing, as if they too felt the air thicken with tension.

Darce stared at her, face twisted. "Where is your honour?"

"My bosun once told me honour won't stop a blade between the ribs, but a hole in the head might." Isla forced a smile. "Now, what was it you said about knowing when to give up?"

Darce released his hold on her shirt, letting her slide down the wall until her feet came to rest on the flagstone ground once more. His mouth drew into a thin line as he stared at her, his face stony and immutable. "All those years out at sea, and this is what you come back with? The integrity of a pirate? I expected more from you, wolf cub."

He pushed the pistol out from under his chin and stalked across the courtyard, leaving behind only the clatter of his claymore against the stone underfoot. The lingering echo of his words chafed at her like the sting of a slap, flooding her cheeks with warmth. This hadn't been what she wanted when she came here this morning. None of this was what she wanted.

"He's right, you know." Lachlan cut through her thoughts. "It was an unworthy way to end the fight."

"He made me look foolish."

"You managed that quite well by yourself." A smirk played across his lips. "Just what *did* you have to drink last night? Whatever it was, I could smell the remnants of it from across the courtyard."

"Tides take you," Isla snapped. "At least I was there. What were you doing that was so important you couldn't attend your own mother's memorial feast?"

Lachlan's gaze turned cold. Isla felt the chill in the air as he looked away, setting his jaw. "What right do you have to chastise me for not showing up after you've been gone for the last seven years?"

"That wasn't what I—" Isla broke off, grinding her teeth. "Lachlan, please. It was never my intention to hurt you, to hurt anyone."

"And yet you manage it so easily." Lachlan drew his mouth into a tight smile. "I believe your cheap trick with the pistol wounded the sergeant more than any of the blows I landed on him." He studied her for a moment, then let out a sigh which seemed to dissipate the tension leadening the air between them. "This wasn't how I imagined our reunion would be. I knew Mother's death would be a shadow over any kind of joy, but I didn't expect I would feel so..."

"Bitter?" Isla supplied. "Resentful?"

"Lost." The lump in Lachlan's throat bobbed up and down as he swallowed. "As if I'm looking for someone who isn't there. As if I'm waiting for someone who isn't coming back."

Isla flinched at the raw emotion in her brother's words. He'd felt it too, then. The unfamiliarity with which they'd been skirting around each other, like a dance they'd forgotten the steps to. The undeniable gulf between them, like they were still on opposite sides of the Adrenian. The ache of realising that memory was no match for time, that even blood could become strange and unfamiliar.

There had been no note of accusation in his voice, only grief, but that didn't temper the sting of it. Every word was a barb under her skin, reminding her this was her fault. For leaving. For coming back. For having the temerity to have changed in the last seven years.

"Was it worth it, at least?" Lachlan asked. "Did you find whatever it was you were searching for out there?"

Isla choked back a laugh. For all his talk of wounding, it was her brother who knew precisely where to strike. "Would it make it easier for you to forgive me if I said aye? If I told you I'd stumbled across what I was missing, that I'd carved out a piece of this world in which I belonged? Or would it give you more satisfaction to know I'm as adrift now as I've ever been, that Mother's letter with her promise of some secret was all it took to lure me away from the life I'd tried so hard to convince myself I was content with?"

"None of this gives me any satisfaction. If that's what you believe, perhaps I've become as much of a stranger to you as you have to me." Lachlan's expression softened. "You're my sister. No matter what else has changed, that hasn't. Not for me, at any rate."

Gentle as his words were, they couldn't stop the grief that seized Isla's heart. Grief for the lad she'd left behind and come back to find long gone. Grief for the years she'd robbed herself of, robbed them both of. "I missed you," she said, realising with a painful swell that it was true.

Surprise flashed across Lachlan's face, and his mouth broke into a half smile. Strained, perhaps, but it offered a glimpse of the boy she once knew, the wee brother who'd looked up at her with beseeching eyes and followed her around the estate like a pup underfoot.

"I know I haven't made your return as easy as it should have been," he said, placing a hand on her shoulder. His grip was tight, as though he was afraid to let her go, afraid she might leave again. "There are old sores I've been unable to leave be, even if time has shown me that resentment is a wound self-inflicted. The fault for that lies with me, not with you." He grimaced. "Even after you left, the shadow you cast was a long one, and I've never been able to find my way free of it."

"Neither have I." Isla sighed. "Why do you think I stayed away for so long? For me, the shadow was this place. It was the weight of their expectations, of what they wanted for me."

"The inherited wealth of the firstborn heir? Aye, how terrible that must have been." Lachlan's voice was tart, but his eyes brightened with mischief. "Speaking of such matters, I should probably warn you our father intends to ambush you about the estate today. He's also invited the young Duke de Frellion for dinner later. I assume he believes an introduction to a member of Breçhon nobility might convince you to stick around for a bit."

Isla wrinkled her nose. "I remember meeting de Frellion at a banquet in Arburgh some ten years ago. I can't say he left much of an impression."

"We crossed paths at the Samhain festival last year. I can't say he left much of an impression on me either, though he did try." Lachlan smirked. "In any case, I thought you might appreciate the information. Just in case you felt the need to make yourself unavailable for the evening."

"I'll take it under consideration. Though judging by your antics last night, our father is sure to send Darce to hunt me down."

"I'll put Galbraith on a false trail. I've become rather good at it over the years." Lachlan hesitated, a troubled look falling over his face. "Isla, I don't blame you for wanting to run. Not then, and not now. But you won't be able to put this off forever. Sooner or later, you'll need to face what's expected of you. As will I." A familiar shadow flitted across his eyes, his features becoming cold and withdrawn. The change reminded Isla of a turn in the weather, the threat of a storm even with fair skies.

Then it was gone, and warmth returned to Lachlan's expression. "I know you need time. Tides, we all do. Allow me to buy you some for today, at least. Consider it my way of trying to put right this unease between us."

He clasped his hand around hers, smothering the bloody gashes on her knuckles with his palm. Isla tried not to wince at the pain, unintentional though it was. Instead, she gritted her teeth at her brother's well-meaning attempt at comfort.

"This belonging you're looking for, the one you spent seven years on the open waters hoping to find..." Lachlan offered her a tentative smile. "It's not as far as you think, sister. It never was."

Isla forced herself to return his smile, even as it bruised the corners of her mouth. "Maybe," she allowed, the word dry and hollow. The lie was a soft one, spoken only to protect the fragile hope of moving past the bitterness and tension their separation had engendered. Yet a lie it was, and the dark, treacle-thick taste of it on her tongue was only a reminder of the truth.

Blackwood Estate hadn't changed. It offered what it always had: a life both comforting and confining, like the anchor that stops the boat from drifting. Isla was made for wilder waters. She *knew* it; she felt it bone deep. If she didn't find them, she feared she would only drown in a life not meant for her.

No matter what Lachlan said, this was not home. And she could not stay.

CHAPTER FOUR

B y the time Isla slipped between the fresh cotton sheets of her bed that evening, she was ready for sleep to fold her into its comforting depths. She'd spent the day in Caolaig re-treading steps of old: counting the bobbing boats moored around the jetty like she was a bairn again, greedily eyeing the fresh catches spread out like glistening wet silver-and-white jewels in the fishmarket, taking shelter in the dimly lit, cosy belly of the Stag's Heid. It was there in the tavern that she'd allowed the evening to pass as she nursed a bowl of skink, the soup smoky and thick with flaky haddock and chunks of potato. She'd pushed a piece of crusty bread around the dregs, stretching out the hours as she listened to the bard in the corner pluck his lute and sing an old shanty about a fisher who'd lost his wife to the sea.

The estate was quiet and lifeless when she stole through the rungs of the iron gates and slunk into the manor through one of the serving entrances. Every creak of the wooden floor underfoot seemed certain to give her away, but nothing stirred as she traipsed up the stairs towards her quarters. Even the wind outside was more of a faraway whistle than its usual raging howl.

But sleep was not the respite Isla hoped for. In her dreams, she imagined herself back in the training grounds, but the clack of wood and whalebone swords drowned beneath a harsh song of steel. Then she found herself in the tavern, where the honeyed notes of the bard's voice turned sharp and pitched, sounding more like screams.

Isla sprang upright. Her nightgown was damp with sweat, and her loose hair clung to her forehead. The room swayed before her eyes until she half wondered whether she'd somehow woken up in her cabin on the *Ondasta*.

The drapes over her windows stirred, and a flash of light shot across the walls. Isla held her breath as the seconds passed. Then came the low, rumbling growl of thunder.

A moment later, the door swung open. It took Isla a couple of dazed blinks to recognise the silhouette against the muted lamplit glow from the hallway, but as soon as she caught Darce's familiar glare, her shoulders relaxed.

"Oh, it's only you. What are you doing barging in at this unholy hour? Surely my father isn't paying you to chase young noblemen from my bedchamber now, is he?" Isla stifled a yawn. "Or if he is, well, you're several hours too late. I kicked out young Duke de Frellion some time ago."

"You might regret the ill-timing of that jest. Young Duke de Frellion is dead."

Isla froze, her hand halfway to her mouth. There was no mockery in Darce's voice, no biting sarcasm. The tightness in his jaw gave him an expression that made Isla want to shrink under her sheets and pray for morning.

She cast her gaze down to the claymore Darce was holding at his side. The blade was dull in the darkness, but Isla could see something viscous sliding along its honed edge. It gathered at the tip and dripped onto the floor, each bead echoing off the stone as the puddle grew beside the sergeant's feet.

Isla wrenched her eyes back to him, all the warmth draining from her cheeks. "What do you mean he's dead? What's going on?"

Darce was at her side before she'd finished speaking, grabbing her roughly by the arm and pulling her out of bed. "We need to move," he said tersely. "Throw on something to keep you warm, then follow me."

"I'm not going anywhere until you tell me—"

"Tides *take* you, Isla!" He rounded on her, his expression contorting into something furious and pained. "For once in your life, would you listen to me instead of thinking you know best? If you don't do as I say, you won't survive tonight. None of you will."

It was only now she noticed his face was covered in blood. She could smell it on him, a sharp, coppery stench that churned her stomach. It clung to his skin like a crimson mask, but no wound marked his face.

Fear seized Isla's heart. "Lachlan...my father..."

"We need to move," Darce said again, releasing her with a shove.

Isla fumbled through the armoire in the corner of the room. She felt like she was still dreaming as she pulled a linen shirt over her chemise and slid her legs into a pair of breeches. It wasn't real. It *couldn't* be real. Any moment now she'd wake up in her bed, panting heavily as the nightmare scattered. This darkness, this terror, would disappear with the morning light.

Darce handed her a fur-lined woollen cloak as she pulled on her leather boots. Isla fastened it around her shoulders, then grabbed her pack from beside the bed. It had lain there waiting, as if it had known this time would come. As if it were inevitable she'd be torn from this place.

Isla followed Darce past the flickering lamps as he led her towards Lachlan's quarters. She couldn't remember the last time she'd visited this part of the manor, but time was not the only thing making her surroundings unfamiliar. The glow from the brass lamps hanging along the walls dimmed, as if the oil had run low. The shadows clinging to the mounted paintings and arching roof beams crept towards her with every step.

Her skin prickled, and she pulled her cloak snug. An unnatural coldness fell over her, seeping into her bones and chilling her blood. When her next breath escaped her dry, cracked lips, it lingered like a faint cloud in the lamplight.

Isla froze. "Darce, do you feel..."

He nodded sharply. It wasn't just her. He must have felt it too. Something was nearby. Something that brought with it an icy terror like nothing Isla had ever known. It whispered at the nape of her neck, like a skeletal hand curling around her spine, paralysing her in place.

Darce stalked forward, hands wrapped around his claymore. It was only now that Isla got a proper look at the blade as it glinted under the dying light from the lamps. It wasn't covered in blood at all—it was dripping with a wet silvery substance.

Isla startled. "What in the tides is that? What did you—"

The next thing she knew, her back was against the wall and Darce's body was pressed against hers, his hand clamped roughly over her mouth. She struggled against him, but Darce only tightened his grip. He met her eyes with a disquieting gaze, then silently gestured across the hall.

Lachlan's door was ajar.

Isla's mouth turned so dry she couldn't swallow. Her breath was caught somewhere between her throat and her lungs, trapped there as she stared at the ominous crack in the doorway.

She slipped through Darce's arms and bolted towards it.

"Isla, no!"

She barely heard Darce's hushed cry as she flung open the door and rushed into the darkness. All she could see of Lachlan was the outline of his body under the sheets and his dishevelled golden hair across the pillow. She'd already taken a half step towards him when the chill set over her skin. It stole the blood from her cheeks and the air from her lungs.

She lifted her chin. There, bleeding from the shadows as if it were made from the black of night itself, floated a wisping wraithlike creature. It drifted through the thin curtains around the four-poster bed like a mist, drawing a ghostly sword from the darkness to clutch between its incorporeal hands, the blade poised over her brother's chest.

The wraith brought its sword down, and Isla screamed.

Everything happened at once. As soon as Isla's cry tore from her throat, Lachlan jerked awake. Isla saw the whites of his eyes as the blade came for his heart. There was a cry and a scuffle, then Lachlan was rolling away. Blood poured from a gash in his shoulder, leaving a crimson trail on the sheets behind him as he scrambled back.

Darce pushed past her, swinging his claymore with such ferocity that it might have cleaved through solid stone. The two swords clashed with a watery sound that turned Isla's blood to ice. Her ears filled with the fury of crashing waves. She could almost taste the spray dancing from the blades as they bit each other again and again. Each time Darce pressed forward, the mist surrounding the wraith grew thicker. It clung to the vaulted ceiling and the corners of the room, turning the air damp. The creeping chill dug its fingers into her, colder with each passing second. Isla rolled back her cloak to see her skin turning blue and frost clinging to the stiff hair along her forearms.

She reached into her pack and drew her pistol. She could barely feel the handle in her palm—her hands were numb and throbbing. Curling her finger around the trigger was agony. The barrel only held a single shot; if she missed, she'd never be able to summon enough strength in her fingers to reload.

Isla steadied her arm, pushing away the sound of her chattering teeth, and squeezed.

The crack of the shot cut through the air, and a shower of splinters rained down from one of the carved wooden bedposts.

She'd missed.

The wraith turned its spectral form on her. It was too shrouded in shadow for her to make out any kind of shape to it, but there was no mistaking the way it crept across the room towards her. The chill seized Isla's breath, freezing her muscles. Whether it was the cold or the terror, she couldn't tell. Whatever sea-forsaken horror this was, it was beyond her.

Tides be kind, she prayed. *At least let it be over quickly.*

She sank to the floor, each breath thinner than the last. There was no time to scramble in her pack and retrieve another lead ball and fresh black powder. She'd had her shot, and she'd wasted it.

The wraith reached for her with wisping fingers, its stench as salty and foul as the washed-up rot of dead crabs at low tide. It suffocated her, dragging her below the depths to drown.

"Get away from her!"

The mist scattered, falling to the floor in silvery puddles. The wraith was gone.

Lachlan stood over her, his bare shoulder dripping with blood. In his hand was a small ornamental dagger.

Isla pushed herself to her feet, her legs trembling as she stumbled towards him. "You're hurt."

Lachlan waved her off, wincing. "A wee nick, that's all. Reckon that thing is hurt more."

"That *thing* is made from the mists," Darce said, a dark look on his face. "It won't remain scattered for long."

"What was it?" The lingering touch of the wraith's fingertips released itself from Isla's skin, but she couldn't help the shiver prickling her neck. "It didn't look like a raider."

Darce pressed his lips into a tense line. "I've fought selkies before. They're monsters, but they bleed the same as we do. Whatever these spirits are, I don't think they can be killed." His eyes drifted to the oozing wound on Lachlan's shoulder. "We, on the other hand, most certainly can. If we want to survive this, we need to get out of here."

Lachlan paused in the middle of pulling his shirt on, the light linen already staining red. "Is our father still upstairs in his quarters? We can't leave without him."

The silence thickened between them, ugly and raw. It confirmed what Isla already knew, what she'd known the moment she'd seen Darce's face covered in blood...her father's blood. She felt like a stone had dropped into the pit of her stomach, leaving her numb. Tides, this couldn't be happening.

Lachlan stiffened his spine. "If you think I'd abandon him to save my skin—"

"You forget, little laird, that I am Laird Cormick's swordmaster, his sworn protector." Darce's voice was quiet, but his eyes glittered furiously in the dim light. "Do you think I'd have left his side if there was any hope of saving him?"

Lachlan paled. When they were bairns, that had been the tell-tale sign of his temper. Anger came to Isla in the form of flushed cheeks and tears of rage; her brother turned cold and ashen. Even now, she saw the vein pulsing in the side of his neck, his fingers twitching as if yearning to grab Darce by the throat.

Darce seemed to have noticed too. When he spoke again, his voice was low and gentle. "Your father gave me my orders. Don't make me break my promise to him by getting yourself killed."

Lachlan shivered, eyes bright and feverish. The bloodstain seeped across his shirt as he clutched the ornamental dagger in one hand. Isla recognised it now, recalling how her father presented Lachlan with the blade on his twelfth name-day. A sgian dubh, though she hadn't realised what it was at the time. All she'd known was it looked a tiny, decorative thing, and she'd teased her brother endlessly about all the sealed letters he was certain to vanquish with it.

The memory brought shame rushing to her cheeks. That dagger had saved her life. Lachlan had saved her life.

"Please," she whispered. "If Father is gone, I can't lose you too."

She saw the shift in his expression. The tension in his jaw slackened. The desperation slid from his features, replaced by something agonised and despairing. It was all Isla could do not to throw her arms around him and tell him everything would be fine. They were no longer bairns, and such words would only be another lie, one they'd both resent.

Lachlan met her eyes and gave a slow, heavy nod. "Let's go."

CHAPTER FIVE

They followed Darce through one of the old servant stairwells leading to the kitchens. The passageway was musty and damp, cobwebs clinging to the low ceiling. Isla couldn't see anything past the suffocating darkness. The stone walls squeezed her shoulders as she navigated the spiral stairs down into the bowels of the estate.

A faint glow crept through the cracks of a heavyset wooden door at the bottom of the stairwell. Darce paused, his hands shifting around his claymore, awkward and unwieldy at his side in the narrow space. They waited, the only sound their rasping breaths echoing off the walls. Then Darce edged the door open.

"Looks clear," he said in a rough whisper. "We'll take the side entrance out into the courtyard. From there, it's a straight line to the main gates. Stay close to me, and whatever you do, don't..."

Darce's words faded on his lips, disappearing into the stillness of the air. Even in the low light from the half-burnt oil lamps, Isla saw the colour drain from his face.

She followed his stricken gaze across the kitchen. A crumpled body lay on the floor, limbs sprawling at unnatural angles. Isla recognised her as one of the estate's cooks—a kind-faced, jovial woman of near sixty who'd taken great pride in her winter broths. Her grey hair spilled across the floor, matted with blood. The simple, unadorned fabric of her dress was ripped open, exposing her back. And her back...

Isla pressed a fist over her mouth, knuckles pushing painfully against her teeth. Part of her wanted to scream. Part of her wanted to retch. But all she could do was stare, as if her eyes were held there by some morbid, petrifying fascination. The cook—*Rowan*, Isla remembered—lay stiff and prone on the floor. Her skin was peeled back on each side from shoulder to waist, stretched out like a pair of bloody wings. The exposed tissue underneath was ragged and red, like ribbons spilling out in frayed strands, torn up by whatever terrible weapon had been used to rip her open.

Tides, she'd been *flayed*.

Lachlan trembled. "This wasn't the work of a wraith."

"No," Darce said, his voice like a blade against Isla's ears. "I've seen this before, during the raids. There's only one tides-damned creature capable of this kind of violence, this kind of cruelty."

He didn't need to say anything more. The word hung in the air, filled with foreboding. *Selkie*. A skinchanger. A creature of the depths, bringing to the surface all that darkness from below.

"Do you think she suffered?" The question left Isla's lips before she could stop it. She didn't want to hear Darce's reply. She didn't need to—she already knew the truth of it. But she'd voiced the horror anyway, and now her words rang between them all, demanding to be answered.

"If you're asking whether she was still alive when this was done to her, then aye," Darce said, his voice bleak. "She suffered."

Isla pressed her lips together. The desecration of Rowan's bloodied body was terrible enough. Knowing she'd been alive as the creatures had torn her open and scourged the exposed flesh and sinew of her back... It was enough to bring the sharp taste of bile to Isla's throat. The room filled with the stench of blood. The walls trembled with the echoes of Rowan's screams, silent though they now were.

She'd never wanted to leave this place as much as she did now. And this time, there would be no returning.

Lachlan's skin took on a sickly grey tinge. "It doesn't seem right that

45

we leave her like this."

"It's not right," Darce said. "But there's nothing more we can do for her. If tides be kind, she's found some peace. That's more than I can say for us if we don't get out of here." He moved towards the narrow door leading out to the courtyard and gestured for them to follow. "I hear fighting outside. The rest of the Blackwood Watch must be holding them back. No matter what you see, you don't stop. You make for those gates, understand?"

"What about you?"

"I'll clear us a path." Darce shot Lachlan a pointed look. "Did you hear me, little laird? Put that sgian dubh back in your boot and stay close to your sister. This isn't the time to be brave. This is the time to stay alive."

Lachlan's face darkened. "If anything happens—"

"You run. Head for the wee copse off the coastal path. Your father told me there's an old smuggler's passageway there that leads through the caverns and comes out near the shore at Caolaig. If we're separated, that's where we'll meet." Darce hauled open the door. "With me, Blackwoods."

Outside, storm clouds wove together like a black canopy, so close they might have brushed the roof of the estate. Isla shielded her face against the lashing rain, but it beat her skin and bled into her eyes until everything was a blur.

She followed Darce down the slippery stone steps to the courtyard, then stopped dead in her tracks, the air leaving her lungs in a single breath. A thick haar had rolled in from the coast, shrouding the courtyard so densely she couldn't see the gates on the other side. It seemed like the whole place was abandoned, like they'd arrived at what should have been a battlefield and found only a grave. Then came a clamour of raised voices and crashing steel, echoing through the haze from every direction.

Darce pulled her along, shaking the rain from his face. "Move, Isla. This is a fight we cannot involve ourselves in."

A rumble tore through the air above them, leaving Isla's ears ringing.

A heartbeat later, the courtyard lit up in a blinding flash. The fog turned white, illuminating the dark shapes dancing within. Selkies. Wraiths. The valiant soldiers from the Blackwood Watch. It was impossible to tell which was which.

"Lachlan!" Darce barked. "Tides take your bloody-minded brother—I *told* him to stay close."

Isla blinked the rain from her eyes. There was no sign of Lachlan anywhere, no sound of his voice fighting against the raging wind. "Where did he go?"

Darce let loose a string of curses, and his fingers tore free from Isla's arm. "Get to the gates. Don't stop."

Then he was gone, disappearing into the haar without a backwards glance. Isla was utterly, terrifyingly, alone.

She stood, swaying slightly. Her cloak was heavy and sodden from the lashing rain, and her face had gone numb. She didn't want to run. She didn't want to do anything. Part of her viciously wished she'd never come back at all, that her mother's letter had been lost on its way to Vesnia, that she could have been somewhere else—anywhere else—apart from here.

Then you would have lost them all, a small voice whispered. *And never known it until it was too late.*

Something tightened in her chest. It had been mere days since the grass and soil had swallowed Lady Catriona's casket, taking her mother out of reach before Isla had the chance to make peace. Now her father had been ripped from her too, their parting tainted by drunkenness and resentment and grief. She wouldn't let them take Lachlan from her. She *couldn't*. If the tides had brought her back here to suffer, they'd drowned her in loss enough already.

There would be no more. Not tonight.

Isla set her eyes on the courtyard. She couldn't see any sign of Lachlan or Darce. The veil of fog might as well have been an impenetrable wall. The flicker of distant flames gave it an ominous orange glow, and it grew thicker with each passing second. Through its density came muffled screams and the dull clunk of swords. She heard the sighthounds howling in their kennels, the fierce crackling of burning wood, the screams of dying soldiers.

Then came the rhythmic clip of hooves on cobbles.

A hazy shape emerged, strong and equine. Trails of vapour wisped from its proud neck as it slowly crept towards her.

Isla stepped back. This was no mount from the Blackwood stables. Its slick mane was not formed of hair, but spray and salt. The brackish stench of seaweed from its watery hide made her eyes sting.

A water-horse from legend. A dread mount.

A kelpie.

The creature pawed the ground, staring at her through ghostly green eyes. No breath came from its nostrils. No sound came from its long throat. Its presence turned the air to ice, bringing crystals of frost to her exposed cheeks.

A flash of lightning lit the sky in a pale white sheet, turning the storm clouds into angry silhouettes.

Then Isla noticed the rider.

Another wraith. It was formed of the same silvery mist as the creature that attacked Lachlan. It wore armour of blackened bone that glistened in the rain. Its face—if it had one—was half obscured behind a skeleton jaw, the mandible long and protruding.

A seal skull, Isla realised with a shudder. Behind it, the wraith wore no expression. Isla could see nothing of its features apart from the grotesque mask and a pair of fathomless, empty sockets where she might have imagined its eyes.

The wraith fixed its face on her, and the black jawbone moved. Tides, it was *speaking*. Not in any tongue Isla recognised, but with the sound of the sea itself. A harsh, rolling resonance like waves crashing off a cliff. An unsettling echo that carried with it the depths of the ocean. All she could do was stare, transfixed, as the creature's watery voice caught her like a current.

Something stirred in the shadows.

A selkie slunk towards her, a bloodstained snarl on its lips. Its hair was dripping wet, pulled back from its face in a tangled knot. She might have mistaken the creature for a man were it not for the feral expression distorting its features. Isla was no stranger to that kind of look. She knew what it spoke of. This selkie was a hunter.

She was the prey.

The selkie stalked closer, bare-chested apart from the lustrous brown pelt across its shoulders. Its sealskin. The thing that allowed it to transform into the monster it truly was.

If she tried to fight, she'd die. The rain was too heavy to draw her pistol. The powder would only get damp. But running meant turning her back on the selkie.

Darce's warning from their sparring match rang around her head. *Taking your eye off the enemy will get you killed.*

She met the selkie's cruel eyes, and its bloody grin widened.

Let it try, Isla thought.

She ran. Her legs forgot their tremble as she forced them to move, forced them to carry her towards survival. The gates were only metres away. If she could reach them, she might have a chance.

The hand on her shoulder was cold and uncompromising. Isla hissed as the selkie's fingernails clawed through her cloak, digging into her skin as it dragged her towards the rain-slick cobbles.

Her chin hit the ground with a crack, and a lancing pain shot through her tongue. A coppery tang filled her mouth as it pooled with blood, but Isla barely had time to spit it out before the selkie was on top of her, wrenching her shoulder to flip her onto her back.

Desperation seized her, and she flung her hands into a protective ward. It was a hopeless gesture, one with no power behind it. But if only one time—if only *this* time—the old magic of the sentinels might sing in her blood, she could throw the beast from her hips and scramble to safety. Tides, maybe she could even kill it.

The selkie laughed. Then it brought a fist down against her cheek with a sickening crack, sending the back of her skull thudding off the cobbles.

Another flash of lightning cast the selkie's features in distorted shadows. For as long as the brief, blinding light lingered, Isla glimpsed its inhuman black eyes. Muscle and sinew over a predator's frame. A strong, parted jaw ready to devour her.

Then came the dull flash of a blade to separate the selkie's head from its neck.

Time seemed to hold its breath. The selkie hung above her, murder in its eyes. In the time it took Isla to blink, its head was gone, sliding from its shoulders in a smooth, swift motion.

She thrashed as the creature's limp body fell against her, pinning her to the stone ground. Something warm and wet splattered her face. The tang of blood still lingered on her lips, but not all of it was her own. It gushed from the creature's cleaved neck like a mountain spring, feeding the streams of rainwater snaking between the cobbles, turning them a violent red.

"Isla! Here, let me help you." Lachlan knelt at her side, his face pallid. Beside him, Darce stood watch, the coils of his dark hair dripping down his cheeks.

The weight lifted from Isla's chest and she took a gasping breath as her lungs filled with air once again. She winced as her brother helped her to her feet, then turned to Darce. The sergeant towered grim and silent over the selkie's headless corpse, his sword slick with the creature's blood. "You saved my life."

He shot her a hard look. "You don't make it easy. Either of you."

Isla pressed her fingers gingerly to her cheek, the tissue already swelling. The back of her head was throbbing from where it cracked against the cobbles. But she was alive. The three of them were alive.

Behind them, the haar had thinned out. Isla could make out the coastal trail past the gates. "Let's leave here while we still have a chance. Together, this time."

Nothing followed them as they slipped through the gates and fled into the night. Isla couldn't help the flinch of fear at every scuff of the soil, every snapping twig underfoot, but the phantom footsteps she heard in pursuit were only an imagined terror. As they ran, all they had for company was the raging rain and far-off rumble of thunder.

After a while, they came across the copse Darce mentioned—a sparse gathering of spindly silver birches off the edge of the trail. Darce pulled back a knot of overgrown brambles to uncover the crumbling remains of an old well, and in it, the hidden smuggler's tunnel.

Isla peered down the shaft. The hole in the middle of the well's maw offered no end, only darkness waiting to swallow them whole. Rough-cut stone steps jutted out in a descending spiral into the gloom.

"Are you sure about this?" Lachlan looked uneasy. "We could end up crushed or buried alive. I'd rather take my chances with the selkies."

The forced humour in his voice fell flat. They all knew the truth of it: Blackwood Estate was lost. They'd left behind a graveyard filled with bones that would never be buried, souls that would never be given peace.

The memory of her father's ruddy, grief-stricken face swam before Isla's eyes. The last moments they'd shared had been heavy with pain. She'd avoided him, never given him a chance to talk. Now that chance was gone. There was no getting it back.

She pushed the thoughts from her mind and followed Darce over the stone lip of the well. Loose flakes of rubble crumbled beneath the tread of her boots as she climbed down, and she tried not to think about the steps falling from under her.

After a time, a narrow opening appeared in the wall, marking the entrance to the smuggler's tunnel. Isla followed Darce through the gap, trailing her hands against the rock as if that would somehow stop the walls from closing in. The darkness was absolute, the air stale and musty.

It was impossible to tell how much time passed as they followed the narrow passage down through the innards of the cliff. Isla's legs soon became sore, and an ache spread across her shoulders from the tension in her nerves. She trudged after Darce until he came to an abrupt stop in front of her.

"Do you hear that?" he said.

Isla listened. The rain and thunder had long since faded from her ears, but she heard something else now, something soft and burbling. "Is that water?"

Darce edged forwards, then motioned for her to follow. There was light up ahead. Not much—just slivers of moonlight through clefts in the rock—but enough that Isla could make out the large cavern they'd come out in. The rugged floor flattened out in front of them, dotted with small puddles. Pillars of rock and ice stretched between the floor and roof like glistening teeth. At the far end of the cave, the black water of the sea churned in a large pool below.

Lachlan stared blankly ahead. "It's a dead end. There's no way out."

"No need to fret, little laird," Darce said. "The entrance is hidden, that's all. It can't be navigated when the water is this high, so we'll need to wait until low tide. It might not be the comforts you're used to, Blackwoods, but this cave is your bed for the night. Get some sleep while you can. We don't know what we'll find out there tomorrow."

Isla shivered. Darce might not have said it out loud, but the truth of it lingered in the damp cavern air. For now, at least, they were trapped. The cave entrance was submerged below the waves. If the selkies followed them down the smuggler's tunnel, if the wraiths drifted through the cliff and descended on them...

She laid her pack against the uneven ground and rested her head on it, curling herself up inside her cloak. The fur around the hood was sodden and musty, but it sheltered her from the draught circling the cave. *Sleep*, Darce had told her. How could she sleep when the sea whispered to her with its shapeless voice from metres away? When her ears rang with strangled screams carried off by the wind? When closing her eyes meant reliving the night's blood and horror?

Sleep would bring her no peace. But exhaustion took hold of her all the same, leadening her eyelids and slowing her breaths. It offered her a respite from her aching body. It didn't matter that the price attached would be terror in her dreams.

For if there was one thing Isla feared more than her nightmares, it was what she would soon wake up to in the cold light of day.

CHAPTER SIX

T he next morning, they followed the tide out of the cavern. The waves had retreated from the rocky shoreline, leaving in their wake fronds of yellow-brown kelp and washed-up driftwood. Isla took care not to slip as she navigated the rockpools and scrambled across the pebble-strewn stretch of coast leading back to Caolaig.

The storm had passed, clearing the way for a periwinkle sky, but the scent of rain, limestone-thick, still lingered as they approached the village. Isla trained her eyes on the harbour in the distance, searching for any signs of selkie raiders lying in wait, but she saw nothing. Perhaps daylight had chased the monsters away like in the stories her mother used to read to her by lamplight.

Lachlan coughed. His skin was slick with sweat, and he grimaced as he pressed his fingers over the wound in his shoulder.

"We need to get that looked at," Isla said. "The doctor in the village should have ointments and bandages for us. I don't have much coin in my pack, but—"

"I don't think anybody will be taking our coin today, wolf cub." Darce nodded towards the harbourfront, his voice grim.

Isla cast her gaze over the jetty. The painted wooden boats were all tied up, bobbing on the water like coloured gulls. It was quiet. Too quiet. Dawn should have brought with it the bustle of the fish market opening, the chatter over the wind, the slapping of oars against waves as boats sailed in and out of the tiny harbour.

Instead, there was only silence.

They traipsed into the village, tight-lipped and wordless. None of them needed to say anything. They all knew what they would find. It was the knowing that made it worse.

Death was worse in the daylight. Isla couldn't ignore the trails it left across Caolaig's gutted heart. The abandoned streets lay still. The gull shite staining the stone pavements had turned red. The stench of rot and filth clung to every home they passed. Outside the Stag's Heid, they found the body of the bard lying face down in a bloody puddle, his back stripped of skin and his broken lute resting beside him, the delicate strings snapped and curling.

"No," Isla whispered.

As the denial left her lips, she knew it was useless. There was no undoing the violence that had fallen upon Caolaig last night. The selkies had swept through the village like a plague, leaving nothing behind but bodies. Some had been tortured and flayed, like the bard. Others washed up from the water onto the blood-soaked shore, bloated and grey. The corpses stared up at them with glassy eyes, their skin wet and translucent.

What would be worse? Isla wondered. *The agony of a blade separating skin from tissue, or drowning with lungs full of water and a stomach full of salt?*

It was Lachlan who broke the stifling silence. He fixed Darce with a rigid stare, his fists clenched, and asked, "How did our father die?"

Isla stiffened, but before she could say anything, Lachlan pressed on. "Was it like this? Did you find him in agony with his back mutilated and put on display like some sick trophy?"

"By the time I reached him, Laird Cormick was badly wounded from an axe to his thigh," Darce said. "The beast that attacked him was already dead, slain by your father. I tended to him as best I could, but the wound was deep. He'd lost too much blood. He knew it. We both knew it."

The words left his mouth calm and practised, his voice steady across every syllable. Isla didn't know whether it was the truth or whether Darce was sparing them from whatever horror he'd seen in their father's chambers. She didn't have any other choice but to accept his word. Believing otherwise would only drag her to a place she wouldn't be able to come back from. The guilt and grief would eat at her until there was nothing left.

It wasn't enough for Lachlan. Her brother stepped towards Darce, his jaw trembling violently. "You were meant to protect him."

"I was meant to follow his orders, and that's what I did." Darce's voice slipped an octave. "I held your father as he died and swore I would get you to safety. I respect you, little laird, but I won't ask your forgiveness for keeping that promise." He closed his eyes, his expression pained. "There was nothing we could have done to prepare for what happened last night. We've suffered raids before, but nothing like this."

"The wraiths," Isla said, her voice tight. "I think the selkies called them here, somehow. I saw one of them speak."

"Speak?" Lachlan shot her a sceptical look.

"Not in any words I understood." Isla frowned. "Did you not see it, either of you? It sat on a kelpie made from sea spray and wore a seal skull over its jaws."

Darce shook his head. "I saw no wraiths in the courtyard, only the selkie attacking you."

Silence fell between them again, filling the spaces between their confusion and fear and grief-laden accusations. The water was unnaturally still now. It seemed impossible that the storm had brought so much terror, so much violence, yet disappeared without leaving a trace.

"What do we do now?" Isla asked. "We can't stay here."

Lachlan gave a dark chuckle. "I suppose I shouldn't be surprised your first thought would be to leave. Ever since you got back, you've been looking for an excuse."

Isla's cheeks burned. "That's not fair."

"Don't talk to me about fair." Lachlan turned to her, his face twisting with pain. "If there was some ill-fate that caused this, it was you who brought it upon us. You who returned carrying it."

"That's enough," Darce said sharply. "Your grief is no excuse for casting blame where it does not belong. Your sister is right—we can't stay here. There's still too much danger."

"We can't abandon our home," Lachlan insisted. "We have to go back. Maybe there are others who survived the attack."

"Look around, lad," Darce said, his voice softening. "Even if the selkies are gone, there is nothing there for you. Caolaig is home to nothing but ghosts now. Without its people, without its trade, Blackwood Estate won't survive. You have no choice but to leave, at least for a wee while."

His words hung over them like a sword about to fall. Isla blinked furiously, fighting to stop the angry tears from brimming. Her throat was too tight to speak. Perhaps that was for the best. There was nothing she could say that would ease the pain. Not while it was still so fresh.

Eventually, Lachlan let out a sigh. "If there is no choice but to leave, then we should go to Arburgh. The capital is our only hope."

Arburgh. An unpleasant shiver scuttled across Isla's skin at the mention of the city. She hadn't visited the capital since she was sixteen. The last time she'd been there... No, she wouldn't think of it, not now. Grief clung too tightly to her heart already without the reminder of false friends and sharpened knives and the weight of betrayal. If Lachlan meant to go back there...

"Why?" she asked, the question wrenching from her throat. "What hope is there for us in Arburgh?"

"The only hope Silveckan has against these selkie raids," Lachlan said. "The Admiralty. If we petition them, they may be persuaded to send aid to the coastal estates. Protection where we desperately need it. It will take time, but with ships and resources, we can rebuild what was lost here. We can resettle Caolaig and take our home back."

Darce pursed his lips. "It's been a while since I was last in the capital, but from what I hear, the Grand Admiral is more concerned about hunting selkies for coin and protecting his new trade routes than what happens to provincial fishing villages up and down the coast. There's a reason you rarely see a sentinel outside the south these days."

"It's worth trying," Lachlan said. "At least in Arburgh we have allies, if nothing else." He glanced at Isla. "And you'll be able to get a ship back to Vesnia, if that's what you want."

It was too much. The bitterness lacing Lachlan's voice, the unrelenting ache holding her heart in its grasp, the bleak exhaustion seeping through her body. Isla turned on her heel without saying a word, storming across the shore and leaving Darce's shouts after her to be carried off in the wind.

The stillness of the village was eerie and unwelcoming. Death's stale breath followed her everywhere she trod, curling the hairs on the back of her neck. She passed strings of seashells dangling from empty doorways, chiming a dreary lament in the non-existent breeze. The villagers hung them up for protection. Isla only needed to look at the bloodied cobbles underneath to know how well that had worked.

It felt wrong intruding into the doctor's house. All she could do was force her eyes from his stiff body as she rummaged in his desk drawer for the key to the supply cabinet. She'd never imagined she'd have to do something as wretched and shameful as picking the bones of the dead, like she was one among the gulls and the crows, circling the carrion.

She filled her pack with bandages and ointments and herbal remedies, pushing away the revulsion gnawing at her. The guilt wasn't enough to stop her, not when scavenging might be the only thing that kept them alive. She swiftly moved on to the market, where she found several decent-sized crabs in the pots along with a handful of spiny sea urchins and some salted salmon still dusted with sand from where it had been dug up.

"He doesn't mean it, you know."

Isla looked up to find Darce towering over her, his eyes dark and troubled. When she didn't reply, he added, "Your brother. He's in pain, both from his wound and losing your mother and father. It's his grief lashing out, not him."

"That doesn't make it hurt any less." Isla pushed herself to her feet, shouldering her pack. Her earlier anger slipped away, leaving behind only a dull ache in the hollow of her sternum. She'd never been able to stand seeing her brother in pain, ever since they were bairns. Maybe because when Lachlan was hurting, he made damn sure she felt it too. But if that was what it took to ease some of his torment, Isla suffered it. She always would.

Darce was still looking at her, his expression steady. "I know it's not my place to tell you, but the little laird needs you more than you know. He'll never admit it to anyone, least of all himself, but he lost part of himself the day you left. I think it scares the lad to hope there might be a chance of getting it back."

A hard lump lodged in Isla's throat. "I can't be what he needs to me to be."

"He doesn't need you to be anything apart from his sister." Darce shook his head. "You're all he has left."

Fresh shame washed over her, churning in the pit of her stomach. The sergeant was right. Blackwood Estate might never have been home to her, but it was to Lachlan. Now, it was gone. Their family was gone. She knew better than anyone what it meant to suffer the heartache of something missing, something forever out of reach. She'd left Silveckan behind—left *everything* behind—in search of it. The sea called to her, but in seven years it had offered no answer.

Maybe she could find it instead in the brother she'd sailed away from.

Something swelled in her chest, pushing past the pain and grief. *Purpose*, she realised. Perhaps this was what she needed.

"You're right," she said. "After everything that's happened, I can't leave him, not like this. He deserves a home to return to. We both do." She swallowed, tears tickling her throat. "Maybe we can help each other find it."

They walked back along the shore to where Lachlan was sitting. His hair wisped across his forehead as he stared out to sea, ashen-faced and unblinking. Isla saw the pain in each crease of his forehead, each twitch of his jaw.

"Here," she said, opening her pack. "I brought some supplies."

He locked eyes with her, his gaze tired and pained. Then he nodded, slipping his furs from his shoulders and peeling off his blood-soaked shirt to reveal the gouge the wraith left behind.

"Looks clean, at least." Darce took the ointment and bandages Isla offered him and knelt at Lachlan's side, his hands working deftly to dress the wound. "I'm no doctor, but I've enough scars of my own to know this will heal well. A good thing, too. It's a long road to Arburgh."

The stony expression faded from Lachlan's face. "You're in agreement then?"

"Both of us are." Isla took a hesitant step towards him, afraid to get too close lest he push her away. "I left you once before. I won't leave you again. Whatever the Grand Admiral says, I'll stay by your side until we have a home to return to. I swear it."

Lachlan's mouth pulled into a slow smile. It was a careful gesture, and Isla found herself wishing his features were more familiar to her, that she might know how strained his smile was, how much of a lie hid behind it. All she could do was return it, and pray her own mask was rigid enough to conceal the doubt and fear she couldn't wear. It was what she had to do to protect him. Even if it meant protecting him from herself.

"We should go north to Cape Dromair," Lachlan said. "I know Tarmouth is closer, but it's too quiet these days. We could be waiting several days for a ship bound for Arburgh."

"I don't like the idea of going to either port." Darce looked out across the water, surveying the waves. "The selkies might be gone for now, but where the tides go, they follow. Travelling the east coast is too much of a risk."

"You suggest we take the capital road?" Lachlan's face fell. "We have no mounts or carriage, Galbraith. It would take us weeks. Besides, it runs just as close to the coast in places, at least until it gets further south."

"I'm not suggesting the capital road," Darce said. "In fact, I'm not suggesting any road at all. If we want to make sure those wraiths and selkies don't follow us, we should head for Kinraith."

"Kinraith is on the west coast. That means cutting through the wilds."

"It's less than fifty miles from shore to shore, and the wilds cover less than half of that," Darce said, folding his arms. "The most important thing is we'll be heading inland."

Isla shuddered. She heard the sense in Darce's words, but that didn't do anything to quell the fear rising at the thought of venturing into the wilds. The edge of the sprawling forest crept along the outskirts of Blackwood Estate, crawling closer each year with new thickets of gorse and bracken. The pines were too densely packed for any kind of road, and curious visitors were warned off with tales of howling cù-sìth stalking the shadows and lonely brollachan spirits waiting to steal their shapes.

"You should decide."

Isla tore herself from her thoughts to find Lachlan staring at her. "What?"

"It's not up to the sergeant. Or me, for that matter." He lifted his chin and fixed her with a measured stare. "Our mother and father are gone. You are firstborn and heir to Blackwood Estate. It's only right you make this decision."

Isla fought the urge to laugh. If she laughed, she feared she might retch. She couldn't decide whether her brother's words were a peace offering or a jab at a raw wound. It was hard to tell past the ever-present bitterness tinging his voice, the reserved tone he used only with her.

You should decide, Lachlan had said. Wasn't this what she'd run from? This responsibility she'd never asked for, this weight around her like an anchor dragging her to the depths?

The lapping of the waves on the sand filled her ears like a promise. The sea still called her; maybe it always would. But there was no running now.

No ignoring what she had to do. She'd told Lachlan they'd find a way to return home. Tides take her if she broke her word.

"Darce is right. The east coast is too dangerous to risk." Isla forced herself to meet Lachlan's eyes, readying herself for whatever resentment still lingered there. Accepting it, if that was the price to pay for keeping him alive, keeping them all alive. "We make for the wilds."

CHAPTER SEVEN

"Are you sure you know where you're going, Galbraith?"

Lachlan stopped again, bending double and wincing as he stretched his injured shoulder. Isla couldn't blame him for finding another excuse to pause. The path was difficult enough without being wounded. The gaps between each proud tree were uncomfortably narrow, the muddy ground obstructed by knotted, sprawling roots and mounds of uneven soil.

"It's so bloody dark in here I've lost all sense of direction," her brother continued through ragged breaths. "We could be heading back towards the estate for all I know."

Isla lifted her chin to the canopy above, where branches wove together to shroud the light. The ancient pines grew tall and regal, with scaly limbs of red-brown bark and evergreen needles that carpeted the forest floor as thickly as they blocked out the sky above.

For the past seven years, she'd learned to navigate the sea using the stars and her sextant, but neither could help her now. Their only hope of making it out of the wilds was Darce.

"See those tracks there?" The sergeant pointed to a disturbance in the soil. There was a depression in the mud, forming the shape of distinct pads and hooked claws. "It's said that cù-sìth roam the forest from one end to another, taking the most direct route. That's how I know where we're going."

Isla startled. "We're following a cù-sìth? Is that wise?"

"Better for us to be following it than it to be following us," Darce countered. "Have no fear, wolf cub. It's only after the cù-sìth's third howl you need worry, and the wilds have been quiet so far."

His words sent an unpleasant shudder down Isla's spine. The cù-sìth's howl was an omen of terror, so bloodcurdling that anyone who heard it thrice would find themselves paralysed by fear, unable to run when the hound came for them.

The thought turned her cold, and she pushed it away, bristling with irritation. "You can't keep calling me wolf cub in the capital, you know. Arburgh isn't like the coastlands. There are certain protocols expected of us there."

"Oh, can't I?" Darce's expression darkened. "Well then, I'll do well to remember that, your highness. Would you like me to curtsey for you too?"

Lachlan snorted, and Isla shot him a glare. "I was only saying—"

"Were you, aye? Well, I'd rather you didn't."

Silence fell between them, ringing like a rebuke as the sergeant turned his back on her and pushed ahead through a clump of ferns.

Lachlan rolled his eyes. "I forgot how much of a talent you have for pissing off Galbraith. Not sure it's the wisest thing to do, given he's the only one standing between us and whatever demon hound might be stalking this forest."

"I hardly intended to—"

"No, you never do." Her brother let out a heavy sigh and wiped an arm across his forehead. "I'm off to take a piss. Try to get our swordmaster in better spirits before I catch back up, will you? The bastard is dour enough at the best of times without you making it worse."

Isla scowled at his retreating back, then turned and fought through the tangle of ferns, her hands scratching as she pushed fronds and branches from her face. Darce had stopped further ahead, arms folded stiffly as he waited.

"Lachlan will be back in a moment," she said evenly. "Perhaps it's a good time to rest. His wound is giving him trouble."

Darce grunted. "As you wish."

Dour bastard indeed, Isla thought. Despite what Lachlan said, she doubted she was the sole cause of the sergeant's mood. Darce had been surly ever since they'd entered the wilds, his features carrying a grim weight and his conversation even blunter than usual.

Still, she could see little harm in trying to make peace. For her own sake, if nobody else's.

"I never properly thanked you for what you did last night," Isla began, hesitating over each word like she was testing unknown waters. "We'd never have made it out of there alive if it wasn't for you."

Darce's face remained as hard as ever, but something loosened in his shoulders, if only a fraction. "I made your father a promise. My word is not something I give lightly."

"I'm grateful. We both are. When I think of what might have happened if you hadn't been there..." Isla ran a hand over the back of her head. Her hair was tangled, matted with dried blood from where the selkie had thrown her against the stone of the courtyard. A second later, and those teeth...

"You're hurt." Darce's jaw tightened.

Isla dropped her hand to her side. "A bit tender, that's all. The cobbles gave my skull a good crack."

"I wasn't talking about your head."

Isla followed his gaze down to her hand, where her knuckles still bore the gashes from their sparring session. Fresh blood welled across her skin, trickling between her fingers. One of the scabs must have torn off during her tussle with the undergrowth. "It's nothing," she said, warmth flooding her cheeks at the way he was staring. "I hardly noticed until now."

A flicker of unease crossed Darce's face. "I pushed you too hard the other day in the courtyard. That was unworthy of me."

"More unworthy than winning a sword fight with a pistol?"

The corner of his mouth pulled into a wry smile. "I suppose not. Though I should have expected you wouldn't give up so easily. It seems you're as stubborn now as the day you left."

Isla raised an eyebrow. "Is that such a bad thing?"

"Only when it gets in the way of me doing my duty." Darce turned away, a pained look settling over his face. "We lost too many of our kith and kin last night. The only comfort I can take in leaving them behind is knowing you and Lachlan are safe. I'd like to keep it that way."

A wave of guilt churned in Isla's stomach. She and Lachlan weren't the only ones suffering under the weight of grief and pain. The Blackwood Watch had been slaughtered fighting to protect her family. Darce had left them to face the selkies alone as he led her and Lachlan to safety.

"I'm sorry," she said. "For those you lost. For the choice you had to make."

"I could never have left you there. Whatever my regrets are, helping you and your brother escape isn't one of them." A muscle twitched in Darce's jaw. "You deserved more time with your father. I wish I could have given you that. I wish I'd been able to—"

The leaves behind them rustled. Isla stiffened, but before she had time to reach for her pistol, Darce stepped in front of her. His hand rested around the hilt of his rapier as he watched the trees, body tense and waiting. Isla sensed the coiling of his muscles as he held himself steady. This close, she could smell the pine residue on his skin, the rich scent of his leather armour. It comforted her in a way she didn't understand. It felt familiar, somehow. *Safe*, somehow.

The leaves trembled again, and Isla braced herself behind Darce.

A crunch broke through the silence, then Lachlan emerged from the thicket, expression pained and arm stiff at his side. When he saw them, he gave a weak smile. "Are we stopping? Tides know I could use some rest."

Isla let out a sharp breath, shoulders slumping at the sight of him. The tension in her limbs dissipated, leaving behind a shaking in her legs and a flutter in her chest.

"You have five minutes, little laird." Darce relaxed his stance and released the hilt of his rapier. "We need to cover more ground before we make camp, unless you want a cù-sìth on our trail before morning."

"Nothing you couldn't handle, right Galbraith?" Lachlan clapped a hand on his shoulder. "Our faithful swordmaster. Sometimes I don't know what we'd do without you."

His words were light, but they sent a foreboding shiver down Isla's spine. Her mind filled with the flash of the selkie's teeth, its breath at her throat. She knew all too well what would have happened without Darce. Growing up, she'd found his proximity stifling. He'd been nothing more than another link in the shackles chaining her to Blackwood Estate. A watchful eye when all she wanted was to slip out of sight. But now...

The strange flutter in her chest lingered, warm and persistent. She could still smell the pine and leather, still feel the way her heart quickened when he'd stepped in front of her. The sergeant's proximity wasn't stifling anymore. Instead, it stirred something far more troublesome, something she wasn't sure if she wanted to cling to or push away as far as she could.

Isla swallowed. There was too much danger in those kinds of thoughts, in trusting she could rely on his protection any more than she had already. Despite the promise he'd made to their father, Darce Galbraith didn't owe her and Lachlan anything. He was a paid guard, and they'd escaped with only the coin they had in their pockets. Sooner or later, they would be on their own.

She pushed away the twinge in her chest and ran her thumb over the handle of her pistol. The next time a selkie came for her throat, it would be up to her to stop it. Next time, she couldn't afford to miss.

The days passed in shared watches and stolen hours of fitful sleep. Darce warned them against starting a fire, so they made do with the parcels of dried fish Isla had taken from the market and scavenged blackberries that burst in their mouths with tart juice, staining their lips red. It wasn't enough to keep the grumbling ache from Isla's belly, but it kept them going long enough to reach the edge of the forest, where the trees thinned out to let in the grey touch of daylight once more.

"How much further until we reach Kinraith?" she asked, casting a furtive glance at Lachlan. He'd barely spoken over the last few days, and his face was still ashen. Though his wound was healing, it had left him weak, and their journey through the forest had not been easy.

"We still have some ground to cover," Darce replied. "There's a stretch of heath between here and Kinraith, but once we get through it, we'll not be far. Don't worry about your brother. He's stronger than he looks."

It was a relief to be under the open sky again, dreich though it was. After a while, they rounded a gorse-covered knoll and found themselves by the side of a loch. The still waters glittered blue-black under the approaching cloak of night, and a small cluster of ash trees ran along its shore.

"We'll rest here until morning," Darce said. "The trees will provide us with some shelter, and we're far enough out of the wilds that I'm willing to risk a fire. Tides know we could do with a wee bit of warmth."

The crackle of burning twigs and fronds of heather soon filled the air, releasing an acrid, mossy odour that Isla couldn't help but find comforting. She inched as close to the flames as she dared, closing her eyes as her cheeks turned rosy. All was quiet, save for the rustling of the leaves and the rumble of Lachlan's snores coming from the log he was curled against.

Isla allowed herself a smile. For the first time since they'd left Black-wood Estate, she felt a sliver of peace.

On the other side of the fire, Darce sat silent and still. The reflection of the flames danced in his eyes, giving them an unnatural glitter. Every line on his face seemed etched from stone, his lips set in the stern grimace that had become so familiar to Isla over the years.

It used to unsettle her. Now, she saw how much it suited him. He was all iron and steel, as sharp as the edge of his claymore and every bit as unyielding.

"You're staring again."

Isla jolted from her thoughts, warmth racing across her skin. "I was only—"

"I suppose it's an apology you're after, isn't it?" Darce released a short breath. "You were right about what you said the other day. I shouldn't be calling you wolf cub anymore. You're Lady Blackwood now."

Isla squirmed. "That's my mother's name."

"It's your name too. And if you're to take over your mother's duties as head of the estate—"

"I'm not." She let out a frustrated sigh. "I don't want an apology, and I don't want any part of the estate. That's not why I came back."

"No?" Darce gave her an appraising look. "You must have known there was a good chance you wouldn't make it home before your mother's illness took her. And once you've given up a place on a good ship, it's not so easy to reclaim it. Why leave the life you made for yourself if not to return to this one?"

Isla watched the sparks from the flames drift off into the night. With a weary breath, she reached into her pack and brought out the crumpled remains of her mother's letter, laying it beside the fire.

Her eyes blurred as she looked down at the tattered parchment. The inside of her pack was damp, leaving the letter a soggy, ruined mess. The ink had smudged, the parchment torn and heavy with rainwater. Even if the warmth of the flames dried it out, the words would only be a barely-legible scrawl. All Isla had was the memory of them in her mother's voice.

"She wanted to tell me something," Isla said. "She said there was something she'd kept from me. I thought if I discovered what she meant, it might help me understand. It might explain why there's always been part of me just...missing. Now she's gone, and it's not just her I've lost, it's the answers she wanted to give me."

Darce raised an eyebrow. "In my experience, nobles tend to hoard secrets like a merchant hoards coin. Why do you think this one held any significance?"

"It's the only thing that makes sense," Isla said. "It sounds foolish, but ever since I can remember, I've felt this call. Tugging at someplace inside of me I don't know how to look for. Like a purpose I've never been able to fulfil. I thought she might be able to explain what it meant."

Darce stared at the flames, his expression distant. "When the selkie attacked you back at the estate, I saw you trying to cast a ward, as if you were a sentinel." He lifted his eyes to meet hers, his gaze steady. "Is that what you thought she wanted to tell you? Is that why you left all those years ago? Did you think being out there on the water would awaken some kind of forgotten magic in your blood?"

Isla shrugged, heat flooding her cheeks. "Would it be so bad if it had? There is purpose in being a sentinel."

"That kind of purpose is not one you should aspire to," Darce said, his expression pained. "Sentinels bind themselves to their captains, to their ships, through blood. They have no fate of their own. Their lives belong to the sea, as do their deaths."

"Whereas mine only belonged to the shackles of Blackwood Estate. Was that so much better? Can you blame me for wanting something more than the life my mother and father so carefully carved out for me?"

"You want something you do not understand," Darce said, his voice quiet. "There is a reason those with the auld blood are feared, a reason the Grand Admiral keeps them on a tight leash in the capital. Sentinels share the same blood as the selkies themselves. They make oaths only death can break. That is a dangerous kind of magic, Isla. A magic the Admiralty would greatly desire to take for itself, if you had it. Would you be so willing to trade one set of chains for another?"

"Not all sentinels serve the Admiralty."

"Aye, but those that don't are too few in number these days." Darce prodded the flames with a blackened stick, mouth twisting. "Silveckan changed while you were gone. Every year, the Grand Admiral claims more and more of the seas for the capital. Every year, the city gets richer from trading in selkie pelts. And every year, the raids across the rest of the island get worse. It used to be we could rely on the sentinels for their protection, but too many of them have flocked to Arburgh. For coin, for the Grand Admiral's favour, for the thrill of the hunt... Whatever their reasons, their allegiance lies more with the Admiralty than the island these days."

"I didn't realise the situation was so dire." Despite the warmth of the flames, cold seeped across Isla's skin. She edged closer to the fire, hands trembling as she rubbed them together. "I remember our parents taking us down to the jetty whenever a sentinel visited Caolaig. They fascinated me. The way they pulled the waves into twisting shapes and made the water dance between their fingers. The way they sent showers of spray sparkling against the sun and cast us all in rainbows."

"Cheap tricks to amuse noble bairns. No wonder you looked up to them." Darce snorted. "But you never fought alongside one during a raid. They can drown a selkie in its own blood, they can cast wards and traps that bind them in place until some sword-wielding bastard like me comes along to strike them down. That's what makes them so valuable to the Admiralty. They're selkie-killers."

Isla's throat constricted as she swallowed back tears. "Perhaps if there had been a sentinel in Caolaig, Blackwood Estate might not have fallen."

"Or it might've anyway." Darce threw the remains of the charred stick into the fire. "There's no use dwelling on things you cannot change.

You're not a sentinel, and where we're going, you should be glad of that. Arburgh is dangerous enough without having to worry about the Admiralty tracking us down."

Isla curled her fingers around the tattered scrap of parchment, scrunching it into the middle of her fist. Her mother's words burned against her palm, the ink hot and angry. "I suppose you must think me a fool."

"I think you want that letter to mean something," Darce said, his voice oddly tender compared to his usual gruffness. "You want to believe it brought you back here for a reason. But you should know by now, the tides don't move for any reason but their own, no matter how much we pray to them. All we can do in the end is go where they take us."

He pulled his cloak around his leather armour and trudged towards the sound of Lachlan's snores, leaving Isla alone at the fire. She watched the flames flicker and dim as they burned low. Soon, there would be nothing left but ashes, and those too would disappear when the rain returned.

Isla lifted her gaze to the still water of the loch. It watched her, as if waiting to see what she would do next. She twisted her hands into a ward, pulling from memory the gestures the sentinels had made that day on the jetty so many years ago. If only a wave might rise with her fingertips, if only she could create the faintest ripple...

The loch remained still and silent.

Isla let her hands fall. Darce was right. She was no sentinel. She'd never make a blood oath to a captain and calm the storms from the deck of a ship. But blood or no, she'd made a promise to Lachlan all the same. Even with no magic binding her to her word, it was a promise she would not—could not—break.

She pocketed the letter, surrendering the parchment to the depths of her woollen cloak. If the answers were out there, perhaps she'd find them one day. Perhaps the tides would see fit to carry her to them.

All we can do in the end is go where they take us, Darce had said.

To Arburgh, then, Isla thought. *Then home, even if I have to fight the sea itself to get there.*

CHAPTER EIGHT

Isla woke the next morning to the dull, thrumming melody of a pebble skipping across the water. She rubbed her eyes to find Lachlan by the loch's grainy shore, his tongue between his teeth as he sent another stone skimming over the surface.

The sight of him brought a smile to her face. "You look better."

"Knowing I'm not about to be mauled by a cù-sìth before I wake does wonders for my sleep," he said dryly, rolling another pebble in his hand. "My shoulder is troubling me less each day as well." A look of chagrin flickered across his face. "I never thanked you for gathering the healing supplies."

"Think nothing of it."

"I was an arse. Those things I said to you back in Caolaig—"

"Think nothing of it," she repeated, her voice firm. "You think I don't remember how much of an irritating wee gobshite you were when we were bairns? If I took to heart half the insults you hurled my way, I'd have throttled you before you turned six."

Lachlan cracked a smile. "I believe you might have tried, once or twice."

"Aye, but my hands are bigger now, so don't tempt me again." Isla stretched, her shoulders popping loose as she arched her spine. Across the loch, the pale light of the morning sun fought to break through the low clouds, chasing away the last vestiges of darkness. It was already some time past dawn, but Darce was nowhere to be seen. "Has the sergeant abandoned us?"

Lachlan glanced at her. "Did you give him cause to?"

"No more than usual." Isla pulled the furs of her cloak around her neck, trying to keep out the shower of rain that had drifted in over one of the rugged knolls. It pattered against the rustling leaves of the towering ash tree and danced off the loch's surface to form a haze across the water, shrouding the far side. Nothing else stirred. The seclusion seemed more unsettling in Darce's absence, like the stillness contained some threat Isla couldn't see.

She didn't know how long they waited. The sun gave up on its fight and retreated behind the blanket of clouds. The rain was relentless, soaking the charred remains of their fire and leadening the wool of her cloak with its weight. Isla was ready to gather the rest of their belongings and set off alone when Darce finally emerged over the summit of the knoll, white-faced and breathless.

"We're being tracked," he said. "The selkies picked up our trail."

Isla stiffened. "How many?"

"I don't know." Darce shook his head. "They didn't show themselves."

"Then how do you—"

"Now isn't the time for questions, wolf cub." Darce slid the claymore from the sling on his back, drawing the great blade from its wrappings. "Wherever they are, they're not far. We need to get to Kinraith before they catch up with us." He turned towards Lachlan. "You too, little laird. Get away from the water and..." He broke off, the rest of his words disappearing as they touched the dreich air. "Lachlan, get away from the water!"

The ripples changed. Moments ago, the water had washed over the loch's edge and ebbed away like a steady breath. Now the waves pushed forward with urgency, dashing off the sand and pebbles faster with each passing second. Something was coming their way.

Isla barely registered the shadow before it burst through the surface. A huge, slick-coated shape leapt from the shallows, sending spray flying. Isla recoiled at the wildness of it: beady black eyes, a rippling, muscular bulk, powerful jaws clamped around the shaft of an axe.

The selkie transformed. Its speckled fawn-coloured fur, glistening with water, shrank back to reveal pale, freckled skin and unkempt hair. Its eyes changed shape and lightened into a stormy grey. It landed in the waves on two legs, bare and wet, covered only by the long tails of the pelt that now sat upon the selkie's broad shoulders. Its long jaws and protruding snout melded into more familiar features, until the creature staring at them had the face of a woman.

The selkie grinned, the axe handle still between her teeth. Then she sprang.

It was over before Isla could flinch. The selkie grabbed her, pressing the axe against her neck with a metal kiss. At the same time, another figure burst from the loch, shedding a white sealskin. He leapt on Lachlan, dragging him to the water and holding him there with a serrated hunting dagger at his throat.

Nobody spoke a word. The only sound was the heavy patter of rain bouncing off the loch's surface. It filled Isla's ears, drowning out the drum of her heart, the echoing of her breaths. The selkie's axe squeezed against her neck so tightly that Isla dared not swallow.

Darce stared at them, a calm, measured fury in the stone of his expression. He didn't move an inch, even as the rain beat down against his face. He just watched the selkies with dark eyes.

"I'd consider carefully what you do next," he said, his voice so quiet Isla had to strain to hear it. "If I see so much as a drop of blood escape their necks, you'll pay for it with your own."

Isla felt the selkie's chest rumble behind her, the laugh punctuated by rattling clicks from the creature's throat. The axe bit fiercely against her neck, the rough edge of it keen and hungry.

"Easy now," the selkie said, her voice rasping at Isla's ear. "Why don't you lay down that blade of yours before you do something daft and get your wee fledglings killed?"

Every breath Isla took was stilted by the nip of the axe against her skin. If she moved, the blade would slice open her throat, leaving her to drown in her own blood. All she could do was hold herself still, waiting to see what Darce would do.

The sergeant's face was as stony as ever as he gripped his claymore in two hands, feet planted carefully in the shifting shingle. He didn't lay down the sword like the selkie asked, but neither did he draw closer.

Isla knew how fast he could move. She'd seen the ferocity with which he swung a blade. But none of that would matter if the selkie opened her throat and let her blood spill across the shore.

Behind her, the selkie turned to her companion and uttered a sharp growl. The other selkie released the blade from Lachlan's throat and pushed him free.

Lachlan stumbled to shore, the water splashing around his ankles. When he reached the banks, Darce stepped in front of him, his eyes as distrusting as ever. "That your idea of a peace offering? I might be inclined to believe it were it not for the blood you've spilled already."

The selkie's voice took on a flinty edge. "Don't talk to me about blood spilled. You might not like where that conversation leads." Then she relaxed, her hand loosening on Isla's shoulder. "In any case, there's no need for violence today. We want to talk."

"Talk?" Rage bubbled in Isla's chest. "You *animals* don't know what it is to talk. You only know what it is to kill. Do you think we'd forget the bodies you left behind? The backs you flayed and left in bloody ribbons? My own father—"

"Isla, don't," Darce called warningly.

She ignored him, craning her neck to look at the selkie. "Let me go and put a weapon in my hand. We'll see how eager you are to talk then."

The selkie let out a low, throaty chuckle and glanced at Darce, her brow quirking. Darce stared back, consternation etched in every line of his face. Then he slowly bowed, lowering his sword to the ground. It nestled against the pebbles with a dull clink.

Darce straightened. "Release her. Then we'll talk."

A rush of air swept across Isla's skin as the axe lifted from her neck. She scrambled back, bringing her hand to her throat. Now was her first chance to get a good look at her captor. The selkie was a head taller than her, with brown-blonde hair and a smattering of freckles colouring her pale skin. She surveyed Isla with grey eyes, twisting her mouth into a smile that almost seemed human.

"Go," she said, resting her axe on her shoulder as she gestured towards the shore. "But don't forget I spared your life today, lass. The auld ways dictate that debt must be repaid."

Isla waded through the waves, heart thumping angrily as she slipped between Darce and Lachlan. Her eyes darted to her pack propped up against the trunk of the ash tree. If she could only reach her pistol, she might have time to fire a shot before the rain soaked the powder. She wouldn't miss this time. She'd put a pellet right between the selkie's eyes. Let *that* be a debt repaid.

She turned back to the loch. The selkie stood knee high in the water, the tails of her pelt drifting around her bare shins. Her sealskin looked different now, so subtly formed that anyone could have mistaken it for a well-fashioned set of winter vestments. The fur draped over her rounded, muscular shoulders, joining across her chest and cascading across her thighs to form something that resembled a dress. It clung to her like a second skin, and though the fur was soaked through, she moved in it like it held no weight.

"My name is Eimhir," she said, inclining her head. "This is my clan-mate, Finlay."

The other selkie's blue-eyed gaze was keen and alert as it darted between them. He was younger than Eimhir, his face marble smooth and his white pelt loose around his shoulders.

"What do you want?" Isla said bluntly.

Eimhir's voice was even in her reply. "I already told you, I wish to talk. I assure you, we *animals* are quite capable of it."

Lachlan barked out a laugh. "You killed our entire family. You slaughtered a village of innocents. The only thing you're capable of is violence."

Eimhir's face hardened. "Neither Finlay nor I were among the selkies who killed your family. We were following the raiders, but we were not part of their company."

"Even if that were true, I fail to see how the distinction makes my family any less dead," Isla shot back. "It was still your people."

Eimhir seemed as if she was about to say something, then snapped her mouth shut, the grey of her eyes flinty and sullen. Isla wanted nothing more than to turn away, but the fear of letting the selkie slip out of sight was worse than the revulsion roiling in her stomach when she looked at her.

Eventually, Eimhir let out a heavy sigh. "You're right. It was my people. And if I am to answer for their crimes, perhaps that is only fair. After all, we tracked you here so you might answer for yours." Contempt flickered across her features. "You made it rather easy in the end. You left something behind for us to follow. Spilled blood that led us right to you." Her eyes flitted to Darce, who stiffened under her gaze. "I imagine it belonged to you, auld blood."

At first, Isla was sure she'd misheard. The selkie's voice came from the back of her throat, rough and guttural, accompanied by a sound that reminded Isla of water streaming over stone. Her speech was strange, the vocalisations harsh and unfamiliar. That was the only way to explain what she'd heard.

Then she saw Darce's face, pale and shaken, and realised she hadn't been mistaken at all.

You want something you do not understand, he'd told her last night as the fire burned to embers.

Auld blood, Eimhir had called him.

Darce Galbraith, her father's trusted swordmaster, was a tides-damned sentinel.

Isla swallowed the rising nausea. No. She didn't believe it. If it were true, if the old magic ran through his blood... Surely he would have *done* something. Surely he'd have used the wards to protect them. A sentinel would have been able to fight the selkies that night. A sentinel would have been able to save them.

"The auld blood runs in selkie and sentinel alike," Eimhir continued. "It sings to us, even when it's faint. I sensed its trail in your home, uncertain and elusive. I knew it was not from one of my kind, for the trail ran away from the coast, not towards it. The closer we got, the more it slipped from us. Yet here you are."

"Here I am," Darce said, his voice firm. "If it's me you came here for, so be it. Whatever blood I owe you, I'll give you a fighting chance of taking it from me, blade to blade. But my promise still stands: lay a hand on either of these two, and tides be my witness, it will be the last thing you ever do."

Eimhir raised an eyebrow. "I have no reason to hurt your fledglings. I spared their lives, didn't I? The lad for honour, and the lass for a debt." She glanced at Isla. "All I want is to give you a chance to repay that which you owe."

"That which *I* owe?" Isla repeated, voice hollow. "Tides take you. Your people soaked Caolaig's streets in blood. Your people desecrated our home with flayed corpses displayed like trophies. What more could I possibly give you on top of what you've already taken?"

"A way to stop it."

Eimhir's words hung between them long after their ringing faded into silence. Isla's tongue dried up in her mouth, her throat thickening around the disbelieving words she wanted to speak. A way to *stop* it? Every year since she was a bairn, the selkies had raided Silveckan's coasts. Every year, they left the waters churning red and shores littered with bloated bodies. They couldn't stop. They didn't *want* to stop.

They were worse than animals. They were monsters.

A knot of fury pulled tight in Isla's stomach. Her palm twitched, itching for her pistol. Her pack was by the knotted trunk of the ash tree, a dozen paces away at most.

"Wait."

The dripping folds of Eimhir's pelt hung loose around her shoulders. The muscles in her bare arms flexed, more powerful than any human's. She was everything Isla expected a selkie to be: brutish and wild like the sea they came from. What she hadn't expected was the crack in her expression, the sliver of something soft and wounded exposed beneath. A pain Isla almost recognised.

Eimhir tossed her axe to the shore. It bounced off the shingle, coming to rest beside Darce's claymore. "On the souls of my ancestors, you have nothing to fear from me."

Isla trailed her eyes over the surrendered weapon. She couldn't trust a selkie. She had no reason to trust a selkie. It went against every instinct. But Eimhir's voice struck at a part of her that ran deeper than grief, deeper than anger. It made her want to stop. It made her want to listen. Eimhir's axe had nestled snugly against her throat. Now it was at Darce's feet, offered freely.

Isla wanted to understand why.

Lachlan said nothing as she turned to look at him, but his tawny eyes glittered with the same anger that had knotted Isla's stomach only moments before. If she did this, it might be more than her brother could forgive. It might be more than she could forgive of herself.

That would be his choice. This had to be hers.

"Very well," Isla said. "Let's talk."

CHAPTER NINE

T he rain eased off as they perched along the moss-covered log and
waited for someone to disturb the silence. Eimhir told Finlay to
retrieve their packs from where they'd stashed them, and the younger
selkie, reluctant at first, finally relented and slunk into the loch, his pelt
melting over his shoulders as he took his seal form again.

Once the ripples subsided, Darce gathered his claymore from the
water's edge. He rested the blade at his feet as he sat opposite Eimhir,
fixing the selkie woman with a glare. *Auld blood*, Eimhir had called him.
A sentinel. How long had he known? How long had he kept this from
them, kept this from their father?

He turned to Isla, eyes dark and troubled. Even with Finlay gone, the
sergeant seemed on edge, his fingers itching for the hilt of his sword. She
gave a slight shake of her head and he stilled, returning his hands to his
side.

If Eimhir sensed the tension, she showed no sign of it. Instead, she
propped her axe against the log and accepted Isla's offer of the wrapped
parcel of fish she'd taken from the market. The selkie snatched greedily
at the cured salmon, the thin pink strips falling apart in her fingers as she
pushed them into her mouth, licking the scraps when it was gone.

"Not bad," she said. "You humans do some strange things to your food
when you take it from our waters, but this is surprisingly pleasant."

She looked between them all, bright-eyed and discerning. Her pelt was already drying, changing colour in the light. Isla found herself unable to tear her eyes from the fur's subtle lustre. Rippling tones of gold and brown cascaded through it, giving the pelt an allure that captivated Isla as much as it repulsed her.

"Let's get on with this," she said, voice brittle. "The sooner you say what you came here to say, the sooner we can part ways. I don't think either of us is interested in keeping each other's company for any longer than we need to."

"Yet here we are," Eimhir said. "Human and selkie, managing to exist together without bloodshed."

"For now," Lachlan muttered.

"For now." Eimhir tilted her head, surveying him with wary eyes. "Still, it's a start. Would it not be in your interest to see an end to the violence between our people?"

"It might be, were I inclined to believe it was possible," Lachlan snapped. "Your ever-increasing raids on our shores lead me to believe otherwise."

Isla placed a quieting hand on his arm. Lachlan stiffened under her touch, but pressed his lips closed, swallowing whatever else he might have wanted to say. Instead, he pulled back, watching Eimhir with a frown.

"My brother is right," Isla said. "You can't blame us for doubting you want an end to this."

"You don't know what you have done to my people. Perhaps if you did, you'd understand." Eimhir glanced between them. "Tell me, what do you know of our sealskins?"

"Besides the fact they allow you to turn into monsters?" Lachlan curled his lip. "What more is there to know?"

"One does not need a pelt to turn into a monster," Eimhir replied, her voice calm. "You humans should understand that better than most." A shadow fell across her face. "These pelts are not just sealskins—they are soulskins. To understand anything about us, you must first understand that. They do not merely allow us to change shape. They contain a selkie's soul."

Isla stilled. "Your soul? How is that possible?"

"It's not something a human can easily understand. Your souls exist within you, bound to you alone." Eimhir buried her hand in the folds of her pelt. "Ours exist in our pelts, our soulskins. They connect us to our ancestors. They ensure we live on long after our bodies perish. They are the most precious parts of ourselves. We can remove our pelts as easily as a human can remove one of their fancy cloaks, and you think that justifies your actions when you steal them from us. But it is not the same. Our pelts may look like simple clothing in our human form, but they are our *souls*."

Her words sent a shudder through Isla's chest. "Your kind has stolen much from us in turn. Caolaig was proof enough of that."

"One is not the same as the other," Eimhir said. "Do you know what happens when a selkie is separated from their pelt? Our bodies cannot exist without our soulskins. We are creatures of the water, and when you prevent us from returning there in our natural form, you destroy us. Our organs shrivel and refuse to sustain us. Our flesh grows hard with salt and crumbles, leaving only our bones behind. Unless we are reunited with that which is taken from us, we wither and die."

"A life is a life, regardless of how it is taken," Lachlan said, his eyes flashing. "It doesn't bother you when you're drowning us or flaying us alive."

Eimhir shook her head. "That's where you're wrong. When we kill a human, we're extinguishing a single life. The harm we do to your people does not extend beyond that body, beyond that soul. But when you take a pelt from us, you carry out an act of violence that echoes through generations."

"Through generations?" Isla furrowed her brow. "What are you talking about?"

"There is power in blood. We've always known it. There was a time your kind did too, though it's been forgotten by all but a few." Eimhir sent Darce a pointed look. "When our children are born they are like humans, naked flesh. For them to become one of us, they must inherit a soulskin from a selkie no longer with us."

Darce shifted, fingers digging into the log. "How can you inherit a soul?"

"It is an ancient ritual, the beginnings of which not even the oldest of us remember. When we die, our blood is spilled onto our pelts, bringing together our body and soul. It is a time for mourning, but also celebration. The passing of the pelt provides new life, carrying with it the souls of our ancestors across thousands of years." Eimhir closed her eyes. "That is why the worst thing a human can do to us is take our pelts. If we're killed in battle, our blood-soaked furs are brought home. If we die of disease or old age, our funeral rites involve spilling our blood into our pelts. But if they are lost or stolen..."

"There's nothing to pass on," Isla finished, her words catching in her throat.

"Aye," Eimhir said. "Our people are dying. It's something we've known ever since the sea blessed us with our souls. We'll never be more in number than we are today. We are not meant to last forever." Her lips pulled into a bitter smile. "We know our time in this world is only a beautiful, transient thing. That is why we cannot forgive you every time you shorten it."

Tension fell like a storm ready to break. The threat of violence hadn't dissipated; it lingered between them, and all it would take to release it was one sharp word, one cutting remark.

"The flaying." Darce spoke quietly, his face ashen. "That's why your raiders strip the skin from our backs and leave the bodies on display. All these years I thought it was wanton violence, but it's more than that, isn't it? It's a message."

"One your Admiralty has yet to take heed of," Eimhir replied. "It used to be we selkies kept to our own waters. The only humans we threatened were those who sailed into our territory. But the seas are getting smaller. Every year, your Grand Admiral opens more shipping routes across selkie waters. The more he charts, the fewer places we have to hide. For where your commerce goes, your sentinels and selkie hunters follow."

"Does the Grand Admiral know?" The words sounded weak to Isla's ears as they left her mouth. "Perhaps if he understood—"

"Tell me, how much gold does a selkie pelt command on the continent these days?" Eimhir chuckled as Isla's face fell. "Aye, I thought as much. I believe your Grand Admiral understands all too well. He'll hunt us until there's nothing left of us to squeeze coin out of. And we'll make him pay for that until the last one of us is salt and spray once more."

"By flaying us," Isla said shakily. "As vengeance for the theft of your pelts. But Caolaig was a fishing village. We didn't have any hunters. Nothing we did could possibly warrant that kind of torture."

"If it was not you, it was still your people," Eimhir said pointedly. "Wasn't that what you said before?"

The echo of her own words flung back at her stung Isla's cheeks like a slap. "You think that justifies the killing of innocents? There were fucking *children* in the village. Don't you dare try to compare—"

"You want to talk to me about children?" Eimhir's voice turned dangerously soft. "Do you know what happens to a selkie newborn with no pelt to inherit? They wither and die within months, and each moment they spend without their soul is one of agony. I watched my mother as she held my baby brother one last time before returning him to the sea. He was so small. His skin wrinkled and dried and became scarred with salt. The water swallowed him and took him to its depths. He was never one of us. All because there was no pelt for him. All because of what you humans stole from him."

Isla froze. She wanted to unhear Eimhir's words, to find the lie in them so she could push them away. But there was no deceit in the broken timbre of the selkie woman's voice, only despair. A grief that was all too familiar, all too *human*.

"I'm sorry," she managed. Her words were hoarse, scraping her throat raw. "For your brother. But that still doesn't justify—"

"Sorry?" Eimhir's laugh was a harsh, painful sound. "A thousand apologies could never put right what has happened between our people. Your kind continue to hunt us, stealing our pelts for trophies with no remorse, no understanding of what you have done. Our numbers dwindle year after year because there are no longer enough pelts to hand down to our children." She clenched her jaw. "And when the consequences of your own greed, your own violence, come from the mists to make things right, you blame *us* for what happens."

"Consequences? What are you..." Isla stiffened, her skin prickling with memories from Blackwood Estate. A blade of vapour and shadow plunging through Lachlan's shoulder. The air turning cold enough to freeze the breath in her lungs. Silvery droplets scattering across the floor. The lone rider in the misty courtyard, its kelpie mount leaving a watery trail across the cobbles.

"You're talking about the wraiths," she said, horror rising in her throat. "What are they?"

"They are the monsters you created." The grey of Eimhir's eyes darkened like a storm rolling in. "We call them the gun-anam—the soulless. Selkies whose pelts were stolen from them, whose bodies turned to salt and wasted away, leaving them as wandering spirits, lost without their souls. They forge their armour from the bones they leave behind. They summon creatures of salt and spray. They bring with them the storms of their wrath and the mists of their sorrow. And when we raid, they follow us, feeding on the blood we shed in violence, in hatred."

Isla forgot to breathe. "You *led* them to us?"

"I told you the truth when I said I was not part of the raid on your home," Eimhir said. "But my family was, ancestors forgive their souls. When my baby brother died, my mother and sister threw themselves into raiding. For years, they've bloodied their hands over and over for what they lost. For years, I've been trying to stop them. I knew it was only a matter of time before they succumbed to the mist sickness."

"Mist sickness?"

Eimhir's face was pale as she spoke, her lips trembling. "The gun-anam are drawn to trauma and pain. The more we raid, the more they follow, and the more their suffering infects us. When the sickness becomes too much, we lose all sense of self. All we can do is continue to throw ourselves against those who have wronged us."

A shiver crawled over Isla's skin. "How many times have *you* come into contact with them?"

"Not enough. Yet too many to bear." Eimhir sighed. "My mother and sister are beyond saving. I am all that remains of my family. Perhaps now you understand why I seek an end to this, an end to the gun-anam."

Isla glanced at Darce. The sergeant sat tight-lipped and dark-eyed as he stared at the charred flecks of ash from last night's fire. Beside him, Lachlan was rigid and pale, a tremor dancing in his jaw. His right hand hung casually by his side, fingers half drifting to where his sgian dubh was tucked in his boot. Isla wondered what Eimhir would do if he leapt at her. The selkie woman presented a calm façade, but rage and grief simmered under every syllable. Maybe she expected this to end in violence. Maybe she was counting on it.

"How would you end it?" The words left Isla's mouth before she realised she'd spoken. They caught her by surprise, leaving her tongue dry and her heart drumming a frantic rhythm against her ribs. Almost immediately, she wished she could take them back. They felt too much like an offer she couldn't bring herself to make, a promise she would only break.

Eimhir's smile was like iron. "With your help."

"Our help?" Lachlan shot her an incredulous look. "You can't be serious."

"Why not? The gun-anam are humanity's mistake. You are responsible for them. It is you who needs to make things right."

"What proof do we have of that except your word? The word of a selkie." Lachlan scowled. "We won't be baited into believing your lies. We already know those wraiths cannot be killed."

"I don't want to kill them," Eimhir said. "I want to end their suffering. Our pelts contain the souls of our ancestors. For most selkies, they come to us only in glimpses. They offer comfort when it is needed, advice when we're in danger. But there are some selkies who can visit the memories of their ancestors, who can see things that came to pass long ago, who can move between our world and the non-existence the gun-anam are trapped in. In your tongue, they would be called dreamwalkers."

"Dreamwalkers." Isla rolled the word on her tongue, trying to make sense of it. "You're saying one of these selkies could stop the gun-anam?"

"They could, were there any who still lived." Eimhir's voice took on a brittle edge. "My aunt was the last one I knew of, and she died shortly after I was born. Killed by your Grand Admiral."

"Not without good reason, I'd wager," Lachlan said coldly.

"She had the most beautiful pelt our people had ever seen. The Grand Admiral coveted it, wanted it for his own. He murdered her for it. He stripped her soul from her back and dumped her body in the sea." Eimhir drew her lips into a sneer. "Tell me, human, does that sound like good reason to you?"

Isla looked at Eimhir's pelt. She'd never seen a sealskin so close before. The fur had a sheen to it unlike the coat of any other creature. It rippled like it was alive.

It was not hard to believe the Grand Admiral would desire such a trophy. His reputation was as fearsome and uncompromising as the seas themselves. He was not the kind of man who would let something he wanted slip through his fingers, even if he had to kill to get it.

"My aunt left behind no children of her own, but her blood runs through me," Eimhir continued. "If I claim her pelt, I may be able to inherit her memories and learn her ability to dreamwalk. I could stop the gun-anam and put an end to this violence before it has the chance to claim anyone else." She held them all in her gaze, unapologetic and unflinching. "This is why I need your help. To take back what he stole."

Isla couldn't speak. She could hardly breathe. Eimhir's words rang around her ears, the absurdity of them leaving her lightheaded. What she was asking was unthinkable, impossible.

Lachlan choked out a hollow laugh. "Oh, this is too much. You're telling us you plan to steal a sealskin from the Grand Admiral, of all people? To lift some alleged curse on these so-called soulless? And you expect us to *help?*"

"My clan tasked me with finding my aunt's stolen pelt and bringing it home. I don't have a chance of getting near it without the help of a human. When I stepped foot onto those wretched shores and saw what the gun-anam did to your home, what they drove my family to do..." Eimhir trailed off, swallowing. "I'd hoped I might find someone who shared my enemy. Someone who had as much reason to want the soulless stopped as I."

Isla opened her mouth—to laugh, perhaps. To tell Eimhir no enemy could ever make her desperate enough to help a selkie. But her words stuck in her throat, unwilling or unable to come out. She remembered the wraith plunging its blade into Lachlan's shoulder while he slept. Its dead, icy breath against her cheek. The silvery droplets it left across the floor.

Tides, if there was a way to stop them...

"If you succeed—" She broke off, her voice lost in a shaking breath. "Are you certain that with this pelt, you can put an end to these gun-anam?"

"I am certain of nothing," Eimhir said. "The knowledge of how to move between this world and the realm of the soulless died with my aunt. That is why I must bring the pelt to my clan. Only they can help me uncover that knowledge by helping me learn to dreamwalk. It will take time, but—"

"Time," Isla echoed, the noise dull in her throat. She knew only too well what time would mean for the Silvish coast. It was a measure not of hours and days, but of blood-soaked shores and flesh torn to ribbons. Bloated bodies, grey and waxy, lungs bursting with salt and seawater. The gleam of an axe against the sky. The stench of iron and rot in every gutter. "And what happens to us after you take your aunt's pelt back to your clan? Can you promise that if we help you, your people will stop their raids on our shores?"

Eimhir hesitated. Isla could see the lie on the tip on the tongue. She curled her fists, ready to tear the deception from her, ready to put an end to this madness before it had a chance to begin.

But Eimhir didn't say anything. Instead, she swallowed and shook her head. "I cannot promise you that. All I can do is try to close a wound that has been killing my people and yours alike. Without that pain, perhaps there is a chance for us to heal. For *all* of us to heal."

"A *chance* is not enough."

"No," Eimhir agreed softly. "But it is a start. Perhaps that's all we can hope for."

Silence fell between them, thick with the weight of Eimhir's words. Isla relaxed her fists and willed her racing heart to settle. It was too much to take in. Too much to accept. Eimhir offered a sliver of hope like bait on the end of a line, thinking Isla was unable to see the glint of jagged hooks underneath. And yet...

Fear crawled over her skin as she thought of the wraith in the courtyard. The memory of it was enough to turn her breath cold in her lungs. The empty sockets in its seal-skull mask. Its armour of blackened bone, holding together mist and spray. The way it turned its head towards her and spoke with a voice from the depths.

They are the monsters you created, Eimhir had said.

Tides, what if she was *right?*

Eimhir rose stiffly. "Finlay has been gone some time. I should check on him. Consider what I ask of you, humans. And remember I spared you instead of wetting the shore with your blood. If you owe me for nothing else your kind has done to mine, you owe me for that." Her gaze hardened as it found Isla. "Help me or not. One way or another, I will see your debt paid."

The warning lingered in the wind as Eimhir walked barefoot across the shingle to the edge of the loch. Her pelt stretched across her skin, sliding down her bare arms, wrapping itself around her legs.

Then she let herself sink into the water and disappeared.

When the retreating ripples subsided, Lachlan leapt to his feet. "We should gather our packs and get out of here before they return. For all her talk, she's ready to draw her axe across your throat. We can't give her that chance."

Isla didn't move. "If what she's saying is true—"

"You can't possibly believe—"

"*If* it's true," she repeated firmly, "then no number of Admiralty ships will ever be enough to protect Caolaig. More raiders will come, and with them, more wraiths. You saw what happened at the estate. You know we can't stand against those things."

"All I saw was a shapeless spirit." Lachlan rubbed a hand over his wounded shoulder, grimacing. "What makes you believe it was anything more than that? You spent enough time when we were bairns terrifying me with tales of will-o'-the-wisps and cù-sìth and brollachan. I'm not denying these wraiths are dangerous, but that doesn't mean they have anything to do with the selkies."

"The one in the courtyard wasn't some shapeless spirit. It wore a seal skull and sat atop a kelpie mount made of salt water and spray. It must have been one of them, one of the gun-anam."

"I saw no such thing when I found you, wolf cub." Darce said gently. "Only the selkie trying to tear your throat out. Believe me, if anything else had threatened you, it would have met my blade."

"But—"

"This isn't the first time I've seen the blood and ruin the selkies leave in their wake," Darce said. "But it's the first time I've encountered anything like those wraiths. Lachlan is right. They are a foul kind of spirit, but there's nothing to suggest their presence among the selkies was anything more than a coincidence."

Lachlan rounded on him. "Speaking of raids, Galbraith, I don't know where to begin with you. All these years you've been by my side and never once did you think to mention you're a bloody *sentinel*?"

A grey look fell over Darce's face. "Now is not the time, little laird. We have more urgent concerns at hand." He flicked his eyes towards Isla.

A shiver ran down her spine at the lingering echo of the selkie's parting words. "From what Eimhir said about their ways, the fact she spared me means I owe her my life. If we don't agree to help them, I fear she'll make me pay with it."

Darce stooped to pick his claymore from the coarse shingle, his hand tight around the pommel. "You know I won't let that happen. She may have got her blade to you once, but tides take me if I let her do it again."

His gaze offered the same steel as his blade. It was just as unyielding, just as resolute. It made Isla want to believe him. It made her want to trust him, like her father had. Darce had protected them, hadn't he? He'd kept them alive this far.

He'd also kept from them a secret that could have saved them all.

"Even you're not infallible, Sergeant," Isla said curtly. "The truth is, until we reach the capital, we're vulnerable. It seems to me we're better off keeping our enemy where we can see them."

Something in Darce's expression faltered, the hard lines giving way to something pained and regretful. He opened his mouth, looking like he was about to say something more, but then pressed his lips together, giving her nothing more than a resigned nod.

Lachlan glanced between them, his face stricken. "Those creatures killed our *father*," he said. "How can you consider trusting them after that?"

The crack in his voice sent an ache through Isla's heart. It was easy to forget her brother's anger only existed to mask his pain. That pain would never leave, not when so much had been ripped from him, not until he had a home to return to, somewhere he could heal.

Somewhere they could *all* heal, like Eimhir said.

The nip of the wind caught the nape of Isla's neck. If what Eimhir said was true, Blackwood Estate would never be safe, not as long as those soulless spirits, those gun-anam, existed. But the bite of the selkie's axe still lingered against her throat. How much could she believe a bargain bought with the edge of a blade?

"I don't trust them," Isla said. "I'm asking you to trust me. I promised I'd stay by your side until we get our home back, and I will, no matter what it takes." She released a long breath and met Lachlan's eyes. "We'll let the selkies join us and go to Arburgh like we planned. We don't have to decide anything more than that, not yet."

Darce folded his arms, a troubled look crossing his face. "You think that will be enough for them?"

"It's what they want to hear, isn't it?" Isla glanced at the loch. The water was still and glassy, its depths dark below the surface. She couldn't help but fear it was listening, fear it would swallow their secrets and spill them back to the two selkies. "Once we're in Arburgh, we'll have more protection. We might even be able to use them to gain favour with the Grand Admiral. Whatever it takes to secure his aid." She turned to Lachlan, taking his hand in hers. "I told you—we're going home at the end of this. Together."

Home. As the word left her mouth, Isla shivered. All she could think of when she pictured Blackwood Estate was creeping mist and spilled blood. It was difficult to imagine ever returning there and knowing peace.

What wasn't difficult to imagine was what might await them in Arburgh if this all went wrong. She pictured it as clearly as if it was there in front of her: the wooden carcass of the gallows waiting to welcome her into its jaws, and a noose swaying in the breeze.

CHAPTER TEN

When they started off again, the three of them had become five. Eimhir returned with Finlay and nodded in quiet acceptance when Isla told her they'd agreed to help. No other words were spoken, and after the two selkies pulled on their clothes and boots from the packs Finlay retrieved, they set out on the final stretch towards Kinraith.

The moor was rugged and exposed, offering no protection from the biting wind. The rain assaulted them from the side in furious gusts, soaking them through. All that grew on the barren ground were coarse swathes of purple heather and yellow gorse. It was a miserable trudge across the sodden, peaty terrain, but when they at last reached the other side, the port of Kinraith was waiting for them.

Isla filled her lungs as they navigated the winding outskirts of the town towards the main harbour. The air was thick with the sea again, full of salt and brine and seaweed. She hadn't realised how much she'd missed it in the few days they'd spent trudging through the forests and heathlands. Pine needles and heather had a pleasant scent of their own, but it wasn't the same as the brackish smell that burned her nostrils now, so sharp she could taste it on her tongue.

Lachlan caught her eye. "I suppose we should go about finding ourselves a ship. Any ideas?"

"Aye—let me do the talking," Darce cut in, sending him a warning glance. "These seafarer types can spot a soft noble lad a mile away. Best let me handle the negotiations unless you want taken for what little coin you have left."

Isla bit back the smile playing at her lips. "Can't argue with the sergeant's reasoning."

"You manage just fine when it suits your purpose." Lachlan rolled his eyes. "Very well. Lead on, Galbraith."

The streets widened as they approached the docks, the cobbles barely visible beneath the bustling of sailors and merchants. Kinraith was at least three times the size of Caolaig, boasting a thriving harbour alive with chatter and noise. There was too much to take in: great wagon-loads of harvested kelp awaiting transportation to the capital; passengers milling around, clutching their ship papers to their chests; a sprawling fishmarket that made Isla's mouth water after days of sour blackberries and cured salmon.

Most of the ships were proud, imposing vessels, blocking out the light as they loomed over the dock. They groaned restlessly against the waves, held in place like wild beasts by thick seaweed-covered mooring lines. It didn't seem right for them to be tied up. They wanted to be out on the water, cutting through the swell with full sails. They wanted to be free.

The closest ship was a formidable-looking thing, the length of its hull lined with gun ports, its tall masts stretching skywards, its black sails billowing in the wind like angry storm clouds.

"Admiring the view?" The voice came from a man leaning casually on the rail at the side of the gangway. His hair was slicked across his forehead, and he was dressed in sturdy leathers and a cloak trimmed in black fur. "If you're headed for the capital, ain't no ship safer to book passage on than the *Stormbreaker* here."

Darce surveyed the ship with an unconvinced scowl. "Not much to admire. And your pitch needs work—most captains would boast of their speed over their safety."

"I ain't most captains. And the *Stormbreaker* ain't most ships." He pushed himself off the post, his chest puffing as he sauntered closer. "We have certain…protections that other ships don't. Protections that paying passengers like yourselves deserve, what with the seas being as they are these days."

Something in the tone of his voice chilled Isla's skin. She cast a furtive glance at Darce, whose expression was growing darker by the minute. "I don't think we—"

"What kind of protections?" Lachlan interrupted.

The captain smirked. "You're not the only passengers to ask. Just so happens, we're about to do a wee demonstration on deck. How about you join us and see for yourselves?"

Before Isla could say anything, Lachlan was already following the captain up the gangway. She hurried after him, cursing him under her breath for being so bloody bull-headed all the time.

"What happened to letting Darce handle the negotiations?" she hissed, tugging on his sleeve.

Lachlan shrugged. "I want to see what this so-called protection entails. The crossing to Arburgh is dangerous, and I don't trust those selkies. If they call on their kind to attack us while we're on the water, I want to be on a ship capable of defending itself."

His words were calm and measured, but that wasn't enough to stop the shudder that ran through her as she followed him onto the *Stormbreaker's* deck. Something about the ship troubled her. She felt it in the creak of timber under her feet, in the shadow of the sails and rigging above. The ship was watching her. It saw how restless she was. It heard the churning in her stomach, the anxious trembling of her heart.

Darce stiffened. "Tides, I need to beat some bloody sense into your brother. We have no business being on a ship like this."

"What do you mean?"

His jaw tightened as he stared up at the masts. "There's something here. A presence, or the echo of one. It's restless. Hungry."

Isla shot him an uneasy look. "Like the wraiths?"

"No." Darce shook his head. "This is different."

"And you know this because you're a sentinel?" She tried to keep her voice even, but the edge of it pierced through, betraying her. "Was that why you were able to get to Lachlan and I so quickly back at Blackwood Estate? Did you sense them coming?"

A flash of pain darkened the sergeant's features. Then it was gone, leaving behind only exhaustion. "Not quickly enough. If I had... Isla, do you think I wouldn't have tried to—"

The rest of his words drowned in a collective gasp from the crowd gathered across the deck. The captain brought forward a young lad bound in chains and sporting a mottled purple bruise on his cheek. The lad struggled against his restraints, eyes wide and frenzied. At first, Isla didn't understand. Then she saw the way he was clutching his furs.

He was a selkie.

The lad's pelt hung raggedly around his bony shoulders, ripped in places it should have been whole. She glanced at Eimhir, who was staring at the young selkie with her jaw clenched so tightly a muscle twitched in the side of her neck.

Darce was right. They shouldn't have come here.

"For those of you who aren't aware, my name is Wilson, and this is my ship you have the honour to be aboard." The crowd hushed as the captain spread his arms. "I named it *Stormbreaker*, for there is no other ship on the Strait of Silveckan capable of repelling a squall like this one."

Wilson shoved the selkie in the back, and the lad fell to his knees. "Some captains will tell you to look for sentinels for protection. But when was the last time any of you saw a sentinel outside the capital fleet?" His grin widened at the murmured assent that rippled through the crowd. "I say we must protect ourselves. And what better way to do that than by using the blood of the tides-damned creatures we need protecting from in the first place?"

The selkie tried to scramble to his feet, but Wilson was too quick. He planted a boot on the lad's torn, shredded pelt, pinning it to the deck. He shot a hand out, grabbing a fistful of the selkie's hair and yanking his head back. "The *Stormbreaker* has made more than a dozen trips to the capital this year, and not once has a selkie breached its hull. You know why?" He leered at the crowd. "They can smell us coming. They know the stench of blood and decay. They know how eagerly the *Stormbreaker* drinks their blood. In its timber lies our protection. And all it takes is one less skinchanger in the world."

The dagger appeared in his hand in the moment it took Isla to blink. Her next breath caught somewhere between her mouth and lungs. She couldn't move. She couldn't do anything but stare at the edge of the blade and the smooth pale skin of the selkie's exposed throat.

"Look away," Darce said, his grip like iron around her arm.

It was too late. Wilson drew back his arm, leaving a thin red line across the selkie's neck. Blood bubbled out, spilling across the deck. It spread in a red pool, dripping through the narrow gaps in the timber and soaking into the wood.

Wilson released his hold on the selkie's hair. The lad's limp body fell with a dull thud, blood splattering across the fur of his torn pelt. Isla stared at it, unable to wrench her eyes away. Darce's hand was still around her arm, squeezing so hard she was sure she'd be left with bruises. A few metres along the deck, Eimhir turned white, holding a restraining hand across Finlay's chest.

"Shit," Lachlan muttered, glancing at them. "When he talked about protection, I didn't think... I didn't know he was going to..."

Wilson wiped his dagger on the end of his cloak. "A nasty business, dealing with these tides-forsaken beasts." He slipped the blade into his belt, sending the crowd a wide smile. "But rest assured, there is no creature of the sea that would dare approach *Stormbreaker* on our journey to Arburgh. Our new blood wards will make certain of that. If you want to ensure your safety between here and the capital, our quartermaster will gladly arrange your papers. Just make sure you have your coin ready."

Some of the crowd shuffled to the gangway, their faces drawn and pale as they left the ship. But more still hurried to the quartermaster, forming an agitated queue as they fished for coin in their pockets and purses.

Darce looked down, cheeks reddening as he quickly released her arm. "We should find another ship. Our new companions aren't likely to take this insult well. Risking the crossing with that kind of tension will only lead to more blood."

Isla didn't reply. The limp body of the young selkie lad lay crumpled on the deck. It shouldn't have disturbed her like it did. The selkies were monsters. A blade across the throat was more of a mercy than what they'd done at Caolaig. But in his dead, glassy eyes, she saw none of the wildness she'd learned to fear. He was a lad younger than Lachlan, his spilled life dripping between the cracks in the deck.

"Isla." Darce touched her shoulder. "We have to go."

She broke herself from her trance and turned to Eimhir. The selkie woman was staring into the distance with a glazed expression, her grey eyes stormier than ever.

Isla skirted through the crowd towards her, half afraid to break her reverie for fear that it would provoke something far more dangerous.

"Let's get out of here," she said tersely. "We'll find another way to reach the capital. Grab Finlay and..." She trailed off, glancing around.

Finlay was gone.

"No, no, no!" Lachlan's face paled. "He'll get us all killed."

Isla saw it now. Finlay had pushed through the crowd and was kneeling by the selkie lad's limp, unmoving body. He muttered something Isla couldn't hear and buried his hands in the fur of the red-stained pelt lying beside him on the deck.

Dread clawed at Isla's stomach. Finlay was shaking with barely contained rage, his eyes glistening. If Wilson turned around now, if he noticed how Finlay was clutching the dead lad's pelt... She imagined the captain's dagger sliding across a selkie throat for a second time. Lachlan was right. It wouldn't just be Finlay's blood soaking the deck. It would be the blood of them all.

Darce's hand was already drifting towards the rapier on his belt. "Head for the gangway. If he tries to follow, I'll—"

Wilson laughed at something the quartermaster said, then turned back. When he saw Finlay crouched over the dead selkie, a frown fell across his face. "What are you doing?"

"Apologies, Captain." Lachlan inserted himself between Wilson and Finlay, giving the selkie a rough kick and hauling him to his feet. "My brother here has a bit of an obsession with selkie pelts. Fancies himself a collector, as you see." He gestured to Finlay's own pelt, lustrous in the sunlight over his shoulders. "You'd think this beauty would be enough, but the brat has a hard time understanding he can't have everything."

Finlay wrestled furiously against Lachlan's grip, but Lachlan twisted his arm into an unnatural angle and brought him into line with a rough yank. Even from across the deck, Isla noticed how tightly her brother's fingers dug into the selkie's arm, pinning it against his back, out of reach of the hunting dagger in his belt.

Wilson glanced between them, a flicker of uncertainty on his face. For a moment, Isla feared Lachlan's bluff wouldn't be enough, that the captain would see through his deception and call his crew down on them. Her fingers drifted towards her pack, to the pistol waiting for her inside.

Then Wilson's face split into an amiable grin, and he let out a guffaw. "A lad of expensive tastes, aye? I can relate to that. It's a shame this one's pelt got damaged when we brought him in, but the wee bastard put up a fight. Still, there's more than a few fools in the capital who will part with good coin for it." He chuckled. "Unless your brother wants to empty his pockets, of course?"

"I'm afraid my pockets would be the ones emptied, so I'll have to decline your offer, generous though it may be," Lachlan said smoothly. "Thank you once again for your demonstration, very impressive."

Wilson grunted. "Aye, well, flattery won't get you a better cabin. If you still want to sail with us, best be seeing the quartermaster before we're full on passengers. We make sail in an hour." He waved them off with a dismissive hand and gestured to one of his crew. "Take care of this mess.

I want the pelt cleaned up and stored properly. Throw the rest of him over the side."

Lachlan waited until the crowd began to disperse, then dragged Finlay towards the gangway. Finlay struggled at first, his lips drawn in a snarl, but Lachlan jerked his arm and pushed him forward, not stopping until they were back on the harbourfront.

Eimhir raced down after them. The selkie's pale cheeks flushed pink as she walked, her brows knitted together in agitation. As soon as she reached Finlay, she pulled him from Lachlan's grasp and stormed off, muttering something unintelligible in their low-toned selkie tongue.

Lachlan stood with his hands on his hips. A trickle of sweat ran down his forehead, and he pushed his crop of golden hair from his face. "I knew this was a mistake."

"Would have been a lot worse if it wasn't for you." Isla glanced at him. "Where did that come from?"

"Did you think I was sitting on my arse for seven years while you were out finding yourself on the sea?" Lachlan snorted. "Our esteemed swordmaster probably believes otherwise, but there *are* ways to resolve conflict that don't involve the end of a blade. I've been training as much in politics and diplomacy as I have my sword arm. A good thing too, where we're going."

The image of Arburgh loomed in Isla's mind, dreich and grey. She hadn't forgotten how small it made her feel. Her parents had always warned her that capital politics were notoriously complex and none too pretty to look upon. Betrayals were as commonplace there as insincere compliments at a noble's dinner party, part of a game with so many rules it was difficult to know which of them you were breaking.

She'd learned that too late, and it had cost her everything.

"I hated that side of the capital," she said, unable to rid the bitterness from her tongue. "The scheming, the lies... I never thought you'd be interested in that kind of life."

"I didn't have much of a choice. The estate was meant to be yours, and I could never have lasted as a glorified steward, a laird only in name. Your shadow was too cold a place for me." A thin smile danced across Lachlan's lips. "No, if I was to step out on my own and make a name for myself, Arburgh seemed as good a place as any. And to survive the capital, you need to hone your tongue as sharp as your blade."

"You've certainly done that." Isla put a hand on his arm. "You saved us, after all."

"No need to sound so surprised." Lachlan grunted, but he couldn't hide the fact he looked rather pleased with himself. "Much though it may irk you to learn your wee brother is capable of handling a situation without your help."

"If you're so capable, you won't mind demonstrating it a second time, will you?" Isla nudged him. "In case you hadn't noticed, we're still in need of a ship. Preferably one that *isn't* crewed by selkie hunters, given our present company."

"I still say they're more trouble than they're worth," Lachlan grumbled. "Fine, I'll go to the harbourmaster's office and find out what other ships are taking on paying passengers." He whistled to Darce. "Galbraith, you're with me. A lot of ships from Bréchon come by the west coast, and they're friendlier with someone who knows the language. I trust my sister to keep our *friends* out of trouble while we speak with the captains." He grinned. "Don't worry, I'll leave the talking to you this time."

"I fear it's you who needs kept out of trouble, little laird. That silver tongue of yours is forever as likely to get you into a mess as it is to get you out of one." Darce's gaze fell across Isla, turning sombre. "I don't like leaving you alone with those selkies. Eimhir may have sheathed her axe for now, but I don't trust her word to be any less fickle than the waves."

Isla forced a smile. "I assure you, Sergeant, I'm perfectly capable of looking after myself. Or did you forget the outcome of our sparring session so quickly?"

"What I recall from our sparring session is how sloppy your swordplay has become," Darce countered. "A single-shot pistol is poor protection against two selkies, wolf cub."

"Then perhaps I should find a sentinel for protection instead. They seem to be hiding in plain sight these days, after all."

As soon as the words left her mouth, she regretted the sharpness of them. They rang through the air, piercing a tension she hadn't realised had thickened.

Darce stared at her, his stone-faced expression giving nothing away. Then he lowered his head. "As you wish. My apologies, Lady Blackwood." He averted his eyes and turned to Lachlan, clapping a firm hand on her brother's shoulder. "Come then, little laird. Let's find ourselves a ship."

Isla watched them melt into the bustling crowd. If she could have called the words back, she would have. They'd escaped her too rashly, too filled with a hurt she didn't understand. Even now, staring at Darce's retreating form, she couldn't help the heat spreading across her chest, the anger pulsing behind her sternum. It wasn't just the secret he'd kept. It ran deeper than that, coming from a place she wasn't sure she wanted to look for.

A low murmur across the crowd on the docks tore Isla from her thoughts, and she turned to the *Stormbreaker* to see two deckhands heaving the limp, naked body of the selkie lad over the top of the gunwale. She bit her tongue as he lay there, pallid and lifeless, before the deckhands pushed him into the murky harbour water with an irrevocable splash.

One less skinchanger in the world, Wilson had said. If only she could take that kind of satisfaction. Instead, something uncomfortably like pity rose from the pit of her stomach. Instead, tides forgive her, she was considering *helping* them.

Eimhir and Finlay were still arguing as she approached, their voices hushed. When Isla cleared her throat, they both looked at her with wary expressions.

"Come on," Isla said. The words sounded like a peace offering. "Let's get something to eat."

The tavern was as busy as the rest of the port, but Isla found a booth in the corner away from the crowds where they could sit in peace, hidden from intruding eyes. She signalled the barkeep and lightened her purse, and a huge wooden platter appeared on the table in front of them, topped with a spread of fresh Kinraith delicacies.

Finlay hesitated, as if waiting for permission, before grabbing one of the crab claws and cracking it open expertly, pulling the meat out and devouring it like he hadn't eaten in days.

Isla followed suit before everything was gone and split open a sea urchin, scooping out the yellow roe with her fingers and sucking hungrily. It was fresh and briny, with that sweet sea flavour she'd never missed until now. The warm sense of familiarity spreading through her was as unsettling as it was satisfying. It might have tasted of home, if only she understood what *home* truly meant.

She glanced at Finlay. It was difficult to look at him and not see some reflection of Lachlan—or at least, the Lachlan she'd left behind seven years ago. He had the adolescent leanness of a face that hadn't quite filled out, and if his display on the *Stormbreaker* was any indication, he shared the same hot-headedness her brother possessed in his own teenage years. It made something lurch in her heart, reminding her of how much time she'd never get back.

"I'm sorry about what happened on the ship," she said stiffly. "I know how difficult that must have been."

Finlay bristled. "You know nothing, human. Do you think just because you witnessed your kind's cruelty this time, that you understand it? If you had any idea..."

He let the empty crab claw fall to the table with a hollow rattle as he pulled his pelt closer. The white fur was thick and shiny, and in the lamplight Isla observed other colours rippling through it: subtle fractals of cloud blue and lavender grey. At a glance, the pelt seemed nothing more than an expensive set of furs draped across the breadth of his shoulders and down his arms, yet it could meld with his pale skin and turn him into one of the creatures she'd been taught to hate and fear.

Eimhir put a hand on his arm. "Fin's parents fell to the mist sickness, as my mother and sister did. We only have each other now."

Isla's throat constricted. "I know too well what that feels like."

She hadn't meant the words to sound like an accusation, but she still tasted the venom on her tongue. Some of it must have escaped in her voice too, for she noticed both selkies stiffen.

After a short, tense silence, Eimhir spoke. "We all knew this wouldn't be easy. There is too much blood spilled on both sides to call each other friend, yet an alliance built on nothing more than a mutual desire to see the gun-anam stopped seems fragile at best. If we are to trust each other, we must bury what came before." She glanced at Finlay. "All of us."

Finlay said nothing, but his mouth pulled into a hard line.

"What about you?" Eimhir fixed Isla with a keen stare. "Can you forgive me for holding my axe to your throat, or should I expect some kind of retribution?"

"If I was planning retribution, I'd hardly tell you to expect it."

Eimhir laughed, the sound rumbling from her throat. "The human can jest. There may be hope for us yet." She leaned across the table, amusement dancing in her eye. "Unless it's not a jest at all. Back at the loch, you asked me to put a weapon in your hand. I have to admit, I did not expect such fighting spirit."

Isla met her stare. "You wouldn't be the first monster I've killed."

The quiet that fell between them drowned out all the bustle and chatter from the rest of the tavern. Across the table, Finlay made to stand, but Eimhir steadied him with a gentle hand before turning to Isla.

"Is that what I am?" she asked, her voice measured.

There was no anger in her question, just a mild curiosity that left Isla more conflicted than ever. Eimhir was the enemy. She *wanted* her to be the enemy. It was her blade that had pressed against Isla's neck, her people who'd murdered Isla's father and slaughtered their way through Caolaig, leaving behind nothing but a bloody grave. She couldn't forget that. But neither could she forget the wraith on its mount, the dread that had frozen her breath and turned her blood to ice.

Isla leaned back, folding her arms. "I suppose I've seen worse."

"Careful, human. That almost sounded like a compliment." A languid smile stretched across Eimhir's lips, then faltered halfway. "Maybe you can pass some of that good humour along to your brother. I feel his anger every time he sets his eyes on me."

"If it wasn't for my brother, Finlay would be hanging on the wall of some Arburgh noble's mansion in short order, and the rest of us would be dead." Isla fought to keep the edge from her voice. "Lachlan is grieving. You cannot blame him for that. Not when your people caused it."

Eimhir made no reply, but her eyes turned hard, scattering the tentative truce between them. Isla felt a ripple of fear. Behind Eimhir's wry smiles were glimpses that reminded Isla of the wildness lurking beneath her skin. The wildness of a selkie.

The tension pulled taut between them, like a frayed rope on the brink of snapping, but then Eimhir sat back and loosened her shoulders. "I suppose we'll see, won't we?" She flicked her eyes across the room. "In any case, it looks like he and the auld blood have returned. Let's hope they bring favourable news."

Isla spun around to see Lachlan and Darce pushing through the crowded tavern. She tried not to dwell on the way her chest flooded with relief at the sight of the sergeant's squared shoulders, his claymore secured between them. Instead, she gulped down the last of her mackerel and said evenly, "I assume you found us a ship?"

Lachlan shot Darce a glare. "*He* found us a ship. Go on, Galbraith. Tell them."

Darce winced. "It's a Sea Kith vessel."

Isla raised an eyebrow. The Sea Kith were a strange folk, claiming no land as their own and spending their lives on the water for as long as their stores allowed. To see one in port for more than a fleeting visit was unusual; to hear of one taking on passengers even more so. "I thought they preferred to keep to themselves."

"They did. But much has changed these last few years. All these new shipping routes the Grand Admiral has established... The waters are getting smaller, like the selkie said." Darce grimaced. "The Sea Kith need coin and supplies to survive like the rest of us. I won't deny there are certain superstitions around them—"

"Like the ability to summon storms and command giant sea birds to do their bidding? It's not superstition—they're dangerous." Lachlan shot a distasteful look at the selkies. "We already have enough trouble on our hands."

"Sounds like we'd be safer with these Sea Kith than the hunters you led us to," Eimhir shot back. "As disappointing as it might seem to you."

"Enough." Isla pushed herself up from the table, glaring between them. "Whatever reasons we have to hate each other can wait until we get to Arburgh. We need to reach the capital—that's something we can at least agree on. Let's focus on getting there in one piece." She met Eimhir's eyes. "Bury it. Wasn't that what you said?"

Eimhir gave her a measured stare, then nodded.

"Then it's buried. Now, let's go find these Sea Kith."

Outside, the swathes of cloud parted, revealing a rare blue sky. The late-summer sun beat down on Isla's cheeks. It should have brought her some relief, but instead, she shivered. Regardless of what the sky said, there was a storm coming. Only time would tell when it would break.

If we are to trust each other, we must bury what came before, Eimhir had said.

If only it were so easy.

CHAPTER
ELEVEN

The *Jade Dawn* was a ship that lived up to its name. Its oak hull resembled a moss-covered stone, the wood stained a seaweed-green. Its sails swallowed the breeze like emerald clouds against the darkening sky. The moment Isla stepped aboard, she felt like she had returned to a place she remembered well. It wasn't the *Ondasta*, but it carried the same familiarities life at sea entailed: the creak of timber underfoot, the salty smell of the wooden hull, the gentle rocking rhythm. Past the gunwale, the waves glistened blue-grey in the early evening light, stretching further than Isla could see. They promised freedom where the boundary lines of the shore never could.

She filled her lungs as the spray dashed over the ship's carved serpentine figurehead and disappeared into the wind. The *Jade Dawn* was quick and agile, its prow cutting through the waves like a blade as it skirted perilously close to the jagged sea stacks littering the mouth of the port. The rocks rose from the water like serrated fangs, jutting out at odd angles to resist the crashing waves.

"They say only the most skilled sailors make berth in Kinraith," Isla remarked. "It's too easy to run afoul of the teeth."

"The teeth?" Eimhir said.

"That's what the locals call the rocks. Legend has it an ancient sea serpent—perhaps even the Cirein-cròin itself—was slain off the coast hundreds of years ago, and all that remains are its teeth poking through the surface of the water."

"Are you certain it's only a legend?" Eimhir raised an eyebrow. "You forget, human, I have spent many years in the depths. It might surprise you to discover we're not the only creatures lurking in these waters." She grinned. "Neither are we the most dangerous."

"I'm not sure about that."

"Aye? Because you're so well acquainted with what's below the waves, are you?" Eimhir joined her at the gunwale, peering over at the crash of salt and seafoam below. "Back at the tavern, you said you'd killed monsters before. Was that true?"

Isla flinched. If this was a trap, it was one she'd walked into herself. There was little she could give now but the truth. "I spent some time among the Vesnian Tidesguard. Our job was to protect the Adrenian coast from threats."

"Threats?"

"Sea serpents, mostly. The old ones usually kept to themselves, but breeding season brought with it a feeding frenzy. They'd swarm fishing boats, even venture to the shallows and prey on the beaches."

"Tides forbid they feed themselves." Eimhir cocked her head. "Better they starved, aye?"

"What do you expect?" Isla said, unable to help the defensiveness seeping into her voice. "That people will not defend themselves when they are attacked?"

"I expect nothing from humans at all. That way, they can't disappoint me." Eimhir fixed her with a keen look, the intensity making Isla squirm. "The question is, what did *you* expect? Those Vesnian trawlers come each year with bigger nets, plundering more than the waters can supply. If you take the serpents' food from them, it should be no surprise when they turn to the shores for sustenance."

"I..." Isla gritted her teeth. "Some of those coastal villages have existed for hundreds of years. They have as much right to the water as the serpents."

"Aye, and if they had it all, it still wouldn't be enough." Eimhir's voice was strangely gentle; there was no malice in the ragged-edged shape of her words. She let out a sigh like a wave breaking. "I don't blame you, Isla Blackwood. In fact, I rather pity you. You've had but one life, and a short one at that. You don't carry the weight of your ancestors on your back like we do. You don't see the years of mistakes, the years of regrets. You don't understand what it is to catch a glimpse of something that should have been done differently, done *better*."

Isla fought the urge to bristle at her words. It was too easy to feel the need to defend herself with Eimhir, like drawing a blade and facing a challenge that had never been hers to answer. But something in the selkie woman's voice stirred an unbidden curiosity in her. She wanted to know more. For whatever tides-damned reason, she wanted to understand.

"What is it like?" she asked. The question left her lips quietly, as if she feared it being heard. "How does it feel having your soul so...bare? So out in the open?"

Eimhir smiled. For once, the gesture didn't seem threatening. It relaxed the edges of her face, brightened the ever-present storm in her eyes. "It's wonderful," she said. "And terrifying. It's like knowing everyone you have ever been, and keeping a promise for everyone you ever will be. Protecting your past while fearing a future too easily stolen. It is mine alone, but only for now. There is comfort to be taken in that. Knowing where you came from, and where you will go."

Isla hadn't expected an answer so honest, so raw. It lodged painfully in the space between her ribs and her heart. Tides, she was *jealous*. Jealous of this woman whose soul could be ripped from her as easily as a cutpurse separated coin from a mark. But what she would give to have that kind of certainty, that kind of belonging. If not to a place, then at least to herself.

"I believe it is my turn to ask a question," Eimhir said, breaking her from her thoughts. "This Tidesguard ship of yours... What was your purpose on it? Did you take joy in cutting down creatures doing nothing more than trying to survive?"

A hundred memories flooded Isla's mind. The sight of frothing waves, the seafoam turning red. The metallic taste of fear at the roof of her mouth. Surprise at the sting in her palm the first time she fired a pistol. The churning in her gut at the smell of burnt powder mingled with siren blood.

None of it had been what she'd left Silveckan for. The wind and waves had promised her something else, something she'd never been able to find.

"I was a navigator. My purpose was helping us find where we needed to go," Isla said shortly. "Anything else I did was nothing more than *me* trying to survive."

She turned her head to the stars, plucking constellations from the darkening sky. Mapping a course usually brought her comfort. Now, she felt more unmoored than ever.

Eimhir followed her gaze with an expression of mild disinterest. "I heard humans use the stars to find their way home, but I never understood it. We follow the currents."

"The stars only help you find home if you know where home is," Isla replied. "That's something that has always been lost to me. I'm starting to fear it forever will be."

The words left her lips unbidden, like spilling a secret she'd never intended to share. She didn't want to think about the silence that fell between them, heavy with things left unsaid. She didn't want Eimhir's scorn or spite. Even less did she want her pity.

As if sensing the change in the air, Eimhir straightened. She gave Isla a nod before turning and traipsing across the deck, the glint of her axe winking in the moonlight. Isla hadn't forgotten its touch against her neck. She couldn't afford to forget it.

"What did she want?"

Isla turned to find Lachlan approaching. "Truth be told, I'm not certain."

A shadow fell across his features. "She's not to be trusted. Neither of them are. In fact, this whole ship—" He broke off, eyes widening. "Did you see that?"

Isla tightened her hands on the edge of the gunwale. She'd seen it—a bird with huge wings carving a silhouette against the silvery light of the moon, its belly a flash of white in the darkness.

It circled the mainmast before swooping to the deck, landing with a clatter. Its webbed feet splayed across the wood, ending in huge curved claws. A throaty caw rattled from its long black-and-white neck as it stared at them with beady eyes.

Isla's mouth turned dry. "That looks like a razorbill."

"Since when have you ever seen a razorbill the size of a grown man?" Lachlan shot back. "Look at its beak—that thing could snap my arm in two. I knew there were rumours about the Sea Kith and their birds, but I never thought..."

He trailed off as the giant razorbill stretched its impressive wings. It let out another cackle from the back of its throat, flapped twice, then was gone, disappearing once more into the night sky.

"Now you've gone and upset it," Isla said, unable to keep the amusement from her lips. "Better head below deck, wee brother. Who knows when it might return?"

Lachlan scowled. "You won't find it half as amusing if we end up becalmed because that bird brought an omen of ill winds. I knew coming aboard a Sea Kith vessel was bound to be bad luck."

"If you're unhappy, take it up with the sergeant. He's the one who struck the deal with the captain, after all." Isla turned towards the bridge where Darce was locked in quiet conversation with the impressive-looking woman at the helm. Captain Nishi, she'd introduced herself as. She had the dusky brown skin of someone from the Karzish Peninsula but spoke in a speckled accent, her voice ringing with the staccato of

Silveckan's southlands to the lilt of the Breçhon coast and everything in between.

"You're not my usual kind of cargo," she'd said as she welcomed them on board, the gold ring through her lip glinting. "Still, it's foolish to turn down paying work when you can get it, especially as we're already headed for the capital."

She stood now at the helm, one hand on the wooden wheel, the other drumming a rhythm on the hilt of her rapier. Her black hair shone like silk as the wind tugged at it from under her tricorne hat, and her eyes gleamed like copper coins as she laughed at something Darce said.

Lachlan sent her a sidelong look. "Are you jealous?"

This time, it was Isla's turn to scowl. "Don't be ridiculous."

"Is it ridiculous? I remember how aloof the sergeant used to be before you left. It seems all those years apart have softened him to you."

Isla brandished her knuckles, still scabbed from the crack of Darce's whalebone training blade. "You call that soft?"

"He saved your life back at the estate."

"He saved *both* our lives, and until now, he's been well paid for it." Isla grimaced. "Believe me, that will change soon."

Lachlan frowned. "What are you talking about? Galbraith has always been loyal to our family."

"All men are loyal to coin. Let's see what happens now we no longer have any."

The words left her mouth with a bitter aftertaste she hadn't realised she'd been carrying. Her family had trusted Darce. *She'd* trusted him. When he'd burst into her room, sword drawn, Isla had never wondered—not even for the most fleeting of seconds—if his blade had been meant for her. She'd taken his protection for granted.

But that was before she knew he had a secret he'd never shared. Before she'd realised relying on him brought with it the fear of him leaving.

As if he'd been able to sense her thoughts, Darce caught her eye, acknowledging her with a silent nod. Lachlan was right; he'd always been

115

aloof with them, keeping them at arm's length. He'd been a teenager vy-ing for position in the Blackwood Watch, all the while being saddled with looking after a couple of spoiled noble brats. Despite their proximity, they'd existed in different worlds.

After what happened at Blackwood Estate, she thought things had changed. Maybe she'd *wanted* them to change. But there was still too much of Darce she couldn't see, too much he kept buried under armour and duty and the promise he'd made to their father.

She didn't know him. Not truly. The only thing she knew for certain was that Eimhir wasn't the only one with a secret hidden beneath her skin.

CHAPTER TWELVE

For the first two days at sea, the tides were kind. Then, on the third day, the winds whipped up and a wall of clouds plumed across the horizon. It brushed the surface of the water as it rolled towards them, turning the sea a dark grey-green as the waves leapt higher.

Isla was alone in the cabin when she heard the rumbling. With only two beds, they'd taken turns using the shared space. She'd been lightly dozing in the late afternoon when the thunder's deep, dangerous growl resounded through her ears, smothering the muffled voices shouting on the deck above.

The floor tipped and swayed beneath her feet as she hauled herself out of bed and scrambled for her boots and furs. She was no stranger to sailing during a storm; the *Ondasta* had seen its share of tempests out on the Adrenian Sea. But they were nothing compared to the squalls that battered the Strait of Silveckan. The waters here were hungry, and they would like nothing more than to swallow the *Jade Dawn*, spitting out its bones as a wreck lost to the bottom of the sea.

Isla pulled her hair into a braid and climbed up on deck. An onslaught of rain pelted down from the black sky above, turning the wood slick and sending the crew slipping as they scurried back and forth. There should have been hours of daylight left, but darkness closed around them like a shroud.

A blinding flash lit up the sky, illuminating the waves, and Isla shielded her eyes. Across the deck, she spotted Lachlan and Darce heaving on a piece of rope alongside several other men, trying to haul up a section of the mast that had collapsed. Part of the sail snapped loose in the fierce wind, making the ship veer into the waves.

"Tides save us!" someone shouted.

"You think the tides will listen to your prayers?" Captain Nishi was up on the bridge, wrestling with the ship's helm. "I'm the only one who can steer us out of this squall, and I can't do that if this wind tears apart our sail. Get it secured unless you want to sleep on the seabed tonight." Another gust rocked the *Jade Dawn* sideways and Nishi braced herself as a wave crashed onto the deck, spinning the wheel through her hands. She whirled it back on course and threw them a murderous glare. "Now!"

The crew hurried towards the shrouds, climbing up the rope rigging with nimble speed. Before Isla had time to think about what she was doing, she joined them.

The wind howled in her ears as she climbed. She half imagined her name carried up on its roar, shouted by Lachlan or Darce below. But if they were calling her, it didn't matter. Her mind was focused on the rigging in front of her as she put one hand above the other and pulled herself skywards.

The ratlines were sodden, but that didn't stop the rough snarl of the rope biting and burning her palms. Isla wrapped her fingers around each one, taking comfort in the pain of it chafing against her skin. Pain was good. Pain meant she was still holding on. It was her feet she was more concerned about—one slip on the rope, one misplaced boot, and she'd tumble to the deck in a crunch of blood and broken bones.

The giant razorbill circled above, its caws drowned by the howling of the wind. Its eerie cries spurred her on, until at last she reached the top of the rigging. She swung both arms over the yard, squeezing her elbows against the long wooden spar as the ship bucked beneath her. The wind and rain were fiercer up here, pummelling her face. She blinked against the water running into her eyes as she slid along the footrope, a chill biting at her skin through her soaking clothes.

Far below, the crew hauled at the clewlines and buntlines as they fought to hoist the sail in. The green folds billowed in the raging wind, inching higher far too slowly. All the while, Nishi was still fighting to keep the *Jade Dawn* from tipping into the waves, shouting instructions and cursing as she struggled to keep the ship under control.

Another flash lit up the sky behind the angry storm clouds, turning them into looming silhouettes against the sheet of lightning. In Isla's mind, the clouds became the skeleton jaws of the soulless, a gun-anam in the sky opening its maw to devour her. The relentless rain became the hooves of a thousand kelpies, the dread mounts charging to knock her from the mast. Her breath seized, and she swayed on the footrope as the mast swam in front of her eyes.

"Pay attention! We're ready to stow."

Isla jumped at the words, barked over the howl of the wind from the Sea Kith deckhand beside her. The sail was folded against the yard now. They almost had it. She pulled the rope of the gasket into place, securing it tightly.

"Good work," the deckhand said, squinting against the rain. "Now let's get back down there."

Isla scrambled along to the shrouds. The rigging felt more unstable on the way down. It bounced beneath her, threatening to throw her off. She slid her feet into the ratlines as quickly as she dared, pausing only to brace herself when the *Jade Dawn* lurched under the crash of a fierce wave.

She was halfway down when it happened. One moment the deckhand was above her, his boots dripping water onto her face as he climbed down. Then the ship roiled, and without a sound, he was gone.

Isla froze, her fingers numb around the rope. The waves below were black and angry, smashing against the hull with all their fury. There was no sign of the deckhand. The sea had already swallowed him.

"Crew overboard!" The words ripped from her throat, fighting to be heard over the wind. She'd never been the one to give the call on the *Ondasta*. She'd never realised how tight her throat would become, how dry her mouth would turn. She gulped down salty air and bellowed the words again. "Crew overboard!"

Nishi snapped her head up as she tussled with the helm. "Eyes on the water," she commanded. "And someone fetch Kerr from the forecastle. Not even he can tame these waves."

Isla slid down the rest of the rigging, water splashing her boots as she landed. Another violent wave rocked the hull, sending her careening towards the gunwale, but a strong grip around her arm held her in place.

She looked up to find Darce towering over her, his dark hair soaked through. He wore an expression Isla had never seen on his face before, and her heart jolted when she recognised it for what it was.

Fear.

A moment later, he recovered. "What were you thinking? You could have broken your neck."

Through the rain and wind, she felt the warmth from his grasp. It spread into her cheeks, bringing with it a sensation that might have been gratitude or irritation or some turbulent mixture of both. "I know my way around a ship well enough to help. Not bad for someone who *learned nothing* while she was away, as you so kindly put it."

Darce flinched, then settled his mouth into a wry smile. "You always did have a habit of surprising me. I suppose I should have learned that by now." He released her arm, his pale cheeks darkening as he stepped away. "If you're going to help, at least do it from down here."

Isla rushed to the edge of the ship and braced herself against the gunwale. When she peered over the side, she only saw waves leaping at the hull.

"He's gone," Lachlan said from beside her, his face bleak. "They'll never find him in these kinds of swells."

"No, they won't." Eimhir's voice rang clear over the wind. She bent down and loosened her belt from her waist. Then she slid off her leather boots until she stood barefoot on the deck with only her pelt around her.

"What are you—"

Eimhir leapt onto the gunwale. A fork of lightning speared the horizon, and by the time it disappeared, she was gone, diving below the churning water.

Isla held her breath. The wind was thick with salt and spray, whipping up the water more and more with each passing minute. Nothing was visible under the surging of the waves. They heaved and crashed with a watery roar, unforgiving in their ferocity. It was difficult to imagine anyone could have survived their wrath, even Eimhir.

"Tides, it can't be." Lachlan stilled. "Do you see that?"

Isla shook the rain from her face and peered into the darkness. Was she seeing things, or was there a figure wrestling with the waves? They seemed impossibly small, like a piece of driftwood at the mercy of the currents. But each second they washed closer, held above the waves by a shadow below.

"Someone throw a rope over." A short, stocky man with white hair barged forward, his flaxen brows tight with worry. "Come now, before it's too late."

The crew moved at his words. One of the sailors gathered the line to toss into the water while the others set themselves around its coiled tail, preparing to pull.

The fallen deckhand was close now, his eyes closed and face pallid as the shape beneath the surface carried him closer. A monstrous wave crashed over his head, but he soon reappeared, joined by the pale human face of Eimhir.

"The rope," Eimhir shouted, spluttering on the water. "Throw it now."

It leapt from the ship like a serpent, writhing and unfurling as it fell towards the waves. Eimhir grabbed hold of it with one hand, looping her other arm around the unconscious deckhand, fighting to keep his head above the water.

Isla moved out of the way as the crew pulled. Time slowed as they hauled in the rope length by length, casting its sodden loops across the deck. Then came a thump, and two bodies tumbled over the gunwale.

Eimhir leapt to her feet, shrinking back with wary eyes. Her pelt was heavy with water, dripping down the bare skin of her legs. Even in her human form, there was no mistaking what she was. No human would have dared leap into those kinds of waters. No human would have survived them.

The deckhand lay on his back, eyes closed and soaked to the bone. There was no colour in his cheeks, no rise and fall to his chest.

Eimhir was too late. He was already gone.

The man with flaxen hair knelt beside him, spreading a palm on the deckhand's chest and murmuring something in a soft burr. A hush fell over the deck; even the wind seemed to subside. Nobody moved. Nobody dared breathe.

The deckhand's chest rose.

Isla pressed a hand over her mouth. The deckhand's eyes were still closed, his head limp and lolling. The swelling in his lungs wasn't a gasp for air—it was something else entirely.

The white-haired man lifted his fingers and curled them in a slow coaxing gesture. The deckhand's chest continued to seize. A moment later, his neck bulged and an awful gurgling noise bubbled from his throat.

No. It was impossible.

Beside her, Darce had gone unnaturally still, watching with glittering eyes. The white-haired man was drawing seawater from between the deckhand's stiff blue lips. Each delicate twirl of his wrists drew more droplets from the man's bloated chest. They hung in the air for mere seconds, glistening, until they were torn apart by the rain or carried off by the wind.

"What is that?" Lachlan shot her a furtive glance. "Some kind of Sea Kith magic?"

"No." Eimhir stood a few feet away, her hair dripping around her bare shoulders as she trembled in her pelt. "That one there has the auld blood, like your sergeant."

Isla turned to Darce, searching his features for some kind of under-standing. His expression was strained, his dark eyes transfixed on the white-haired Sea Kith. A vein pulsed in the middle of his forehead. A muscle twitched in the side of his neck. Still he stared, like he couldn't look away, even if it was agony.

"Sergeant? Are you all right?" When he didn't answer, Isla reached for his hand, trying to break him from his stupor. She could barely feel his fingers through the numbness of her own, but for a fleeting moment, they tightened around hers.

Darce gathered himself, wild-eyed and white-cheeked. He pulled his hand sharply from her grasp and stepped back. "I am nothing like him."

Isla wasn't sure whether it was an apology or an accusation. "I was only—"

"Look," Lachlan snapped, cutting through them all.

Isla turned back to the deckhand. The water streaming from his throat slowed to a trickle, disappearing into the air as soon as it passed his lips. The white-haired man let his hand fall limply to his side. Everything was still.

Then the deckhand coughed.

The ripple of relief around the gathered crew was palpable. Isla felt it in their hushed whispers, in the loosening of their shoulders. Relief, but not surprise. The white-haired man was a sentinel. *Their* sentinel.

The deckhand spluttered some more, groaning as he arched his back and rolled over. His eyes were bloodshot, bursting with red, and his skin was as pale and deathly as ever. Tides, he'd *drowned*. His lungs had filled with salt water, leadening his body as the depths pulled him towards his end. Yet here he was—pallid and weak, but alive.

"Back off, all of you. Give the man some space." Captain Nishi knelt at the deckhand's side, running a hand over his forehead. "You're colder than death itself, MacKinnon. The fathoms have surely been robbed today, and we will pay for that insult. But I cannot say I am not glad. You are much too fine a prize to surrender to them."

The deckhand drew his mouth into a watery smile. "They'll call for me one day, cap'n."

"They'll call for us all. But not today." Nishi cast a discerning glance to where Eimhir was shivering in her pelt. "It seems I have you to thank for that. Come here, so I may look closer upon the face of the woman who saved my crew."

"That might be a problem," Eimhir said evenly. "It appears your sentinel has called on your ship's sea spirits to bind me in place. I cannot move from this part of the deck."

Isla's heart turned cold. Eimhir stood with an unnatural stiffness, the muscles of her calves taut. Her bare feet planted firmly on the deck, anchored there by a presence Isla couldn't see.

"Release her, Kerr." Nishi's words carried the gentle sting of a rebuke, but a smile danced around her lips. "We're in no danger from her, not on this ship. Isn't that right?"

Eimhir matched the captain's amusement with a storm-eyed glare. "So it would seem." She waited for a moment, then walked across the deck, water splashing her feet. When she came face to face with Nishi, she stopped, jutting her chin out as her seaswept hair flew around her face.

Nishi's gaze darted towards Eimhir's pelt. There was a gleam in her eyes, but it was not one of hunger or greed. Instead, all Isla saw in the captain's expression was understanding, perhaps even respect.

"You saved one of my crew and that is enough to call you kith, regardless of what else you might be," Nishi said, extending her arm. "If ever the time comes you find yourself in need, call on the *Jade Dawn*, and we shall answer as swiftly as the winds allow."

Eimhir looked down at the captain's arm. Her expression was so stony, so immutable, that Isla wondered whether she'd dare push Nishi's outstretched hand aside. A Sea Kith's offer didn't seem like one that could be so recklessly dismissed. Not without consequence.

Silence thickened the air. Isla measured each passing second in the fearful thump of her heart against her ribs and braced for what might come next.

Eimhir drew her mouth into a slow smile and grasped the captain's forearm. "Humankind already owes us a great many debts. What is one more?"

The question hung in the air between them, leaden with contempt and requiring no answer. Eimhir's low, gravelly voice scratched on every syllable, turning each word to stone as it left her lips. This was no mere bargain struck. This was a promise, wrapped in a threat, carrying the weight of spilled blood and stolen souls.

Eimhir shifted her eyes past Nishi, locking her gaze with Isla. Reminding her of their own bargain.

That was the thing about debts, after all. Sooner or later, they had to be paid.

CHAPTER
THIRTEEN

Isla slept fitfully through the night and woke some time before dawn. She left Lachlan snoring in the bunk above her as she slipped on her boots and padded out of the cabin in search of the fresh tang of salty air.

The waves still leapt at the *Jade Dawn's* hull, but they were tamer now the wind had calmed. Above, the sky was clear and filled with the fading twinkle of stars as the beginnings of daylight bled into the darkness. Isla retrieved her sextant from her coat pocket and held it against the vanishing constellations, lining up the horizon in the frame. She murmured calculations into the wind, the words stinging her cracked lips.

"Making sure I'm taking you to the right port?"

Isla startled as Captain Nishi appeared at her side, tired-eyed but sporting a shrewd smile. She nodded at the sextant in Isla's hands. "Go on then, tell me our position."

"Somewhere in the Corran Narrows, if I'm not mistaken." Isla hesitated. "I was surprised. Most sailors would skirt around the isles to avoid the whirlpools."

"Most sailors aren't Sea Kith." Nishi's brown eyes sparkled in amusement. "Whirlpools are no danger to a crew who know what they're doing. We'll shave off half a day taking the more direct route through the Narrows. A good thing too, after that storm."

She looked out over the horizon, her silken black hair dancing in the wind. Though the morning breeze still had a bite to it, the captain loosened her linen shirt at the collar and pushed her sleeves up her arms. It was only now daylight was creeping into the sky that Isla noticed the ink patterning her skin in swirls of terracotta and ochre. The intricate motifs were subtle against the dusky brown of her forearms and lower neck, as if the markings were part of her.

Nishi caught her staring. "You've never seen a Sea Kith up close, have you?"

Isla shook her head. "Can you tell me what they mean?"

"We get a tattoo every time we make port to chart the time we spend on the water," Nishi replied. "It reminds us where we've been, the storms we've endured, the crew we've sent to the fathoms. Each one tells a story, and that story is for us alone to understand."

"They're beautiful." Isla stole another glance at the marks on Nishi's arms. A constellation of voyages written in flesh-toned ink, legible only to the one who bore them. A chart of where they'd been. No, it was more than that. It mapped who they were.

Not for the first time, a pinch of jealousy pulled at Isla's heart. First Eimhir, now Nishi. How comforting it would be to look at her own body and know exactly who she was, exactly where she belonged. To see her life written in a language she could comprehend on a canvas that promised empty spaces for more.

When she tore her eyes away, she found Nishi staring at her expectantly. "This isn't the first ship you've set foot on, is it? I saw how you climbed the rigging during the storm, how you helped stow the sail. You know your way around deck better than most."

"I was navigator on the *Ondasta*. We sailed out of Vesnia."

"One of the Tidesguard? Big ship." Nishi nodded. "On the *Jade Dawn*, I am captain and navigator both. It's often how it is on smaller vessels. It's hard work, but there's nothing that tastes like freedom quite like a ship that fits you and a crew loyal to you both."

"The admirals in the capital are afraid of you. Some call you pirates."

Nishi snorted. "The admirals in the capital wouldn't know a bowsprit if it found itself wedged between their arsecheeks. They're old men and women who made their names on the sea and forgot what else it gave them. What they call us is of no concern to me." She shot Isla a pointed look. "I heard you're heading to Arburgh to ask the Grand Admiral for ships. Tell me, does that include one for yourself?"

"I'm not a captain."

"You could be. You know how to chart a course. You know how to stow the sails in a storm. You raised the call when MacKinnon fell before anyone else." Nishi gestured along the deck. "Most importantly, you already have a sentinel."

Darce stood by the starboard gunwale, deep in conversation with the white-haired sentinel. His brow furrowed as they spoke, his forehead marred with lines of worry.

"How did you know?" Isla asked.

"He told me last night. Asked for my permission to speak to Kerr, as if I could control anything that man does." Nishi rolled her eyes. "Too many people think a sentinel's blood oath makes them a servant to their captain. If anything, it's the opposite. Something to keep in mind, if he spills his for you one day."

Heat rushed to Isla's cheeks. "It's not like that. Darce would never—*I'd* never..."

"I wouldn't discount it, were I you. Being bonded to a sentinel makes a captain valuable. The Breçhon Admiralty practically begged to give me the *Jade Dawn* in return for accepting a single contract. And once you have a ship of your own, you answer to nobody and nothing, except the tides." A pensive expression fell over Nishi's face, her lips curling into a thoughtful smile. "The sea is the home we choose for ourselves. But a captain cannot survive the tides without her crew."

Nishi returned to the helm, spine straight and tricorne hat bobbing atop her head. As she took the wheel, the first slivers of sunlight began to peek over the blue line of the horizon. The light glittered off the waves like shards of glass, filling Isla with desperate longing. Perhaps Nishi was right. Perhaps the thing she'd been missing all these years *was* home. Not Blackwood Estate, but a home on the waves, one that was utterly hers.

She would never be a sentinel, but she could be a captain. All it would take was chaining someone like Darce to her side with a bond of blood only death could break.

A chill seeped into Isla's bones. It was something she'd never dare to imagine. She knew too well the drag of an anchor. She knew how easy it was to drown under its weight. She could never ask that of anyone, least of all the sergeant.

Across the deck, Darce was still talking to the white-haired sentinel, Kerr. The low burr of their voices carried across the breeze as Isla approached.

Kerr snapped his head up, an amiable grin brightening his features. "You're the one who spotted MacKinnon's fall last night. That call you made saved his life."

"You're the one who saved his life. You pulled the water from his lungs." Isla shook her head. "I've never seen a sentinel do anything like that."

As she spoke, Darce shifted his body away from her. Dark lines circled his eyes, and his features were drawn and pale, like he'd not slept in days. Isla half considered telling him to go rest in the cabin, but he'd only resent her for it. He was wary enough of her presence without it seeming like she was trying to get rid of him.

If Kerr noticed the prickle of tension between them, he didn't show it. "There's more to being a sentinel than throwing up some protective wards," he said, turning out to the sea. "It's a capricious kind of magic, one that cannot be defined from one of us to the next. We call on the sea spirits to aid us. Sometimes they answer, sometimes they don't. They are fickle things, after all."

"They answered last night."

Kerr shrugged. "If I asked this morning, I might face a different answer. The sea does not bow to the whims of humankind, not even those of us with the auld blood. It only listens, and then decides for itself. Sometimes it allows us to call on currents and riptides. Sometimes it sends us creatures of salt and spray to drag our enemies to the fathoms' embrace. But without its blessing, all we can do is pray to the tides like the rest of you."

A shrill caw broke through the conversation, and the giant razorbill landed on deck, ruffling its feathers as it folded its impressive wings. Its long beak boasted a ribbon of white like the dazzling patch on its belly, but apart from that, it was as black as night, from the tips of its wings to its great webbed feet.

"This is Shearwing," Kerr said, gesturing to the razorbill. "It is our scout, our guidebird. Where it flies, the *Jade Dawn* follows. This is the way of the Sea Kith."

As Isla observed the bird, it opened its beak in a wide yawn, exposing its yellow gape. "I thought your people would follow a creature of the sea, not the sky."

"Have you never seen a razorbill dive?" Kerr chuckled. "They are as swift and agile beneath the waves as they are above it. They are creatures of the sea as much as we are."

Shearwing's beady eyes darted between them all, and it let out a croon from the back of its throat. Then it was gone again in a rustle of wings.

"I better return to the captain." Kerr pushed himself away from the gunwale, a slow smile unfurling across his lips. "She likes to believe she runs this ship herself, but the *Jade Dawn* is good at letting me know when I'm needed." He winked, then made off for the bridge, leaving her and Darce with only the wind and the waves for company.

The quiet between them was more peaceful than Isla thought it would be. She found herself loath to break it. Breaking it would only lead to words she wasn't ready to exchange. It was better to enjoy this fleeting calm. Darce stood close enough that she caught the lingering scent of pine needles and heather from the wilds. It mixed with the leather from his armour, becoming something familiar, something comforting. It thickened in her throat, sending an unwelcome flutter through her heart.

"Strange to see it so still now." The sergeant barely seemed to realise he'd spoken, so distant were his eyes. "It's almost enough to make you forget the storm ever happened."

"I feared the fathoms would claim us," Isla said. "Nishi was right when she said they were robbed. If it hadn't been for Kerr and his magic..." She trailed off, sensing the blade edge of the conversation between them, sharp enough to cut with.

Darce remained silent, his spine stiff. Then he loosened his shoulders, hanging his head low. "This is it then? The part where I'm forced to account for keeping this from you?"

Isla kept her voice steady. "If you have an explanation, I'd like to hear it."

"To what end?" He met her eyes for the first time, fixing her with a look both tired and pained. "There is nothing for you to gain from this. The auld blood might run in me, but I'm not a sentinel. I've never sworn an oath to a captain. If I had my way, I never would."

"What does that mean?"

Darce rubbed a hand across his forehead. "There's so much I didn't know. So much I still don't know, though Kerr explained some of it. All I know for certain is this—a sentinel's magic only truly awakens once they make a blood oath to their captain." A dark look fell across his face. "Kerr says we don't have a choice in the matter. He says the blood in my veins will compel me to spill it in service eventually. It might take years—decades even—but sooner or later, I'll find myself pledged to some captain, bound to do their bidding until one of us dies."

"You didn't know?"

"Of course I knew. Everyone knows about sentinels and their oaths. Only, I thought it was a *choice*. I thought it was something I could walk away from." Darce's hands tightened on the gunwale, knuckles white. "I spent most of my life trying not to think about it, trying to push aside what it might mean. Sometimes I heard stirrings, like the sea itself was whispering in my ear. Then those wraiths descended on Caolaig, and I couldn't ignore it anymore. I *felt* them. I felt the restless souls of those wretched selkies slaughtered on the *Stormbreaker*. I felt the sea spirits answer when Kerr called on them to bind Eimhir to the deck. They're not stirrings anymore. They're real."

"All the years you spent with my family..." Isla fought to keep her voice steady. "You never said a word."

Darce cocked his head. "And rob myself of the chance to suffer this interrogation?"

"It's hardly a—" Isla cut herself short. "Be as glib as you like, but the truth of the matter is my family trusted you. I'm trying to determine whether we still can. You hid this from us. It rather makes me wonder what else you might be hiding."

Darce laughed, the sound thin and devoid of humour. "You told me you spent years wishing for something I never asked for, never wanted. I had no desire to bear your resentment for that. I'll tell you the same now as I did at the loch: this isn't something you want. This is no gift. It's a curse. If you had any sense, you'd understand it was something to fear."

"I have nothing to be afraid of."

"That's not true." Darce slid his hand along the gunwale as he closed the distance between them. "You're afraid of the selkies. Afraid of Eimhir sticking a knife in your back. Afraid of the things your brother might say, and more afraid of the things he doesn't. Afraid of the rope around your neck in the gallows if this all goes to shit." He leaned closer, trailing his eyes over her like he was searching for something in her expression. "You're afraid that me being a sentinel has somehow changed me, that I am not the loyal swordmaster on whom you thought you could rely."

"Are you so loyal?" Isla fought against the tremor in her voice. "Or will that change when we are no longer paying you?"

"Ah." A tight smile flitted over Darce's lips. "There it is. Now I understand what this is about. You think once we're in the capital, I'll sell my services to the highest bidder."

"You said it yourself—the Admiralty pays its sentinels handsomely."

"The Admiralty can go fuck itself." There was a bite to Darce's voice now, a ripple of anger. "I won't chain myself to any captain. My life is my own." He let out a breath and stepped back. "The last thing your father asked of me was to protect his children. That is the only oath I choose to honour. I won't betray his memory by failing him."

"My father is dead."

"That might be enough reason for some to break their word, but not me."

Isla bit back the impatience on her tongue. "The Blackwood Watch were paid soldiers. You fought for our coin and hospitality, not out of any love for us. What did my father do to inspire such loyalty in you?"

Darce frowned. "He never told you how I came to be at Blackwood Estate?"

"I assumed it was the same as all the other squires. A paying job for a lad with less than two coppers to rub together."

"It was more than that." Darce turned to the water, his jaw tense. "I meant it when I said my life is my own now. But that wasn't always the case. There was a time it belonged to those who only wanted to use it for their own ends."

The bitterness in his voice curled Isla's stomach. "What do you—"

"You wanted to know if you could still trust me, didn't you? Then perhaps you should listen." Darce took a steadying breath. "My father was a kelp harvester who lost his life to bloodlung and left nothing behind but debt and a Bréchon mistress. My mother found herself alone in a cold, strange land with no coin to her name, only a bastard son. She was only too happy to wipe her hands of me when the Vane Company came calling."

"The mercenary band?" Isla pursed her lips. "I've heard rumours about them. Turning orphans into weapons, finding them positions in the households of prominent families."

"For a substantial fee, of course." Darce's eyes glinted. "Your father would have turned them away at the gates like he always did when they showed up touting their wares. Only this time, they had me."

"They knew what you were?"

"Not at first. Even I didn't know what I was at first." His expression clouded. "I still remember the day I felt the auld blood wake in me. There was this girl, a young lass only a few years older than me. The bigger lads used to pinch and bruise me when the captains weren't looking. Then it turned into beatings. One night they came after me with blades, and she took the axe that was meant for me." He pressed a hand to his shoulder. "There was so much blood. I couldn't tell mine apart from hers. I thought we were both dead."

"She saved you."

"She died for me. When I woke up, she was gone, and everything had changed. I felt things I couldn't before. The change in the wind, the smell of a storm before it broke. I tried to hide it, but it wasn't long before they suspected me for what I was. Every estate we visited, they did their best to beat me into a demonstration. It never worked. I never showed them what I was capable of, and no laird or lady ever believed this scrawny, ragged twelve-year-old lad was worth the coin the Vane Company was asking."

"Except my father." Isla froze. "He knew? All these years, he knew you were a sentinel?"

"I reckon he took pity on me. He paid twice what they wanted for me, then pulled me aside and told me as long as I proved myself with a blade, he'd never ask me to use my magic, nor share my secret with another soul. In almost twenty years, he never brought up the matter again. That was the last he ever said about it." Darce shook his head, his brown eyes dark and solemn. "I owe him more than my life. I owe him my freedom."

Something constricted in Isla's chest, love and grief and resentment all tightening their strings around her heart. "He refused to force you into a life you didn't want. I cannot blame him for that. I *love* him for that, even if he couldn't afford the same understanding to me."

"I was a simple soldier. You were his daughter. Were I to wager, I'd say everything your father did was to keep you safe."

Isla laughed. "Clip a seahawk's wings and tell the bird it's safe."

"Yet you flew anyway."

"I did. At least for a while."

"And now?" Darce fixed her with a piercing gaze. "What happens next?"

"I suppose we'll discover the answer to that in Arburgh, won't we?" Isla paused. "If you decide to stay with us, that is."

She hadn't meant for it to sound like a question, but the moment the words left her lips, she tasted hope on them. Despite the bite of the morning breeze, warmth raced to her skin, and she swallowed the embarrassment at the back of her throat.

Darce stared at her, a faint smile playing across his lips. "I'm not going anywhere, wolf cub. You may not want to admit it, but you and your brother need me, and I have no intention of letting you fend for yourselves in a place like the capital. I'm as much yours as I was your father's. Perhaps in time, you'll learn to believe me."

She searched his expression for some kind of doubt, some kind of uncertainty. "You cannot expect me to believe that's the kind of life you want."

"It's the life I've chosen," Darce replied. "And having that choice means more to me than you know. As for wanting..." He let out a dry chuckle. "I know the only reason you agreed to sail for Arburgh was for Lachlan. But even if you succeed, even if you make it back to Blackwood Estate with a fleet to defend it, how long will you be able to stay there? What is it *you* want, Isla?"

Isla tightened her fists, pressing the rough edges of her nails into her palms. Nishi's words echoed in her head, and for a fleeting moment, she imagined herself at the helm of a ship—*her* ship. The wheel sliding through her fingers and the breeze tugging at her hair. The sea in front of her, open and welcoming. The thought swelled within her like wind filling the sails.

Then she imagined the sentinel at her side, and the unbidden glimmer of that life was gone, dashed against the rocks with guilt and shame. She could never ask that of Darce, never allow herself to think about it, not even in the darkest parts of her heart.

I won't chain myself to any captain, he'd said. *My life is my own.*

Isla understood that feeling all too well.

"It doesn't matter what I want," she said, her voice thin. "You're not the only one who places value on their word. I promised Lachlan we'd go home together. That's all that matters to me now."

"Home," Darce repeated. "Are you sure that means the same to you as it does to him?"

Isla couldn't answer.

CHAPTER
FOURTEEN

L ater that day, the stern façade of Arburgh's dreich harbourfront loomed on the horizon, waiting for them with the disapproval one might reserve for unwelcome guests.

Isla shivered at the sight of it. As a bairn, she'd spent a fair time in the capital, and she'd never forgotten how its dreary bearings precipitated a certain downturn in her spirits. A perpetual drizzle clung to the air, leaving spiderweb trails of moisture beading along her hair and her cloak. The dampness was like a cold hand cupped against her cheek, its lingering touch turning her skin dewy with its residue. Even where the city was grand, it was grey, as if the gloom leached all colour from it.

The length of the gangway seemed to stretch forever as Isla shouldered her pack and followed Lachlan and Darce down to the docks. Not for the first time, she felt an anxious tug, as if the simple act of stepping onto land stirred an ache for the part of herself she left behind, the part of herself that somehow belonged out there on the sea.

Behind her, the *Jade Dawn* rocked in its moorings, its emerald sails faded and drab in Arburgh's grim surroundings. Isla let the others go on ahead and waited for Eimhir, who'd been held up by Nishi at the bottom of the gangway. The captain clapped Eimhir on the shoulder and turned back towards the ship, leaving the selkie with a disgruntled look on her face.

"Problem?" Isla asked.

"She wanted to remind me of the favour I can call on. Pointless, really." Eimhir glowered. "I don't intend to go anywhere near that ship again now I know there's a sentinel among its crew."

"How is it you didn't realise before? You knew Darce was a sentinel when we met."

"We can only hear the song of the auld blood when it is spilled," Eimhir said. "Finlay and I picked up its call at your estate, but by the time we tracked you to the loch, we could no longer hear it. All we had to go on was your trail. But then your swordmaster friend came looking for us. Part of him must have been able to sense us, even if he didn't realise it. That's how we knew he was of the auld blood." She tilted her head, expression thoughtful. "I didn't understand why he didn't use his gift to protect you. But he's different from that bastard on the *Jade Dawn*, isn't he?"

"Kerr?" Isla raised an eyebrow. "He seemed a reasonable sort."

"Many humans seem reasonable until their true nature reveals itself." Eimhir's lips curled. "You didn't know the sea spirits were there. You have no idea what it's like to have them reach out and grasp your soul in their hands, to bind you in place through the force of their will. We are creatures of the sea. They should be *our* allies, yet instead they answered to that human." She shuddered. "I'll never understand the power the auld blood has over them, over us all."

"Yet you risked your life to save the deckhand." Isla searched her hard-edged features for some kind of understanding. "You didn't have to reveal what you were. You could have let him drown, and Nishi and Kerr wouldn't have been any wiser."

"Let him drown?" A harsh laugh tore from Eimhir's throat. "Is that the kind of person you think I am? I suspect it would be easier for you if I were. Easier for us both, perhaps." She drew her lips into an unhappy smile.

Isla hurried to change the subject. "What else do you know about sentinels? Some Silvish folktales say they are the descendants of selkies who left behind their wild nature and gave up their pelts to live on land. That some measure of selkie blood still lingers within them, and that's what gives them their magic."

Eimhir snorted. "Silvish folktales are full of shite. We may share the auld blood, but we are not the same. How do you suppose we could ever willingly part with our souls? Selkies who lose their pelts wither and die. We cannot survive without them. Our children, our brothers and sisters, they cannot…" Her voice cracked, and Isla could almost hear the shards of grief caught in her throat.

"I'm sorry." She reached for Eimhir's arm, surprised when she didn't pull away from the gesture. Her skin was ice to the touch, and it was all Isla could do not to flinch. Instead, she allowed her hand to rest around her arm and wondered how a creature so cold could feel so familiar…so *human*.

"I know there's nothing I can say to make up for that kind of loss," she said, her voice low. "Only that I understand. I know what it's like to love a brother. If anything ever happened to Lachlan…" Her words died in her throat, shrivelling into a grief she couldn't give voice to.

Eimhir fixed her with a keen stare. "He may be your brother, but I do not trust him."

Isla dropped her hold on Eimhir's arm. "Aye? Well, he doesn't trust you either. But that doesn't mean there's any reason for us not to be at peace. At least for the moment."

"And if the moment passes? Will you use that?" Eimhir gestured to the pistol on Isla's belt. "I see the way your hand drifts to it when you're afraid, the way your fingers twitch. It's not the kind of weapon that offers any kind of compromise, any kind of second chance. Tell me, Isla Blackwood, is that the kind of person *you* are?"

Isla pressed her lips together. She was no stranger to the smell of black powder and the crack of a shot fired. She'd felt the kick of a pistol in her palm. She'd seen the splatter of blood across deck. But her enemies had been different on the *Ondasta*. Silver-scaled sirens with curved claws and needle-like fangs. Young broods of sea serpents with shell-encrusted hides, leaping from the waves onto the deck in a feeding frenzy. They'd never looked at her with storm-grey eyes and a questioning smile. They'd never worn faces so familiar they might have been human.

Monsters were easy to kill when they looked like monsters, when they *acted* like monsters. What happened when they didn't?

Isla shook herself free from her thoughts. "It's best we don't put ourselves in the position where that question needs answered."

It sounded like a threat. She'd *meant* it as a threat. But Eimhir only gave a full-throated laugh, rumbling from deep inside her.

"Careful, human," she said. "I might find myself starting to like you."

They left behind Arburgh's sprawling harbourfront and followed the tail of the firth as the river snaked into the city, splitting the capital in two. Here in the southside, the streets were lined with slippery cobblestones and bustling with bodies. Steep stone stairways led down to the tunnels of the city vaults. Arched bridges connected winding streets over a maze of canals. Each narrow wynd, each cobbled close, formed an intricate web around the beating heart of the capital.

Isla tried not to think about the stone buildings closing in around her. The city was suffocating; everywhere she looked was another alley, another dead end. She couldn't see the horizon here. She could barely see the sky. If Blackwood Estate had been a cage, Arburgh was a coffin.

Ahead of her, Finlay froze, a string of indecipherable words spilling from his throat in his rough selkie tongue. Before Isla could say anything, Eimhir was at his side, a warning hand around his shoulder. She murmured something, but the softness of her voice wasn't enough to temper the murderous glare darkening her eyes.

Isla pushed forward to see what they'd stopped for. An old man wrapped in filthy rags hugged his knees at the side of the street, spitting at the feet of strangers as they walked by. His sunken eyes were too large for his face. His cracked, pale lips seemed fused together. And his skin was scarred with salt, withered and dry like crumbling paper.

"He's one of us," Eimhir said quietly. "Or was, at least. After what's been done to him, I'm not so sure anymore."

Finlay let out a furious breath. "He must have got away alive when the thieves stole his pelt. Better he'd died fighting. There's no worse fate for our kind than this."

"This is what happens when a selkie is left without a pelt?" Darce blanched, his expression uneasy. "He's dying, then?"

"All of us are dying," Finlay said, voice sharp. "Some of us more quickly than others."

Isla forced herself to look at the old man, though all she wanted to do was tear her eyes away and walk on by. He was a broken, pitiful thing, left with nothing but pain and anger. She tried to summon the familiar hatred for the creature he was, but not even that was enough to chase the ache of shame and pity.

"There's nothing you can do for him?" she asked. "You couldn't find him another pelt?"

"It is no simple thing, to inhabit another's soul," Eimhir said. "It is a gift tied to blood. We cannot inherit a pelt without the blood of the selkie it belonged to."

"But the pelt you want to steal, the one the Grand Admiral took..."

"It belonged to my aunt. Her blood runs in my veins, and I can spill it in place of her. I am the only one who can claim it. I have no more siblings. No pups of my own. If I don't inherit her pelt, my aunt's dreamwalking gift died with her." Eimhir turned to the old selkie. "There is nothing left for him now. Soon, the call of the sea will become too much and he'll return there to die."

"That's it?" Darce still looked troubled. "He'll just go off to drown?"

"It's a brave thing to seek out death before it comes to claim him," Eimhir said. "It's all he has left."

The old man shied away but continued to stare at them long after they passed, humming behind his tight-pressed lips.

Finlay muttered something in his strange tongue, punctuated with clicks and whistles, and kicked a loose stone so viciously it clattered off the wall and broke up into angry dust.

"Watch your mouth," Lachlan hissed. "If somebody hears you making those kinds of sounds, there will be no hiding. Do you want to get caught?"

"What do you care?" Finlay glowered, but Isla didn't miss the fear darting across his face.

"I care because we'll fare no better if somebody thinks we're harbouring a pair of tides-damned selkies." Lachlan shot Isla a pointed look. "I told you this was a mistake. With the way the lad runs his mouth, I give it three days before he's hanging on some noble's wall."

"You think your threats frighten me, human?" Finlay drew his dagger from his pelt. "I can take care of myself."

Lachlan eyed the blade in contempt. "It was a warning, not a threat. And if you're not afraid yet, you should be. Maybe it's time you understand what kind of fate lies in store for you if anyone in this city discovers what you are."

He pushed ahead and turned up one of the steep cobbled stairways. Isla followed him, the muscles in her legs burning. The city was hard and unforgiving underfoot, punishing every step. Her feet were raw and chafed, blisters rubbing against the heels of her boots. The ache of exhaustion leadened every part of her. They'd been running ever since escaping Blackwood Estate. Sooner or later, they'd have to stop.

"Lachlan," she said, reaching for his arm. "Slow down. Where are you taking us?"

"He needs to see this." Lachlan's voice took on a cold edge. "You all do."

It wasn't until Isla reached the top of the steps that she realised where they were. She emerged from the shadows of the wynd and all her breath left her lungs, as if squeezed out by a violent grip.

Gallowgate.

A shudder crawled over her, burrowing beneath her skin. She remembered all too well the time she'd ventured here as a stubborn youth, slipping away from her parents to catch a glimpse of the place they'd forbidden her from visiting. It hadn't taken her long to understand why. The creak of the gallows' wooden jaws. The stench of blood and loosed bowels. The bleak granite buildings surrounding the square like faceless spectators. She'd covered her mouth with her hand and gagged. Then she'd run.

Laird Cormick and Lady Catriona never punished her that day. The pallor on her face told them she'd already learned her lesson. It wasn't until years later her parents banned her from visiting the capital, and that was only because...

Isla pushed the thought aside. That time was over. There was nothing she could do to change it now. Today at least, the square was still. Nothing moved save for the knotted loop of the noose drifting back and forth with the gusting wind. The rusting iron bars of the gibbets held no bodies, only bones. Somehow, that made it worse. The gallows were hungry, waiting for their next chance to feed.

"Is this what you want?" Lachlan said, turning to Finlay. "Because this is where you're heading. That old selkie back there will never make it to the water. They'll drag him here and leave him in one of these cages to rot. The crows will feed off the salt on his skin. He'll die a slow, painful death, because that's what the Grand Admiral does to those who threaten Silveckan."

Finlay blanched, but said nothing. Beside him, Eimhir's face turned cold as she cast her eyes over the gallows.

"This is what you wanted to show us?" she asked. "Another example of the cruelty humans are capable of?"

"I wanted to show you what will happen if you go through with this mad plan of yours. The Grand Admiral will show no mercy." Lachlan glanced at Isla and lowered his voice. "We should cut them loose before we get ourselves killed."

Isla said nothing. It was difficult to deny the truth in her brother's words. Difficult not to consider them.

She pressed her fingers against her throat, imagining the bite of the noose as it tightened around her neck. At least for her, it would be over quickly. The selkies would not be as fortunate. Their pelts would be stripped from them. The cages would drip with their blood, staining the cobbles red. They would leave behind only salt and bones.

Not even a week ago she might have taken some satisfaction from the thought of any selkie strung up in the gibbets, wasting away until death came to claim them. Now, she wasn't so sure. Eimhir had found a way under her skin, steering her like a ship blown off course. It was enough to make her hesitate. Enough to make her doubt.

Beside her, Darce turned deathly white, his eyes slack and unfocused as he stared out over the square. He seemed caught in the same trance as on the *Jade Dawn*, filled with the same anguish.

This time, when Isla reached for his hand, he didn't pull away.

"I can sense it," he said, voice straining. "The stench of blood spilled here. The keening of their cries. The agony of a rotting body separated from its soul. Tides, no wonder they hate us so much."

"We didn't do this, Darce."

His fingers turned cold, slipping out of her grasp. "You think that matters to the ghosts in this place? They want somebody to answer for what was done to them." He shook his head, his hair damp with sweat. "It was never like this before. The call is getting stronger. I feel it in my blood, like it wants to be spilled."

A shiver ran down Isla's spine. "You're talking about the blood oath?"

"Aye." A shadow fell across Darce's face. "I thought I had more time. But every time I look over my shoulder, it creeps a wee bit closer. I don't know what will happen when it catches up. All I know is we shouldn't linger here."

Isla pulled the woollen folds of her cloak together, though the gesture brought her little warmth. Gallowgate had struck her with a chill, and Darce's words only left her more unsettled. "You're right," she said. "We're already losing daylight, and the Tolbooth district isn't somewhere we want to be wandering after dark."

"Tolbooth?" Lachlan shot her a questioning look. "Why would we... Surely you didn't think we were going to Muir for help? When I said we had allies in Arburgh, our uncle wasn't exactly who I had in mind."

"I..." Isla paused, reaching in her cloak for the tattered remains of her mother's letter. Her heart tightened as her fingers brushed against the scraps buried in her pocket. Lachlan was right. Muir was a disgraced officer, cast out from the Admiralty. He'd never be able to help them. But that hadn't mattered. Her only thought, selfish as it might have been, was that he might be able to help *her*. "He's the only family we have left."

"That may be so, but Muir has been stuck at the bottom of a bottle for years, and we don't have the time to help him out of it." Lachlan sighed. "Trust me, sister. This is my world. I know how to move in it. If we play our cards right, we might be able to leverage my connections to get close to the Grand Admiral. After that, well... The rest is up to you. You'll know what to do next."

For once, there was no underlying bitterness in Lachlan's words. Whatever distance had come between them these last few years seemed to scatter in a heartbeat. He had her back. More, perhaps, than she'd ever had his. He trusted her to do what was best for them, what was right.

If only she could be as certain of that as he was.

"Very well, brother," Isla said. "Let's meet this ally of yours."

CHAPTER FIFTEEN

Nathair Quinn.

Tides-damned *Nathair Quinn*.

Even in her head, the name was enough to send a wave of irritation through Isla. Lachlan hadn't mentioned his connections in the city involved a decade-long friendship with a merchant viscount, or that the viscount in question was the same duplicitous bastard she'd once counted as a friend before he'd stabbed her in the back. The last time they'd met only solidified the feeling that the smiling jaws of the capital and all its games were the opposite of what Isla wanted from her life.

The setting sun drenched the upper city's townhouses in a red glow by the time they reached Arburgh's northside district. On this side of the river, the cobbled streets widened and the buildings stood tall and proud, their granite faces made elegant with grand columns and stone carvings. Mosaic tiles and hanging baskets spilling over with flowers cut through the dreich grey, offering rare bursts of colour. But even that wasn't enough to brighten Isla's mood.

"He was a lad," Lachlan said, attempting to mollify her.

"He was a snake," Isla retorted, and her brother made no further mention of the matter.

They stood in a pristine lobby with grand windows stretching from floor to ceiling and marble tiles patterned in diamonds of black and white. Isla fidgeted with the hem of her cloak as they waited. She'd been wearing the same clothes for more than a week now, and she was all too conscious of their reek, thick with sweat and dirt and seawater. Her fingernails were black with filth, her hair knotted and grimy. She looked like she belonged in the gutters of a dockside tavern, not an upper city townhouse.

"How well do you know this man?" Eimhir asked. "Can he be trusted?"

"He was a childhood acquaintance, nothing more," Isla replied stiffly. "And he's absolutely not to be trusted."

Darce shot her a questioning look, but she turned away, squaring her shoulders. It was strange how quickly the sense of betrayal returned. Not one day out on the water had she wasted thinking of Nathair Quinn. He'd been banished to a distant part of her mind, the intervening years diminishing him into little more than an unwanted memory. He hadn't been worth her anger, or so she'd thought. Yet once unpicked, she found the wound as raw and weeping as the moment it had been inflicted.

"Lachlan Blackwood, I hardly dared to believe it was you."

As if summoned by her thoughts, Nathair Quinn appeared at the top of the marble staircase, his face split into a wide grin. Life as a viscount was treating him well, it seemed. His red hair was perfectly coiffed, and he stood tall and straight-spined in a doublet and shining dress boots.

"Mind you," Quinn continued, "I could be forgiven for not daring to believe it was you. After all, how could my dearest friend have possibly returned to the capital without informing me?"

He sauntered into the lobby with the same self-assured poise Isla remembered from years ago and pulled Lachlan into a rough embrace. Her brother returned the gesture with a thump on Quinn's back, then pulled away, grief darkening his eyes.

"I would have written to you, but the circumstances under which we left Blackwood Estate were…" Lachlan trailed off, his voice catching on the words. "I'm afraid we come to you carrying some misfortune, and I find myself in the uncomfortable position of having to ask you for help."

"The only uncomfortable thing about it is your mistaken assumption of thinking you have to ask." Quinn put a hand on his shoulder. "We are friends, are we not? Whatever you need, you shall have it, as long as it is within my power to give."

Isla couldn't help the scoff that escaped her mouth. Her cheeks flooded with warmth that came as much from anger as it did from embarrassment as Quinn turned to stare at her.

He smiled, all teeth and charm. "Isla Blackwood. I see your propensity for assuming the worst of me hasn't abated over the years. Can't I want nothing more than to offer aid to an old friend?"

"I doubt it, given your propensity for not doing anything that doesn't benefit you."

"You wound me."

"I'm tempted."

He laughed at that. Threats of violence, no matter how thinly veiled, were a certain way to lose such games. The northside nobility would rather talk circles around each other for hours than lower themselves to using such crude instruments, and Quinn no doubt felt pleased he'd picked up the points in this particular exchange. Isla didn't care. If there had ever been a time when coming off worse in a war of words had been enough to anger her, it had long passed.

Upon seeing her expression, Quinn held out his hands. "I understand your concern, given our history. All I ask is that you accept my hospitality, if not my word." He sank into a deep bow. "I'll have my staff prepare rooms and bring you some fresh garments. Please, use the baths and explore as you desire before dinner. It is my wish for you to feel most welcome here."

"Thank you, Nathair." Lachlan grasped his arm. "I won't forget this."

Neither will he. The thought came sharp and unbidden, like the warning flash of a blade. It didn't matter how many years had passed. It didn't matter how well Lachlan thought he knew him. If Nathair Quinn did something, it was something that would serve Nathair Quinn. Perhaps it would be a day from now, perhaps a decade—eventually, it would reveal itself. Until then, he would appear to be whatever he needed to be long enough for his schemes to take root. Isla knew only too well that by the time he showed his true colours, they'd be so entrenched in his debt it would be impossible to dig out.

This time, it was up to her not to let it get that far.

The lapping of water against the edge of the porcelain tub was almost enough to send Isla drifting off to sleep. The bath had lost much of its heat, and the fragrance of perfumed oils had long since faded, but something about submerging herself beneath the surface weighted her with comfort. For the first time in weeks, she allowed the tension in her shoulders to loosen, allowed her mind to find some quiet as she sank into the water. She could forget where she was. She could forget everything that had happened.

A rap at the door was all it took to jolt her back to her senses.

"I'm to remind you dinner will be served on the hour." Darce's muffled voice came through the door. "Your brother seems to think you might intend on being purposefully late."

Isla sighed, hauling herself out of the tub and patting her skin dry with a towel as she eyed the gown one of Quinn's attendants left hanging up for her. Its fabric was a rich burgundy trimmed with gold, more expensive and elaborate than anything she'd worn in years. Another reminder of the life she'd left behind, the life she'd never wanted to come back to.

Slipping into the silk underdress was enough to make her skin crawl.

She'd been grateful for the chance to clean up and change out of her filthy clothes, but accepting Quinn's generosity felt like entering a negotiation she hadn't agreed to. Here in his home, wearing the gown he'd chosen for her... It was too much like being caught in a web, waiting for the spider.

She reached for the silk ties at the nape of her neck, her fingers fumbling with the cords as she tried to pull them into place. "Darce, are you still out there? I can't fix the back of this tides-damned dress."

For a moment, there was only a weighted silence. Then Darce's voice came through the door again, coloured with gruff embarrassment. "Aren't you supposed to have attendants for that kind of thing?"

"I sent them away. I don't trust Quinn, or his attendants."

The door creaked open and Darce walked in, shoulders square and rigid. His tousled crop of black hair had been cleaned and tamed, the stubble that darkened his jaw shaven clean. Gone was his leather armour, replaced with a charcoal doublet and a kilt in the blue-and-green of the Galbraith tartan. The only thing reminding Isla that he was a swordmaster, not a steward, was the glint of a steel rapier hanging at his belt.

His eyes trailed over the loose cords at her shoulders, and his cheeks reddened. "Go on, then. Burl yourself around and let me get this done."

Isla turned away as Darce worked the silk cords at the nape of her neck. She braced herself for the roughness of a soldier's hands, but instead she found his touch deft and gentle with the same care he'd taken when he'd stitched Lachlan's wound back in Caolaig. The brush of his fingers against her skin made the hairs on her neck stiffen, sending a tremble down her spine that wasn't entirely unpleasant.

A familiar feeling rose in her chest, resurfacing all the more insistently every time she tried to push it away. Ever since the sergeant had burst into her room that night at Blackwood Estate, something had changed. He'd brought his sword down on the neck of a creature intent on taking her life. He'd shepherded her and Lachlan to safety. Without her realising it, Darce Galbraith had become one of the few things in her life she feared to lose.

The thought stirred something uneasy in her. The sergeant wasn't hers to give up. There was nothing stopping him from leaving apart from a word given in grief to her dead father. A word that might be broken once the call of the sentinel's blood oath became too much for Darce to ignore. Sooner or later, he'd be bound to someone else.

Isla wasn't sure she wanted to dwell on that.

"Well, that's as good a job as I can make of it," Darce said, drawing back. "Let's hope the viscount isn't offended by my efforts."

Isla snorted. "If Quinn is offended, he won't squander the opportunity to tell me so. Which will give me the satisfaction of telling him how little I care for his over-sensitive sense of propriety."

Darce raised an eyebrow. "What did he do to cause you to hate him so much?"

"My father never told you?"

"You forget I was still a lowly soldier back in those days. Not exactly the kind of person who was privy to petty squabbles between nobles."

"Perhaps it was petty, though it didn't feel like it at the time." Isla grimaced. "I thought I'd found in him a friend unlike all the other young nobles. We could talk for hours. Though looking back on it, perhaps it was me talking and him listening. Quinn always could carry a conversation without saying too much. I wouldn't realise that until later."

"You spoke to him of something you shouldn't have?"

Isla nodded. "By the time I was sixteen I already felt trapped by the walls of Blackwood Estate, already planned on making my escape. On my last trip to the capital, I showed him the letters I'd written for all the great Arburgh captains, asking them for a chance at an apprenticeship. Quinn encouraged me to send them." She squeezed her fingers into fists. "I thought he was supporting me, but he paid off one of the dispatch boys to intercept my letter and brought it to my parents."

"Ah." Darce's eyes flickered with understanding. "It was him, then? The reason your parents stopped bringing you on their visits to the capital?"

"Aye, it was him. Quinn's deception won him my parents' gratitude. They believed his tattling was out of concern for me, but I knew better. Quinn doesn't do anything that doesn't benefit himself. My father wrote him a recommendation for the Merchant's Union, and it seems that favour paid off, given his current position. As for me..." Isla shook her head. "Blackwood Estate became more confining than ever. A prison of my own making, for being foolish enough to trust someone like Nathair Quinn. For the next two years, my mother barely let me out of her sight. She became hysterical at the mere mention of me leaving, and for each tear she shed, each cross word spoken, my resentment towards her only grew. It wasn't until I was walking up the gangplank that she realised how much of a push she gave me. She..." The words caught in her throat. "She ran to the harbour from the estate. She called after me from the jetty, her words half swallowed by the wind. She said she was sorry. Said she understood, and that she'd see me when I returned."

Something lodged itself in her chest at the memory, squeezing the air from her lungs. "Took me months to push that image from my mind," she murmured, half to herself. "Mother waving goodbye from the end of the quay, smiling through her tears. Never thought it would be the last time I saw her."

Isla forced herself in front of the mirror, pulling the edges of the lace overlay into place. She barely recognised herself. It was like looking at someone she had long forgotten. Even fresh and clean, with her hair neatly tied, the gown didn't seem to fit her. She still imagined saltwater clinging to her skin and the wind snarling her hair.

"People always said I look like her," she whispered. "I've never been able to see it."

In the reflection of the mirror, she saw Darce's hand rise to smooth the fabric into place across her shoulder. His fingers brushed lightly over her arm, trailing across her skin like a shiver and making her hair stand on end.

"You look like you," Darce said gently. "That should be enough for anyone."

His hand still lingered on the back of her arm, his touch so faint it didn't feel real. She watched through the glass, waiting for him to pull away. *Wanting* him to pull away, to ease this tightness seizing her chest, the nerves flitting in her stomach.

That should be enough for anyone, he'd said.

But it hadn't been. Not for her.

It was as if the glass shattered. As if through the broken pieces she could see what might have been, if only she'd turned around and walked back down the gangway that day. Perhaps Lady Catriona would still be alive. Her father too. Perhaps none of this would have happened.

Tides, she still hated Nathair Quinn, even after all these years. But all he had done was expose a rift already years in the making. The decision to leave, to walk away without making peace with her mother, had been hers. No matter how hard she tried to pretend otherwise, there was only one person she could blame for that.

"Let's go," Isla said, wiping her eyes. "We have a dinner to attend."

The spread on the dining room table was as grand and luxurious as everything else in Quinn's townhouse. Isla's stomach groaned at the fragrant scent of each steaming dish. Every mouthful she gulped down soothed a hunger she hadn't known she'd had. Garnished mussels and hunks of crusty bread. Rich black pudding scattered over wedges of fresh apple. Sweet octopus in a lemon vinaigrette, raw and tender, sliced so thinly it melted on her tongue. Had there been anybody else at the head of the table, she might have been able to set aside her misgivings and bask in the comfort of it all. But with Quinn, each delicious morsel carried a bitter aftertaste, reminding her of the poison to come.

He met her eyes from across the table. "Glad to see you're enjoying the food. Such a shame your friends didn't feel up to joining us."

His tone was pleasant enough, but Isla couldn't help but squirm at the way his mouth curled around the word *friends*. "Lachlan told you of our journey. I'm sure you can understand how exhausted they are."

"Indeed. Not to mention them being strangers to the capital." Quinn nodded. "Were I you, I'd remind them to keep those pelts of theirs close when wandering the city. It's only good sense these days."

Isla fought to keep her eyes from darting to Lachlan. She didn't believe her brother could have been so bone-headed as to tell Quinn the truth about Eimhir and Finlay, but there was a barb to the viscount's questioning that caught at her skin. "What do you mean?" she asked, struggling to quell the stiffness in her voice.

"Oh, just that the Merchant Quarter is booming this summer, and high-quality furs command a fair amount of coin," Quinn said, his voice light. "Of course, that means everybody wants a share. Only last week a particularly febrile mob beat a man to death in the Tolbooth district because they thought his expensive fur coat was a genuine selkie pelt." He snorted. "Of course, it turned out to be ermine. Not that you can expect those southside types to know the difference."

Isla tightened her grip around her fork, knuckles white. "But you do, I presume?"

"I own a significant portion of the merchant fleet. It's my job to know the goods we carry." Quinn drew his lips into a delicate smirk. "Tell your friends their pelts are some of the finest bearskins I've seen."

It should have been enough for her to loosen the tension across her shoulder blades, to sink back in her chair and let the air escape her lungs in relief. But Isla knew the sharpness of Quinn's smile. A decade wasn't long enough to forget the danger that kind of look carried. Maybe Lachlan hadn't told him, but tides, he *knew*.

She stabbed a piece of apple with her fork and averted her eyes from his smug expression. The dining room and all its opulence felt like it was closing in around her. The polished wood panelling on the ceiling, the patterned wallpaper half hidden by grandiose oil paintings, the row of glittering chandeliers winking down at her... Everything felt wrong, like being trapped in a cage with a snake ready to strike.

Perhaps it was time to show Quinn he wasn't the only one with fangs.

"Do you know what selkies do to people who steal their pelts?" she asked sweetly, fighting to keep the rage from her voice. "Would you like me to tell you?"

She reached for the wine, fingers trembling, but before she could fill her glass, Darce wrestled the bottle out of her grip.

"Easy, wolf cub," he said, the words spilling from his mouth far too loudly. "We all know what happens when you overindulge on a Breçhon vintage."

Isla glared at him, cheeks flushing. Before she could untangle her tongue and snap back, Quinn shot her an arched eyebrow. "Wolf cub, did you say? I imagine there must be a story to tell behind that particular moniker."

"None of your damn—"

Darce cut her off. "Aye, there's a story. Not one she's particularly fond of hearing, mind you."

Quinn laughed. "All the more reason to tell it, surely?"

The look Darce sent her was fleeting and impossible to understand. It flashed across his face, twisting his features with something that might have been regret. Then it was gone, replaced by a brash smirk. "Well, you see, when Isla here was nothing but a bairn, none of the Blackwood squires would fight her properly for fear of who she was, or rather who her mother and father were. Didn't do her any favours, of course—only led to the wee brat thinking she would always win."

Across the table, Lachlan's mouth pulled into a smirk, and Isla's cheeks grew hotter.

"Then a new lad gets transferred to the Watch, barely twelve years old," Darce continued, leaning back in his chair. "And what does the young lady of the estate do? Needles him, saying she's already beaten everyone else and she'll beat him too." He rubbed the back of his neck. "Of course, I didn't know who she was at the time, only that some feral wolf cub half my age needed to be put in her place. When I realised I'd bruised up the laird's wee girl, I expected to hang for it."

"You might have, were it not for Isla refusing to drill swords with any of the other squires from then on out," Lachlan cut in, eyes flashing with amusement. "Apparently Galbraith here was the only one who could give the so-called wolf cub a *real challenge*. So instead of sending him to the gallows, our father promptly rewarded him by naming him our personal squire."

"Rewarded?" Darce grinned. "Sometimes I wish he'd hanged me instead. The tides must enjoy seeing me suffer."

Lachlan choked into his goblet, and Quinn let out a roar, pounding his fist against the table. Isla could do nothing but stare between them as their cheeks turned ruddy with wine and laughter. It was too much. All the exhaustion and tension and grief of the past few weeks barrelled into her at once, snapping whatever composure she had left.

Her chair scratched against the floor as she pushed back, cutting through the raucousness like a blade. "If you'll excuse me, I'll take my leave. It seems the Bréchon vintage has gone to my head after all."

She marched out of the dining room, fighting to steady her breathing over the rage and embarrassment. Tides take them all, she was *done* here.

"Isla, you're a bloody fool."

She spun halfway up the grand marble staircase to find Lachlan at her heels. "Aye," she said quietly. "It appears I am. I thought we'd buried whatever ill feeling there was between us, but you couldn't resist the opportunity to see me humiliated."

"Believe me, I took no pleasure in witnessing what transpired. Though I should be grateful at least that your storming out put an end to the situation before anything worse came to pass."

"What does that mean?"

Lachlan fixed her with a measured look, all humour gone from his face.

"You don't trust Nathair."

"That's obvious."

"You could do with making it less so." Lachlan rubbed a hand across his forehead. "Did you forget where we are? At least Galbraith had the sense to—"

"Don't talk to me about Darce Galbraith."

"Isla, he was *protecting* you." Lachlan climbed the last few stairs separating them and grabbed her shoulders. "You were thrown off by Nathair's questions about the sel—about our two other guests. Everyone could see it. All Galbraith did was take the attention away from your slip-up."

"I didn't ask for his help."

"You wouldn't, would you?" Lachlan sighed. "But that doesn't mean you didn't need it. Or did you want to give away their secret?"

Her brother's words hit her squarely, the accusation stinging. "I didn't give away anything. In fact, I'm certain Quinn already knows."

"Not from me, I assure you." Lachlan's face hardened. "And if he does know, he'll speak nothing of it."

"You trust him that much after what he did to me?" Isla paused. "How did the two of you become so close? Is there something more between you than simple friendship?"

Lachlan chuckled. "Nathair is a singular kind of man, I admit, but he's far too valuable an ally to risk for the sake of a tumble between the sheets. I know it may be difficult for you to accept, but he's far from the foolish, ambitious lad who saw an opportunity to exploit all those years ago. He made a mistake in how he treated you; he admitted as much to me earlier this evening."

"How convenient." Isla folded her arms. "Nathair Quinn has an impeccable sense of timing."

"Nathair Quinn has power, influence, ships. The kinds of things we'll need if we're ever to rebuild what we lost. If we're ever to go home." Lachlan's voice strained on the word, pain clouding his eyes as he spoke.

"Blackwood Estate needs to be restored. Caolaig needs to be resettled. He can help us do that."

"For what price?"

"Let me worry about that." He locked his eyes with hers. "I'm not asking you to forgive him or cast aside your suspicion. All I'm asking is for you to trust my judgement like I'm trusting yours with Eimhir." He reached for her hand. "We're family, Isla. There's nothing they can do to get in the way of that, as long as we have each other's backs. You know that, don't you?"

Isla let out a heavy breath, her fingers slack and reticent in his grasp. She wanted to push him away again, but already her anger was disappearing, loosening the ache in her chest more and more with every earnest word that left her brother's lips. Lachlan was right. She'd asked him to trust her. How could she do anything but the same without fracturing what she'd been trying so hard to rebuild?

He kissed the top of her head. "Go on, you should get some rest. Tides know we all need it after these last few weeks."

It wasn't until Isla reached the top of the staircase, her legs stiff and weary, that she realised Lachlan hadn't waited for her to reply. Perhaps he assumed her trust was something beyond question. Perhaps he knew better than she did the only answer she could possibly give.

We're family, Isla. There's nothing they can do to get in the way of that, as long as we have each other's backs.

His words echoed around her head as she slipped beneath the sheets and drifted off to sleep. But though it was her brother's mouth that spoke, all she saw in her dreams were the grinning lips of Nathair Quinn.

CHAPTER SIXTEEN

A pleasant chill in the morning air bit at Isla's lungs with each breath. Its sharpness cleared her head, chasing away the previous night's discontent as she stole through the narrow confines of the townhouse garden.

She slipped along the flagstone path towards the gates, grateful to be back in breeches and boots. The Tolbooth district wasn't the kind of place she could blend in wearing Quinn's expensive finery. One slip on the shite-stained cobbles, one look at the wrong kind of person, and she'd find herself in one of the canals, drowning under the sodden weight of a gown with too many layers. Her new linen shirt and long-tailed coat might have been well-made, but at least they were inconspicuous enough for her not to draw any unwanted attention.

Or so she hoped.

"Going somewhere?"

Isla cursed inwardly, her hand inches from the handle of the gate. "I needed some fresh air."

"Don't insult my intelligence."

She turned to find Darce watching her with folded arms and a half smile. He was clad once again in his leather armour, the Blackwood sigil worn and faded. Ever the loyal soldier, it seemed, even when she'd been too scorned to see it herself.

Isla sighed. "It's not your intelligence I wish to insult, Sergeant, merely your insufferable need to smother me like a bairn. I'm certain I can manage a short walk across the city without your presence."

Darce stared at her, jaw set in a hard line. "If this is about what happened last night—"

"Lachlan told me you were only trying to throw off Quinn," Isla said. "As much as I hated it, I have to admit it was quick thinking."

"For a low-born lout like me, you mean?" The corner of Darce's mouth pulled into a smirk. "I've spent the last seven years with your brother for company. It's little wonder I've picked up on his silver-tongued habits, as shameful as it is."

"He's changed a lot since I've been away."

"Aye, that's bound to take a bit of getting used to. But take it from someone who knows—he's still the same lad you left behind. A good one, with his heart in the right place."

Isla smiled. "You speak as if you've become friends."

"I suppose we have. Or as close to friends as you can get with the arrangement of one man paying another." Darce shrugged. "I never got to know you the way I got to know Lachlan. I wasn't old or experienced enough to be your mentor, nor young or well-born enough to be your friend. You were less a person to me back then and more of a charge."

Isla arched an eyebrow. "Or a pain in the arse?"

"That too." His eyes glinted. "Something I'm afraid remains true to this day."

Isla couldn't help but laugh. The sting of the previous night faded, leaving behind a tension of an altogether different sort. She hadn't realised how disarming the quirk of the sergeant's mouth could be, how the rare humour in his eyes could leave her feeling like the ground was unsteady beneath her feet. "And here I was about to forgive you."

"So easily? You're far too gentle-hearted." He tilted his head. "Most people would make a man beg."

"I'm not most people."

Darce watched her, holding her in place with the quiet command of his gaze. When Isla was younger, that look made her want to squirm. Now, something different seized hold—a nervous flutter that took wing and thrummed against her heart.

"No," he said eventually, the barest trace of a smile on his lips. "You're not." He held her in contemplation, looking as if he was on the brink of saying more, then shook his head.

Isla stepped towards him, leaving the townhouse gate and its promise of freedom behind. Each thump of her heart resounded in her ears as she drew closer, and her tongue turned dry around the question burning in her mouth. "You said last night the tides must enjoy seeing you suffer. Am I truly such a burden to you?"

"A burden? Isla, I—" Darce looked away, a frown worrying his brow. "You were never a burden, not even back then. I admit, it was churlish of me to accuse you of having learned nothing while you were at sea. Watching you on the *Jade Dawn* made me realise how wrong I was. The way you climbed the rigging, helped pull in the sail..." He hesitated, meeting her eyes again. "I don't think I understood why you left Black-wood Estate until I saw you on deck. Like you were meant to be there, like you belonged there."

"There was a time I thought so too," Isla said softly. "I was happy on the *Ondasta*. But it still wasn't enough. Part of me wonders if anything will ever be enough." She reached into her coat pocket, scrunching the parchment in her hand. "You want the truth? I'm going to see Muir. He was my mother's brother. If there was something she wanted to tell me, something I needed to know, maybe she told him." She lifted her chin. "I appreciate you doing your duty, but this is something I have to do alone."

Darce didn't say anything, but his frown deepened.

"You have to look out for Lachlan too," Isla pointed out. "And believe me, Nathair Quinn is more of a danger than the capital in broad daylight. Unless your sword arm can be in two places at once, you won't always be able to protect both of us."

A pall fell over Darce's face. "I have not forgotten Blackwood Estate. I know all too well what it means to fail someone I was sworn to protect. I would do anything to ensure it doesn't happen again."

Isla flinched. "Darce, I didn't mean—"

He closed the remaining distance between them, grasping her arms with a force that left her wondering if he was trying to hold her or keep her away. He smelled of leather and sheepskin and the oil he used to sharpen his claymore. His breath was warm against her forehead. The hard lump in his throat bobbed up and down under his stubble-coated chin. His lips parted, and she braced herself for the rebuke, the warning, the reminder of the promise he'd made to her father.

Then the moment passed and he stepped back, tightening his jaw. "Go to your uncle. Just...be careful, wolf cub. You're not a stranger to me anymore. We've been through too much these last few weeks for that to be true. If anything were to happen to you...or your brother..." His neck flushed red. "What I mean to say is I don't think I can stand to lose any more Blackwoods."

Before Isla could say anything else, he turned on his heel and walked back to the townhouse, leaving her with the painful ache of his words and a tightness in her sternum she could neither understand nor explain.

Part of her wanted to chase after him. But the townhouse's iron gate was only fingertips away, promising her freedom if she were to walk through it.

Isla took a breath and pushed aside her thoughts of the sergeant. Tolbooth was waiting, and with it, perhaps the answers she'd been searching for.

Southside's rotten stench burned Isla's nostrils as she followed the street signs towards the seedy heart of the capital. Here, the river was green-brown and murky, skulking alongside the grim tenements and crumbling moorings. The gloomy wynds grew ever narrower as she walked, the cobbles under her feet becoming slick with filth and grey seafoam spilling over from the snaking canalways. It was difficult to imagine she was still in the same city. Tolbooth was a world unto itself, one riddled with poverty in every doorway and danger in every dark close.

When at last she found herself at the bottom of the rickety wooden steps that led to Muir's last known address, Isla hesitated. Her hand drifted to her coat pocket, her fingers finding the scrunched remains of her mother's letter.

She forced herself up the steps, mouth dry and legs trembling. The wooden door at the top waited for her to knock, its paint faded and flaking, its brass handle covered in grime. She'd never been here before. This wasn't her home. Yet, in the strangest way, it was the closest she'd felt to it since leaving the *Ondasta*.

Isla took a breath and rapped on the door.

Nothing stirred. The echo of her knuckles on the wood faded into silence.

Then the door creaked open, and she was met with the gaunt, tired face of her uncle.

Muir stared at her, glazed and distant. There was no warmth in his gaze, no joy of recognition. Isla half wondered if he might close the door on her without a word leaving his lips.

Then his eyes widened, and an ashen pallor fell across his dark brown skin. "Isla," he said, and somehow it sounded breathless to her ears, like hers was not the name he'd expected himself to speak. "You shouldn't be here."

It was not the welcome she'd anticipated. "Can I come in, at least?"

Muir moved to block the doorway, his broad shoulders stiffening. He opened his mouth to say something, then shook his head and stepped back, pushing the door just wide enough for her to squeeze past him.

Isla looked around the cramped confines of the room. The wallpaper was drab and peeling, the ceiling thick with cobwebs. The only furnishings were two sturdy chairs sitting at odd angles and an overturned footstool lying in the middle of the room. Muir seemed to have decorated the place with bottles, most of them lying empty apart from one or two with candles forced halfway down their necks, wax drippings caked onto the glass. In the corner sat a huge barrel with a makeshift tap, dripping a brown liquid onto the wooden floor with an erratic *tip-tip*.

Muir retrieved a cane from beside the door and used it to hobble to one of the chairs, limping gingerly. A painful twinge caught at Isla's heart. It was difficult to understand how it had come to this, how a once-decorated admiral could have found himself brought so low. She remembered her uncle as a dashing figure in his embroidered tricorne and sailor's coat of teal brocade. He'd been a seafarer with no equal save for the Grand Admiral himself. The Cirein-cròin they'd called him, after the sea serpent of legend—such was his fearsome reputation on the waves.

Isla didn't see any of that man in him now. It wasn't just age, though that had caught up with him—his dark brown skin was weathered and marred with creases, and the coarse hair escaping his sailor's braids had turned seafoam white. No, it was the way Muir hung his head low, the way his once-proud shoulders sat hunched and drawn.

He gestured at the other chair. "Might as well take a seat, seeing as you're here. Just don't go helping yourself to my barrel."

Isla raised an eyebrow. "I'm surprised you're letting so much go to waste dripping on the floor."

Muir muttered something under his breath and fetched a dirty tankard, plopping it under the tap with a loud clunk. Then he sat in his chair, watching her with wary eyes.

"You look like you saw a ghost," Isla said.

"Aye. Part of me thinks I'm still seeing one." He stared at her. "Why are you here?"

Isla tightened her hand around the fragments of parchment in her pocket. "Mother is dead."

The words tore from her lips with more pain than she realised she'd been carrying. Talking to Darce the previous night had brought back the rawness of her loss, the ache of regret. Regret for the time she'd lost to coldness and resentment where there should have been joy and laughter. All of it for the sake of something Isla had held more dearly than her own family, something she'd never been able to find.

Muir slumped in his chair. "Aye, your father wrote to tell me as much. But reading it isn't the same as hearing it." He lowered his head, running his hands across his braids. When he looked up again, his eyes shone with unspent grief. "I still remember when my own father—tides watch over him—brought Cat home from the workhouse in the Merchant Quarter. She was a tiny wee thing, so small she didn't seem real. I loved her from the start. Didn't matter that she didn't look like me, that we didn't share blood. She was my sister the moment I laid eyes on her."

"Yet you didn't come to the funeral." Isla fought to keep the bitterness from her voice, but it rose anyway, sharp and unpleasant. "Father said you'd lost yourself at the bottom of a bottle. I didn't want to believe him, but here we are."

"My presence wouldn't have been kind to anyone. Cormick never did think much of me after...after I lost my place in the Admiralty. I don't blame him for that. There's much I have to be ashamed for. A lot of things I did, he never understood. He's a good man. A better man than me."

"Was," Isla corrected gently. "He was a good man."

165

"You can't mean..." Anguish darkened Muir's features. "I thought it was only Cat who'd been struck by the malady. He never mentioned anything about—"

"It wasn't sickness." Isla swallowed. "There was an attack. Selkie raiders came from the mists. They slaughtered every villager in Caolaig, then came for Blackwood Estate. Our swordmaster helped me and Lachlan escape, but the rest..."

She rubbed her arms. She couldn't forget how the wraith had frozen the air in her lungs. Couldn't forget how the selkie's jaws had parted above her throat, how her mouth had filled with its blood as Darce severed its head from its neck above her. It was more than a nightmare left behind. It was an omen of what would come if they didn't stop it.

Muir closed his eyes. "I'm sorry, lass. I didn't know."

"That's why we're here. We have nowhere else to go. Blackwood Estate isn't safe for us anymore, not unless..." Isla trailed off, biting down the rest of the words. She couldn't tell Muir about Eimhir and Finlay. A drunken slip of the tongue was all it might take to bring a noose around their necks. "Lachlan is working with an old friend to petition the Grand Admiral for ships. If we ever want to return home, we must have the means to protect it."

It was a half-truth, the words leaving her mouth sour. Not for the first time, a wave of doubt washed over her at what Eimhir had asked. If Isla refused, she might pay for it with her life. But to follow through on the selkies' plan? To steal from the Grand Admiral himself? Dread rose like the tide in the pit of her stomach at the thought of Gallowgate waiting for them. It was not only her life at stake. It was Lachlan's. It was Darce's.

"You should stay far away from the Grand Admiral."

Isla snapped her head up to find Muir watching her with a hard, sober gaze. The tired slur had disappeared from his voice, leaving only the sharpness of a warning.

"Arburgh is an unforgiving place, and he is an unforgiving man. I know that better than most." A shadow passed over Muir's face. "You and your brother are better off finding somewhere you can start over. Somewhere your name...my name...won't carry so much danger for you." He let out a weary sigh. "Ah, lass, why did you come here?"

"I already told you." Isla fought to bite back her impatience. "And I don't understand why—"

"No." Muir cut her off. "Why did you come *here?*"

Isla reached into her pocket and pulled out the scraps of parchment that had once been her mother's letter. Some of it had crumbled entirely, and the larger pieces were ragged and torn. The ink and parchment held no meaning anymore. All she had left was the memory of the words written there and the hope her uncle might understand what was meant by them.

She passed the pieces to Muir. His brow furrowed as he ran his fingers over the faded ink.

"She was dying," Isla said, her words a whisper. "She wanted to tell me something. She wanted to give me something she'd kept from me."

Muir stared down at the scraps of parchment with an unfathomable expression.

"Everyone else who might have known about this is gone." Isla's throat burned with tears. "You're my last chance, uncle. Do you know what my mother meant in this letter?"

Muir turned over the remains of the letter in his hands, a tremor dancing along his jaw. The silence between them became so thick Isla feared it might smother her. Her heart thumped against her ribs. Blood pounded in her ears.

"Please," she said. "I need to—"

"Aye." Muir folded his hand around the letter. "I know what she meant. But I cannot tell you."

Isla couldn't breathe. Muir's words hit her like a blow, bruising her lungs.

Muir placed the letter back in her hand, closing her fingers around it with his own. His touch was gentle and filled with sorrow, but Isla barely felt it. Her skin was numb, her mind reeling with grief and confusion. The room blurred as she blinked back the hot tears pricking the corners of her eyes.

"I don't understand," she said hoarsely.

"It's better you don't." A pained look fell across Muir's face and he turned away, running a weathered hand across his white braids. "Whatever manner of sickness Cat suffered must have struck hard. She would never have sent you that letter if she'd been in her right mind."

"You don't know that. You *can't* know that." Isla's throat constricted around each word. "She wanted to tell me something. She wanted to give me answers. What right do you have to deny me them?"

"That's the thing about answers, lass. Once you find them, there's no going back to not knowing, no matter how much you wish for it." Muir grimaced. "There is too much danger in what you're searching for. Too much pain. Believe me, Isla, some things are better left buried."

"That should be for me to decide." She pressed her nails into her palms. "You can't expect me to walk out of here and leave this behind, not after what I've been through. Not after what I gave up to come here."

Muir shook his head. "I can't give you what you're looking for. I promised her. I promised them both I'd do whatever it took to keep you safe."

"Tides take everyone who's ever made a promise to keep me *fucking safe!*" Isla leapt to her feet, pushing the chair from under her. Her cheeks burned as she stared down at her uncle. The sight of him shirking back from her, face twisted in distress, only squeezed the ache tighter. "I am so bloody sick of people trying to protect me. None of you understand what this is doing to me. None of you understand what it's like knowing there's something out there I can't find. It's been eating at me ever since I can remember. I fear one day, there will be nothing left of me for it to consume."

She sank back into the chair, her anger dissipating as quickly as it had arrived. It seeped from her skin, leaving her empty. Her heart felt drained, even as it thrummed painfully in the hollow of her chest.

"Do you have any idea," she whispered, "what it's like to feel so lost?"

Muir looked around the room, his gaze falling across the scattered collection of bottles. His expression twisted into something dark and pained, and he reached into his pocket to retrieve a small brass compass Isla recognised from his Admiralty days. It had been a shining thing then, a distinguished trinket that made her eyes sparkle. Now, its casing was dull and grimy, its chain tarnished.

Muir stared at the compass, fingers trembling as they closed around it. "Aye," he said quietly. "I believe I do."

When at last Isla made for the door, Muir didn't try to stop her. He didn't ask her to stay. Tides, he didn't even mutter a goodbye. He was all too willing to let her go.

Maybe she should have understood that better than anyone.

CHAPTER
SEVENTEEN

T he next few weeks passed like the black skies of a storm shrouding the passing of day into night. No brightness came with dawn each morning, and the evenings held no more darkness than Isla already carried with her. In the wake of Muir's refusal, it was difficult to bring herself to care about what happened next. Returning to Blackwood Estate felt like a far-off dream that had never been her own, and her grief for what had happened there turned to numbness in the frozen cavity of her chest. None of it seemed to matter anymore.

At least, not until Eimhir took it upon herself to remind her.

The townhouse roof had become Isla's place of respite. She often slipped through the loft hatch once the others retired for the night, wrapping her furs around her to keep out the midnight chill as she gazed out over the harbour. Tonight, the water glittered, moonlight fracturing off the waves. The capital fleet sat in the firth, their great hulls swaying, waiting patiently to be called upon. The stars winked at her from above, reminding her where she was, providing her with bearings she no longer needed.

The icy bite of a steel axe blade sliding under her chin was all it took to shatter the tranquillity.

Isla stiffened as Eimhir crept beside her. The selkie's mouth curled at the corners, revealing the flash of a smile as she pressed the axe further against Isla's throat.

"I thought you might need a reminder of the debt you owe me," she said, her rasping voice light with amusement. "I expect you'd rather keep your blood in that skinny wee neck of yours, but I can still spill it if you wish."

Isla reached two fingers behind the head of the axe and pushed it firmly away. "That won't be necessary."

"No?" Eimhir's smile stretched wider. "We had an agreement, you and I. Your life for my aunt's pelt. I'm getting fair scunnered waiting for you to do your part."

Isla flinched, the sting of the accusation all the worse for how true it was. "It's not that simple. We don't know where the Grand Admiral is keeping the pelt. Even if we did, it would be foolish to rush in. We'll only get one shot at stealing it, and if we fail..." She let the rest of her words hang between them. "Well, you saw Gallowgate for yourself. I shouldn't need to explain what will happen if we're caught."

Eimhir lifted her axe, a frown settling across her brow as she sat cross-legged beside Isla. The angles of her face were hard and uncompromising as she stared out over the city. "I've no desire to rush headlong towards death, but neither can I wait forever. My clan needs me."

Her knuckles turned white as she buried her fists in her pelt. It had a lustrous sheen to it, the moonlight dappling across the fawn-coloured fur. It was beautiful. Vulnerable. The longer Isla looked at it, the more she understood why someone like the Grand Admiral might covet it so, why someone like Eimhir would drown the city in blood to protect it.

After a while, Eimhir sighed. "I'm sorry. I didn't come here to make threats."

"No?" Isla rubbed her neck, her throat still tingling from where the axe had bitten her skin. "That's how you begin all conversations?"

Eimhir barked out a laugh. "Seems I'm developing a habit." She sat for a moment, grinning in the darkness. Then the humour fell from her face. "Finlay overheard Quinn talking to your brother."

"Overheard?"

Eimhir shrugged. "Aye, all right, he was spying. Can you blame us? We've been here for weeks and still haven't got any closer to finding my aunt's stolen pelt. We took matters into our own hands."

Isla couldn't help but shiver. "What did Finlay hear?"

"Quinn was complaining of a spate of recent thefts from his stores in the Merchant Quarter. He said there were whispers of selkies in the capital, an underground network of my people." Eimhir's eyes gleamed. "They steal and smuggle supplies for the clans. They help selkies escape the city if they get into trouble. Quinn suspects they're being aided by a group of sympathetic humans."

"That's hard to believe."

"Is it? And here I thought we were proof that human and selkie can put aside their differences for a common cause. If the gun-anam aren't stopped, more and more of my people will fall to the mist sickness. The raids on the coast will only get worse. I don't believe either of us wants that."

A familiar chill crawled across Isla's skin, leaving dread in its wake. Within Arburgh's walls, the threat of creeping mists and the gun-anam seemed elusive and out of place. Even when the skies turned dark, no wraiths emerged from the shadows. It made it easy to forget.

A few words from Eimhir were all it had taken to change that.

"Lachlan doesn't believe you," she said, surprised at how easily the admission spilled from her mouth. "About the gun-anam, I mean. My brother thinks you'll say anything to get what you're after."

"And what do you think?"

"I don't want to believe you. I don't want to believe those tides-damned wraiths are what you say they are." Isla steadied herself with a long breath. "But I do, and that terrifies me."

"It should." The lingering traces of Eimhir's smile disappeared. "Isla, what your brother believes doesn't concern me. It's you I came here for. Help me find these selkies hiding in the capital. They might have information we could use to find my pelt."

"They're your people. Why do you need my help?"

"Your friend Quinn seems to think they use the city vaults to move around. Finlay and I don't know this place well enough to risk going there alone." The edge to Eimhir's voice faded, leaving behind only quiet desperation. "Please. I need to speak to them."

"And if I don't agree?" Isla folded her arms. "You'll bring that axe across my throat and call it a debt repaid?"

Eimhir's face fell, a hollow look in her eyes like Isla had disappointed her. "Tell yourself that, if it's what you need to convince yourself to do this. We both know the terms of our bargain have changed, whether you want to admit it or not."

Isla bristled at the way her words burrowed under her skin, but it was useless to deny them. Sometime between the moment Eimhir first pressed an axe to her throat and where they sat together now, things had changed. She believed Eimhir. Tides, maybe she was starting to *trust* her. It was difficult to see her as the enemy she'd once feared, once hated.

She imagined Lachlan's expression, the betrayal on his face. A hundred justifications danced on her tongue, ready to be released. Helping Eimhir was only a means to an end, a way to protect the coasts from the wrath of the gun-anam and mist-sick raiders. This was for her brother. This was for their home. It didn't need to be anything more than that.

"I hope you don't make me regret this." Isla gritted her teeth. "All right. I'll help you find your people."

They slipped out of the townhouse a few hours later, before the grey light of dawn crept through the city streets. Not that daylight made much of a difference in Arburgh's underground vaults. The sprawling labyrinth of tunnels was buried deep, accessible only through steep winding stairways and rusting ladders. They reeked of damp, their stone floors slick with sewage and canal water. The only light came from the occasional oil lamp or the glimpse of daylight through the sturdy bars of a grate high above. The vaults formed a city within a city, a patchwork of capillaries below the grey and granite of the capital, the dark echo of its beating heart.

Isla led them through the narrow wynds as best she could, stepping cautiously around loose cobbles and spills of waste. She'd never been allowed down here as a bairn, and all she had in terms of directions were the vague rumours Finlay had relayed. The curved stone ceilings were obscured by lines of clothes, though there was no sun to dry them. Each wooden doorway lining the grim walls held another secret, another forbidden space hidden from the world above. Flophouses filled with the disease-ridden and desperate. Gambling dens where losses were paid in blood. Makeshift morgues used by gravediggers and bodysnatchers.

And perhaps, if the rumours were true, a place where selkies gathered in secret.

"We've been down this way before. I can smell it." Finlay let out a low snarl. "I told you she's not here to help us. All she's doing is leading us in circles."

"I'm trying my best," Isla said shortly. "You haven't given me much to go on, and the vaults are a maze. I don't know which part of the tunnels your friends might be hiding in."

Finlay shot her a sullen glare but said nothing. Isla felt his eyes on her as they walked, the sensation like a breath at the back of her neck. She didn't like how often she caught him watching her, his lip curling into a sneer he didn't seem to notice.

The path split up ahead, and Isla stopped in her tracks. Finlay was right. They had been this way before. There were so many branching tunnels, so many hidden passageways, that it was impossible to keep track of the places they'd already been. She could not navigate down here.

Something on the wall caught her eye, and she froze. "Did you over-hear anything else Quinn said about the humans who are supposedly helping your people down here?"

Finlay frowned. "Not much. He suspected they were organised by a smuggling ring. He mentioned a name. Some lower city bottom feeder called the Eel."

"The Eel? You're certain?"

"That's what I said." Finlay scowled. "What does that have to do with anything?"

The oil lamp in front of her flickered, sending shadows dancing across the wall. Isla drew her fingers across the stone, wiping away the dust and grime under her fingertips.

There on the wall, illuminated by the dim light of the lamp, was a crudely drawn mural. The paint was sloppy and devoid of detail, but Isla could still make out the long, writhing shape of the creature it depicted. An eel of the canals, its gaping jaws pointing towards the tunnel on the left.

She exchanged a glance with Eimhir. "It's a marker. It's showing us where to go."

Eimhir gave a tight-lipped nod. "Then let's follow it."

They pressed on, leaving the more populated section of the vaults to venture deeper into the abandoned tunnels. Every time they reached another fork, they found another mural, the eel's jaws pointing them in the right direction.

Eimhir put a hand on her arm. "I smell something."

Isla sniffed the stale air but could discern little but the reek of rat droppings. "What is it?"

Eimhir's reply came in a breath of excitement. "Home."

It wasn't until they ventured closer that Isla smelled it too. Bitter and brackish, filling her lungs like the reminder of an old friend.

She lengthened her stride to keep up with Eimhir, who'd already rushed ahead. Under her boots, the cobbles yielded to rockier ground.

The walls grew slick and wet, their lower reaches stained green with moss and fronds of seaweed. With each step, the darkness retreated, chased away by a light streaming in the distance. Then came the unmistakable yawn of a wave breaking upon the shore.

Somehow, they'd found the sea.

The mouth of the tunnel spilled out into a wide cavern, limestone walls curving on either side of them. In the distance, the blue line of the horizon sat against the brightening dawn sky, half swallowed by a jagged maw of overhanging rocks. The wind whistled past her ears. The water lapped against sand and pebbles.

But it was not the existence of the cavern that unnerved Isla. It was the presence of the creatures gathered within it.

"Ancestors forgive me," Finlay muttered. "I didn't dare believe it."

Scattered around the cave were a dozen or so selkies. Some gathered at the mouth of the cave in their seal forms, flippers splayed on the flat rocks. Others huddled in small groups, talking in hushed tones. Pelts of every colour lay draped across their shoulders: furs of glistening white, dappled grey, brown and sandy and everything in between.

"A sea cave, here. Right under the city." A delighted laugh burst from Eimhir's throat. "Right under the Grand Admiral's nose."

Isla looked around. She was in a secret cavern leading to the heart of the capital. A hidden entrance the Grand Admiral couldn't have known about. For if he knew, there would be slaughter—of that much, Isla was certain. The rocky walls splattered, the water clouding red. Slain bodies left to rot amongst the rockpools, fit only for the crabs to feast upon. That was what these selkies risked gathering here. That was the secret she was now privy to.

It felt like a betrayal.

"We should speak with them," Finlay said, then sent a wary look towards Isla. "She shouldn't be—"

Isla waved him off. "You two go ahead. Even if there are humans around these parts helping them, I'd rather not risk provoking anyone.

I'll wait here."

She found a flat ledge near the tunnel entrance to serve as a place to sit while Eimhir and Finlay spoke with the other selkies. The rock was cold and damp through the fabric of her breeches, but it was not that which caused ice to run down her spine. It was seeing the creatures who'd killed her father, who'd slaughtered a village of fishers and traders and simple kelp harvesters who'd never raised a weapon in violence.

At least, that's what she told herself she believed. Watching the selkies now, it was harder to recognise in them the horror and bloodlust she'd witnessed at Blackwood Estate. They chattered in low-pitched voices, their strange tongue punctuated with guttural clicks and piercing whistles. They embraced each other with bright eyes and laughter. They kissed before disappearing into the water, fur melting over their bare skin as they took their seal forms once more.

Eimhir was deep in conversation with two selkies on the far side of the cave. One of them peeled back the folds of her pelt to reveal the swell of her belly, her brown skin smooth and stretched over the life inside. Eimhir's lips parted in wonder, her eyes lighting up with an expression Isla had never seen before. The wide smile transformed her face, blunting the hard angles, softening the stone in her expression. She pressed her palm against the pregnant selkie's belly, and even from across the cavern, Isla couldn't mistake the tremble in her fingers, the yearning on her face.

She turned away, the sting of heat rushing to her cheeks like she'd been caught watching something that wasn't hers to observe. When she dared to glance back, Eimhir was looking at her with a ponderous expression. She murmured something to the pregnant selkie, then gestured for Isla to join them.

Isla hesitated, fingers digging into the edge of the stone slab. This was not her world, and these were not her people. Being here felt like intruding on a place she had no right to be in. But the selkies still waited for her, their expressions serene and expectant.

She traversed the rocky floor of the cavern, skirting around rockpools as she made her way over. The pregnant selkie sent her a cautious smile, then nodded, gesturing to her belly.

Isla stilled. She couldn't—she *shouldn't*.

Eimhir took her hand, gently placing Isla's fingers on the selkie's stomach. Her skin was like ice to the touch, but even so, Isla could feel the faintest trace of warmth, of life, beating from within. For a moment, she was a bairn of only three years again, deep in the embrace of her earliest memory: her mother snuggled between the bedsheets, holding Isla's hand over her swollen belly, whispering to her of the brother she was soon to meet.

Isla snatched her hand away from the selkie, her heart aching. "I... I'm sorry."

She hurried back to the slab on the other side of the cavern. Her fingertips were numb from the selkie's cold skin, but the lingering echo of the heartbeat underneath still pulsed against her own blood. It was too familiar. Too much like her own.

Tides, how could she have got everything so fucking *wrong*?

Eimhir joined her, pale cheeks flushed pink. She hopped onto the ledge beside Isla and let out a long breath, her eyes shining. "Thank you for bringing me here. For being here."

Isla bit her tongue until she tasted blood, not trusting herself to say anything.

"You seem troubled," Eimhir said. "Was this not what you expected?"

"I don't know what I expected." The words sounded hollow to Isla's ears. "It was easier before. Easier when I hated you. But seeing you like this... It all seems so—"

"Human?" A half smile tugged at Eimhir's mouth.

Isla nodded. "The look you had on your face when you were talking to that selkie over there..."

Eimhir faltered, the curve at the edge of her lips tensing. "I've not felt that kind of joy for a long time. But it was bittersweet. Happiness for something I'll never know myself."

Isla stilled. "You can't..."

"Won't." Eimhir shook her head. "There is nothing I would love more than a pup to call my own. I've never had much interest in the act itself, of lying with a mate, but to bear a child..." Her throat squeezed around the words, smothering them with grief. "But I won't. Not when there is a chance they will be born into this world with no pelt to inherit. I couldn't bear to surrender them to the sea like my baby brother. I still see his salt-scarred skin, his bloodstained lips. I still see him sinking into the black depths. I couldn't..."

Something broke in Isla's heart, shattered by grief and guilt. She lifted her head, blinking away tears. Finlay was still in hushed conversation with a selkie by the mouth of the cave, his white pelt loose around his shoulders as he sat by the water. "He reminds you of your brother, doesn't he?"

Eimhir let out a choking laugh. "It's hard not to think about the kind of selkie he might have been. I hope, had he lived, that he'd be burdened with less anger, less pain, than Fin. Though I cannot blame him for it. He has lost so much. We all have."

Isla placed her hand over Eimhir's. Her skin was cold, sending a shiver through her. "Back in Kinraith, you told me we must bury what came before. Do you believe it's possible for friendship to exist across such wounds?"

Eimhir said nothing. Then her lips pulled into a familiar wry line. "I want to. Ancestors forgive me, but I want to."

Silence fell between them, ringing with words unspoken. It stirred something inside Isla, like a shifting current pulling her off course. She couldn't do this anymore. Not after what she'd seen. Too much had changed, or perhaps she had.

When Finlay at last returned and they ventured back into the lamplit tunnels of the vaults, Isla steeled herself with the thought of what she must do. It didn't matter that Eimhir had bought her help with the edge of her axe—Isla would give it anyway. If that made her a traitor, perhaps it was a price worth paying to make right what was wrong. Perhaps that was the first step on the path to friendship, the path to peace.

"Did you get what you came here for?" she asked, glancing at Finlay. "Did the selkies have any information on where the Grand Admiral might be keeping the pelt?"

"Rumours." Finlay shot her a hard look. "Nothing for you to concern yourself with."

"We need her help," Eimhir said, a tired rebuke ringing in her voice. "The only hope we have—" She placed her hand in front of Isla. "Wait. Did you hear that?"

Isla listened, but all she heard was the rasping of her own breaths, the shifting of cracked, loose cobbles under her feet. "What are you—"

The shot came without warning. One moment, there was silence. The next, the crack of a pistol and the whistle of a shot flying past her head. She didn't see where it lodged itself, only heard the crack and crumble of the pellet hitting the stone wall.

Eimhir grabbed her arm. "Someone followed us."

"A selkie?"

"Our people don't use your weapons of fire and powder," Finlay snarled. "They don't work in the water. It must be one of your kind."

Isla wanted to push the accusation away, but her denial turned to ash on her tongue. Someone had come after them. Someone who didn't care about getting their hands bloody, regardless of whether it was human or selkie they felled.

"What do we do?" Eimhir's eyes were wide and desperate.

Isla stared into the darkness of the tunnels. "We run."

CHAPTER EIGHTEEN

I sla's ears pounded with the thump of her boots against the cobbles as she sprinted through the tunnels. Her lungs burned in an effort to keep up with Eimhir and Finlay. All she could hear was the frantic gasps of their breaths, and occasionally, another crack of a shot fired.

Whoever was pursuing them was close. Too close to risk slowing down. There wasn't enough time to search for the murals and retrace their steps—all they could do was run.

"You did this," Finlay snarled, flecks of spittle flying from his mouth. "You had someone follow us."

Isla didn't have enough breath in her lungs to argue. The only thing that mattered was escaping these tides-cursed vaults.

When they reached the steep steps of a spiral staircase, Isla dropped her hands to her knees. "Wait," she said, straining against the pain in her chest. "They'll be expecting us to go up, to make for one of the entrances that come out in the city. I'll wait here and lead them that way. You two should go down. Find another route, and we'll meet at the townhouse."

Eimhir's eyes flashed, though whether it was in suspicion or concern, Isla wasn't certain. "They'll catch you."

"It's not me they're after." Isla drew her pistol from her belt. The mother-of-pearl casing glinted in the dull light, and the wooden stock nestled comfortably in her palm. "You said your people don't use weapons of fire and powder. Well, if this pursuer expects their quarry to be a selkie, they're in for a nasty surprise when they catch up to me."

Eimhir hesitated. "Why would you—"

"Go. Before it's too late for us all."

Eimhir nodded, a worried expression twisting her features as she followed Finlay down the winding stairway into the shadows below.

Isla waited, hand around her pistol. If she moved too quickly, whoever was chasing might not follow. They might go after Eimhir and Finlay instead. She had to let them see her. She had to be the bait.

Something in the darkness stirred, and she ran.

The tunnel wall exploded above her head, showering loose chips of stone. She'd waited too long. Long enough to catch a glimpse of a lean, gaunt-faced man levelling a pistol at her and firing a shot that only missed her by inches.

She pushed herself up the steps, willing the screaming muscles in her legs to give her more. The bastard was right behind her. If she didn't put some distance between them, the next shot would find the back of her skull.

As she ran, the light from the oil lamps dimmed, leaving her in darkness. Isla slowed as much as she dared, dragging her hands along the rough stone walls on either side of her, feeling them narrow and widen and change direction. She must have made a wrong turn somewhere. This section of the vaults was abandoned—there was no light from the lamps, no sign of life apart from the rats scurrying at her feet. She might find herself trapped at a dead end, or with a broken neck at the bottom of a drophole, or—

"Shit!" Isla let out a hiss as she slipped on a loose cobble, her ankle twisting. She stumbled, gritting her teeth against the pain as she hobbled into one of the branching tunnels. The stone wall was cold as she pressed herself against it. She listened, but only the breath of the tunnel's musty air replied. Perhaps she'd managed to lose him. If she doubled back now, maybe she could find a path to the surface.

Then she heard it. The shifting of loose rubble underfoot.

Isla froze. The slightest sound, the smallest movement, would give it all away. She couldn't run, not with the pain twinging in her ankle. If she wanted to get out of here alive, there was but one way to ensure it.

She held her breath until she heard his footsteps scrape again. He'd passed the mouth of the tunnel she was hiding in. This was her only chance.

Isla stepped out of the darkness and placed the barrel of the pistol against her pursuer's neck. "My bosun told me never to waste your shot if you're not close enough for the kill. I learned that lesson well." She pulled the hammer back, the click echoing off the walls. "You're going to wish you had, too."

The man stiffened. "Where are the skinchangers?"

"Gone. Count yourself lucky. They would have made this more painful than I will." She pressed the barrel more firmly against his neck, her finger curling around the trigger. "Why were you following us? Who sent you?"

"You won't do it." The man chuckled. "You like your lessons, lass? Here's another one for you—people willing to use a pistol don't waste time talking about it. If you were ready to bloody those wee hands of yours, you'd have done it already."

Isla stilled. The pistol felt warm, the polished wood of the stock pulsing against her palm. He was right. She'd never killed like this before. She'd never been an executioner. Every time she'd pulled a pistol, every time she'd drawn a blade, it had been a matter of survival. Serpents, sirens, storm harpies. All of them monsters.

And what of selkies? a voice whispered to her. *Are they no longer monsters?*

She pushed the thought away and tightened her fingers, the pistol quivering in her grip. What choice did she have? The man still held his own pistol by his side, though his arm remained still. The dull glint of a dagger winked from his belt. This wasn't something she could run from. It was survival. Only this time it was not a monster at the end of the barrel, but a man.

A laugh spilled from his throat. "Aye, I thought as much. Takes a certain kind of person to stomach killing another in cold blood. A lesson you've left too late to learn, by my wager." He turned his head, lips twisting into a cruel smile. "Never mind, I'll take my time teaching you. It's not just the skinchangers who can make things painful. You know they flay their victims? Maybe you deserve a wee taste of that for trying to help them. I'll slide my blade under that pretty skin of yours and peel it back piece by piece. I'll cut your tongue out when you scream. By the time I'm finished, you'll be begging me to put you out of your misery, you wretched little cu—"

Isla squeezed the trigger.

It was such a quiet thing, the death of a man. No keening wail from a serpent's throat, no writhing tail or thrashing wings. Just the crack of a pistol and the dull thud of a body crumpling against stone. He collapsed at her feet, his blood pooling around her boots. It seemed too easy.

"Thank you," she murmured to the lifeless corpse at her feet. "It appears you taught me a lesson after all."

The stench of singed powder burned her nostrils. Blood splattered her cheeks, dripping with tiny fragments of bone. She already felt the twisting in her gut, the bile threatening to rise. Later, when her frantic heart returned to normal and the numbness of her shaking fingers wore off, she might regret what she had done.

Worse still, she might not.

The sun had long risen by the time Isla hobbled up the flagstone path to the front door of Quinn's townhouse. The brightness fought in vain to break through the clouds in beams of scattered light. Down in the vaults, she'd lost all sense of time. It was only now she realised how exhausted she was, how her stomach growled with hunger. Her legs were stiff and sore, her ankle swollen and throbbing. A cool wind nipped at her neck, and she pulled the lapels of her longcoat tighter, noticing the dried blood under her nails. There would be no hiding what had happened. One way or another, she'd have to answer for it.

The others were gathered in the drawing room when she returned, talking in hushed voices. Darce saw her first, relief washing over his face as she limped through the doors. His eyes darkened as they trailed over her. Isla could only imagine how she must look—her clothes coated in grime, her face and hands stained with blood that was not her own.

Lachlan stormed over, pale and shaken. "Where have you been? When we woke to find you and the—the others gone, we feared the worst."

Isla glanced to where Quinn stood in the corner of the room. "We were followed. Someone was after Eimhir and Finlay."

"And you," Darce said, expression stony. "What happened, Isla? Where are they now?"

"They didn't make it back?" Isla's heart dropped. "We split up. I thought they got away, but—"

She broke off at the sound of the drawing room doors bursting open, the wood rattling on its hinges. Standing between them, hair dishevelled and shoulders heaving with ragged breaths, was Finlay. His lip was torn and bloody, the white fur of his pelt stained red around his shoulders.

He fixed her with a glare that contained only fury, only hatred. "This was you. You did this."

Isla froze. "Where's Eimhir?"

"You tell me." He stalked back and forth, his fists clenched so tightly his hands were shaking. "You were the one who led us into a trap."

"I had nothing to do with—"

Finlay let loose a snarl and leapt towards her. Before Isla had time to scramble for her pistol, he grabbed her by the throat and slammed her against the wall. His dagger was in his hand, the tip of the blade pressing into her neck with an unrelenting bite.

"Tell me where they took her." His hand was like ice around her throat as he squeezed, crushing her windpipe. He was so close she could smell the salt on his breath. All it would take was one wrong move, and his dagger would slide across her throat, spilling her blood across Quinn's perfectly polished marble floor.

"Take that blade away from her." Darce's voice cut through the room, dangerously soft. The sound of it was like a blade of its own, cold-edged and unforgiving. "I warned you once before that if you spilled a drop of her blood, you'd pay with your own. Don't make me follow through."

Finlay flared his nostrils as he held her. Isla wondered if he'd even heard Darce. If he even cared. Maybe he'd rather slit her throat anyway, damn the consequences.

Then he relented, releasing his fingers from her neck. Isla collapsed against the wall, clutching her swollen throat through bruised gasps.

Darce rushed to her side, grabbing her arm and holding her steady. He tilted her chin back and slowly drew away her hands. His fingers were warm against her skin where Finlay's had been like ice, his touch oddly tender for how insistent it was. Isla shivered as he traced the curve of her throat, then winced as he found the scratch where the dagger had pressed against her skin.

His dark eyes met hers, and Isla stilled. The pulse from his fingertips beat against her skin, making her heart quicken in response. There was a question in his gaze, a promise of retaliation, if she only asked for it.

She shook her head, the gesture so slight it was all but imperceptible. This was not the time for reckless blades and threats of violence. There was too much at stake.

Darce's jaw tightened as he pulled back and turned to Finlay. "You're lucky I don't cut you down where you stand."

Finlay's lip curled. "You're lucky I still need her."

"Enough," Isla said, the word rasping from her aching throat. "We have greater concerns than whatever ill feelings and resentment we may harbour towards each other. You said Eimhir was taken. That's the only thing that matters now. We need to find her."

"Do we?" Lachlan folded his arms, blunt and unyielding. "I don't know what trouble you managed to get yourself into this morning, but it's clear it was at their behest. I won't let you put yourself in any more danger because of their mistakes." His brow softened. "Don't forget why we came here."

His words tugged at her chest, but she pushed them away. "They are not to blame for what happened. Finlay is right—we were led into a trap. Only it was not I who laid it."

Quinn had been watching the exchange with an expression of mild amusement. When Isla's gaze fell on him, his mouth pulled into a thin smile. "Always so quick to accuse me of treachery, dear Isla."

"Hardly surprising, given your eternal inclination towards it."

"Only when it serves me." Quinn shrugged. "What could I possibly gain from arranging the deaths of those living under my own hospitality? My reputation would be tarnished among the nobility, not to mention with your brother."

"He's right." Lachlan shot her an irritated look. "Whatever you think of Nathair, he is my friend. He would not allow for any harm to come to you under his watch, let alone order it. You're letting your past grievances affect your judgement."

"Then let him prove it by helping us find Eimhir."

Quinn's smile didn't falter. "How should I have any idea where she is?"

"Because you know *what* she is." Isla cut him off with a wave of her hand before he could protest. "Oh, let's not do this dance, shall we? We don't have time for it. You know she and Finlay are selkies. You've known it since we walked through those overly-ornate front doors of yours. You might have hidden it better, but you never could resist dangling your knowledge in front of someone's nose to see if they had the wits to sniff it out."

He slipped for the briefest of moments, his mask of composure giving way to surprise that she was no longer playing by their old rules of engagement. Then it returned, quicker than anybody could have noticed. But Isla was not anybody. She knew him as a lad, knew the man he'd become. She, more than anyone else, knew what he was capable of. It was past time she turned that to her advantage.

Quinn inclined his head. "I admit, I had my suspicions. But if she is a selkie like you say, I fear she is beyond your reach."

"I'll be the judge of that. All I need from you is to know where they took her."

Quinn pulled his lips into a thoughtful line. It was an expression Isla recalled only too well, one that brightened his eyes as he considered and calculated and schemed. If he decided to help, it was only because there was something to be gained from it. She couldn't let herself forget that.

"Well?" she asked, biting back her impatience.

Quinn sighed. "There is a district gaol here in the city's northside. The warden is an enterprising sort, offering bounties for selkie pelts. A profitable means of earning some coin on the side, for those willing to risk the wrath of the Grand Admiral's tax collectors. If your friend isn't dead already, it's likely she's been taken there."

Isla gave a firm nod. "Then that's where we have to go."

"Have you lost your mind?" Lachlan paled. "Why not walk to Gallowgate right now and tie the noose yourself?"

"I can't leave her there."

"Why not?" Lachlan said, his expression pained. There was no understanding in the crease of his forehead, nothing in his eyes but hurt and confusion. "You don't owe her anything. Risking your life to save hers... It's not worth it, Isla. She wouldn't do the same for you. None of them would. Remember what her people did to our home, to our father..." His voice cracked on the words, splintering with a grief that was still too raw for Isla to bear.

She glanced at Darce, but his expression was made of stone as he stared blankly ahead. He'd watched her father die. He'd seen his friends slaughtered and flayed. Perhaps he thought the same as Lachlan. Perhaps asking either of them to put this aside was too cruel a request to make.

Isla turned back to Lachlan, taking his hand in hers. "I wish I could hate her for what they did. Tides know I've tried. Hating her would be easier. But she's not responsible for what happened to our home. It was the wraiths. The gun-anam."

"This again?" He pulled his hand away, shaking his head. "Have you forgotten the bodies the selkies flayed and left in pieces? The selkies brought this violence upon us, not the wraiths. All you have is Eimhir's word that the two are connected, and I'm not as convinced of her ghost story as you are. At least if we get ships from the Grand Admiral, we can protect ourselves."

"Can we?" Isla's neck prickled with the memory of frost permeating her skin as the wraith reached its spectral hand towards her. Looking at her through the empty eyes of a seal skull. Speaking with the voice of the ocean, like it was promising to drown her in it. "Even if you don't believe her, you saw how that wraith passed through the walls like mist. You still bear the wound from its blade. How are *ships* to protect us against such things?"

Lachlan's hand drifted towards his shoulder. "Your scream saved me that night."

"And your sgian dubh saved me. We have each other's backs, remember? That's what you told me."

He looked at her, mouth drawn. He'd never been so solemn when he was a lad. His tawny eyes had been ever-bright and full of mischief, attached to a permanent grin. Now, his face carried the same lines as hers—marks of sorrow and doubt and regret etched in the folds of their brows and the edges of their lips. Part of her wished she could pinch his cheek and tousle his hair and take it all away like she'd done when they were bairns. But the time for such things had long passed, for both of them.

Lachlan rolled his head back with a resigned expression. "You'll go regardless of what I say, won't you?"

"I have to."

"Then I have no choice." Lachlan straightened, glancing towards Quinn. "I'm sorry for putting you in this position, Nathair. I should have told you who you were harbouring. If your door needs to close to us after this, I understand. All I ask is that before it does, you tell us everything you know about this gaol."

Quinn blanched. "We are friends. My door shall never close to you. But I would be a poor friend if I didn't try to dissuade you from this foolishness. Your sister"—Quinn cast her a scathing look—"has clearly made up her mind, but there's no reason for you to risk your standing and your life over this. You don't need to get involved."

Lachlan gave Isla a sidelong glance. "I'm afraid it's a bit too late for that. If my sister has made up her mind, I already am involved. There is no force in this world that can change that, for better or worse."

Isla's heart swelled painfully at his words, bringing tears to her eyes. Ever since she returned, she'd been fumbling at the threads of an old life, thin and fraying, finding too many missing to ever have a hope of weaving them back together. Now, for the first time, she realised she was wrong. She'd lost so much, but she still had him. They still had each other.

She gave him a wide smile. "Glad to have you on board, brother. Finding ways to get into trouble isn't the same without you."

Lachlan snorted. "I don't think finding trouble will be the issue. How do you expect to break into a district gaol anyway?"

"That's the easy part." Isla turned to Finlay, waiting for the flicker of understanding to dawn across his expression. "We walk right through the front door."

CHAPTER NINETEEN

T he district gaol was a blocky granite building in the west of the capital. Isla could have walked past its featureless walls a dozen times without giving thought to what it was. There was nothing to suggest that festering in its bowels were countless prisoners awaiting their fate. Knowing that only a few feet of stone separated those within from the oblivious cityfolk passing by only made it all the more eerie.

Lachlan held himself stiff beside her as they walked. He'd swapped his new shirt and doublet for an ill-fitting stained tunic and a woollen cloak frayed along the hem. No longer a northside noble, but the hard-faced mercenary he needed to be for this to work.

"I still can't believe I agreed to go along with this," he muttered, shooting her a dark look. "If it wasn't for the fact you and Galbraith would have gone ahead without me..."

"There's still time to turn back. Darce and I can handle this on our own."

"I'm not leaving you. I only—" Lachlan sighed. "Just promise me we'll get out of there if we come across any sign of trouble. No matter what you think of her, Eimhir isn't worth our lives."

Isla pulled her cloak close, shielding herself against the night wind.

Inside the folds, her fingers drifted to the pistol on her belt. It was more of a comfort than it had ever been, now she knew what she was capable of with it in her hand. But that didn't mean she wanted to use it. Not unless there was no other choice. "Agreed," she said. "First sign of trouble, we leave."

The gaol's entrance loomed in front of them: heavyset wooden doors with thick iron brackets holding them in place, flanked by two guards in silver cuirasses and feather-rimmed bicorne hats. Each of them held a musket in their hands, blades attached to the end of the barrels. Once they approached, it would be too late to turn back.

Isla cast a glance at Finlay's manacled wrists. He'd agreed to her plan out of desperation rather than trust—that much was clear. His lip was bloody and eyes sunken as he looked at her, his expression one of revulsion and hatred.

At least one of them would find it easy to play their part.

"Are you ready?" she asked.

Finlay clutched the filth-stained white fur of his pelt as best he could with his bound hands. "Let's get this over with."

Lachlan and Darce took an arm each, knuckles white as they dragged Finlay across the cobbles. The selkie thrashed, letting out a string of harsh words from the back of his throat, barked out in a language she couldn't understand.

The guards straightened as they approached, observing Finlay with wary expressions. "Look here," one of them said. "Another skinchanger, if I'm not mistaken. As if the cells aren't full enough already." He snapped his head up. "What are you doing with a creature like that?"

Darce gave Finlay a violent kick, sending him to his knees. "Found him down the docks trying to break into my stores. Heard this was the place to come for compensation. Could do with the coin—not sure how I'm supposed to sell my catch after I've had vermin in my wares."

The guard folded his arms. "That doesn't sound like our problem."

"Now, let's not make any rash decisions," the second guard said. "That pelt might be a wee bit dirty, but I can tell it's a fine one. Not to mention it would be our second one this week—the commander will be fair chuffed."

The first guard ran his eyes over them. "I suppose you're right. I'll put it in the storage room along with the rest of them. Head inside and the overseer will make sure you get your coin."

He reached for the pelt, but Finlay kicked out at him, glaring with wild eyes. "Get your hands off it, human scum!"

The guard aimed his musket, but Darce twisted Finlay's arm behind his back and pushed him to the ground with a sickening crack. "Should have warned you, this one's fierce for a young lad. Nearly took a chunk out of my partner's hand with those teeth of his. But what can you expect from a beast like that?" He pulled the pelt from Finlay's shoulders and tossed it to the guard. "Here you go."

The guard sneered at Finlay. "Not as brave without this, are you?" He turned back to Darce. "Maybe you should bring him in. I don't want to take any chances if he's a biter. I heard a guard on one of the southside patrols lost a leg from the poison in their teeth."

The second guard snorted. "Poison in their teeth? That's the most ridiculous thing I've ever heard."

"It's true! They were talking about it for weeks. Turned his leg black, so it did."

"It was an infection, nothing more."

"Aye, well, I'm still not taking any chances." The guard grimaced. "Go on. The overseer is at the far end of the corridor. She'll take the prisoner for processing. Here, dump his pelt in storage while you're at it—it's on the left as you go in."

Isla followed Darce and Lachlan as they dragged Finlay inside. The hallway stretched the entire length of the building, the end so far away it dissolved into darkness. The only features lining the walls were the bars keeping the prisoners caged.

"Human scum?" Isla asked under her breath. "Were you trying to make a scene?"

The hint of a smile appeared on Finlay's lips. "I thought it prudent to be convincing."

"If I didn't know better, I'd say you were enjoying this."

It was oddly silent as they approached the cells. Isla had been expecting more of a clamour, with prisoners shouting or cursing the guards. But the noises were muted. Faint shuffling against the floor, aching gasps of laboured breaths, moans and whimpers of a body in pain.

As they passed the first set of bars, she saw why. The cells were suffocatingly narrow, with barely enough room for outstretched legs. One of the prisoners had bloody stumps for fingertips, and the walls of his cell were covered in scratch marks and trails of red. Another was deathly thin, with sunken cheeks and bloodshot eyes, covered in his own bile. The stench of blood and stale sweat made Isla want to retch.

A low growl rippled from Finlay's throat. For once, Isla didn't have it in her to warn him to be quiet. Quinn was right—most of the prisoners here were selkies, stripped of their pelts. Scars of salt encrusted their flesh. Flakes of skin peeled from their bodies, scattering the cell floors. They were wasting away, withering like empty husks.

"Isla, over there."

Lachlan pointed at one of the cells further ahead. Isla could only make out a mess of brown-blonde hair behind the bars. As they got closer, the prisoner looked up and Isla was met with a pair of sunken, storm-grey eyes she recognised only too well.

"Eimhir. You're alive."

The selkie eyed her warily. "What are you doing here?"

"Freeing you, of course." A painful lump caught in Isla's throat. "I didn't betray you. And I would never leave you here, not in a place like this."

"My pelt..." Eimhir's voice sounded thin and fraying. "All of this is for nothing if I don't get it back. I'd rather die than suffer the life that awaits me without it. I won't become one of the gun-anam."

Isla moved closer to the iron-wrought gate. Eimhir's broad shoulders and ropy arms seemed smaller behind the bars of the cell. She huddled in the centre of the stone floor, holding her knees to her chest. There was no sign of salt scarring her skin yet, no wasting of her pale flesh, but the shadow darkening her features chilled Isla's blood all the same.

"We'll find it," she said. "They're keeping them in a storage room nearby. Hold on until we get the keys from the overseer. We'll be back soon."

She hurried after Lachlan and Darce, who were dragging Finlay after them in a bundle of white fur. As they approached the end of the corridor, the gloom retreated under a row of hanging lamps, revealing a sturdy wooden desk and the sour-faced woman sitting behind it.

The overseer met them with an irritated scowl. "Why is this creature still wearing its pelt? The guards didn't direct you to storage?"

Lachlan shrugged. "Must have missed it. We'll take it from him now."

He reached for Finlay's shoulder, just like they'd planned. And just like they'd planned, Finlay responded with a grin as he drew back and threw a vicious headbutt.

Bone connected with bone in a sickening crack, and Lachlan stumbled, blood streaming from the bridge of his nose. Darce leapt forward, eyes flashing as he wrestled with the white fur of Finlay's pelt, making a show of trying to pull it from his shoulders. Finlay pushed him and Darce staggered back, rolling across the overseer's desk with more force than Finlay's bound hands could have possibly mustered.

By the time the overseer realised the position she'd been caught in, it was too late. Darce sprang up behind her, unharmed, and slid his forearm around her throat. Her lips parted, but no sound came from them save for a weak, wheezing gasp. Her eyes widened, then glazed over as she fell limp in Darce's grasp.

"Quickly," Darce said. "I can only keep her out for a minute or so."

Lachlan unhooked the keys from the overseer's belt and tossed them to Isla. "We'll lock her in Eimhir's cell. That should give us enough time to get out of here before someone raises the alarm. Now let's move, before it's too late."

Isla hurried to Eimhir's cell, fumbling with the keys. The metal screeched and scratched as she tried one after another until finally one caught, releasing the lock with a dull clink.

Eimhir pushed herself to her feet, a strained smile worrying the edges of her mouth. She looked different without her pelt around her shoulders. Not smaller, but diminished somehow, like the stiffness in her spine had been stolen too. Her muscular arms were smeared with grime, her bare feet crusted with filth and dried blood. Eimhir had been in this place less than a day, and already she bore the marks of it. If they hadn't come, if they'd left her here...

"Thank you," Eimhir said, her voice a low, ragged rasp. "You had no reason to risk yourself for me, yet you came anyway."

"I did not need a reason." Isla swallowed. "A friend should not need a reason."

"A friend?" Eimhir rolled her tongue over the word like she was tasting it, and the smile at the edge of her lips stretched into something more than relief. "A caraid—a *friend*—was not what I was expecting today."

She limped out of the cell, wincing each time her bloodied feet touched the stone floor. When she saw Finlay, her eyes brightened, and she pulled him into a fierce embrace.

"Touching as this is, we have to go," Lachlan said, grunting as he helped Darce drag the overseer's limp body into the cell. Already she was stirring, eyelids fluttering as she writhed against the filth-covered floor.

Eimhir glanced at the gloom of the corridor. "What about the others?"

"We don't have *time* for the others," Lachlan snapped. "As soon as the overseer comes to her senses, she'll start screaming for the guards."

"He's right." Isla put a hand on her arm. "I know you don't want to leave them here, but if we don't go now, we may lose our only chance of finding your pelt."

The sunken lines around Eimhir's eyes seemed to darken. "So we should forfeit their souls for the chance to save mine?"

"Aye." It was Finlay who answered, the word ringing bitterly. "Ancestors forgive me, but aye. You know what it is you need to do. You know you're the only one who can do it. We can't lose you." He swallowed. "*I* can't..."

Eimhir's expression softened. She turned back to Isla, wearing a grimace heavy with pain and regret. "My pelt. Do you know where they're keeping it?"

Isla nodded. "Follow me."

As they hurried down the hall, Isla tried to avert her eyes from each cell they passed. Some of the selkies might make it to the gibbet, might live to have their blood spilled across the cobbles and the carrion pick at their wounds. Others would wither with only harsh stone walls and the smell of their own shite for company. Their skin would crumble. Their organs would waste away. Whatever was left would be a spectre of what they were before, a soulless wraith existing only for revenge. One of the gun-anam.

"These guards have no idea what they're doing here," Isla said, fighting against the tightness in her throat. "This is only a promise of more pain."

"For your people and mine alike." Eimhir's face was drawn in weary lines, her eyes bleak. "And there lies the truth too terrible to admit: the men are the monsters, and the monsters men. This violence belongs to all of us. It will continue as long as we let it."

Isla closed her eyes. Eimhir's words only brought back memories she wished she could forget. The kitchenhand's back stripped bare, the chalky-white knobs of her spine pushing through flayed ribbons of flesh. The bard in Caolaig lying prone in a puddle of his own blood. A pair of jaws coming for her throat, cut down by the swift stroke of Darce's sword. And at the centre of it all, a creature of salt and spray wearing armour of bones and a mask of its own skull. A creature that might have been born in the bowels of a place like this.

She lengthened her stride and pushed open the door to the storage room. It was cramped and dark, the odour thick with must and stale fur. Pelts hung on the teeth of rusting hooks and spilled out of stuffed wooden crates. Some coats were dull and haggard, while others had been ripped and mutilated. They looked nothing like the lustrous white fur around Finlay's shoulders, which gleamed even when streaked with dirt. They were pale shadows of what they were before, each of them a soul stolen.

"We better start searching," Lachlan said, eyes darting around the room. "There are a lot of pelts here, and we don't have much time."

Isla joined him in sifting through one of the crates, heaving out folds of fur in search of Eimhir's speckled fawn-coloured pelt. Each time she plunged her hands in, a sharpness pulled at her gut. It was impossible to ignore the brush of fur against her skin; it was like nothing she'd felt before. As firm as leather and rich as velvet, soft and brittle all at once. More than anything, it felt *wrong*. These pelts didn't belong to her. They'd been stripped from someone else, and that now she held the most precious part of them in her hands felt like a violation she could neither understand nor explain.

"So much waste," Eimhir murmured, her voice rasping. "So many souls that could have been passed on. But I fear the owners of these pelts have no blood left to spill. They are already gone, lost beyond our reach."

"It's not here." Finlay's voice cut through the silence, the edge of it rough and jagged. He whirled around. "It's not *here*."

Isla's stomach turned cold. "Quinn said the warden sold pelts for bounties. If he already had a buyer lined up…"

Finlay lunged for the nearest crate, toppling it over so the pelts tumbled out in a dust-covered heap. The wooden frame slammed against the floor with a crack, making Isla jump.

"Quiet!" Lachlan hissed. "You'll draw them down on us."

Finlay barked out a harsh vocalisation from the back of his throat and aimed a vicious kick at another crate. The frame buckled as the crate skittered across the floor, the rattle of wood and stone echoing around the dense walls.

From outside the storeroom came the groan of the heavy front doors and the hammering of footsteps against stone. "Too late," Isla said. "We're out of time."

Lachlan paled. "We subdue them, then get out. We are *not* killing members of the city guard over this. Galbraith, make sure you—"

The warning had barely left his lips. There was nothing Isla could have done—nothing *any* of them could have done—to stop what followed.

The first guard entered the room, cheeks ruddy. When he caught sight of Finlay, wrists free from his manacles and pelt draped over his shoulders, he reached for his musket.

He was too late.

Finlay moved in the time it took Isla to suck in a horrified breath. One moment he was in the middle of the storeroom, eyes wild and hair dishevelled. The next, he'd unfurled a vicious grin and leapt for the guard's throat.

No crack of powder escaped from the long barrel of the musket. There was only a wet squelching sound, then a gurgling, punctured gasp. The guard sank to the floor, his musket rolling from his limp hands as blood pooled around his lifeless body.

His throat was gone.

Isla's heart stuttered, each thump bruising her ribs. She couldn't tear her eyes away. The guard's exposed throat. Finlay's red-stained lips and dripping chin. The splatter of blood bright across his pelt.

Tides, what had she done by bringing him here?

"Fin..." Eimhir's voice sounded scraped to the bone, ready to break. "Do you have any idea what you—"

The second guard burst into the room, her fingers trembling around her musket. She didn't look down at the fallen guard, not even when her boot splashed in the seeping pool of his blood. Her attention was fixed on Finlay alone.

"Monster," she spat.

As Isla waited for the shot, her eyes found Eimhir on the other side of the room. Her gaze was torn with agony. She could see the resignation in every line of her brow. She could see her despair in the way her lips parted around the ghost of Finlay's name.

She was too far away.

It all happened at once. The crack rang in Isla's ears. The pistol leapt in her palm as the shot loosed, and the guard collapsed, the pellet lodged in the blooming red centre of her forehead.

Lachlan's eyes widened. "What did you *do?*"

Isla couldn't answer. Horror rose in her throat, putrid on her tongue. She tried to swallow, but instead it threatened to suffocate her. What *had* she done? How had her fingers twitched so quickly around the trigger?

She shoved her pistol into her belt, her hand burning like it had left a brand on her skin. Tides, she'd *killed* her. It wasn't like before. This wasn't about survival. This was a choice. A choice she'd made the moment she'd seen the pain and desperation on Eimhir's face. A choice to spare her friend—her enemy—from losing the only family she had left.

The ghost of Isla's own grief fell across her heart like a shadow. When she looked up, Eimhir was staring back at her. A sliver of understanding passed between them, acknowledging what she'd done, what she'd sacrificed for this.

She couldn't bring herself to look at Darce. Lachlan's dismay had been difficult enough to bear without imagining what she might find in the sergeant's gaze. The cold edge of disappointment would cut her as surely as a blade. Worse still would be if his eyes betrayed nothing, if he looked through her like he no longer recognised the person she was. Like she was a stranger.

Maybe she was. Maybe whatever it was she'd spent years searching for was that which she'd carried with her all along, buried somewhere deep beneath her skin until all the horror clawed through the surface.

The men are the monsters, and the monsters men, Eimhir had said.

Aye, Isla thought. *And the women too. Every tides-forsaken one of us.*

She barely registered Lachlan's low, urgent tones as he grabbed her arm and pulled her along beside him. The thump of their boots against the floor was muffled and distant, like she'd been dragged to the depths. It wasn't until they burst through the gaol doors and the bite of the night air met her cheeks that she snapped out of her stupor. Her aching chest pulled tight, squeezing her lungs. If she took another step, she'd retch.

The frantic slap of boots against cobbles forced her to lift her head. She only had a moment to glimpse Finlay retreating, his bloodied white pelt the last thing to disappear.

"I must go with him," Eimhir said. "Consider yourself free of our bargain. It went against everything I am to claim it in the first place. I should never have..." Her words faded into the wind, and she straightened her spine. "Do what you have to do, and I'll do the same."

Isla grabbed her. "Forget your tides-damned bargain. You no longer need to hold an axe to my throat to convince me to help you. I believe you about the gun-anam. I trust you. We can still help each other."

A strange expression flickered across Eimhir's face, something strained and yearning and full of regret. "I cannot abandon him now. But I'll return, if I can. That will have to be enough for now, caraid."

She pressed her lips against Isla's cheek, then turned to follow Finlay into the shadows of the city, leaving nothing behind but the icy touch of a half-whispered promise against her skin.

CHAPTER TWENTY

T he townhouse was still sleeping when the three of them slipped
through the front doors. The oil lamps burned low, and Isla heard
no tread of footsteps from the floors above or the cellar below. Neither
was there any sign of Quinn or his attendants. Not that she'd been
expecting a reception at this hour. Outside, the cloak of night clung fast;
not even a hint of grey morning light had crept between the buildings as
they'd skulked back through the northside streets.

She followed Lachlan across the marble-tiled floor to the kitchen, her
tongue pressed to the roof of her mouth. Part of her longed to break
the silence, but she dreaded too much what it might bring. Instead, she
watched as he filled a crystal pitcher with water and found a washcloth
to dab at the bloodied cut on the bridge of his nose where Finlay had
struck him.

He pulled the rag from his face and met her with an accusing glare.
"You promised me."

"I know."

"The only thing I asked was that we do this quietly. That we not
draw attention to ourselves by leaving a trail of bodies behind. What that
vicious bastard did..." He broke off, the traces of his voice thick with

revulsion.

Isla couldn't blame him. She couldn't unsee it. The slow grin unfurling across Finlay's face. The swiftness he'd leapt with. The parting of his jaws, the bursting of flesh beneath his teeth. It stained her mind with red. It clawed at her gut until her stomach churned. "I didn't want this either. I had no idea Finlay would—"

"That's the problem. I warned you about him, and you didn't listen. I told you he would get us all killed, and that damn near happened. And you..." Lachlan's mouth tightened with disgust. "After what he did, you still saved him. By killing a guard in cold blood."

"I had to do something. Her musket would have been aimed at us next."

"That wasn't why you did it. It was for Eimhir. It seems everything you do now is for Eimhir." He threw the washcloth onto the table with a slap and spun away, knuckles white. "I've been trying to make things right for us, for our family. I thought that's what you wanted too." He turned back, eyes overcast. "When did that change? When did it stop being about us and start being about her?"

"That's not—" Isla swallowed the rest of her words. Denying it would only make things worse. She could hear the hurt in her brother's voice, the bitterness lacing every accusation. The worst part was, he was right. Something *had* changed. It had been easier when Eimhir was nothing more than a means to an end, when all that connected them was the bargain she'd made. Now, it was more than that.

A friend was not what I was expecting today, Eimhir had said.

Neither was Isla. Yet impossibly, it was what she had found.

"I had to save him," she whispered. "I would have wanted her to do the same for you."

"Oh, Isla." A choking laugh tore from Lachlan's throat. "Do you honestly think she would?"

A heavy silence stretched out between them, laden with grief and guilt. Lachlan let out a sigh and pressed his hands against the table. "I suppose it doesn't matter now. They're gone, and good riddance. We need to forget about them and focus our efforts on petitioning the Grand Admiral for aid."

For the first time since they'd returned to the townhouse, Darce piped up. "And how is that going for you so far? It seems to me your friend Nathair Quinn has done little of what he promised in that regard."

Lachlan looked as surprised as Isla at the bite behind Darce's question. "He's trying," he said tersely. "Quinn has connections but he's not part of the Admiralty, and there's only so far coin can carry a reputation. He means to use our family's standing for leverage, but we're not the only nobles who have arrived in Arburgh from villages up and down the coast, bringing with them tales of death and misfortune at the hands of the selkies. The Grand Admiral has been hearing petitions for months."

Isla's throat tightened. "Yet still he does nothing. All he cares about protecting are his precious trade routes between the capital and the continent. The same trade routes driving the selkies to our shores."

"You're starting to sound like Eimhir."

"And what if I am?" Isla folded her arms. "It doesn't make what I'm saying any less true. Arburgh has never known wealth like it does today. Why would the Grand Admiral spare any of his ships for the sake of a few coastal villages?"

"Quinn can be persuasive. As can I, for that matter. We just need more time." Something in Lachlan's expression softened as he met her eyes, leaving behind only traces of weariness and desperation. "I know the waiting is difficult, but this is our best chance."

"Waiting is the one thing I cannot do," Isla said. "Unless Eimhir's pelt is returned to her, she'll die. I won't let that happen."

"It was not you who took her pelt," Lachlan retorted, heat in his voice. "You are not responsible for her. The only thing you are responsible for is ensuring our home—the home our parents' bodies *still lie in*—does not fall into ruin. That should be your priority, not some selkie who threatened her way into our lives. If it isn't, perhaps you were right to leave all those years ago."

The blunt edge of his words rocked Isla back on her feet. She couldn't argue. Couldn't blame him, no matter how much she wanted to. She'd made him a promise. A promise she was willing to risk breaking, all for the life of a selkie who should have been nothing but an enemy to her.

"I won't abandon Eimhir," she said firmly. "Not any more than I could abandon you. There's still a chance to save her. If we can't find the buyer from the gaol, her only hope is the sealskin that belonged to her aunt—the one the Grand Admiral stole. Either way, I intend to help her."

She waited for his cheeks to pale with rage, for the anger and hurt to flash in his eyes. She braced herself for the acid in his voice and prepared to suffer whatever pain he lashed out with. But Lachlan just pinched the bridge of his nose, his shoulders rising and falling with each heaving breath.

"If you persist in this, I will stop you," he said quietly. "Even if that means giving up Eimhir to the Admiralty. I'm not prepared to lose the last person in my life who I can call family, not for the sake of a selkie. If you cannot forgive me for that, I hope you can at least understand it."

Before Isla could say anything else, he was gone, footsteps fading on the marble tiles until all that remained was the ringing of his words in her ears. Part of her wanted to shout after him, but it was too late, and the words would have been too filled with pain. Instead, she stared at the floor, fighting to keep her tears from spilling. It was too much, this aching in her chest. Like a hook beneath her sternum, tugging her in every direction. The more she fought, the more it would tear her apart.

"Isla."

She couldn't bring herself to meet Darce's eyes. His presence filled the room now they were alone, suffocating her with all the things between them that remained unsaid.

"Please, look at me."

She lifted her head. There was no sharpness in his gaze, no steely edge of disapproval. Some of the fear melted, loosening the tightness around her lungs. But the look he gave her was dark and troubled.

"You're asking a lot of him." He spoke firmly, each word ringing with a warning. "It worries me what might happen if you push him too far."

"It worries me too." She wrung her hands together, trying to wipe away the black powder and flecks of blood clinging to her fingertips. "All I wanted was to make things right between us. I didn't intend for any of this to happen."

"Then *stop*. Eimhir released you from the debt you owe her. This is your chance to walk away from this, walk away from *them*."

"How can you ask me to do that?" Isla pressed her hands against the table, trembling. "I saw your face in the square at Gallowgate. You felt their suffering. That's what will happen to Eimhir if we don't get her pelt back. She'll become one of the gun-anam. Is that what you want? To be responsible for another one of those wraiths?"

Darce blanched. "Of course not. If the Admiralty and its sentinels really are the cause of those wretched creatures, tides take every one of them. But you don't know that for certain. You don't know anything about what this pelt can truly do, apart from save Eimhir's life."

"Is that not enough?"

"Not for me. Not if it puts your life at risk." Darce looked away. "I understand why you want to help Eimhir. She's lost part of herself, the piece that will make her whole again. Maybe you think if you help her, there's a chance you'll find whatever it is you're missing."

Isla flushed. "It's not about that."

"It is. It always has been. First with Lachlan, now with Eimhir." Darce's face twisted, his expression pained. "I just hope when you find whatever it is you're looking for, you'll not be disappointed. I know too well what it means to discover a destiny you never asked for with a price you never wanted to pay. You deserve more than that, wolf cub."

She hadn't realised how close he'd drawn until he brushed his hand against hers. The touch was so light she might have thought it accidental, but then his fingers wrapped around hers, slow and hesitant. The beat of his blood against her palm stirred something in her chest, thrumming against her heart.

"Do I?" she whispered.

Darce edged towards her, close enough that she could see the worry in every crease of his brow. His fingers tightened around hers. He lifted his chin, fixing her with a dark-eyed gaze.

"Aye," he said softly. "And if I knew a way to give it to you, I would."

The squeeze he gave her hand was too relenting, too resigned. All Isla wanted to do was clutch onto his retreating fingers as they slipped from her grasp, leaving her palms warm with the lingering memory of his touch. A tingling heat spread through her, rising into her cheeks.

She opened her mouth, but her tongue turned dry around the words. *You can*, she wanted to say.

Instead, she stared after him as he headed for the door. Her ribs constricted painfully around her heart, bruising it with each beat. She couldn't say it. Darce didn't have the option of walking away. He'd pledged his life to hers and Lachlan's for the sake of the promise he'd made to their dying father. She couldn't ask him for anything more, especially when the call of the sentinel's blood oath would one day be too much for him to ignore.

He'd never truly be hers. He'd always belong to somebody else.

Unless it was you, a voice in her head whispered. *Why couldn't it be you?*

She pushed the thought away, shame burning her insides. Darce had never wanted the magic running in his blood. If he spilled it for her, there would forever be part of him that resented her for it. Living with that would be harder than watching him bind himself to somebody else.

Who? the voice whispered again. *Somebody like Lachlan?*

A shudder ran through Isla's body. She hadn't considered that this rift she'd opened with her brother might leave the sergeant unmoored, drifting between them. Hadn't considered that one day, he might have to choose which one of them to chain himself to.

If that time ever came, Isla wasn't sure she wanted to know what decision he'd make.

Exhaustion held Isla in the depths of sleep for most of the following day. It wasn't until the late-afternoon glow from the sun slipped between the townhouses that she woke up, blinking at the light intruding through a crack in the embroidered curtains. She found her chemise wringing with cold sweat as she propped herself against the pillows. Sleep hadn't done anything to cure her fatigue. If anything, it had only made it worse.

She closed her eyes briefly, as if returning to the nightmare might be what she needed to chase away its lingering presence. Her dreams had been filled with mist and shadows, haunted by the gun-anam. She'd stood frozen as the creature from Blackwood Estate drew near on the watery ridge of its kelpie mount, holding her in place with its fathomless gaze behind its seal-skull mask. She imagined it reaching for her, turning the breath in her lungs to ice, drowning her with its touch.

Even now, awake once more, Isla couldn't shake the chill. The hairs on her arms stood on end as she shivered under the quilted blankets. It wasn't just Eimhir's life at stake—it was every villager up and down the length of Silveckan's coast. As long as the dreamwalker pelt remained in the Grand Admiral's clutches, the gun-anam would never be stopped. They'd come with their weapons of salt and spray, leaving behind bloated bodies with lungs filled with seawater and ice-encrusted flesh. They'd infect more and more selkies with the mist sickness, driving them to shore.

It would never end. Not unless she did something about it.

Isla threw off the bedsheets and pulled on fresh buckskin breeches and a linen shirt, her fingers fumbling with the buttons in her haste. If she found Lachlan, perhaps she could put right some of this tension between them. He was right—they'd both lost too much to lose each other too.

We're family, Isla. There's nothing they can do to get in the way of that, as long as we have each other's backs.

Lachlan believed that. She had to do the same.

She hurried down the marble staircase, ignoring the aching grumble in her stomach at the waft of braising venison drifting out from the kitchens. There would be time to satiate her hunger later. For now, all that mattered was finding Lachlan.

Down the corridor, Darce emerged through the mahogany doors of the drawing room, a grim expression on his features. When he saw Isla, his frown deepened. "Have you seen your brother?"

"I came to look for him. He's not here?"

"No, and he's not in his room either." Darce's face hardened. "The little laird always did find it amusing to sneak off, but after what happened last night, I can't believe he'd be so reckless. Where do you suppose—"

"Your uncle's, I believe." Quinn appeared on the marble stairs behind them. He took each step slowly, trailing a hand along the banister as he reached the bottom. "He left a short time ago."

Isla stilled. "He went to Tolbooth? At this hour? He'll lose the daylight before he makes it back."

"I have someone tailing him, naturally. He's in no danger, I assure you."

"Forgive me if I don't take your word for it." Isla nodded to Darce, who gave an assenting grunt in return and headed towards the front doors, stopping only to retrieve his claymore from where it stood propped against the panelled wall.

She turned back to Quinn. "Why did my brother go to see Muir?"

"He was looking for you." He cast her an amused glance. "I might have given him the impression you'd gone to visit your uncle."

Isla's stomach turned cold. "Why would you—"

"I wanted the chance to speak to you alone." Quinn motioned to the drawing room, and Isla had no choice but to follow as he pushed through the doors. He gestured for her to sit while he went to the large wooden cabinet in the corner of the room and returned with a bottle of wine.

When he'd finished pouring the two long-stemmed glasses, she folded her arms. "You first."

Quinn drew a long gulp. "You don't think much of me at all, do you?"

"Can you blame me?" Isla brought her glass to her lips. The flavours were too tart from the confines of the bottle. It left her with a sour taste on her tongue instead of the sweet relief she'd been craving. With Quinn for company, perhaps that was more appropriate. "What did you intend by sending Lachlan to my uncle's tonight?"

Quinn waved a dismissive hand. "Lachlan's excursion southside is nothing more than a harmless deception, though a necessary one. You and I have matters to discuss. And since you insist on speaking plainly, allow me to do the same." His leaned forward, flashing his teeth. "I want you to leave Arburgh."

The mask had come off. The sight of it slipping made Isla wonder how she'd never seen beneath it before. Gone was Quinn's amiable smile. The amusement in his eyes turned into something sharp, promising an edge Isla knew well to avoid. This was the man who lurked underneath. The man she never saw coming before he plunged the blade into her back.

Isla sipped her wine. "That's not what you're really asking, is it? You're asking me to leave Lachlan."

"Is that such a surprise?" Quinn narrowed his eyes. "You drag your brother down like an anchor. You're willing to risk his reputation—not to mention his *life*—for a skinchanger you barely know. He follows you without question, yet you offer him no loyalty. You never have."

"Do not speak to me of loyalty. It is a concept with which you are entirely unfamiliar."

Quinn knitted his fingers together. "Despite what you may believe me capable of, I'd never do anything to hurt Lachlan. Your brother and I are friends."

"We were friends, once." Isla couldn't help the anger creeping through her chest. "That friendship was wasted on you."

"That's not true. I treasured it, while it lasted. Valued it in the only way I knew how."

"Valued what I could do for you, you mean. Valued using me for your own ends. You cared for me less than your own ambitions. I didn't realise that until it was too late." Isla tightened her fingers around the stem of her wine glass. "I won't let you do the same to him as you did to me."

"Whatever mistakes I made in the past, I learned from them." Quinn steepled his fingers. "I'm trying to *help* him. I am from merchant stock, and there is only so far someone like me can rise in the capital. Lachlan is a noble. He could do great things for Arburgh if he only knew what he was capable of. But as long as you remain by his side, he'll only ever see himself in your shadow. He deserves more than that. More than you."

A heavy weight settled around Isla's heart. Perhaps Quinn was right. She hadn't thought of her brother when she'd sailed from that jetty seven years ago. All she'd thought about was the belonging she'd always been searching for, always craved. Never realising Lachlan had been looking for the same thing. Never realising she took it with her when she left. Never realising it had pushed him into the clutches of someone like Nathair Quinn.

"I heard about your friend's lost pelt." Quinn's voice was velvet-soft, full of folds and ripples as he spoke. "You know I own half the merchant fleet. Not much moves in this city without me knowing. If I were to track it down and return it to her..."

Silence hung between them, disturbed only by a far-off rumble in the distance. Isla gritted her teeth. Another promise. Another bargain. Another debt to be made and repaid. "You'd ask me to abandon my brother to save Eimhir?"

"Is it really so difficult a choice?" Quinn curved his lips into a pitying smile. "You left him once before. It shouldn't be too difficult for you to do so again."

Isla tried to brush his words aside but they burrowed under her skin, cutting all the deeper for how true they were. "And if I went back on my word? If I stayed with Lachlan anyway?"

"You don't need me to answer that." A silken laugh spilled from his throat. "You never did."

It was as close to a threat as Quinn would ever admit to, and that alone was enough to send a tremble of fear down Isla's spine. He'd never needed to brandish a blade to make a point. He was more subtle than that, more dangerous than that. All this time, she thought she'd managed to stay out of his reach. Now, she knew the truth: Quinn had ensnared her the moment he'd ensnared her brother. There was no escaping him now.

Outside, the thunder rumbled again, rattling the glass in the windows. The storm was getting closer. Isla heard the pattering of rain—haphazard at first, then lashing down with more wrath each passing second. It battered against the windows, joined in a chorus by the howl of the wind.

"That came on quick," Quinn remarked. "I suppose it's about the right time for our first autumn storm of the year."

Isla pushed her chair back and moved to the window. Another deep, monstrous growl rippled through the sky, something in it stirring a memory in her, a prickle of unease. The last traces of daylight had been swallowed by storm clouds, plunging the rows of townhouse roofs into shadow. But it was more than darkness; small fractals of frost began to crawl across the windows, and the flicker of the streetlamps outside disappeared behind a curtain of mist and drizzle.

This was no autumn storm, Isla realised. The selkies were coming for them.

CHAPTER
TWENTY-ONE

B y the time Isla grabbed her woollen cloak and dashed out into the storm, the cobbles were already slick underfoot. Rivers of rain washed down the northside streets, streaming over the uneven stones and splashing her boots as she ran.

The Admiralty Bridge was ahead, its stone arches spanning more than a mile across the churning river. She could barely make out the far side; the fog crept in, shrouding everything. From here, it seemed like the bridge simply disappeared into the mist.

Isla leapt up the steps two at a time. The bridge was still and eerily quiet as she ducked under its vaulted wooden roof. Even in this weather, there should have been people crossing, trying to find shelter. But the only other soul she could see was a lone sentry, not dressed in the silver steel of the city guard, but the leather armour and jewel-toned cape of the Admiralty.

He raised his musket. "Bridge is closed. Grand Admiral's orders."

Isla fought to keep her hand whipping towards her pistol, tucked under the sodden folds of her cloak. This was an Admiralty officer. If her powder had got damp, her pistol would misfire, and she'd be dead.

Not to mention the fact he's only doing his job. Lachlan's voice echoed around her head, snide and cutting. *Or is shooting people without justification what you do these days?*

Isla shook her head, sending rainwater flying from her soaking hair. "Closed? Arburgh's seen worse squalls than this."

"The Grand Admiral makes the decisions, not me. He's imposing a city-wide curfew, so you best get back to where you came from and buckle down for the night."

"But I need to—"

Boom.

The capital bell. Strange how easily Isla could recognise something she'd never heard before. Its solemn toll vibrated through her, making her shudder with the warning it carried across the city.

Boom.

The resounding brassy knell was soft and loud all at once. *Return to your homes*, it intoned. *Take shelter. Weather the storm.*

Isla hurried down the steps. If the bridge was closed, Lachlan and Darce were trapped. The southside was on lower ground, bisected with branches from the river and its network of canals. If the selkies were to strike tonight, that was where they'd hit first.

She had to find another way across.

Most of the boats tied up at the northside marina were already secured by knots of rope by the time Isla reached the bottom of the city steps. She rested her hands on her knees as she caught her breath, flicking her eyes over the bobbing shapes. Further down the jetty, a man was loosing a rope from one of the wooden posts. He was a fisher, his leathery skin weather-bruised and brown from the sun.

As Isla approached, his expression soured. "What are you doing out here? Didn't you hear the bell? You should be getting home, as I am."

"You're headed southside? I need to cross the river."

The fisher's eyes trailed suspiciously over the expensive cut of her cloak. "What business has some noble like you got over in the southside?"

"Family." Her throat constricted around the word. "Please. I need to find them."

The fisher sighed and gestured towards the boat. Isla clambered in and braced herself near the bow. The wind and rain still raged as the fisher pushed off from the jetty, sending the boat across the roiling water towards the merchant docks.

Away from the shore, the bite of the wind grew ever fiercer. Isla pulled her cloak higher, sheltering her face from the nip against her skin. The fisher's grey hair whipped in every direction as he wrestled with the oars to keep them on course.

"The worst of it hasn't hit yet," he called out over the howl. "When we reach the docks, you should find shelter. If your family has any sense, they'll have done the same."

Isla peered into the darkness, the spray stinging her eyes. Across the gaping mouth of the firth, the mist continued to roll in, thick with salt and drizzle. All she could make out on the far side of the river were the faint outlines of the ships moored in the merchant docks, their creaking masts jutting above the frothing water.

The storm was already here. How long until the selkies followed?

A knock on the underside of the boat jolted her from her seat, and she flung out a hand to steady herself. "Did you feel that?"

The fisher grappled with the oars as the boat bucked again. "Probably a piece of driftwood. You get all kinds of things floating in from the sea."

Isla craned her neck over the edge, trying to spot what they'd hit. Beneath the waves and the wake of the boat, there were only shadows. "Can we go any faster?"

The fisher barked out a laugh. "Only as fast as my arms can take us. Don't worry, lass. This isn't the first time I've made the crossing in a storm."

A low rumble rolled through the air. Then came a flash of lightning, rupturing the sky from the storm clouds to the raging waters below.

The fisher heaved at the oars, but the wind was whipping up fiercer by the minute, howling around their ears. Isla fought to quell her rising panic. The merchant docks were almost within reach. If they got off the water, they might have a chance.

Isla's hands shook as she gripped the edge of the boat. The river was so dark she could barely see her own reflection. She leaned over as far as she dared until another flash lit up the depths long enough for her to see a shape shoot past.

"Give me an oar," she said, climbing alongside the fisher.

"You don't have to—"

"Give me a bloody oar!"

She wrestled it from him, but no sooner did she have the handle between her fingers than it slipped from her grasp, wrenched away by something that moved too quickly to see. She snatched at the air but could only watch as the oar disappeared below the waves.

The fisher shot her an accusing glare. "Now look what you've done."

"I didn't drop it. Something took it." She fought to steady her frantic breathing. "Tides, we're too late. They're here. The selkies are here."

The fisher scoffed. "Everyone knows the skinchangers keep to the open waters. Storm or no, they wouldn't dare breach the harbour, not with so many Admiralty ships protecting it."

Isla didn't reply. It didn't matter what the fisher thought. She'd seen it before. The storm, the mists...

The blood, she reminded herself. *The bodies.*

Something barged into the boat again, tilting it sideways. Isla braced herself as she tipped towards the wall of black water. She shot out a hand and grabbed the fisher, hauling him back in time to stop him falling. For a moment, they hung there, as though time had frozen still. Then the boat crashed down on the waves, settling upon the swell.

The fisher gripped the bench, skin paling. "It can't be. Not here in the capital. The Grand Admiral would—"

This time, there was nothing Isla could do. The boat rose, sending her into the air. Then she was falling, falling until she hit the water.

The cold was immediate and unforgiving. It squeezed the breath from her lungs and sent icy pain through her limbs. She thrashed below the waves, gulping in salt water as she struggled against the pull of the depths. Her woollen cloak became an anchor around her shoulders, dragging her deeper and deeper.

She fumbled with the ties with one hand, desperately fighting to swim with the other. Then she was free, the cloak falling from her as she squirmed out of its drenched folds towards the far-off glimmer of the surface.

Her lungs burned as she burst through a break in the waves. She pushed her bedraggled hair from her face, gasping for air as she treaded water and darted her head around. Through stinging eyes, she saw the fisher grab hold of the overturned boat, fighting to keep his head above the waves. Isla began to swim towards him, but before she could reach the boat, the fisher disappeared with a scream swallowed by the waves.

"No!" Seawater filled Isla's throat, cutting short her cry. She spluttered it out, choking for breath as she searched the river for any sign of the fisher. The gloom shrouded the depths. Wherever the fisher was, he was out of her reach.

A wave crashed over Isla's head, pulling her under. She writhed and flailed until she fought to the surface, sucking in precious air.

The docks, she thought. *I have to make it to the docks.*

She stretched her arms through the water and swam towards the closest pier. Even the short distance seemed hopelessly out of reach as the waves rose and fell, dragging her with them. Still she swam, trying not to think of the panic on the fisher's face as he'd plunged beneath the waves.

The pier was agonisingly close now. Isla could see its green-stained posts, the barnacles encrusting its wooden struts. A few more strong strokes and she'd be able to haul herself up.

Something brushed against her leg, and she thrashed in panic. The frenzied movement set her plunging below the surface again, and she fought the urge to scream into the water as another shape rushed past.

She kicked out and caught something soft. Without hesitating, she kicked again, this time propelling herself towards the surface. She heaved one arm after another, not stopping until she pulled herself up over the wooden struts of the pier.

Her palms were bloodied from the razor-edges of the barnacles, her fingers stuck with splinters. But she'd made it. She was out of the water. She fell on her hands and knees, retching up wine and seawater. The clouds hung low, turning into fierce dark shapes every time the lightning flashed between them. Rain fell fierce and heavy against the pier's wooden planks. All she wanted to do was close her eyes and hope it washed her away.

No, she told herself. *Lachlan. Darce. I can't lose them too.*

Isla forced herself to her feet. Her boots squelched with every step and her drenched clothes clung cold and tight to her body. If the selkies didn't get her, the chill from the water might. She knew how quickly bloodlung could set in. She had to find shelter soon. But first, she had to find Lachlan and Darce. If anything happened to them...

"You there! What are you doing out here?"

A middle-aged sailor ran down one of the gangways, barely able to keep upright. He dumped the large crate he was carrying at her feet when he reached her.

"I'm looking for someone," Isla said, raising her voice over the wind.

"Well you won't find them out here. Everything is shut down, harbourmaster's orders. No ships are setting off, and all crews have been told to find shelter in the Merchant Quarter."

He hoisted the crate into his arms and set off again down the pier, gesturing for her to follow. Isla hesitated, then ran after him. If Lachlan and Darce had found the Admiralty Bridge closed off, maybe they'd returned to Muir. Tolbooth wasn't far from the docks. If she could get there, they could all sit tight until the storm passed.

Waves crashed against the hulls of the moored ships, bucking them up and down like restless beasts. The timber groaned and creaked like it was about to burst. It was like the firth had come to life, rising around the ships with its grey-green spine, a sleeping sea serpent roused.

Through the mist, the silhouette of the dock offices towered above them. They'd almost reached the end of the pier. Almost found themselves back on dry land.

Almost was not enough.

A dark brown shape leapt from the water, sliding across the slick wooden decking in front of them. The creature's slippery mottled coat glistened with water as it pressed itself up on its front fins, baring its yellow teeth.

Isla jumped back and held out a hand to stop the sailor. "That's no harbour seal." She shifted her balance and waited as the creature stared at them with beady eyes. It threw back its head and barked out an eerie wail that cut through the roar of the wind.

"Tides take you!" The sailor dropped the crate and charged, reaching for the sabre on his belt.

The selkie was too fast. Even as the sailor started to move, the creature's wet fur melted into bare skin and a human emerged, grizzled and muscular. The only trace of the animal was the mottled brown pelt around the man's shoulders, draping across his scarred chest to his bare feet.

The sailor cursed as a strong hand shot out and grabbed him by the throat. He tried to fight the selkie, but the creature shrugged off the glancing blows and dragged him to the edge of the pier.

Isla remembered Eimhir's grip around her neck, the taut muscles of her forearm twitching, stronger than any human's. She'd seen the swiftness Finlay could leap with, the raw power behind his jaws. Even in their human form, selkies carried a strength no human could match.

The helpless sailor clawed at the hand around his throat. Then the selkie dropped him into the churning water below.

There was nothing Isla could do but watch. Even as the sailor resurfaced, thrashing wildly, another selkie rose from the waves. It clamped its jaws around the man's neck and hauled him towards the depths. There was a cry and a splutter, then the sailor was gone, leaving no trace behind but the tinge of red amongst the seafoam.

The first selkie turned to Isla with flinty eyes and a seaswept mane of hair. His brown pelt hung across his bare chest, his skin marble white and marred with old scars.

Isla stiffened. Her pistol was no use. Her fall into the river would have soaked the black powder through. All she had was the cutlass she'd taken from Quinn's armoury.

Darce's jibe from the training grounds resurfaced in her mind. *It seems all those years at sea have amounted to little more than a sloppy sword arm.*

He was right. It hadn't been a lesson that day back in the courtyard; it was a humiliation. He'd cracked open her knuckles with a whalebone training blade and pushed her until she'd retched because he knew she was in no shape to fight. Because he knew if she ever faced something like this, she stood no chance of escaping with her life.

That had been a warning. This was survival.

Isla drew her cutlass. The sword felt heavy in her hand, nothing like the easy grip of her palm around her pistol. To hurt the selkie, she'd have to get close. She'd have to pit the edge of her blade against his strength. Even that might not be enough.

The selkie stalked forward. He had no weapon. He didn't need one. Isla knew that only too well.

She scrambled back, slashing as she moved. The blade swished harmlessly through the air, nowhere near enough to the selkie's chest to threaten blood. It didn't matter. As long as she kept some space between them, she was alive.

The selkie closed the distance with another prowling step. This time, when Isla edged back, she felt the terror of empty air below her heel. She was at the end of the pier. There was nowhere else to go.

The waves leapt angrily, throwing themselves against the wooden struts of the pier, showering her with spray. She couldn't see what lurked beneath, but she imagined it all the same. Jaws around her ankle, dragging her to the depths. Her lungs filling with salt water. Darkness taking her, drowning the pain.

Above the waves or below, death beckoned. At least here, she could make this bastard bleed for it.

The selkie flicked his tongue as he advanced. Only the length of her cutlass separated them, and that wouldn't be enough to keep him at bay long, unless...

A shrill cry cut through the air and the selkie looked up, confusion falling across his features. Isla leapt forward and slashed. Her strike was wild and uncontrolled, but it opened up a deep red gash across the selkie's chest, splattering his brown pelt with blood.

She whirled away, slipping past him to get clear of the edge. It was then she saw what had distracted him: a huge bird, black as the swirling storm clouds and twice as dangerous. It gusted over them in a fury of wings, flashing the brilliant white of its belly as it circled and landed beside her.

When Isla caught its eye, it clacked its beak and let out a familiar trill from the depths of its gullet.

Shearwing.

"Looks like you could use some help."

Isla spun to find Nishi behind her, hair coiled and wringing under her tricorne hat. The gold ring in her lip glinted as she smiled and pulled her needle-bladed rapier from her belt. Beside her stood the pale, flax-en-haired figure of Kerr, his expression as amiable as ever as he twisted his fingers into a protective ward.

The selkie backed away, sliding his bare feet across the wooden slats of the pier until he reached the edge and threw himself into the furious waves. By the time he hit the water, his pelt had melted across his skin again, transforming him into his long, lithe sea-shape. Then he was gone, disappearing below without a trace.

Nishi stared after him. "He won't be the last."

"What are you doing here?" Isla asked, glancing between them. "I thought you'd have been long gone by now."

"Believe me, I wish we were. Our mainmast was damaged in the storm during the crossing from Kinraith, and Sea Kith ships aren't a priority in the capital when it comes to repairs. We've been stuck here far longer than any of us would like." Nishi's copper-toned eyes gleamed. "Though I suppose it's lucky for you, at least."

Isla shivered. Her breeches were sodden and wrinkled, her linen shirt plastered against her skin. "Thank you. I should have known the Sea Kith would never leave their ship to take shelter inland, Dock Admiral's orders or not."

Nishi scoffed. "We have no need of shelter. If the selkies think they can fight us on the decks of the *Jade Dawn*, they are welcome to try. There's more protecting that ship than a timber hide and stores of powder."

Shearwing let out an assenting screech, ruffling its wings as it shifted its weight on huge, splayed feet. Kerr scratched the bird under its beak before turning to Isla, his gaze every bit as shrewd as the razorbill's. "The real question is what are you doing out here? The docks are no place for you tonight, especially without your sentinel."

"He's not *my*—" Isla curled her hands into fists. She could barely feel her fingertips. Her toes were numb inside the soaking soles of her boots. Every breath tore from her lungs thin and shallow, like there was little left to give. "Lachlan and Dar—I mean, Sergeant Galbraith, were out when the storm hit. I came to find them."

"You braved the river in this weather? Many Sea Kith would have thought twice before doing such a thing." Kerr's voice softened as he turned to Nishi. "We should help find them."

"They're not our problem." Nishi glanced at Isla, her expression hard but not unkind. "I'm sorry, but your brother and lost sentinel are not my kith. I can't risk the lives of my crew for the sake of two strangers."

"That's not your choice to make. It's mine." Kerr put a steady hand on Nishi's forearm, pulling her around to face him. His white hair clung to his cheeks as he fixed his captain with a pointed look. "There are too few of us sentinels left. Even fewer who haven't pledged their services to the

Admiralty. The sergeant may not be Sea Kith, but he knows the call of the auld blood, even if he doesn't understand it yet. As the waters grow ever smaller, that is too precious a gift to abandon. You *know* this."

Each second stretched longer than the last as Nishi stared him down. Whatever passed between them needed no words, no movement.

Nishi's brow furrowed in a pained expression. "I know only that I cannot deny you. Even when I wish I could. Even when fear turns my blood to ice at what might happen if I do not." She let out a long sigh. "Fine, go with her. I'll return to the *Jade Dawn* and gather the rest of the crew. Shearwing will lead us to you."

"Captain..." The word caught in Isla's throat. "You don't have to—"

"I do." Nishi turned to Isla, a tight smile curving her lips. "I think you understand that, perhaps more than you want to admit. Darce Galbraith may not be your sentinel, but he has a hold over you all the same. Why else would you risk so much to find him?"

Isla flushed. "It's not just him. Lachlan is out here as well."

"Aye, but your bonnie cheeks don't turn red every time I mention your brother, tides be grateful." Nishi chuckled. "Blood oath or no, you're willing to risk your life for him, and that is a powerful thing. A dangerous thing."

"Dangerous?" Isla frowned. "In what way?"

"Sentinel, selkie, human... When it comes down to it, we've all got one thing in common." Nishi sheathed her rapier and straightened her tricorne hat. "Once you give someone part of your soul, it's not so easy to get it back."

CHAPTER
TWENTY-TWO

N o screams yet sounded over the roaring wind as Isla led Kerr from the docks towards Tolbooth's criss-cross canals. Drizzle and fog cast the narrow walkways in a pale shroud, snuffing out the light from the oil lamps and clinging to the murky green surface of the canals. The rain petered out, leaving behind an eerie silence. It was like the entire district had been abandoned, like they were walking through a graveyard filled with ghosts. The only sound came from the gentle slapping of the water snaking along beside them.

Then a shrill yell cut through the air, turning Isla's blood to ice.

She started forward, hand on the hilt of her cutlass, but Kerr pulled her back. "The rain has stopped. Any reason you're not using that instead?" He gestured to the pistol on her belt.

"The powder got soaked when I fell in the river. It's useless now."

"I can fix that." A slow grin unfurled across his face as she handed him the pistol. He curled his fingers into changing shapes, drawing a steady trickle of seawater from the barrel like he'd pulled the water from the deckhand's lungs on the *Jade Dawn*. The droplets shimmered and fell to the cobbles like rain.

"There you go." Kerr handed her the pistol.

She wrapped her hand around the stock, unsettled by how comforting it felt in her grip. She'd killed twice with this gun. Not serpents or sirens or even selkies, but humans, like her.

The men are the monsters, and the monsters men, Eimhir had said.

Perhaps that was the worst part of all. Seeing herself in them only made it easier to pull the trigger.

Another cry came from the blanket of fog. Isla quickened her step, her boots sliding across the slimy surface of the cobbles. The canal water lay unnaturally still, as if it were lying in wait for her to slip and fall.

"Is there anything in there?" she asked.

"I don't know." Kerr pursed his lips. "The sea spirits have quietened against my call. They care little for squabbles of cut flesh and spilled blood, and I fear the further I tread from the *Jade Dawn*, the less inclined they are to listen."

"Can you still—" A metal clang tore through the mist, ringing in Isla's ears. They no longer needed the sea spirits to tell them what was coming. The selkies were here.

The steel bite of blade against blade echoed off the overhanging stone buildings. The fog was dense, but through it Isla could make out a trio of shadows dancing violently at the edge of the canal. One wielded a sword, another swung wildly with an axe. Then, through the haze, she caught a glimpse of a formidable blade held in a familiar two-handed grip.

"Darce!" His name tore from her lips before she could stop it. He spun around, eyes widening at the sight of her.

"Tides, Isla," he growled. "How could you be so bloody—"

It happened quicker than she could blink. One moment, Darce was staring at her, ashen-faced and mouth agape. Then he was reeling back, blood pouring from his arm from the unforgiving edge of an axe.

Isla froze. She hadn't seen the selkie move. It had been a distraction at the corner of her vision, lost amongst the mist. Now she saw the man in the midnight-black pelt, his hand around the hilt of the axe dripping with Darce's blood.

225

Isla didn't hesitate. Her thumb brushed the hammer, pulling it back with a click as she raised her arm and levelled it at the selkie. One shot. She had to make it count.

She squeezed the trigger. The flint sparked. When the smoke cleared, the selkie was on the cobbles, blood pooling from his neck.

Isla dropped her arm, smoke still wisping from the pistol's barrel. This time, no guilt churned her stomach. The only tightness in her chest was a grim knot of satisfaction at what she had done, at what she had *meant* to do.

"Galbraith!" Lachlan appeared beside her, his face pale and clothes stained red. When he saw Darce, he sheathed his sword and drew the blade of his sgian dubh from his boot, ripping a length of fabric from his cloak to bind around the sergeant's bloodied arm.

Isla moved closer. Fear thrummed in her at the pallor across Darce's skin, the sweat beading under his tousled hair. Darce grimaced as Lachlan pulled the blood-soaked cloth tight around his wound, then dropped his eyes to the gun, still lightly smoking in Isla's grip.

She met his gaze. "Told you I prefer pistols."

Darce gave a begrudging smile. "For once, I'm not complaining. I'm just glad your aim is better than your sword work." He winced as Lachlan finished the knot on the makeshift bandage. "Not that your brother's wound dressing is anything more to be impressed by."

"Next time I'll leave you to bleed to death, will I?" Lachlan turned to Isla, the corners of his mouth twitching. "I shouldn't be surprised you're here. It's just like you to come in and steal all the glory after Galbraith and I did all the hard work."

The glint in his eyes brought a hoarse laugh to her throat. "I wouldn't want to disappoint, wee brother." She pushed his hair from his face, the golden strands damp and bloody. Underneath was a nasty gash across his temple. "You're hurt."

"I'll live, though that's more than I can say for some of the other poor bastards out here tonight. They're everywhere. Leaping from the water, dragging people in. Tolbooth's streets are running with blood, and the canals are thirsty for it."

Isla's stomach lurched. "Muir?"

"We left him holed up in that midden of his, told him to bar the door after we'd left," Lachlan said. "It's the safest place for him. A decade ago, we might have been able to count on his help, but looking at him now... He's not who he used to be."

None of us are, Isla thought as she stowed the pistol in her belt, but she pressed her lips together and said nothing. Now was not the time for reopening old wounds, not when the selkies were so eager to inflict new ones.

She turned to Kerr. "What now?"

The sentinel lifted his gaze upward. Though the rain had stopped, the black storm clouds still hung across the sky, flickering with blanket-flashes of lightning in the distance. "We should return to the *Jade Dawn*," he said. "It's the safest place to shelter until this squall passes. On our deck, we have the advantage."

Isla braced for Lachlan's resistance, but for once, her brother didn't argue.

"After what I've seen tonight, I'll take my chances with the Sea Kith," he said. "The selkies are out for blood. Let's not make it any easier for them than we have to." He wiped the red trickle from his forehead. "To the docks, then?"

Isla nodded. "To the docks."

The rain-soaked streets echoed with screams as Lachlan led them through the narrow wynds. Every corner they skirted, every alley and floating canal mooring they passed, brought with it a new kind of horror. Pale bodies left on the stone steps leading down to the water, their skin waxy, lips blue and frothing. Blood coursing through the gaps in the cobbles, streaming from another back torn open and flayed. The selkies left behind a warning with every drowned soul, every mutilated corpse: *you are not safe from us.*

Overhead, Shearwing let out a throaty caw, the sound piercing through the mist. The cramped streets left the giant razorbill little room to spread its imposing wings; instead, it circled above them, heralding their approach to the docks.

"Nearly there," Lachlan said, breathing heavily. "Keep away from the water until we get to the ship. The selkies—"

He halted, the rest of his words lost to the wind. Isla stopped and placed her hand on his arm as she cast her eyes over the docks. Through the lingering drizzle, she could see the fighting. The selkies moved like the storm itself, a blur of iron and fur as they struck with thick-hafted axes. In amongst them was the jewel-toned regalia of the Admiralty, swirling in hues of sapphire and teal as musket-wielding soldiers fired off precious shots before trading their guns for blades.

"Over there." Kerr gestured further along the dock to where a band of Sea Kith were locked in a tussle with a particularly brutish pair of selkies. Captain Nishi was among them, moving like the water itself as she thrust with her rapier, fluid and nimble.

Isla slotted a lead ball into her pistol, praying the remaining powder was enough to fire another shot. She glanced at Darce. His face was drawn as he shifted his grip around the hilt of his claymore. "Leave the sword behind. You'll only risk aggravating that wound of yours if you try to swing it with an injured shoulder."

"I might be inclined to listen to your orders if you'd ever demonstrated yourself capable of heeding mine." Darce lifted the claymore into a defensive position. "Don't worry about me, wolf cub. It will take more than a lucky blow to finish me off."

"Must you always be so stubborn?"

"Fine words, coming from you." He smiled tightly. "Your father put this blade in my hands to keep his family safe. I won't abandon it. I won't abandon you."

Isla tried to ignore the tug of his words, the flutter that filled her chest at what they might mean. They were too close to a promise of all the things she wanted from him, all the things she'd never have.

Kerr was already moving, striding across the open docks with a straight spine and steady gait. When a selkie stormed towards him, dagger in hand, he didn't stop. He didn't need to. Before the selkie could raise her blade, a blur of black feathers plummeted from the sky, throwing itself upon her with a horrifying screech. The hooked claws on the end of the razorbill's great webbed feet raked across her back, taking bloody clumps of fur from her pelt.

The selkie spun around, an agonised snarl on her lips as she slashed with her dagger. Shearwing swatted off the lunge with a flick of its wing, then jabbed with its enormous beak. The white ribbon across the tip flashed as it caught the selkie's arm and yanked sharply.

The sound of splintering bone cracked through the air, followed by the selkie's agonised howl. Her dagger clattered to the ground at the razorbill's huge feet, and Shearwing bared the yellow gape of its beak with a cackle of menace.

"Leave her," Kerr said. "She'll carry that injury into her selkie form. Let the fathoms decide whether to claim her."

Shearwing stretched its massive wings and hauled itself skyward once more, circling as they scrambled through the fighting towards the *Jade Dawn*. For every metre they gained on the ship, they lost as much between each other. Lachlan was boxed in near one of the warehouses, fighting back-to-back with a young Admiralty officer against the group of selkies who'd surrounded them. Darce lagged behind, his face contorted as he swung in laboured strokes. Kerr was almost at the gangway where Nishi whirled and jabbed with her rapier in an elegant dance.

Not much further, Isla told herself. *Just a wee bit more and then—*

She stopped in her tracks as a gleaming white shape leapt from the waves onto the slick wooden slats of the pier. It slid towards her with beady eyes and a snarling muzzle, its yellow teeth clamped around the hilt of a serrated hunting dagger. It straightened, growing tall on a pair of lean-muscled legs. White fur shrank back and settled around pale shoulders. Black eyes filmed over and turned ice-blue, burning with a glare Isla recognised only too well.

"Finlay." Her mouth turned dry around his name. "This was you?"

"So quick to cast blame on others, aren't you? Never thinking you might be the one responsible." A dark chuckle escaped his lips. "This was *you*."

"Me? All I've done is try to help you."

"Liar," Finlay hissed. "I know you arranged for us to be followed that day at the sea caves. Eimhir was taken because of you. She's *dying* because of you."

The accusation stung her cheeks like a slap. "Where is she? Does she know you're here?"

"I'm not telling you anything." Finlay bared his teeth, shifting his feet forward one step at a time. "I came here so that she might taste vengeance before she surrenders herself to the sea. So the people of this accursed city might suffer the way she'll suffer before she dies." His eyes gleamed. "I didn't think I'd get the chance for some vengeance of my own."

"Vengeance? That's what you think Eimhir wants?" Isla choked out a hoarse laugh. "Tides, you're a fool. As am I, for saving your life."

"Hold on to that regret, human." Finlay leered. "I'm only getting started."

She knew how fast he was. By the time he moved, she'd already aimed her pistol and curled her finger around the trigger.

The gun sputtered in her hand. There was no spark of flint, no crack of the shot flying loose from the barrel. The black powder was spent, and she was without the weapon she'd always relied on.

Isla leapt back, drawing her cutlass from her belt as she cast a desperate glance across the docks. It was chaos. All she could see was a blur of bodies and the dull flash of steel as the fighting spread. Nishi and Kerr had retreated to the *Jade Dawn's* gangway, holding position against the encroaching selkies. Lachlan was still pinned down by the warehouses. Darce was lost in the middle of a scrum of bodies, selkie and Admiralty alike.

She was on her own.

Finlay lunged, dagger in hand. Isla parried with a desperate push, already staggered by the fury of his attack. Before she had time to gather herself, he was on her again, the blade aimed at her throat. She swiped wildly, hoping to knock it loose, but Finlay dropped the dagger to his other hand and brought it up in a swift, sweeping stroke.

Heat lashed across Isla's face and she stumbled back, her left eye stinging from the blood pouring into it. Her vision clouded, leaving Finlay to dissolve into a red blur in front of her. *Shit.* She pressed her fingers to her cheek, wincing as they came away wet and bloody. *Shit, shit.* She could barely see a thing.

The blow came out of nowhere, too fast for her to stop it. The curve of his bare heel connected with her chest, sending her sprawling across the pier onto the stone cobbles of the docks. Her cutlass flew from her hand as her spine bounced off the ground with a sickening crack. Her chest ached from the brutal impact of the kick. All she could see above was the black blanket of clouds, then Finlay's twisted smile as he knelt his weight across her.

"She'll die slowly. You know that, don't you?" Finlay pressed the dagger into the flesh below her eye. "Salt will build up across her skin, scarring her more painfully than any blade. Her body will crumble. Her organs will wither and die. Her dried flesh will peel from her bones. Do you want to know how that feels?"

He dug the blade deeper into her skin, and Isla screamed. Pain burned the left side of her cheek as something dripped down her face, a luke-warm mixture of blood and tears.

He was going to flay her.

"Eimhir never should have trusted you," he said. "If only she'd listened to me... I told her you were just like the rest of them."

Isla thrashed, but the pressure of his knees against her arms was too forceful. He drew back, smiling as a droplet of blood trembled at the tip of his blade, then fell.

"You should stay still for this," he crooned. "I want your bone-headed brother and lovesick sentinel to recognise what's left of you. Let them see how they failed, how they—"

The dagger tore from her skin as something barrelled into Finlay, knocking him across the cobbles with a hefty blow. Blood rushed back into Isla's arms, leaving them tingling as she propped herself up with one hand and wiped her eyes.

Her heart stopped. "Lachlan!"

Her brother pushed himself to his feet, his forearm grazed from where he'd tackled Finlay to the cobbles. His sword was missing, his shirt ripped and bloody, but that did little to temper the unbridled rage on his face.

He swept his blood-soaked hair from his forehead and rounded on Finlay. "Don't you *ever* lay a hand on my sister again."

Finlay staggered up from the ground, teeth stained red. He spat a glob of blood to the cobbles and turned to Lachlan with a grin.

Too late, Isla realised what was about to happen. Lachlan was too close to the pier, too close to the churning waves. Her warning scream died in her throat as Finlay lowered his head and charged.

She couldn't stop it. Even as she scrambled to her knees, Lachlan was already tumbling backwards, Finlay's arms wrapped around his waist. In the time it took for her cry to leave her throat, the two of them disappeared under the roiling waves.

Isla staggered to the edge of the pier. There was no sign of either of them. The waves leapt against the jetty, breaking against the wood and scattering spray into the wind. She couldn't see what was beneath. She could only imagine.

"Lachlan!" His name tore from her throat into the screaming wind.

"*Lachlan!*"

Only the crash of the waves answered. Then something rippled, and her brother's soaking crown of golden hair burst through the surface.

Isla jolted, heart in her mouth as he lurched through the water, pale lids closed and head hanging limply. His cheeks were pallid and lifeless, his lips blue, yet still he somehow returned towards her, carried by the waves or something below them.

Only when he reached the edge of the pier did Isla see the strong arm under his chin, the lithe shoulders fighting through the swell. The next wave subsided, and a pair of familiar storm-grey eyes stared out at her, holding her in their grasp.

Eimhir. Tides, it was Eimhir.

She was a strong swimmer, even in her human form. She battered through the final few metres and grabbed the wooden strut under the pier with one hand. With the other, she hauled Lachlan out of the water and dragged the two of them up and over the edge.

Isla dropped to her knees and rolled over Lachlan's cold, unmoving body. His skin was slimy and grey, so translucent she could see the purple webbing of veins under his eyes. She placed a hand over his chest, but her fingers were too numb to search for the beat of his heart under the soaking folds of his shirt.

"I can't tell if he's breathing," she said. "We need a sentinel. We need Kerr."

Eimhir crawled beside Lachlan, her icy skin pebbled all over as she shivered in the sodden rags she'd escaped the district gaol in. She leaned across, holding her ear above his mouth as her hair dripped seawater over his cheeks.

"He's breathing," Eimhir said. "It's faint, but it's there." She straightened her back, casting her eyes over him. "That's not what we need to be concerned about."

Isla stiffened. One of Lachlan's boots was missing, exposing his bare leg. Or at least, what was left of it.

She clamped a hand to her mouth, fighting the urge to retch. Beneath the end of his breeches, Lachlan's leg was a bloody, ragged mess. The skin was ripped to shreds, some gashes so deep they exposed the white of his shinbone. Muscle and tissue hung in frayed ribbons, dripping red. The parts of his leg that hadn't been eviscerated were marred with punctured bite wounds—bloody holes gaping across his pale flesh.

Isla brushed his forehead, wiping sweat and saltwater from his skin. "Finlay did this," she choked, the words furious in the back of her throat. "He did this to my brother."

"He told me he was leaving, going back to the clans," Eimhir said. "I couldn't follow without my pelt, so I waited for him in the sea caves. I knew he would come back for me, but I never imagined it would be like this."

Before Isla could reply, a distant rumble tore through the air above. The storm had not yet passed. A far-off flash of lightning danced between the clouds, illuminating the fading mist.

Illuminating the shadows within it.

Isla stilled. The gun-anam. Tides, she should have known. Where violence spilled over, the soulless followed.

Fear rose in her throat as the wraithlike figures wavered in the mist across the harbour. Her eyes fell upon the spectre haunting her dreams, the gun-anam from Blackwood Estate. It stared at her from eyeless sockets behind its seal mask of blackened bone, whispering across the wind in its watery voice. A deathly touch of ice crept across her skin as it reared up on its mount, the kelpie's hooves making no sound atop the waves.

Eimhir followed her gaze. "They're not coming any closer. Something must be—"

Before she could finish, the mists broke apart, scattered by the prow of a ship so large it shrouded the length of the docks in the shadow of its hull.

Isla scrambled to her feet as the huge vessel crawled past. Its timber groaned as it pushed through the churning water, as slow and steady as

234

if the raging wind was little more than a light breeze. Towering masts pierced the remains of the mist like obsidian blades. Midnight-black sails rustled where they were stowed, as if yearning to billow free.

It wasn't until the ship passed that Isla caught the gold-plated carving along the side of its formidable hull.

Vanguard of the Firth. The Grand Admiral's warship.

She knew the stories. How the ship wasn't really black, just drenched in decades' worth of dried selkie blood. How the wolfen figurehead came to life on the water, scouring the deck for prey. How the Grand Admiral kept an entire regiment of captains ready on the bridge, each one of them with their own sentinel.

Isla snapped her gaze to the mouth of the harbour, heart hammering as she searched the mists. The lingering wisps clung to the tips of the waves, but no ghostly shadows stirred within. She saw no sign of the gun-anam in the seal-skull mask, no trace of the kelpie's watery hide. "Where did they go?"

"The mists are retreating," Eimhir said. "They won't linger without them."

Isla let out a shaking breath. "Then it's over."

"No." A harsh voice snarled behind her, and Isla spun around to find Finlay staring at her, his white pelt clinging to his wet shoulders.

"Fin, stop." Eimhir leapt to her feet and pushed between them, her face drawn and exhausted. "The clans are fleeing—you can see it as well as I can. Whatever you thought you were doing by coming here, you failed. You lost." She grabbed his shoulders, knuckles white. "Please, if you have any love for me, you'll leave while you still can."

He stared at her with shining eyes. "I'm doing this *for* you."

"You're going to get yourself killed. And I won't let you hurt—Fin, stop!"

Finlay wrenched Eimhir's hands from his shoulders, fingers wrapping around her wrists. Then he gave her a broken, cracked smile and shoved her to the ground.

Eimhir landed on the cobbles, the back of her head hitting them with a crack. Before Isla could call for her, Finlay turned his attention to her instead, his cold hands wrapping around her throat.

He pushed her to the ground slowly, thumbs pressing against her neck. All the air left Isla's lungs in a feeble gasp. She spluttered as she tried to suck in another precious breath, but the squeeze around her windpipe was too tight. Already her vision was turning blurry. Her head lolled across the stone as Finlay laid her down, using his weight to crush her throat.

"Drowning is too good for you," he spat. "This will have to be enough."

Isla blinked, trying to peer past the haze clouding her vision. Eimhir lay on the ground, arms weak as she fought to push herself to her knees. Somewhere in the distance, Darce was struggling to fight through a group of selkies. She imagined the roar from his throat, his mouth forming the shape of her name. All of it was fading before her eyes.

Out of the corner of her vision, she saw her brother. Lachlan lay metres away, his face contorted. He writhed against the ground, reaching for the bloodied ruin of his leg.

Rest, wee brother, Isla thought, her head thick and distant. *It will be over soon.*

But it wasn't his injured leg he was stretching towards. His fingers found the heel of his other boot, closing around something Isla couldn't see. Then he straightened, his eyes meeting hers for only a second before he slid something across the cobbles towards her.

The clink of metal skittering against stone cut through Isla's heavy-headed stupor. She shot her hand out and closed her fingers around a slim hilt. Her thumb brushed over the intricate ornamental carvings and found the edge of the blade, no less sharp for how delicate it was.

Lachlan's sgian dubh.

Finlay's eyes filled with horror, but it was already too late. Isla swung her arm and sunk the blade into the crease of his neck.

The pressure lifted from her throat. Finlay drew back, clutching the gushing blood spilling around the blade. Gone was the hatred in his eyes. Now there was only fear. Panic. He looked nothing more than a lad who'd found himself face to face with something he couldn't take back.

His eyes widened, and Isla pulled the blade out.

It was over quickly. Even as his skin turned ashen, even as he fumbled desperately at the gash, Finlay was falling, sinking across the cobbles in a wilting heap. A frantic, wheezing breath escaped his throat, the sharp finality of it making Isla tremble. Then he stilled. Nothing moved save for the spreading bloom of red soaking deep into his glistening white pelt.

"Fin?" Eimhir crawled towards him. She bent her head and buried her hands in his pelt, staining her fingers red. "You didn't listen. Why don't you ever listen?" A choking sob tore from her throat as she shook his limp, lifeless body. "Fin, *please.*"

Isla slipped the sgian dubh into her belt and stumbled over to Lachlan. Death's shadow had already crept across him. His pallor was bone-pale, greying around his cheeks. A purplish hue darkened his fluttering eyelids, and a sheen of sweat had broken across his forehead.

"Hold on," she whispered, cradling his head. "We'll get through this."

She lifted her head at the sound of footsteps. Darce rushed towards her, followed by a young Admiralty officer.

Darce faltered, his gaze drifting between her bloodied face and Lachlan's limp body. When he spoke, each word came in a shattered breath. "I couldn't reach you. I couldn't reach either of you."

Lachlan let out a moan, pain stretching his voice thin.

Isla shuddered. "We need to get him to a doctor."

"We can bring him northside to the barracks." The young officer glanced between them, the boyish curls of his brown hair dripping onto his nose. "He saved my life over by the warehouses. If there's anything the Admiralty can do to save his..."

Isla felt a light brush on her arm and turned to see Eimhir, exhaustion and grief battling on her face. "You need to find somewhere closer. He won't make it back across the river."

Dread wound itself around Isla's heart, chilling the air in her lungs. "Muir," she said through trembling lips. "We'll take him to Tolbooth."

The Admiralty officer helped Darce heave up her brother's limp form, looping his arms around both their shoulders as they carried him slowly across the slick stone. Isla was about to follow them when she caught Eimhir in the corner of her eye, a bundle of red and white fur in her arms as she knelt by the edge of the pier.

Eimhir bowed her head, cheeks stained with tears. Her arms loosened as she allowed Finlay's pelt to slip from her grasp into the water. It floated for a moment, lingering beneath the surface like a ghostly white shadow. Then came the wet head of a seal to take it gently in its jaws and disappear below the surface.

"Until our souls meet again," Eimhir whispered, staring into the churning waves.

CHAPTER
TWENTY-THREE

The narrow, grimy walls of Muir's home had felt cramped the last time Isla visited; now, they were suffocating. Her uncle ushered them in with a half-glazed expression, sparing only a disgruntled glare for the young Admiralty officer and promptly barring the confines of the doorway.

"I've got no room for your sort, lad," he said gruffly. "Not anymore."

The officer didn't protest. Instead, he sent a troubled glance towards Lachlan and gave a nod, retreating into the shadows of Tolbooth with a whirl of his jewel-toned cape.

Muir ground his teeth, then slammed the door shut. A pallor fell across his dark brown skin as his eyes flicked to Lachlan moaning and writhing in the middle of the floor. "The lad needs a proper doctor. What tides-forsaken reason could you have for bringing him here? I thought you had friends in the upper city."

Isla watched as Eimhir knelt by Lachlan's side, inspecting the mangled ruins of his leg. "There wasn't time to go northside. This was the only place I could think—"

A groan escaped Lachlan's throat as Eimhir poured water over his leg. Some of the blood cleared, washing from his skin in puddles of red.

Isla stilled. The skin around the puncture wounds was mottled, turning Lachlan's leg a sickly purple-grey. The veins working their way up his leg swelled through his skin, almost black. "I don't understand. What's happening to him?"

Eimhir kept her gaze locked on Lachlan. "Sometimes we apply sting-fish poison to our teeth before raids. It doesn't affect selkies, but if it gets into a human's blood…" Her jaw twitched. "I'm sorry."

Isla's eyes darted to Muir, but her uncle said nothing. He looked from Eimhir back to Lachlan, a flicker of understanding crossing his face.

Isla let out a sharp breath. "I don't want your apology. I want you to save him."

"The poison is spreading too quickly," Eimhir said. "The only way to save him now is to stop it."

Silence settled over the room, punctuated by the gasping breaths from Lachlan's throat. Horror clutched at Isla's heart. Tides, Eimhir was talking about cutting off his *leg*. How could there be no other way? How could this be the choice she had to make?

"Isla, please." Lachlan cracked open his discoloured eyelids, his tawny eyes glistening. "Don't do this. I don't *want* this."

"I know." She dropped to her knees, brushing his hair from his face and taking his hand. He was already cold, his palm clammy against hers. She could feel the warmth bleeding out of him.

"Take me to Quinn instead," he said, his voice little more than a whisper. "Some of his merchant ships deal in medicines. He'll have some antidote, some remedy. You have to try."

Isla shot Eimhir a desperate glance, but Eimhir only shook her head, her lips pressed together in a grim line.

"It's too late for that, wee brother." Isla pressed a kiss against his temple. "I can't lose you. If this is the only way to save your life, we have to do it."

She lifted her chin, meeting Darce's eyes. A stricken look fell over his face, his cheeks grey. He clenched the hilt of his sword, fingers trembling, but made no move to lift it.

Isla turned to her uncle, a lump catching in her throat. "Muir?"

"I'm no surgeon. Best I can do is get him something to dull the pain."

"I'll do it." Eimhir straightened her spine. "I have known selkies whose flippers were maimed in hunts. When they shed their sealskin, their human limbs were often beyond saving."

Her words hung in the air, turning the room cold. Isla wanted to push them away, but they burrowed under her skin, bearing grief and guilt into her bones.

"Do it." The words left her mouth in a harsh bite, leaving the lingering bitterness of betrayal.

"No." Lachlan squirmed on the floor. "Isla, please…"

"Are you sure about this?" Darce said. "Do you trust her with your brother's life?"

There was nothing in the hollow of Eimhir's face but grief and exhaustion. Her brown-blonde hair was limp and tangled, blunting the edges of her jaw. Not so long ago, Isla had only been able to see her as one of the monsters she'd once feared. So much had changed.

"I trust her," she said, and with those words there was no turning back.

Muir moved away, returning with his cane and a tankard of swill from his barrel. "Here," he said, pressing the edge to Lachlan's mouth. "This first."

Lachlan gulped it down, the liquid spilling across his skin as he spluttered. "Couldn't you at least stretch to the good stuff, uncle?" he asked faintly, then froze as Muir brought the cane to his teeth. "No, you can't. I told you, I don't want—" He jerked his head towards her, eyes wide. "Isla *please*. Don't do this. Don't let them do this."

Isla choked out a sob, clutching a hand to her aching chest. Lachlan's grip tightened around the other, squeezing her fingers as Muir placed the wooden length of the cane between his teeth.

She couldn't watch as Darce fixed his belt around Lachlan's thigh as a makeshift tourniquet. She couldn't watch Eimhir dousing the head of her axe under a stream of sharp-smelling liquor from one of Muir's half-opened bottles. All she could do was clutch her brother's weak, feverish hand and hold it tight, both of them bracing for what was to come.

Darce held the tourniquet steady. Muir adjusted his hands around the cane. Eimhir wrapped the hilt of her axe in a white-knuckled grasp and lifted it to her shoulder.

Lachlan turned his eyes to her, the grime across his skin streaked with tears.

"I'm sorry," Isla whispered. She pressed her lips to his forehead and drew back.

The axe fell.

It was over in a crunch of iron and bone. A heartbeat of silence reverberated in its wake, seeming to Isla as though it might last for eternity.

Then came her brother's screams.

Muir wrestled with the cane as Lachlan's back arched, his chest swelling with a tortured howl. Each cry tore from his throat like it had been ripped out, raw and unbearable. Everything else became a muffled hum between Isla's ears. All she could hear was Lachlan and the sound of his pain. The echoes of what she had done.

She focused on her hand in his, ignoring the ache as her fingers crushed together. Isla knew how to bear his pain. She always would.

After a while, Lachlan's hand fell limp against hers and his cries subsided, giving way to slow, ragged breaths. She wiped the sweat beading his forehead. His lids lay heavy and still, and Isla felt a pang of twisted relief that this exhausted slumber had eased his suffering, if only for the moment.

She pushed herself to her feet, bile rising at the back of her throat at the blood soaking into Muir's floorboards. The tourniquet was fastened tight, and Darce had wrapped the bloody stump in rags, but the stain of red across everything was more than Isla could bear. It didn't matter that Finlay had been the one who'd poisoned him, that Eimhir had been the one to bring the axe down. Lachlan was *her* brother. She'd made this decision for him. His blood was on her hands.

She moved to the fireplace, laying her pistol and Lachlan's sgian dubh on the mantelpiece as she held her hands over the flames. Even with the fire, she couldn't shake the numbness bleeding into the tips of her fingers and ends of her toes.

Muir peered over, his eyes widening as they trailed over the sgian dubh. A flicker of dismay crossed his features, then disappeared, replaced by a frown deeper than before. "Where did you get that?"

"It's Lachlan's. Father gave it to him the year he turned twelve. A family heirloom, he said." Isla trembled. "That's twice it's saved my life now. Twice *he's* saved my life. And this is how I repay him."

"A family heirloom." Muir gave a low chuckle. "Aye, you have the right of it. But that sgian dubh wasn't Cormick's. It belonged to your mother."

By instinct, Isla's hand drifted towards her pocket, then stilled. Tides, *no*. The letter wasn't there. The tattered remnants had been in the pocket of her woollen cloak, the cloak she'd surrendered to the river. It was lost.

She was lost.

Grief squeezed her chest, but the pain was dull and distant. She would feel it later, of that she was certain, but there was no room for it in her heart now. Not when Lachlan lay weak and wounded on the floor, barely clinging to life.

Muir's mouth drew into a pensive line. "The sgian dubh was meant to protect you. I'd say it ended up in the right hands."

Isla glanced at him sharply. "What do you mean by that?"

Muir pinched his lips. "Never you mind. Best leave the past where it is, for there's no changing it."

"Whatever it is you think you're protecting me from, I don't care. I deserve to know. I *need* to—" The rest of her words collapsed into a deep hacking cough, sending pain through her sternum. She wiped her mouth and fought to catch her breath, each gasp a struggle.

Muir's brow furrowed. "You're bloody soaked. Go through to the bedroom and get out of those clothes. I'll not have your lungs wasting on my watch."

Isla hobbled away, another cough wracking her chest as she closed the door behind her and tore off her sodden layers. In the corner of the room, she found a pile of rags and a woollen blanket to wrap herself in. It had a stale, musty odour, but Isla bundled herself into the folds of it anyway, shivering against the chill that settled into her bones.

A knock at the door broke through the quiet.

"I'll be out shortly," she called. "I need a moment to—"

The rest of her words were lost to the creak of the door as it slowly opened. Darce slipped through the gap, his expression dark and worried.

"Forgive the intrusion," he said. "I wanted to speak to you away from the others. After what happened—"

"I'm fine." The words soured on her tongue. Hot tears pricked her eyes and she turned away, blinking furiously. "There's no need to concern yourself."

"Isla." Darce pulled her around. She saw his gaze trail over the left side of her face, felt him stiffen at the bloody gouge Finlay had left. "You should let me see to that. It doesn't take long for such wounds to turn foul."

"You think it's *my* wounds I'm worried about?" She choked out a laugh. "I took his *leg*, Darce. He begged me not to, and I took it anyway. Or rather, I let Eimhir take it, because I couldn't do it myself. Perhaps that makes it worse."

"You were trying to save his life. He'll under—"

"Don't. *Don't* tell me he'll understand." A sob wrenched from Isla's throat. "I let this happen. He tried to warn me, and I didn't listen. I... I didn't..."

Her voice constricted around the words as the tears came, blurring the room. There was nowhere left for her grief to go. It spilled out of her in violent bursts, each one more painful than the last.

She didn't know if she was the one who moved, or if it was Darce. All she knew was by the time the next cry wracked through her, his arms were around her. She buried her face into his chest, tears spilling against his leather armour. He smelled of sweat and blood and death, but all that mattered was the fierceness of his arms, the way they wrapped around her and held the pieces together.

"You had to make a decision." Darce's voice was soft at her ear, brushing against her skin as he spoke. "Sometimes that's harder than having no choice at all."

Isla tried to stifle the gulps and gasps straining at her throat. It would be so easy to accept this comfort, to lean further into Darce's arms and lose herself in the way they tightened around her back. She could press her cheek to his and close her eyes against the warmth of his skin and pretend he was right, that what she'd done was right, that she hadn't—

In her mind, the axe fell. Bone splintered. Lachlan screamed.

Isla wrenched away, her head reeling. "I'm sorry, I—"

Darce caught her, his hands firm but gentle around her wrists. His mouth was barely a breath away, offering a comfort more than words. All she had to do was take it.

He'll never truly be yours, the voice in her head reminded her. *He has the auld blood. Soon, he'll belong to somebody else.*

Anguish welled in Isla's chest and she pulled away, ignoring Darce calling after her. Her name rang in her ears as she stumbled through to the main room. Lachlan was still on the floor, whimpers pulling from his throat as he shivered under a blanket. Eimhir watched over him, expression unreadable. On the other side of the room, Muir sent her a knowing look.

"I need a drink," Isla muttered, grabbing an empty tankard from the mantelpiece and running it under Muir's barrel. The liquid frothed in the tin mug, the sight of it turning her head hazy before she'd brought the ale to her lips.

She pushed through the door leading to the tiny rooftop terrace overlooking the canals. The stairwell was thick with dust and cobwebs, the steps worn to splinters as she climbed. At the top, she pushed open the second door and stumbled onto the stone terrace, spilling ale over her hands as she sat on the rickety wooden bench.

The storm clouds had scattered, leaving a clear sky made bright by the fullness of the moon. Its glow danced off the still surface of the canals, fracturing the water with changing patterns. The only reminder of the violence that had fallen over Arburgh's streets was the bloodstains splattered across the cobbles.

The door creaked behind her and Muir hobbled over to the bench, leaning heavily on the cane that had moments ago been wedged between Lachlan's teeth.

He lowered himself beside her, clutching a tankard in one hand. In the other, he held his old Admiralty compass. The brass casing shone dully as he fumbled with it between his fingers, every movement tense and agitated. They sat wordlessly, sipping the frothy ale, pretending there was nothing to discuss. It was a comfort when Isla's head grew heavier and the world started swaying.

Eventually, the alcohol untangled her tongue enough to release the words she'd been too ashamed to give voice to. "I've got myself into a fine old mess, uncle."

Muir gulped down his ale. "Aye, I can see that. It's a story I know all too well. I hope you find your way out of it better than I did."

"I'm not sure I know how."

"Neither do I." He slipped the compass into his pocket. "All I know is you can't change any of it. You can't go back just because you don't like how it turned out."

Something churned in Isla's stomach. She wasn't sure if it was Muir's sorry excuse for ale or her own guilt eating at her insides. "I killed the selkie who did this to him. I sank Lachlan's sgian dubh into his neck and watched him die. And when I saw Lachlan's face tonight, when I saw the fear and panic in his eyes, I couldn't help but think of him. He was barely more than a lad."

"From what I heard, he left you no choice."

"Aye, and that's the worst of it. Despite everything, some part of me still wishes he had."

Muir tipped the dregs of ale from the bottom of his tankard. The liquid splattered on the ground in a tiny puddle at his feet. "The things we do don't matter as much as who we choose to be. There's a lesson to be learned in how a respected Admiralty captain ends up a drunkard squandering his life in the lower city." He shrugged. "You killed the lad. You saved your brother, and yourself. All those things can be true. It's up to you which one you let dictate what comes next."

Isla looked at him, tracing the weathered lines of his face with her eyes. There was still so much he was keeping from her—she saw it in the crease of his brow, the strain in his mouth. But tonight, she no longer cared. Tonight, all she saw was someone who understood.

"I've not met many respected Admiralty captains," she said. "But as far as lower city drunkards go, I wouldn't change you for anyone."

The corner of Muir's mouth twitched. "You're a piece of work."

"I only followed your example." Isla kissed him lightly on the forehead. "Goodnight, uncle."

She'd almost reached the narrow wooden stairwell when he called after her.

"Isla." Muir propped himself up on his cane, face grim. "I can't help but worry you're caught up in something much bigger than you're telling me. The lad you killed, this selkie lass you're somehow involved with—aye, I know what she is, so don't give me that look." He rolled his cane from one hand to the other. "Cat... My wee sister is gone. Cormick is gone. You and Lachlan are all I have left. Don't go getting yourself into trouble that will get you killed."

Isla nodded, unable to speak.

I'll do my best, she promised silently, hoping it would be enough.

Isla spent most of the following morning paying the price for the copious amount of ale she'd drunk. Even after kneeling over the side of the canal and retching into the water, the remnants of it still sloshed around her stomach, threatening to reappear.

Muir looked rather grey but was otherwise in a much fresher state than she was. He shook his head when she pushed through the door for the third time, wiping her mouth with her sleeve. "Sometimes I wonder if you truly are my niece."

Isla groaned. "Because I don't have your tolerance for this poison you call ale?"

"It did the job, didn't it? If you wanted something more refined, you should have gone to your friend's estate in the upper city." Muir limped over to the barrel, holding a dirty tankard underneath the meagre trickle of ale. He took a long slurp before holding it underneath to refill. "You've got that look on your face. I remember it from when you were a bairn. Usually means trouble."

"It's none of your concern, uncle. Don't worry about it."

"Telling me not to worry does little to reassure me." Muir sighed. "I've reconsidered. You must be my niece after all. You've certainly picked up my habit of ignoring all good sense when you put your mind to something." He lowered his voice. "I meant what I said before. Stay away from the Grand Admiral. He's not the kind of man you want to tangle with, especially given your...present company."

He looked pointedly at Eimhir, and Isla bristled. "She's a friend."

"That's a dangerous kind of friend to have. You don't understand—"

A rap at the door cut off the rest of his words. Grateful for the distraction, Isla opened it and ushered in Quinn's attendants. Darce had sent a runner first thing that morning, and Quinn had answered swiftly, sending a carriage to retrieve Lachlan.

She stood aside as the attendants lifted her brother from the blood-soaked sheets on the floor and settled him in the rear of the carriage. His face was still pale, his breathing thin, but the sweat had cleared from his forehead and Eimhir assured her the stump of his leg showed no sign of lingering poison.

Darce joined her at the doorway. "We should go," he said gently, touching her shoulder. "The sooner one of Quinn's surgeons can see to him, the better."

"Wait for me in the carriage. I'll be there in a moment."

Darce flicked his eyes between her and Eimhir, then nodded, making his way down the wooden steps.

Isla turned to Eimhir. The marble white of her skin seemed harder than usual, each line etched with grief. It was not for Lachlan, Isla knew. But it was a pain they both shared, a pain they both understood.

"Tell me there was no other choice," Isla said, the words catching in her throat. "Tell me he would have died if you hadn't brought that axe down on his leg."

"I can tell you whatever you want," Eimhir said quietly. "It won't stop the doubt. It won't stop you blaming yourself."

Isla released a long breath. "I know I should thank you. But—"

"But all you can see is me swinging that axe," Eimhir finished, voice hollow. "Just like all I can see is your hand around the blade in Fin's neck." She closed her eyes. "You asked me before if I believed friendship was possible across such wounds. My answer remains true. I called you caraid, and I meant that." When she opened her eyes again, her gaze was clearer than before, reflecting the grey morning light. "Perhaps neither of us will ever be able to forgive the things that have happened to us. Perhaps such scars are inevitable when it comes to friendship between human and selkie. But I don't want to surrender myself to the sea with only hate in my heart. When the time comes, I would like you to be there. As my caraid. As my friend."

"Are you certain this is how it must end? I thought..." Isla swallowed, half afraid to give voice to the words. "Finlay's blood was spilled on his pelt when he...when I... Why didn't you take it?"

Eimhir looked away. "You saw what he was like at the end. That hatred, that rage, that pain... It would have become part of my soul too. That's not what I want to become. I have to believe there is more hope for my people than that, even if I do not live to see it."

"What about your aunt's pelt, the one the Grand Admiral has locked away? You said the selkies in the sea cave heard rumours."

"Less than rumours. Whispers, maybe. They told me the smuggler your people call the Eel spoke of a map to an island where the Grand Admiral keeps what he treasures most." Eimhir shook her head. "Even if such a thing exists, it would be impossible to lay hands on. According to the Eel, the map is kept in the Admiralty Garrison."

"The Admiralty Garrison..." The words dried on Isla's tongue. "It's impenetrable. They'd catch us before we made it through the gates. The only thing waiting for us would be a noose around our necks."

"Then it's over." Eimhir gave a bleak smile. "And perhaps that is for the best. I swore to my clan I would return with my aunt's pelt. If I am to break my word... What is it you humans say? Tides take me?" She blinked. "And so they shall."

Isla reached for her hand. Eimhir's skin was as cold as ever, her pulse slow under her fingertips. "This doesn't seem fair."

"It isn't. None of it is. But that doesn't change it." Eimhir squeezed her hand, then slipped her fingers out of Isla's grasp. "I must leave you now. It's not safe for me back at the townhouse. I'm not sure it's safe for you either."

"Lachlan is there. Safe or not, it's where I have to be."

"I understand." Eimhir straightened, the pain and grief across her face smoothing out as she settled her expression into the stony composure Isla remembered from their first meeting. "I should have learned by now there are places each of us have to go where the other cannot follow. I wish it were not so, but—"

"But that doesn't change it," Isla finished softly. "Go, Eimhir. And when the time comes..."

"The sea caves, at next month's new moon." Eimhir's eyes glistened with tears. "If you wish to say goodbye, that is where you'll find me. If tides be kind."

"If tides be kind," Isla echoed, the whisper pulling painfully at her heart.

The will-o'-the-wisp. The gun-anam walking out of the mist. The roiling black waters of the harbour. Ever since she'd returned to Silveck-an, all the tides offered was their cruelty.

If kindness still existed amongst the waves, it was difficult to believe it was destined for her.

CHAPTER
TWENTY-FOUR

T ime became a knot in the pit of Isla's stomach, pulling tighter with each passing week. The weight of inevitability, of delayed grief, sat heavy around her shoulders, following her wherever she went. Walking the floors of Quinn's townhouse was like standing atop the trapdoors of the gallows. All she could do was wait for them to spring open and drop her towards the end she knew was coming.

She kept herself busy taking care of Lachlan, ushering away Quinn's attendants to sit by his bedside and clean his stump herself. Each time she peeled back the bandages, her heart stilled; she half expected to see his skin mottled and purple, his veins turning black. But the poison was gone, leaving her only with the reminder of the decision she'd made for him. The decision he'd live with for the rest of his life.

"You don't have to make that face every time you come to see me, you know." Lachlan hoisted himself up on his elbows, mouth twisting into a grimace. The colour had returned to his cheeks in recent days, breathing some of the boyishness back into his features. When he turned his irritated glare to her, Isla could almost pretend nothing had changed.

"What face?" she asked.

"That one. The one where you're looking at me like I might fall apart."

He shifted against the pillows. "Stop searching for a way to fix something that can't be undone. This will be difficult enough without suffering your guilt every time you walk into the room. I told you already—I don't blame you for what happened."

If words were all it took to assuage the squeeze around her heart, Isla might have been able to breathe easier upon hearing them. But louder still were the things that went unsaid: the way the air turned cold when she met his eyes, the way his smile strained too tightly at the corners of his mouth, the muffled cries of pain and grief and anger permeating the wall between their rooms. Her brother was suffering, and for the first time she could remember, he was trying to shield her from it. No sharp-tongued accusations, no words of anger. That, more than anything, was what worried her the most.

She pulled the bedsheets over his leg. "I'm lost, Lachlan. I don't know what to do anymore."

"I do." He wrapped his fingers around her hand and squeezed. "We came here for Caolaig, for Blackwood Estate. We came here to make the Grand Admiral listen. We can still do that. When we go home, it will be with a small fleet at our backs. We'll rebuild what we lost. Together."

The words rang in her ears for the rest of the day, a distant echo of the promise she'd made to him on the blood-soaked shores of Caolaig. So much had changed since then.

"Together," she said, the word leaving the taste of a lie on her tongue.

Even when Lachlan recovered enough to leave the confines of his bed and hobble about with the aid of a polished rosewood crutch Quinn commissioned for him, Isla only felt the cold seeds of dread grow. Too often a veneer of distance fell across her brother's eyes when he looked at her. The warmth of his smile became too easy, too practised. In between the flashes of the Lachlan she knew was a stranger of her own making.

I don't blame you for what happened, he'd said. But then the tension in his voice pulled tight, threatening to snap, and Isla wondered if she'd heard a lie behind it.

Quinn, for his part, had engaged her with hollow pleasantries since returning, even if each of his words dripped with insincerity. He'd made no move against her, though whether that was out of genuine concern for Lachlan or a lack of opportunity, Isla couldn't be certain. All she knew was the shadow of his threat hung over her still, prickling her neck every time she met his eyes. The townhouse walls were closing in. If she didn't leave soon, she'd be crushed between them.

And where should I go? she thought. Leaving would only be another betrayal, one she could never come back from. No matter Quinn's demands, she wouldn't abandon Lachlan. Not when all that held them together was this final thread of the promise she'd made, ready to break with the lightest touch.

A rap at the door broke Isla from her thoughts. The sound echoed up the marble stairs like a gunshot, and her heart thudded as she ventured down to the foyer balcony to see what the commotion was.

The front doors swung open in the vestibule below, and up drifted the clack of dress boots against the floor. Isla leaned over the balcony to catch a glimpse of the small cohort marching through to take their places in a uniform line, their jewel-toned capes swirling as they came to a halt. They stood straight and tall, gold-handled cutlasses gleaming from their ornate leather belts.

Her heart seized. What was an Admiralty regiment doing here?

One of them stepped forward and met Quinn with a deep bow. As he straightened, Isla recognised him from the attack at the docks. It was the young officer who'd fought with Lachlan, the one who'd helped carry him to Muir's and left when her uncle ushered him away.

Unease swirled in the pit of her stomach. *Stay away from the Grand Admiral*, Muir had told her. Now, the Admiralty had arrived at Quinn's door. Was it because of her uncle, or was there something else at play here?

The young officer caught sight of her, recognition brightening the solemnity in his blue-grey eyes. Light-brown hair poked out from his woollen Admiralty bonnet, coiling around his cheekbones. "Lady Blackwood, if I'm not mistaken. Forgive me for not having realised before. I understand you have not visited the capital in some time."

Isla stiffened, though whether it was at the unwanted title or unexpected easiness with which the young officer spoke, she couldn't be sure. "You have me at a disadvantage, I'm afraid."

"Of course. Allow me to introduce myself." He removed his bonnet, fingers fidgeting with the tartan band around the rim. "Second Lieutenant Blair Cunningham. I would have come sooner, but I didn't know where to find you. Your uncle wasn't exactly forthcoming with your whereabouts."

"No, I don't imagine he would be." Isla frowned. "Dare I ask what this is all about, Lieutenant? I assure you, whatever Muir has done in the past, my brother and I—"

"No, it's not like that." Cunningham waved her off. "You and your brother are precisely the reason I'm here. I wanted to thank you both in person for your service in defending the merchant docks. Your brother in particular, he..." Cunningham trailed off, a hesitant look falling across his features. "Well, it's unlikely I'd be speaking to you now were it not for him. I owe him a debt. My family owes him a debt."

Quinn had been quiet as he watched the exchange. Now, Isla sensed his attention prick up as he turned towards the young lieutenant with a discerning gleam in his eyes. "Cunningham, you said? I know it's far from an uncommon Silvish name, but given the circumstances, I have to ask..." A shrewd smile pulled at the edge of his lips. "Would you be of any relation to *Alasdair* Cunningham? Our city's very own Grand Admiral?"

A flush darkened Cunningham's cheeks. "His nephew, in fact. But that has no bearing on this matter. I've come here in my position as lieutenant to extend the gratitude of the Admiralty for your service to the capital. The Grand Admiral is holding a civil reception next week to celebrate those outside the Admiralty who stood in defence of the capital last month. It would honour me to have you attend."

"Will there be dancing?" Lachlan's voice drifted from the stairs behind her, light and drawling. He edged down each marble step with a grimace, crutch buried in his armpit. When he saw the young lieutenant, his face pulled into a tight grin. "Sorry to disappoint, but I don't think you'll catch me in a Lowland Reel anytime soon."

Cunningham's eyes trailed up the staircase, falling across the pinned-up breeches around Lachlan's stump. Isla braced herself for the flinch, for the surprise to twist at the lieutenant's mouth, but Cunningham only let out soft laugh. "That's hardly an excuse. From what I observed of your swordplay at the docks, I expect you to move better on one leg than most men on two."

"I might need you to repeat that when Galbraith is in earshot. He always did have something to say about my footwork." Lachlan hobbled forward, joining Isla at the balcony and slipping his free arm through hers. She moved to help steady him, then froze at the squeeze he gave her arm.

"This is what we need for an audience with the Grand Admiral," he murmured under his breath. "This is the opportunity we've been waiting for." He released her arm and turned back to the lieutenant. "I have to admit, I never expected that pulling you out the path of a selkie's longsword would result in an invite to some fancy ball, but if that's the reward for rescuing royalty these days, who am I to refuse?"

Cunningham's mouth tightened at the mention of royalty, but his eyes brightened nonetheless as he ushered over one of his fellow officers and pulled out a small stack of envelopes. "I'm certain you won't regret it. Not many civilians are given the chance to see the inside of the Admiralty Garrison, and the main hall is a wonder. Of course, the rest of your household is more than welcome to accompany you. Let me know how many invites you need and I'll..."

The rest of his words faded from Isla's ears. All she could think about was the way the lieutenant's voice lingered around a certain phrase.

The Admiralty Garrison.

A cold twinge of fear pulled taut. Only weeks ago, she'd told Eimhir it was too much to risk. Perhaps it still was. But now, at least, they had a way in. A way to get closer to the Grand Admiral and the map that might lead them to the pelt he'd stolen all those years ago.

Fresh hope swelled in her, so fragile Isla hardly dared believe it. The new moon was only a few days away, but there was still time to tell Eimhir what she'd learned, to convince her to hold on. It might be her last chance—her only chance—but it was a chance nonetheless. She could find the pelt. She could save her.

Isla's throat thickened as Lachlan reached the bottom of the curved staircase, his mouth stretched into a smile as he engaged Blair Cunningham in conversation. Her brother had saved the Grand Admiral's nephew. If there was any hope of petitioning the Admiralty for ships to protect Caolaig and Blackwood Estate, Lachlan couldn't have done anything more to secure it.

This is what we need, he'd said. *This is the opportunity we've been waiting for.*

But it wasn't just about Caolaig anymore. It wasn't about Blackwood Estate and the promise she'd made to her brother. It was about saving Eimhir. It was about stopping the mists once and for all, no matter the cost.

Lachlan's eyes found hers from the vestibule below, their tawny colour gleaming in the light. Isla smiled at him, even as the cold grip of betrayal wound its fingers around her aching heart.

No matter the cost, whispered a knowing voice at the nape of her neck. *And what if the cost is him?*

Isla swallowed the guilt and grief rising in her throat. She didn't have an answer. She feared if she ever did, it would only come when it was already too late.

Hours later, Isla returned to the dark gullet of Arburgh's vaults with a stuffed pack around her shoulder and a pristine envelope tucked into her longcoat pocket. This time, no footsteps trailed after her in pursuit as she wound through the narrow, cobbled streets. This time, she was alone, following the murals towards the seaweed-soaked tunnel leading out to the sea cave.

Eimhir sat alone on one of the flat rocks overlooking the lapping water, her shoulders bundled in an old set of furs. The dull brown-grey colour lacked the lustre of a true soulskin, and as Isla moved closer, she saw the marks of its loss upon Eimhir. Her hair hung ragged around her shoulders, the lengths of it as dry and brittle as yellow beachgrass. Purple shadows half circled her eyes, giving her a gaunt, sunken look.

The worst of it was the salt scarring. Flaky white crystals crawled across her pale skin, encrusted there like stubborn barnacles clinging to a hull. The flesh around the salt was pink and tender, peeling back in places as the scars spread.

All of us are dying, Finlay had said once. *Some of us more quickly than others.*

It was only now Isla understood what he meant.

Eimhir's cracked lips split as she pulled them into a smile, blood welling in the centre. "You're early. So eager to see me give myself over to the tides, are you?"

"You know that's not true." Isla skirted around the slippery, sea-weed-strewn rockpools and hoisted herself onto the flat slab beside Eimhir. Outside the overhanging mouth of the cave, the water lay flat and calm, stretching across the horizon. "It's quiet here today."

"It's been quiet for a while. My people risked their lives coming here, and after the attack..." Eimhir trailed off, face sickly grey. "Have you visited Gallowgate recently?"

Isla winced. No part of her wanted to return to the execution square, but that hadn't stopped word flying to the townhouse of what was happening there. Any selkie that hadn't fled or been killed during the attack had been lashed bloody and strung up in the gibbets. The iron bars held countless bodies, caging together corpses with those still clinging to life. Blood soaked into the cobbles below, staining them red. Some of the more fanciful gossip-mongers said not even the weeds forced themselves up through the cracks anymore. Nothing would grow where such tides-damned blood was spilled.

"You warned us," Eimhir said. "You and your brother told Finlay what the Grand Admiral would do to anyone who threatened his port. If we'd listened, those selkies might still be alive. Fin might…" She pinched her mouth shut, eyes darkening. "But what's done is done. None of it can be changed. I just thought it would be easier to accept, here at the end of all things."

"It doesn't have to be the end."

"Is that why you came?" Eimhir gave her a bleak smile. "To talk me out of this? Believe me, caraid, there is nothing I would like more. The sea is my home, yet without my pelt, it frightens me. I don't want to feel the depths turn my blood to ice. I don't want to drown in saltwater and sorrow. I don't want to surrender myself to it, not like this. Knowing that part of me is out there somewhere, out of my reach, in the hands of someone who has no right to it…"

Isla reached for her hand. It was cold and dry, her skin peeling off her knuckles like flaking fish scales. "Then let's get it back."

Eimhir's hand stiffened under hers, all ice and bone. "What are you talking about?"

"Your pelt might have been sold before we could retrieve it from the gaol, but there is another. The one the Grand Admiral took from your aunt." Isla steadied herself with a breath. "I say it's past time it was returned to where it belongs."

Eimhir narrowed her eyes. "You said—"

"That it was too dangerous, I know. But that was before I had a way into the Admiralty Garrison." Isla slipped a hand into her coat pocket and pulled out the envelope. The card inside was printed in black and gold, with swirling motifs surrounding the Admiralty heraldry.

Eimhir's brow furrowed as she trailed her eyes over the printed script. "You're going to a ball?"

Isla loosened her pack from around her shoulder, setting it down on the rock and pulling it open. Inside was a bundle of fabrics and matching adornments she'd hastily snatched from Quinn's wardrobe. The material peeked out in rich-toned layers of silk and lace, out of place here in the damp, salty air. It belonged to a different world—a world Eimhir had never been part of, a world Isla had tried to sail away from. Yet it was a world they would both need to navigate to survive this.

"*We're* going to a ball," Isla corrected, a smile unfurling across her lips. "Then, we're going to steal the pelt back."

CHAPTER
TWENTY-FIVE

I sla shuffled forward, gathering the gossamer folds of her dress as she fought to keep her balance against the gusting wind. The Admiralty Garrison sat proudly at the highest point in the northside district, perched on the edge of the sheer, rocky ridge that dropped to the sea below. Tonight, its courtyard was lit with braziers and bustling with bodies trimmed in silk and woollen tartan. A burr of excited chatter echoed off the stone as invited guests made their way towards the main hall, smiling beneath ornamental masks of porcelain and leather and lace.

In front, Darce cut a fine figure in his tailored charcoal doublet and Galbraith tartan sash as he helped Lachlan. Her brother edged up the stairway on his crutch, spine stiff in a long-tailed coat of red velvet and a dress shirt fashionably loose at the neck. When he reached the top, he handed over a carefully folded envelope to the attending guard.

"Tides, the invite." Isla made a show of rummaging in her pockets. "Surely I can't have been so daft as to forget it. No, I'm certain I picked it up from my nightstand. Where is it then? I can't find it..."

Lachlan snapped his head towards her, eyes narrowing behind the goldleaf mask pinned across his nose. "Isla, it was the *one thing* you had to remember."

"Don't worry, I'm sure I'll find it in here somewhere. Otherwise you go ahead with Darce and I'll return to the townhouse to—"

"That won't be necessary." A tall figure in an emerald tunic pushed past the waiting guard, blue-grey eyes twinkling from behind a glittering obsidian mask. "I can vouch for these guests personally. Please, make yourselves welcome."

Isla stifled a triumphant smile. She'd been counting on one of the guards being lenient enough to let her in without an invite, but that Blair Cunningham himself had been waiting for their arrival was a stroke of fortune she hadn't dared to anticipate. He offered Lachlan his arm as he led them into the main hall, leaving Isla to trail behind with Darce.

The sergeant sent her a pointed look. "You *forgot?*"

"Is that so hard to believe?"

"I'm no fool, wolf cub, no matter how many times you insist on treating me like one." He fixed her with a dark gaze, the sharpness of it sending an uneasy shiver down her spine. "Whatever you've set in motion tonight, I suggest you reconsider. This is too dangerous a game to be playing."

"It is no game," Isla said, her voice taking on an icy edge. "It is a matter of life and death."

"For Eimhir?"

"For all of us." She adjusted the black mask around her eyes. "The gun-anam still haunt my dreams. I see their leader sitting on its kelpie mount of sea spray and rot, looking out at me from behind a skull of blackened bone. It's only a matter of time before they return."

"You still believe Eimhir can stop them, don't you? That's what this is about. You're going to help her find her aunt's pelt."

"It's better for us both if I don't answer that." Isla gathered the layers of her gown together. "We should head in. Lachlan will be wondering where we are."

"If you think I'll stand by and do nothing while you—Isla, wait!"

She ignored him, lengthening her stride as she stepped through the huge oak doors leading into the main hall. At once, her breath stilled. The parquet pinewood flooring was polished so cleanly she could see her own reflection. White columns lined either side of the room, the entire height wrapped in intricate carvings as they stretched to the curved ceiling.

Tell me, how much gold does a selkie pelt command on the continent these days? Eimhir had asked her once.

Isla grabbed a crystalline flute from a passing attendant to wash away the acrid taste on her tongue. She didn't have an answer for Eimhir then. Now, it was obvious. The ever-expanding trade routes across the continent, the wealth and riches funnelled back to Arburgh—it had all been paid for in selkie blood. She imagined the wax on the golden chandeliers dripping red, the paint-stained windows refracting the lamplight in a crimson glow, the towering pillars white as bone. The worst part was how nobody else noticed but her.

"There he is." Lachlan appeared at her side, resting on his crutch. "Up at the high table."

Isla followed his gaze to the dais halfway down the hall. The long table was draped in sapphire brocade and surrounded by high-backed chairs padded in velvet. She trailed her eyes along the admirals and dignitaries smiling behind their masks with wide grins and painted lips. Her gaze fell across the man at the centre of the table, dressed in a silver-and-white dress tunic and emerald cravat. When he brought a goblet to his lips, Isla caught a glimpse of the black pearl set in the middle of his silver Admiralty ring.

Alasdair Cunningham. The Grand Admiral himself.

A tremble worked its way down her spine, pebbling her skin with icy gooseflesh. Steely eyes glinted behind his porcelain mask, and his smile was wide and wolfish. Even with his face half obscured and a brown-grey beard dusting his jaw, there was a regality to his features, as if the lines and creases held the memory of something handsome from years past.

Isla pushed the thought from her head. She'd learned all too well how the things that made a monster lay beneath the skin. She wouldn't underestimate what the Grand Admiral was capable of. She couldn't.

"I already spoke to Blair," Lachlan said, voice hushed. "He'll get us an audience with his uncle. All we have to do is convince him, and we'll have the ships we need. We can go home."

Isla arched an eyebrow. "It's *Blair* already, is it? I didn't realise you and the lieutenant had become so familiar."

Lachlan's cheeks turned rosy beneath the gold of his mask. "It's not like that. And even if it was, it's hardly any of your business." He smirked. "Why don't you find the sergeant to keep yourself busy? I'll find you when it's time."

"It's not like that eith—Lachlan!"

Her brother skirted away, cutting through the bustling bodies with surprising finesse as he pulled himself forward on the heel of his rose-wood crutch. Dancing couples and circles of chattering guests parted on either side of him like the tides drawing back from shore, and as he moved between them, their heads followed.

Isla shivered. It was the attention Lachlan always wanted, but at what price?

A hand slipped around her waist, and she spun to find herself in Darce's steady grip. He moved his hand to the small of her back and wrapped her fingers in his with the other, guiding her across the pinewood floor with a smooth stride.

"I never took you for a dancer, Sergeant."

"The way I see it, it's no different to swordplay." Darce cocked his head and swept her around in a half circle. "All about the footwork."

"I'm impressed. We'll make a noble out of you yet."

Darce snorted. "I don't have the patience for such things. Or the temperament. I like problems I can solve at the end of a blade. When it gets more complicated, well..."

"You're lost," Isla said. "I know that feeling well."

The skirl of pipes and thrum of fiddles settled into a gentle rhythm, and Isla leaned closer into Darce's hold as they swirled among the other dancers. The brush of his hand against the exposed skin of her lower back sent a tingle racing up her spine. All she could concentrate on was their proximity. The pressure of his chest against hers, close enough to feel the pulse of his heartbeat. The brush of his stubble against her cheek. The warm scent of his breath, so near she could taste it.

He looked down at her, brown eyes half hidden behind his mask. "This is as close as you've allowed me to get to you ever since the night of the attack. I can't help but feel you've been avoiding me."

Because every time I'm near you, I forget how to breathe, Isla thought. *Because I'm afraid all I am to you is a promise you made to my father. Because I can't bear the thought of losing someone else I...*

"There are more important concerns right now," she said aloud. "I don't know what Lachlan is planning, but—"

"*You* are my most important concern," Darce said as he spun her. When he caught her again, his fingers tightened around hers. "If you don't know that by now, I'm not sure what else I can do to make it clear to you."

Isla's breath stilled. "I... Darce, this isn't—"

He let her fingers fall from his grasp and brought his hand to cup her cheek, tracing along her jaw. When his touch brushed over the gouge Finlay had left below her eye, she pulled his hand away.

He grimaced. "Does it still pain you?"

"No, I..." The traces of his fingertips against her skin brought heat to her cheeks, leaving her fighting to find her voice. "I know what it's like to look at someone and see only a reminder of the ways you failed them. I don't want you to look at me like that. There is no beauty to be found in guilt."

He tilted her chin towards him, eyes dark and unwavering. "When I look at you, at that scar on your face, I only see a reminder that you survived. A reminder I didn't lose you. That is all the beauty I could ever need in this world, Isla. There's nothing I wouldn't do to protect it. To protect you."

Isla opened her mouth, but found her throat dry and wanting. There were no words she could summon over the frantic thumping of her heart, the quickening of her breath.

"You of all people should understand." Darce's voice was strained against her ear, unbearably gentle. "You spent the last seven years searching for a place to belong. Are you really so afraid to believe I have found mine?"

There was no space left between them but a shared breath. Isla felt the thrum of Darce's pulse, each beat sending a tremor deep into her core. Part of her wanted to push him away, to push away the longing ache against her ribs. The other part of her wanted to lean in, to close the distance and—

"I do hope I'm not interrupting."

Isla drew back from Darce with a sharp breath as Lachlan appeared beside them. His mouth pulled into a smirk as he glanced between them, a knowing glint in his eyes. "I hate to cut short whatever this is, but it's time. The Grand Admiral agreed to speak to us." He turned to Isla. "Or, more specifically, to you."

The warmth drained from Isla's cheeks. "Me? Whatever could he want to speak to me for?"

Even behind the mask, Isla couldn't mistake her brother's hesitation, the flicker of guilt dancing across his features. A moment later it was gone, and Lachlan straightened his spine, holding himself tall with his crutch under one arm.

"This was never going to be easy," he said. "The Grand Admiral isn't the kind of man to hand out favours without something in return. That's why I need you, sister. I need both of you." He shot a look at Darce. "We need to offer him something he can't refuse. Something that's worth as much as the ships we're asking for."

"What do we have that would possibly—"

"A sentinel." Lachlan slowly turned from Darce back to her. "And a captain."

Something cold lodged in Isla's gut. She tried to speak, but all her breath escaped at once, leaving the roof of her mouth dry. A horrible silence hung between them, turning her lips to stone, her tongue to ash. This couldn't be happening. He couldn't have meant it. Tides, what had he *done?*

"Lachlan," she managed, his name bruising her lips as she whispered it. "How could you ever think I would agree to this?"

"How could you not?" An edge of disbelief crept into his voice. "I know returning to Blackwood Estate was never your dream. For a while, I resented you for it. I kept hoping you would change your mind, that you would want to go home *with* me, not *for* me. But I understand now that the only way you'll ever be happy is to be free. I'm giving you that chance." His brow furrowed above the edge of his mask. "I thought you'd understand. I thought you'd be pleased."

Isla barked out a laugh. "Pleased you'd sell me to the tides-damned Admiralty?"

"You'd have a ship of your own. You'd have the freedom of the seas. All you'd have to do in return is—"

"Come running every time the Grand Admiral calls? Aye, that sounds like my idea of *freedom*." She glared at him. "And what of the sergeant? Did you consider what this would mean for him? You're asking him to give up his soul for the sake of a few ships."

"I'll do it."

Isla froze. The words reached her ears in Darce's soft burr, but the sound of them was like the voice of a stranger. "What?"

"I swore to protect both of you. If this is the best way of doing that, how can I refuse?" Darce shrugged. "My soul is forfeit anyway. It's only a matter of time. At least this way, it will mean something when I give it up."

Isla's heart pounded, the fitted bodice of her dress pulling tighter with each painful breath. The sergeant's eyes were fixed on Lachlan, his jaw as tense as she'd ever seen it. Even half hidden behind the mask, there was no mistaking how stony his expression had become. Every grim line, every sharp angle, was as unflinching as his words had been. All the warmth she might have imagined as he'd held her in his arms was gone, leaving behind only the cold embrace of duty.

She pushed the ache aside and turned to Lachlan. "Was this your idea, or Quinn's?"

"What does it matter?" The edge to Lachlan's voice yielded to weariness. "It's a good plan. It's the only way for us to get what we want."

"What *you* want," Isla snapped. "Not me. If the Grand Admiral needs a captain so badly, let it be you. It doesn't take long to get acquainted with life aboard a ship. I'm certain the young lieutenant would be only too happy to help you find..." She broke off, swallowing her guilt.

"My sea legs? Was that what you were about to say?" Lachlan gave a bleak smile. "Well, if that had been an option, it certainly isn't anymore. Eimhir took that from me."

You let *her take it from me.* The words went unspoken, but Isla heard them anyway, ringing in her ears with resentment. They echoed all the louder for how quiet Lachlan had fallen, how brittle this silence was between them, ready to break under the slightest touch.

"I'm sorry," Isla murmured. "I didn't mean it. I didn't mean for any of this to turn out the way it has. I only wanted to make things right with you."

Lachlan's expression softened. "You still can. We can still do this, together. You'll have your freedom, and I'll look after our parents' legacy. And when you come home, Blackwood Estate won't be a prison, but a safe haven. A place where you can rest before returning to the sea."

"As a pawn of the Admiralty?" Isla lifted her head, fighting the tremor in her throat. "And what good will my new position be when the gun-anam sweep past the ships you bargained for and turn their blades of salt and spray on Caolaig once more?"

"The gun-anam?" Lachlan's mouth pinched. "I thought we were done with that nonsense."

"They were there again the night of the attack on the docks. They're real. And a handful of ships won't be enough to stop them." Isla stepped back, tears thickening her throat. "I truly am sorry, wee brother. But if I am to be bought and sold, it better be for something more than false hope. I can't be a part of this."

Lachlan grabbed her wrist. "Don't walk away. You don't get to do that, not again. After everything that's happened, this is the least you can do. For me, for our family."

Even as his fingers dug painfully into her skin, Isla couldn't help the way her heart broke at the pain in his words. The sting of them lashed at her, stripping her of any remaining anger. There was no room left for anger, only regret.

"That's enough," Darce said, his voice as gentle as it was steely. "Take your hand from her, before you do something you can't take back."

Lachlan released his fingers from her wrist, a dark chuckle escaping his throat. "All these years you've been by my side, Galbraith, and all it takes is her coming back to change everything. I don't know why I expected anything else."

"I have not left your side, little laird. I am as much your friend now as I ever was." Darce put a steadying hand on Lachlan's shoulder. "Do not look for enemies where there are none. We are all together in this."

"Are we?" Lachlan's mouth pulled into a bitter line. "I'm not sure we ever were."

Isla stilled. "Lachlan—"

"Go." He shook his head. "If it's what you truly want, then leave. I'm tired of trying to make myself matter to you. I'm tired of trying to convince you to be part of a family you never wanted in the first place. You don't belong at Blackwood Estate anymore. Maybe you never did. I'll finish this on my own, without you."

Isla's throat constricted. There were no words left, nothing more she could possibly say that hadn't been laid bare between them already.

Anything else would only worsen this rift between them, already so deep she knew not where the bottom lay, or how to navigate it.

She turned on her heel and marched towards the doors. The stuffy warmth of the room and the biting reminder of Lachlan's parting words were making her head spin. She needed to fill her lungs with the cliffside air. She needed to taste the drizzle and the salt on the wind. She needed to get away from this tides-forsaken nightmare she'd woken up in.

"Don't do this. Don't leave again, not like this."

Isla halted, cheeks burning at the sound of Darce's voice. She turned slowly, fingers curling into fists. "How could you agree?" she said, fighting against the quake in her voice. "How could you possibly accept something like that?"

Darce fixed her with a steady look. "Would it have been so terrible?"

She adjusted her mask, blinking away the tears threatening to spill. She wouldn't let him see. She couldn't.

"The thought of having you by my side could never be terrible," she whispered. "But I know too well that kind of chain would only break us both."

Darce reeled back, his face pale. Isla whirled away before he could speak, before he could form the shape of her name between his lips. If she heard it now, she'd be undone. She'd take everything he offered her, and tides damn what it might mean for them both.

He couldn't help her, not in the wild waters that lay ahead.

Only a selkie would do.

CHAPTER
TWENTY-SIX

M isting rain cooled Isla's face as she entered the courtyard and fought to steady her breathing. She pulled off her mask and closed her eyes against the drizzle, for once appreciating the damp touch of Arburgh's weather. Returning to the main hall seemed impossible. She'd left too much there she couldn't bear to face: the twist of betrayal on Lachlan's mouth, the hurt in Darce's gaze, the last chance to return to a home that was never hers. All she had left now was a desperate gamble that hinged on the word of a woman who should have been her enemy.

Isla swept her eyes across the courtyard. The light from the braziers danced across the silvery puddles forming between the cobbles, making them twinkle like stars. There was something beautiful about the stillness of the place, dreich as it was. The weather had chased most of the loitering guests inside, their skirts sodden and shoes splattered. The only other person out here was a solitary figure standing by the fountain wearing a dress Isla recognised well.

Eimhir stood stiffly, her shoulders square and hair pulled into a knot at the nape of her neck. The gown Isla had stolen for her covered the length of her arms in intricate swirls of golden lace to hide the crystals of salt across her skin. Her face was hidden behind a full mask, the porcelain visage as pale and hard-featured as Eimhir's own.

Isla slipped her mask back on and joined Eimhir. After glancing around the courtyard to make sure they were alone, she whispered, "Did you find a way onto the residential floors?"

Eimhir shook her head, the movement blunt and stilted. "There are Admiralty guards posted at the foot of every staircase. I doubt we'd be able to slip past them." She shivered, the lace of her gown clinging to her skin. "This was a mistake, caraid. I should never have let myself hope there was a way for this to end without me surrendering to the tides. I fear if we go through with this, all I'll succeed in is getting you killed too."

Her voice was low and gravelly, each word stretched thin as it left her lips. Eimhir's body was wasting away, and there wasn't enough golden lace or polished porcelain in Arburgh to hide it for much longer. This was their only chance.

"If we *don't* go through with this, all I've done has been for nothing," Isla said. "You said if you return your aunt's pelt to your clan, they'll teach you how to dreamwalk, how to stop the gun-anam. That's what I'm fighting for. Can I still trust you?"

Eimhir's eyes were barely visible through the mask, but Isla didn't mistake their earnest gleam. "Aye," she said. "You can still trust me."

"Then let's find another way up to the Grand Admiral's quarters." Isla slipped her arm through Eimhir's, wincing at how icy her skin had become. The selkie had always been cold to the touch, but now her body exuded a chill that reminded Isla of the mist-like breath of the gun-anam. How long would it be before she could ignore the call of the sea no longer? How long until she became a creature of salt and spray like them?

"We're not going back inside?" Eimhir asked as Isla pulled her past the towering oak doors of the main hall.

"You said there were Admiralty officers at every staircase."

"There are. But I don't see—"

"Then we'll have to find a way in from the outside." Isla led her along the outskirts of the courtyard, her eyes trailing along the granite walls.

The front façade of the main hall jutted out into the square, but down each side of the building the cobbles were shrouded in shadows, cloaked by the formidable height of the residential complex. "There, do you see?"

The window was small, but Isla spotted a sliver of space between its wooden fittings, the frame shifting slightly with the wind's breath. It was open. It was a way into the heart of the Admiralty, to the Grand Admiral's rooms.

Eimhir followed Isla's gaze up the height of the wall. "How do you expect to reach that?"

"The ivy." Isla pointed to the creeping vines winding across the cracks in the granite.

"You mean for us to *climb?*" Eimhir asked.

"I've climbed more treacherous rigging in far worse conditions. Remember the *Jade Dawn?* I am not afraid of falling."

"You may not be, but I am." Eimhir grimaced. "Though I suppose we have little choice if we are to reach the Grand Admiral's rooms. We must find that map."

"We will. And when we do, we'll go after your pelt together. I'll help you reclaim what was taken from your family."

Eimhir reached a hand to her face and removed the white porcelain mask. Her skin was pale, her cheeks marred with salt and red scratches. But the fearsome glint in her eyes was as sharp as ever as she drew her lips into a smile. "When you speak like that, I believe there is another way for this to end. Like you alone can hold back the tides from claiming me. Let's do this, caraid."

Isla kicked off her shoes and fumbled at her waist, loosening the floating layers of overskirts from her gown until she stood in nothing more than a light sheath of chiffon and lace. The bitter breath of the wind skittered across her skin, prickling the hair on her arms as she bundled the fabric and thrust it into Eimhir's arms. "Find somewhere to hide those for now. When I reach the window and signal that it's clear, you'll know it's safe to follow me up."

Eimhir nodded. "I wish you luck. For both our sakes."

Isla waited until the tap of her footsteps faded across the cobbles, then turned to the wall. The granite towered above her in a patchwork of rough-edged blocks thick with ivy. Sturdy vines stretched along the building, the green of their leaves ink-black in the darkness.

She buried her hands into the foliage and tugged the vines to test their strength. The stems were slimy from the drizzle as they slipped through her fingers, but they held fast, clinging to the stone.

Just like the ratlines, Isla told herself. *Just another climb.*

She hauled herself off the ground, swinging to the side as she adjusted her feet in the draping ivy. Each time she reached for a new handful of vines, she held her breath, waiting for the stems to snap between her fingers and send her tumbling to the cobbles. The leaves slid against her palms, crushed in her grip as she pulled herself up, one aching arm after another. This wasn't just another climb at all. No rigging was this fragile, no mast so precarious.

The window was within reach now, its wooden frame jutting from the stone. Isla sank her foot into another tangled clump of ivy, steadying herself as best she could. The vines in her hands pulled tight in protest as she hauled herself up the final few inches and planted her elbow on the windowsill.

A dull orange glow flickered beyond the glass. Isla nudged the window open and leaned forward, peering into the corridor. The oil lamps burned low on the walls, casting shadows across the floor, but the length of the hallway was otherwise empty.

Tides, she'd made it.

She scanned the courtyard below for Eimhir, gesturing for her to follow. Moments later, Eimhir appeared at the window, slipping through with a heavy thud. The muffled noise sent a warning shiver down Isla's spine and she quickly pulled the window closed behind her. If they were caught, the mercy of a noose would be the best they could hope for. She knew too well by now what the Grand Admiral did to traitors.

"We should split up," Eimhir said in hushed tones. "We'll be able to cover more ground that way. I'll take the eastern wing."

Isla set off down the west corridor, her bare feet sinking into the carpet. The doors along the hallway were set in oak and ebony and pine, brass handles gleaming in the dim light. Isla waited outside each one, listening for stirrings within. None of these belonged to the Grand Admiral. They all faced onto the courtyard, onto the city, and whatever else Alasdair Cunningham was, he was a man of the sea. She understood him in that sense.

At the end of the corridor, she found herself facing a set of double doors. These were wider than the rest, the wood ancient and knotted, adorned with gilded hinges and rings set with black pearls. This was the Grand Admiral's private office. It had to be.

Isla wrapped her fingers around one of the handles. The ache between her ribs sank deeper than fear. It lodged itself in her sternum like the spears of a fishhook. This was a place she didn't belong. Yet somehow, she knew she was meant to be here.

Isla pulled open the door.

For a moment, she thought she was mistaken. She'd braced herself for a crude collection of selkie pelts on display, with fur in colours of russet-brown and sable and fawn. But as she stepped into the room, she found no trace of the bloodlust and greed she'd expected to find. There were no chandeliers hanging from the ceiling, no glittering ornaments or carved sculptures. Instead, her eyes found reflections of a man she almost recognised. A simple brass sextant lying on a table. A small-scale carving of the *Vanguard of the Firth*, black sails set against a non-existent breeze, wolfen figurehead snarling at the fireplace. A portrait of a dark-haired woman looking out to sea, grey furs hanging loose around her bare shoulders.

Was this truly the domain of a man so terrifying that even the mists retreated from his presence?

She closed the door behind her and padded through the room, the lacquered wood floor cold beneath her bare feet. The hearth held little more than faintly glowing embers, and a draught brushed the nape of her neck as she noticed three enormous windows stretching from floor to ceiling at the rear of the room, overlooking the sheer drop to the churning waves below.

Where are you? she thought. *Where is he hiding you?*

Her eyes fell across the huge ebony desk by the windows, scattered with maps and charts. It was the only extravagance in the room, the wood no doubt imported from the Karzish Peninsula. As she approached it, she noticed the view through the adjacent window. The rocks fell away below, dissolving into the sea. It was like being at the top of a mast with no deck below.

This was the place. It was where she would choose.

The thought crawled across Isla's skin. There was something too familiar about the Grand Admiral's quarters, something recognisable. It offered her a glimpse of the man behind the fearsome reputation. A man who lived for the sea. A man she feared might not be all that different to who she might have been, had she only stayed.

Isla fumbled with the drawers. She expected them to remain stuck, but they slid out easily as she pulled, spilling over with instruments and compasses and sheets of parchment. She rifled through them, furrowing her brow. If the map Eimhir spoke of was so precious to the Grand Admiral, surely he'd have locked it away. But the desk had no key, and none of the charts looked anything like what she was searching for.

"Tides take him," she muttered. "Where is he hiding it?"

She straightened her back and rested her hands on her hips as she trailed her eyes around the room. There were no expensive cabinets, no sturdy lockboxes or wooden chests. The only piece of furniture that stood out to her was the desk. She'd been drawn to it. It was *important*. She knew it by its place at the window, overlooking the sea. She imagined the Grand Admiral sitting in the velvet padded chair, letting out a sigh as he spared a glance over the horizon every time he looked up from...

Isla stilled. The desk was strewn with rolled-up charts, with stacks of paper and waxy seals. She hadn't yet seen what lay underneath.

She gathered up the materials and shifted them to the side, her fingers trembling. The desk was a rich black, so dense Isla could barely see the grain of the wood. It stretched out in front of her, spread beneath her hands.

That was when she saw it. A glimmer of silver ink.

At first, she thought she'd imagined it—it must have been some reflection of the moon across the ebony surface, some glint from a nearby lamp. But the moon was new and dark, the sweet fragrance of the oil unlit. This was something else, something carved into the smooth surface of the desk with a needle-point blade, tracing silver lines so faint she had to squint to make sense of them.

It was like a spider's web across the black wood, spindly and shimmering as it formed shapes Isla began to recognise. The outline of the coast. The landmarks of the capital. The stretch of sea to the southwest, drawn in flowing silver waves. It was Silveckan. Her island as she'd never seen it before, glittering in ink and wood. She traced her fingers along the shoreline, finding her way back to Kinraith, to the wilds, to Caolaig. Back to Blackwood Estate, which had never been hers, no matter how hard she'd tried.

The image of Lachlan's pained expression swam in front of her eyes, and she snatched her hand away like the table had burned her. Blackwood Estate wasn't what she was searching for. It never had been. She needed to discover where the Grand Admiral had hidden the stolen pelt. Nothing else mattered now.

She peered over the desk once more. Silveckan shimmered before her, as perfectly charted as it was on any map. Rivers and rugged coves bit into the coast. Scattered islands drifted to the north. It was all so familiar, yet something about it felt strange.

There. A spit of land southwest of Arburgh, isolated in the Strait of Silveckan. It wasn't an island she was familiar with, not one she recognised from her charts. It rose in jagged lines of silver, surrounded by a stylised sketch of a fearsome sea serpent.

She rummaged for a ruler and a reference chart, sliding them against the glittering ebony tabletop and murmuring calculations between her lips. If this uncharted island was where the Grand Admiral was keeping the pelt he'd stolen, Isla could afford no mistake. This was not some scrap of parchment she could take away and keep in her pocket, waiting for it to tell her something. If she didn't find the answer now, she never would.

A muffled thump came from the corridor, jolting her from her concentration. She froze, hands hovering above the desk as the oak doors shuddered. Someone was coming. If they found her in here, it was over. But she hadn't yet had time to discern the location of the island. Without it, Eimhir would die, and all this would be for nothing.

The doors rattled again, and Isla braced herself. All she could hear was the rasp of her own breathing.

But when the doors finally burst open, it was Eimhir who stumbled through.

Her mask was gone, exposing red raw skin and the jagged trails of salt across her cheeks. Her gown was bloodied and torn. The knot of hair at the base of her neck had come loose, falling around her shoulders in brittle, snarling strands. Her fingers wrapped around the hilt of a dagger as she stormed forward, desperate. "Did you find it?"

Isla gestured to the silvery etchings on the tabletop. "In a manner of speaking. But unless we want to take the whole tides-damned desk with us, I have to make a copy of the charts."

"We don't have time for that." Eimhir wiped a trickle of blood from her nose. "I ran into some guards. I managed to fight them off, but more will be here soon."

"But I'm so close. I only need a few more minutes to—" Isla broke off at the urgent thud of footsteps from the corridor.

Eimhir leapt towards her, grabbing a fistful of hair and bringing the dagger to her throat in a single fluid motion. The edge of the blade bit against Isla's neck, so keen she didn't dare swallow.

"What are you doing?" she hissed.

Eimhir spun her to face the door. "Making sure I don't take you down with me."

"You know, this is becoming far too familiar a situation for my liking." Isla winced as the dagger slid across her throat, releasing a trickle of blood down her collarbone. "You were gentler with your axe."

"Shut up." Eimhir gave her a rough shove. "They're coming."

The doors rattled on their hinges, then flew open as half a dozen Admiralty officers stormed into the room and raised the muzzles of their rifles to point squarely at her chest.

"Stay back." Eimhir's voice was low and gravelly against Isla's ear. "I've no problem spilling this human's blood across your Grand Admiral's floor."

The senior officer narrowed his eyes, regarding Eimhir with a tight expression. "One might call that a fair price to rid our city of another skinchanger."

"And here I thought your kind valued nobility." Isla squirmed as Eimhir drove the dagger deeper into her neck. "This human is one of your guests of honour. Her brother saved the Grand Admiral's nephew. She killed the selkie responsible for the attack on the docks. But if her life holds no value, then I'll gladly end it before you now."

The officer's eyes darted towards Isla before focusing on Eimhir. "If you do that, you'll never get out of here alive."

"One might call that a fair price to rid this world of another human." Eimhir paused, then lowered her voice to whisper at Isla's ear. "Can you get us to the island?"

"I don't know."

"I need you to know." Eimhir's fingers tightened in her hair. Isla felt the desperation in her grip, the pain as she pulled the knots around her knuckles. "Can you get us there?"

Isla tensed, the edge of the blade digging into her throat. "I can try."

"Good, good." Eimhir released a breath, her grasp loosening around Isla's hair. "You know where I'll be. Find me, caraid. I'll be waiting for you."

"Eimhir, what are you—"

The edge of the dagger whipped away from Isla's neck, leaving behind only the sting of where it brushed her skin. The next thing she knew, Eimhir shoved her in the back, sending her staggering towards the line of muskets pointed towards her.

There was a cry, then the shattering of glass.

By the time Isla spun around, it was already too late. Glittering shards from the broken windowpane flew into the darkness, hanging against the cloak of night like stars. In their midst was Eimhir, ragged and bloody, a feral grin twisting her lips as she fell.

"No!" Isla rushed to the window and braced herself against the empty frame. She leaned out, wincing as the broken glass sliced open her palms. Below, the granite wall of the garrison building gave way to a sheer, rocky drop. The waves below thundered and roared, breaking themselves upon the rocks, sending spray into the wind.

The Admiralty officer placed a rough hand around her arm, pulling her back as he peered over the churning water. "It's done," he said. "If the rocks didn't get her, the currents of the firth will. Nobody could survive that fall."

Isla barely felt the squeeze of his grip as he fastened a pair of shackles around her wrists. Her gaze remained fixed on the gaping maw of the broken window, splintered glass jutting out of the frame like fangs. Eimhir had thrown herself through it, knowing what lay waiting to swallow her below.

Nobody could survive that fall, the officer had said.

No human, perhaps, Isla thought. But Eimhir was no human. She was a selkie.

Pelt or no pelt, if there was anyone Isla would gamble on the tides spitting back out, it was her.

CHAPTER TWENTY-SEVEN

Time lost all meaning in the festering bowels of the Admiralty prison. The cells were windowless, severed from the outside world. Day turned into night and back to day again, the darkness unyielding, and Isla stopped trying to count the hours. There was no morning grey or sun-cast shadows, just a gloom smothering her in its dense embrace.

She shifted on the ground, aching from the unyielding stone floor beneath her. The clinking shackles around her ankle echoed off the walls, another reminder of how she had failed. Another reminder of what awaited her when they came to drag her from her cell.

It was all too easy to imagine the noose swaying in the breeze. The scratching of the rope around her neck. The wooden floor beneath her quaking in anticipation, waiting to welcome her into its open jaws.

"You should have left when you had the chance."

Isla lifted her chin to find Quinn standing beyond the bars, eyes glittering in the torchlight.

"You always were stubborn," he continued. "Never understanding when something was meant for your own good. You could have avoided this if you'd only listened to me."

"I've never had any desire to listen to you, Quinn," Isla replied stiffly. "Not then, and even less now."

"But I have so much to tell you." Quinn's smile widened, his teeth flashing in the darkness. "Winning isn't nearly as enjoyable when the losing side doesn't understand how they were beaten. And make no mistake, Isla—you are beaten."

It was difficult to argue. The iron shackles bit into her bare ankles. Her skin was purple from the cold. She was stuck in the depths of a garrison prison, and Eimhir was dying, waiting for help that would never come.

"If you came here to gloat, save your breath," she said tiredly. "I already suspected your hand in too many of my misfortunes. I know you had something to do with the attack in the city vaults."

"Ah yes, your adventure to the sea caves." Quinn arched an eyebrow. "I knew your selkie friend had taken to eavesdropping in the evenings, so I fed him the information in the hopes it would remove the two of them from the townhouse and give me the chance to get rid of them. I must admit, I didn't expect you would be foolish enough to accompany them. That was the first time you exposed your weakness, your affection for the wretched creatures." He curled his lip. "Can you guess what gave you away the second time?"

"Breaking Eimhir out of the district gaol, I wager."

"Look at that—you are capable of learning after all." Quinn tilted his head, appraising her through half-lidded eyes. "I sent one of my buyers ahead, offering a tidy sum for any selkie pelt that had been brought in that morning. An expensive move, but one that paid off rather handsomely, I must say. All this time you spent searching for it, and I had it right under your nose."

"Why? What could you possibly need—"

"Leverage," Quinn answered smoothly. "At first, I thought I might be able to trade it in exchange for your word that you'd leave Arburgh. But after our conversation the night of the storm, I realised you'd never leave your brother, not even for her. You weren't ready to betray him, not then. That would come after." He chuckled, the sound churning Isla's stomach. "I held on to the pelt until a new opportunity presented itself. You see, the Grand Admiral doesn't like it when his trophies are threatened. When he realised what your friend was trying to steal from him, he was only too grateful to receive some leverage of his own."

Isla's heart stilled. "You gave him Eimhir's pelt?"

"I certainly did. He knows what she's after. Now, he has a means of bargaining with her." Quinn ran a hand through his coiffed hair, smiling. "In return, he elevated me to the ranks of nobility. I am no longer a member of the merchant class, but a baron. For now, at least." A wolfish grin spread across his lips. "Now I've made it to the ladder, there's no limit to how far I might climb."

Isla slumped against the wall, the stone chilling her skin. Quinn was right—he'd had the upper hand from the beginning, and she'd been too distracted to see it. Too preoccupied with chasing Muir for answers. Too wrapped up in Eimhir's desperation. She'd lost sight of Lachlan and the snake that had wound around his shoulders, whispering in his ears with a silver tongue.

"What will you do with me now?" she asked.

"Lachlan no longer trusts you, but he still loves you, so I can hardly jeopardise our alliance by throwing you to the Admiralty," Quinn said. "In fact, I've been doing all I can to help him release you. The beauty of the situation is I don't need to do anything, dear Isla. You've lost. You'll be shipped back to that lonely little estate you detest so much while your brother and I take care of matters in Arburgh. Together, we'll carve out real power in this city—power the Admiralty won't be able to contend with."

Isla forced out a dry laugh. "Lachlan doesn't care about power. All my brother ever wanted was to go home, to reclaim what our family lost. By the time I took notice of that, it was too late. If you want to make the same mistakes I did, go ahead. It will be your undoing."

"We'll see." Quinn cocked his head. "I believe that's him coming now.

I'll give you some privacy to say your goodbyes. I wish I could say I'll miss you, but we both know that ship has long sailed. Rest assured, I'll do here what you could not. I won't fail Lachlan like you did."

He disappeared down the corridor, dress boots clacking on the stone as he walked away. Isla buried her head between her knees. Tides *curse* her, she should have known better. Quinn had always been capable of this. Now, he'd outplayed her for the second time. For the *last* time.

As she pressed her knees against her head, she heard the muffled clink of the metal lock as a key turned and the gate scraped across stone. There was another jangle, and a key fell to the floor beside her.

"I'd free you myself, but I have trouble bending over these days." Lachlan said.

The sound of his voice seized Isla's heart, bringing hot tears to the back of her eyes. Tides, how had it come to this? How had she *let* it come to this?

She fumbled with the key, letting out a hiss of relief as the irons around her ankle fell free. Lachlan's hand appeared in front of her, and she slipped her fingers into his, allowing him to help her to her feet as he fought to keep his balance on one leg. When at last she dared to meet his eyes, she found no anger there, no resentment. Only the reminder of everything she'd given up.

"How did you get me out?" she mumbled.

Her brother gave a tight smile. "I told you I could be persuasive when I needed to be."

"Lachlan."

"All right." He let out a long breath. "As far as the Admiralty are concerned, you were an unwilling participant in the events of the other night. They believe Eimhir threatened you into helping her, that you only went along with it to save your own skin. They may think you a coward and a fool, but not a traitor."

"That's not what happened."

"I know." Lachlan's expression darkened. "But they don't, and that's the most important thing. Fortunately for you, I convinced Blair—I mean, Lieutenant Cunningham—to release you into my custody. You're free on the condition that you take up your duties at Blackwood Estate and don't return to Arburgh."

A terrible silence followed his words, lingering in the stale air of the cells like a noose tightening around Isla's neck. Her heart turned cold, deadening all feeling in her chest. Part of her had hoped Quinn was lying, that his words were nothing more than a way to twist the knife one last time.

"I've already arranged a ship," Lachlan continued, bringing his eyes to meet hers. "You'll have protection and a full complement of staff from the capital to help get the estate back to its feet. Galbraith will accompany you and make sure you stick to the terms of the arrangement."

Isla flinched. "You would have me trade one prison for another?"

"Blackwood Estate is not a prison."

"It didn't need to be, but our mother and father made it so. Now you're doing the same." She swallowed, throat thick with tears. "Please, brother. Don't make me resent you the way I resented them. I have no room left in my heart for such things."

"I am not doing this to punish you," Lachlan said, reaching out a hand to brush her cheek. "I'm doing this to save your life."

"I never asked for it to be saved, not like this."

Lachlan drew back. "And I did? You should know better than anyone what it means to sacrifice something that doesn't belong to you." He gestured to his leg, mouth twisting. "I cannot blame you for this. Just as you cannot blame me for the course you decided on. I begged you to stay away from Eimhir, but you didn't listen. *That's* what caused this, not me."

"Did you ever once consider that I wasn't helping Eimhir to spite you, but because it was the right thing to do?" Isla said, heat rising in her voice. "If the gun-anam continue to—"

"And there it is. You can't even see it, can you? The moment she offered you some kind of meaning, some kind of purpose, you couldn't help but cling to her, as if she could give you the belonging our family never could. You know, these last few months, I thought what we were doing was enough for you." A disbelieving laugh tumbled from Lachlan's lips as he rubbed a hand across his forehead. "I thought *I* was enough for you. But the truth is, I never was. That's why you found it so easy to leave all those years ago."

"Wanting to help Eimhir isn't the same as wanting to hurt you," Isla insisted. "There could have been room for both."

"Not after what you did at the garrison." Lachlan fixed her with a bleak stare, his eyes dull and distant. "I looked up to you. Truth be told, your shadow wasn't all that cold a place until you left. That was when I felt it most. All our mother and father could see was what they'd lost, not what they still had. Quinn was the first person to take notice of my worth. He saw things in me they didn't. He showed me what I could be." He pressed his lips together and turned away. "I love you, sister. I always will. But I won't allow you to destroy what is left of this family."

"Lachlan, we *are* what's left of this family."

"I'm no longer sure that's true, no matter how much I wish it was." He turned back to her, his face softening. "I'll work with the Admiralty to resettle and protect Caolaig. When that's done, I'll return to Blackwood Estate. Perhaps then, you'll understand better why I had to do this. Perhaps then, we can start afresh."

"You really believe that's possible?"

"I have to." Lachlan straightened, glancing down the corridor. "But for now, this is goodbye. Galbraith is waiting to collect you from the holding area. He'll take you back to the townhouse so you can gather your belongings before the ship departs later this afternoon."

"That's it?" Isla's voice sounded dead to her ears. "You're willing to let things end like this?"

Lachlan stooped low, adjusting his crutch under his arm as he placed a kiss on the crown of her head. "Farewell, Isla. If tides be kind, we'll see each other again soon."

The uneven echo of his footsteps and scratch of his crutch resounded in her ears like a heartbeat gone awry. Perhaps she deserved to watch him walk away for once. Perhaps this was how he'd felt when she left him all those years ago.

The realisation turned the hollow of her chest cold. She'd lost him. And in losing him, she'd lost the last part of herself tying her to Blackwood Estate, to the place she once called home. Maybe if things had been different, she could have found it within herself to return there with him. But without him, the empty rooms would be nothing more than a reminder of the life she'd run from. The life that had led her here.

She couldn't go back. Not now. And if the tides were determined to fight against her, Isla would meet them head on.

CHAPTER
TWENTY-EIGHT

I sla fumbled with the leather straps of her bag as she packed what she needed for her journey to Caolaig. Some fresh garments, tightly-wrapped parcels of dried venison, a thick woollen scarf. One by one, she slid them into the pack, fingers trembling at the finality of it all. She'd forgotten how simple it was to leave a place behind, to compress her life into something she could carry and walk away from everything else.

This was the first time it hadn't been easy.

She paused, brushing her hand over the wooden stock of her pistol where it lay on the bed. The mother-of-pearl casing glinted in the fading afternoon sun. The freshly polished metal of the barrel shone like new, forgetting the blood and black powder that had stained it.

Use it well, Lucrezia had told her. *Though I pray you'll never need to.*

It seemed like a lifetime ago that she'd stood on the jetty with her old bosun, readying herself to return to the life she'd sailed away from. Caolaig had a way of drawing her back when she wanted it least, like a fish hooked in the gills, unable to escape the pull of the line.

"Are you ready?"

Isla stiffened. She hadn't heard Darce enter the room, but now she knew he was there, his presence was unbearable. It tightened around her chest, squeezing the breath from her lungs. All she wanted to do was push it away—push *him* away. Anything but suffer a moment more in this tension taut with pain and betrayal.

"Won't you look at me?" he asked.

She shoved the pistol into her pack with more force than she intended, then lifted her chin. "I have no more desire to look at you than any prisoner desires to look at their guard, Sergeant Galbraith. Though it seems I have little choice. You and my brother made certain of that."

Darce blanched. His face was drawn and pale, his eyes circled with bruise-coloured shadows as he stared at her with a hollow expression. "They would have hanged you, even with the story Lachlan spun. Getting you out of the capital was the only way he could save your life. I can't apologise for playing my part in that, not if it means keeping you safe."

"I don't expect an apology. As long as you don't expect my forgiveness."

"Isla—"

"No." She spun away as he reached for her, heart thumping furiously against her ribs. "I am no longer your wee wolf cub or a bairn in need of protection. I thought you understood that. I thought you'd begun to see me as the person I've become, not the soft noble lass I might have been if I'd never left." She let out a sharp breath. "I am not afraid of sailing into a storm, Darce. But you keep trying to be my anchor, when all I ever needed was a wild wind to carry me through."

He faltered, dropping his arm to his side. He was still too close—Isla could feel the echo of his heartbeat in the aching sliver of space between them. Part of her wanted to push him away, but more of her wanted to lean into everything his proximity offered: the comforting warmth of his body, the strength in his shoulders as she folded herself into his arms.

"Tell me how to fix this," Darce said, his voice rough and fraying. "Tell me how to make things right."

"It's too late for that."

"It doesn't have to be." He clasped his hand around hers, brushing his thumb over the fading scars on her knuckles. "It was only a few months ago these were bloody gashes because you didn't know when you were beaten. I don't think you're soft, Isla. You're the most stubborn person I know. That's the one thing about you that never changed, the one thing I..." He clenched his jaw. "I was afraid of losing you. But if I go through with what Lachlan wants, I lose you anyway. So I'll ask again—what can I do to make this right?"

Heat rose in Isla's chest at the low urgency of his voice. The force of his gaze stirred something she no longer wanted to push away. It made her want to forget everything beyond the walls of this room, everything she stood to lose.

If she let him in, was there a chance they could save some of it together?

She steadied herself with a breath. "Are you sure about what you're asking? You might not like what I have to say."

"I rarely do." Darce's mouth pulled into a wry smile. "Still, I offered you my word, and I won't go back on it. Whatever you need from me, it's yours."

"I need a ship capable of outrunning the Admiralty fleet. And a crew willing to risk harbouring a dying selkie."

Understanding crossed Darce's face. "You know where the Grand Admiral is keeping the pelt he stole. The one that belonged to Eimhir's aunt."

"I do." Isla gathered up the woollen cloak she'd laid on the bed and threw it around her shoulders. "But before we steal it back, I have an uncle I need to draw some answers from."

Tolbooth was quieter than usual for this time of day. The canalways and cobbled streets still bore the scars of the selkie attack from a month ago, left in the form of boarded windows and barred doors. Half-sunk barges clung to their moorings on frayed lengths of rope, their hulls splintered and seeping with murky brown water.

Isla pulled the fur-lined hood of her cloak over her head, drawing it close around her cheeks. No matter how still the streets were, she couldn't take any chances. The Admiralty wanted her gone. If anyone saw her here, of all places, it wouldn't be a ship to Caolaig waiting for her—it would be the bloodstained cobbles of Gallowgate.

Darce flicked his gaze back and forth across the canals, his mouth set in a grim line. He'd traded his Blackwood armour for a new set of sturdy leathers and a light travelling cloak, the stone-blue fabric worn and fraying at the end. He might have seemed inconspicuous were it not for the fearsome length of his claymore wrapped in cloth and strapped to his back, waiting to be called upon if needed.

"What makes you think your uncle knows anything?" he asked. "From what I understand, he isn't exactly on friendly terms with the Admiralty these days."

"That's why I need to speak to him. Something happened between him and the Grand Admiral, something that cost him his career and nearly his tides-damned life." Isla shook her head. "He warned me to stay away. I want to know why."

"What does that have to do with getting to this island you found?"

"Maybe nothing. Maybe everything." Isla slumped her shoulders. "The tides have already taken too many goodbyes from me. Whatever happens next, Muir is the only family I have left. I don't want to walk away knowing there's something more I could have said."

After a while, they reached the rickety staircase leading up to Muir's apartment. Some of the steps still bore dark stains where Lachlan's poisoned blood had soaked into the wood, turning the graining an ugly red-black.

A tremor worked its way down Isla's spine. There was too much about that night she wished she could forget. Too much she carried with her still, an ache that wouldn't fade.

Darce placed a hand on her arm, holding her back. "Wait. Do you see that?"

Isla followed his gaze, then froze. Muir's door was already open, the edge cracked like it had been forced. They were too late. Someone had got to Muir first.

Darce drew his rapier as he crept towards the door. Isla paused only to slip her hand into her cloak and slide her pistol from where it was tucked into her belt. Then she followed, the wood creaking under her weight as she edged up each stair.

Tides be kind, she thought. *Don't take someone else from me. Not now, not like this.*

At the top of the stairs, Darce nodded. Then he reared back and pushed through the doorway into Muir's apartment.

Isla stumbled after him, chest seizing as she darted her eyes around the room. Someone else had been here. The two moth-eaten chairs lay strewn across the floorboards, collapsed at odd angles. Broken glass and old wax drippings littered the area by the mantlepiece. Fresh bloodstains soaked part of the rug in the middle of the room. But the place was empty. There was no sign of Muir or anyone else.

"He's gone." The words tore at her throat. "We're too late."

Darce glanced around the room. "Whoever came for him didn't have it easy. There was a struggle. Your uncle could have escaped."

"Or he could be in the depths of an Admiralty prison cell, waiting for the noose," Isla shot back. "If the Grand Admiral suspects he was involved in some way, I might have got him killed."

A painful silence stretched between them, punctuated only by the *tip-tip* of ale dripping from the barrel at the side of the room. The stale dregs formed a puddle underneath the tap, foamy and brown, and Isla couldn't help a reluctant smile at the thought of Muir's expression if he'd been able to see so much of the swill wasted.

"Old sot would be scunnered to come home and find it empty," she muttered, sidestepping around the puddle. The tap was stiff and sticky as she screwed it tight, cutting off the last droplets. "There, that should mean there's at least something waiting for when he..."

She trailed off as a glint caught her eye from behind the barrel's stout wooden legs. Something had fallen underneath, its dull, tarnished gleam barely visible amongst the shadows. Isla stooped low and slid her hand under the barrel. Her fingers found something cold and round attached to a delicate chain, and she brought it out to see Muir's old Admiralty compass dangling between her fingers.

A twinge of grief pulled tight as she rolled the brass casing over in her palm. Muir would never have left this behind without good reason. It was the one part of his old life he still clung to.

Isla dug her nails into the seams and prised the compass open. The metal shell was sticky and stained from the ale seeping across the floorboards. Inside, the needle stuttered, swinging one way and the other with no purpose, no true pull. Perhaps it had been damaged by the ale. Perhaps the compass was every bit as broken as her uncle was.

Darce frowned. "What's that?"

"A reminder," Isla said, "of someone I fear no longer exists."

She wrapped her hand around the casing and slipped it into her pocket. Whatever answers she'd come here for, it was too late. It was *always* too late. Her mother and father were gone. Lachlan had slipped through her fingers. Muir had disappeared, leaving behind only the trace of a man she never really knew.

The only person left, the only person she might still be able to save, was Eimhir.

"Let's go," Isla said. "We have a ship to catch."

CHAPTER
TWENTY-NINE

The merchant docks were awash with bustle and chatter, bathed in the golden glow of the fading late-afternoon sun. It was a far cry from the night of the attack, when the storm had whipped up crashing waves and the mist-shrouded piers lay abandoned. Now, Isla marvelled at the normality of it all: the racks of furs and silks and woollen coats huddled under a tarpaulin roof; the creels scraping across the cobbles, cages bursting with fresh catches; the bickering of a cross steelworker bartering with a trader over the cost of ore. Mouth-watering scents of spices and sweet treats wafted from makeshift stalls, making her stomach rumble.

"We need to keep moving," Darce said, his voice low. "The crew of the *Midnight Crest* were told to expect us at high tide to take us to Caolaig. I wouldn't be surprised if the Admiralty sent officers to ensure we get on that ship."

Isla raised an eyebrow. "You don't think Lachlan trusts you?"

"He's shrewder than either of us gave him credit for. He won't leave anything to chance, especially not this." He gestured across the docks. "See for yourself."

In amongst the heaving crowds surging back and forth across the jetty,

Isla spotted the unmistakable jewel-toned capes of a dozen Admiralty officers. They cut through the mass of bustling bodies in blurs of emerald and sapphire, their movements fluid and purposeful. They were searching for something. Searching for her.

Her hand drifted to the reassuring grip of her pistol, hidden beneath the lining of her cloak. One shot wouldn't do any good against a dozen muskets, but the stock against her palm gave her comfort nonetheless.

"If we're to make our move, we should do it now," Darce said.

Isla shrank her face into her hood as she followed him across the docks. She kept her chin tucked as she weaved between merchants and sailors. Now and then, she risked a fleeting glance up, scanning the bustle for the vibrant colours of the Admiralty. Part of her wondered whether Blair Cunningham was among the officers, whether Lachlan's influence with the Grand Admiral's young nephew stretched further than she realised.

Darce tugged on her sleeve. "There it is."

The *Jade Dawn* sat impatiently in dock, its green-stained hull swaying restlessly. Distant figures marched across its deck, casting off sodden ropes thick with seaweed and pulling in the wooden lengths of the gangways. The low groan of timber filled her ears and the splashing of the waves leapt higher as the ship crawled away from the pier.

Isla's heart stilled. They were too late.

She pushed forward, barging through the tangle of bodies, ignoring the indignant glares and angry shouts from the people she pushed out of her way. All that mattered was catching up to the Sea Kith before they sailed out of reach.

At last, the crowd thinned and Isla stumbled through, careening on the slippery wood as she ran to the end of the pier. The *Jade Dawn's* stern was still alongside, slipping slowly through the grey-green waves.

She craned her neck, unable to see anyone over the lip of the gunwale high above. "Captain Nishi?" she shouted, her voice rasping into the wind. "Kerr?"

No sound came from the ship but the deep creaking of its hull as it gathered speed. Isla was close enough to see the stain of the waterline, the coating of kelp and barnacles clinging to its dark belly below the surface. In a few more minutes, it would be beyond her, cutting through the waves in search of the horizon.

"Please, we need your help!" Her throat burned as she screamed the words above the crashing waves. "Eimhir needs your help. You owe her."

"It's over, Isla." Darce put a hand on her arm. "You tried. I'm sorry."

Fear caught in Isla's throat as a dozen Admiralty officers lined up across the pier, muskets levelled at her. One of them stepped forward, wind tugging at the light-brown curls of his hair as he approached with open hands.

Blair Cunningham. The Grand Admiral's nephew had come after all.

"You should listen to your swordmaster, Lady Blackwood." The young lieutenant spoke firmly, but there was no malice in his voice. He fixed her with a look as sympathetic as it was steely. "Your brother warned me you might try something like this. It comforts me to know at least someone among your family remains loyal to the Admiralty."

Before Isla knew what she was doing, her pistol was in her hand, pointed at Blair Cunningham. Her thumb pulled the hammer into place with a click, echoed a dozen times over as the Admiralty officers readied their muskets.

"What are you doing?" Darce whispered. "I know you've got bite, wolf cub, but you can't take on the whole tides-damned Admiralty by yourself."

Cunningham faltered, eyeing the barrel. "Please, put your weapon away and board the *Midnight Crest* like you were instructed. I have no desire to deliver your body back to your brother, but there are only so many lines you can cross. Believe me when I say this is your last chance."

"We have no choice," Darce said at her ear, voice low. "All we can do now is stay alive. Once we're back in Caolaig, we can—"

"Eimhir will be dead before we reach Caolaig." Isla's voice cracked as she tightened her hand around the pistol. Darce was right. They were outnumbered and surrounded, their last chance at freedom slipping through the water behind them. Whatever hope she had left would be carried away in the sails of the *Jade Dawn*, out of reach before she had time to grasp it.

A shadow flickered across her eyes, and she lifted her head to glimpse the familiar silhouette of curved wings against the pink-orange sky. A shrill caw rattled from the bird's throat as it circled above them, gliding back and forth with the wind.

Cunningham fixed her with a solemn gaze. "See reason, Lady Blackwood. Think how disappointed your brother will be should this turn ugly."

Isla unhooked her finger from the trigger, keeping her eyes firmly locked with the lieutenant's as she slid the pistol carefully into her belt. "I'm ashamed to admit I've already disappointed Lachlan more times than I can count. After all that, what is one more?"

Before Cunningham could reply, a terrible screech cut through the air, and Shearwing plummeted from the sky. The razorbill's black-and-white feathers became a blur as it snapped out its wings and pulled from the dive with inches to spare, sending the Admiralty scattering. The sound of musket shots cracked through the air, and another ear-splitting cry spilled from the bird's throat as it banked, coming at the officers with hooked claws.

Isla whirled around. The *Jade Dawn* had peeled away from the pier, slowly turning towards the firth. The stern rose above her, impossibly tall, but all the same she caught a glimpse of Kerr's flaxen hair peeking over the edge of the gunwale. He heaved a coil of rope from his shoulder, then tossed the end, sending it slithering through the air like a serpent.

"Grab on!"

The thick length of rope hit the wooden planks of the pier with a dull thud. Isla snatched it up, the fraying fibres rough against her hands.

Darce gathered a section of rope in his own hands. "It's never easy with you, is it? Though I'm not sure why I expected anything else, given your unfortunate knack for pissing off everyone who—"

The rest of his words drowned in the crack of a musket. A shot whistled past Isla's head, and she craned her neck to see Blair Cunningham staring her down, rifle between his hands and determination in his blue-grey eyes.

Isla tightened her hands around the rope and jumped.

The rope slid through her hands as her weight dragged her down, burning her palms raw. Isla squeezed harder, bringing her legs up to hook around the knot at her knees. Below her, Darce let out a muffled yell as he hit the water, his lower body dragging through the waves as he fought to keep hold.

The green-stained hull hurtled towards them. Isla uncrossed her legs and threw her feet out at the encroaching wooden wall. Her boots slammed off the timber with a painful thud, rattling her knees. She barely had time to readjust her position before the rope yanked. Then she was hurtling up towards the deck, shoulders and legs battering against the hull with every heave.

When at last she reached the edge of the gunwale, strong hands hauled her over, dumping her unceremoniously on deck. She staggered to her feet and rubbed her aching arms as Darce followed, accepting Kerr's help back to his feet.

"Thank you," she said. "I don't know what we'd have done if—"

The rest of her words gave way to a grunt as something caught her in the chest, sending her stumbling backwards. Before she had time to draw breath, Captain Nishi slammed her into the bottom of the mainmast, elbow across her throat and pistol pressed to her temple.

The hammer clicked into place at Isla's ear, sending a wave of fear through her. "Nishi, please. We didn't intend any—"

"Tides take what you intended." Nishi pressed the barrel harder against her head, the metal cool and unforgiving. "Twice now you've asked my crew to put themselves at risk to save your own skin. I'd be a fool to let there be a third time." Her eyes flicked towards Darce. "Stay right where you are, Sergeant. I don't doubt your willingness to die for her, but I'd rather not spill any auld blood if I don't have to."

Darce shrugged off Kerr's restraining hand on his shoulder, face thunderous. "Let her go."

"It's a wee bit late for that." Nishi turned back to Isla, a thin smile on her lips. "You made the choice to come here, after all."

"I didn't come here for myself." Isla swallowed painfully, the pressure of Nishi's elbow hard against her throat. "You told Eimhir if she ever needed your help, you'd answer."

"That promise was made to the selkie, not you. You cannot call in someone else's favour."

"She's dying." The words tore from Isla's throat, brittle and raw. She spat them out like they were poison, the taste lingering on her tongue like a truth she never wanted to admit. "They stole her pelt, and now she's dying. It is not a favour I ask for, but the chance to save her life, as she saved the life of your deckhand during the storm. Would that not satisfy what you owe her?"

Nishi stared at her, copper-brown eyes unyielding. After several tense seconds, she released her elbow from Isla's throat and dropped her pistol. "We Sea Kith do not hunt the selkie folk, but that doesn't mean we're unfamiliar with the fate that befalls them when their pelts are stolen. Too often has the *Jade Dawn's* bow knocked against drifting corpses bearing no wounds but scars of salt. Too often have we disturbed their floating graves, collecting bodies along our keel among the seaweed and barnacles. The selkies may not be friends of ours, but they are of the sea. I respect them more than I respect those so-called admirals in the capital."

Isla rubbed her throat. "The Grand Admiral is keeping her aunt's stolen pelt on an island southwest of Silveckan. If we can take Eimhir to it, she'll be able to claim it as her own. It's her only chance."

"Where is she now?"

"In a sea cave on the south side of the firth. She told me she'd wait for me there."

A frown knit across Nishi's brows, her expression distant. Then she let out a short breath. "She saved MacKinnon, and I named her kith for it. We owe her a life."

Relief flooded Isla's chest. "Thank you, Captain."

"I need no thanks. The tides witnessed my word, and they'll not forgive me if I break it." Nishi glanced at Kerr. "Since you got us into this, you can be the one to prepare the tender to go out to the sea caves. Send Shearwing to scout ahead. I'll need a deckhand to fetch me my charts too."

"I'm afraid your charts won't do us much good," Isla said. "The Grand Admiral wanted to keep this island hidden. You won't find it on any standard map."

Nishi narrowed her eyes. "Then how do you expect us to get there?"

Isla moved to the edge of the ship, running her hand along the rough wooden surface of the gunwale. The *Jade Dawn* groaned and sighed, timber creaking as it picked up speed through the waves. Its emerald sails fluttered overhead, full with the wind. This was not her ship, yet its deck felt as familiar as the *Ondasta's*.

"I'm a navigator." Something fierce swelled in her as she spoke, and the words left her mouth like unsung truths, finding freedom in the wind. "I'll get us there."

Nishi snorted. "I like your spirit, but this isn't the Adrenian Sea. You're used to clear skies to map the stars, no mists to obscure the horizon and render that pretty sextant of yours useless. If your island is where you say it is, we'll be sailing deep into the Strait of Silveckan. Wild be those waters, and unforgiving too. Do you really think you can navigate them?"

Ahead, the horizon lay waiting. The sun's pale light slipped out of sight, leaving behind only a lingering glow across the tips of the waves. For now, all was calm, but Isla could already imagine the storm gathering in the distance. It would spread across the sea like a shroud, blocking out the horizon. It would do its best to drag the *Jade Dawn* to the fathoms, and all of them with it.

Something lurched in her heart. There was a time she might have thought it fear, but now she knew better. These Silvish waters might have been wild, but she was meant for them.

"Aye," she said. "I believe I can."

Night fell across the waves as the *Jade Dawn* slipped from the firth into the open waters. A blanket of purple-black clouds draped across the sky, snuffing out all light from the stars and waxing moon. If any Admiralty ships had set off in pursuit, they would find no sails on the horizon, no trace of their wake among the churning swell. The cloak of darkness had ensured their escape, but that was not enough to quell the frantic thrumming in Isla's chest.

Eimhir was out of time.

Only a few days had passed since the night of the civil reception, but they weighed on Eimhir's face in scars and shadows. She'd all but collapsed on deck after being carried off the tender, barely able to hold her own weight. The ropy muscles of her arms had lost their shape. Her skin stretched over her face, peeling around her cheekbones and the strong line of her jaw with bloody scabs of salt.

Isla sat beside her and pulled a sheepskin blanket close around them both. "If you won't go below deck, you need to stay warm. There's a chill in the air tonight."

Eimhir shifted her weight and pulled the blanket to her chin. Her shoulder brushed against Isla's, sharp and bony. "I appreciate the thought, caraid, but the cold cannot hurt me now. I am already numb to its touch. What has taken root inside me will take more than a blanket to chase away."

"We'll get you to the pelt. We'll make this right."

A faint smile spread across Eimhir's lips, splitting open the cracks until droplets of blood welled from them. The trails of salt across her skin gave her a strange glisten, like she was petrified in stone. Isla was half afraid to look at her for fear she might crumble before her eyes.

"If I didn't believe you, I might surrender myself to the fathoms tonight," Eimhir said, her voice dry and rasping. "But I know better by now than to doubt you. Sometimes I think your will outmatches that of the waves themselves."

Isla chuckled. "Darce calls it stubbornness."

"Aye, but the sergeant is as blunt with his words as he is sharp with his blade," Eimhir said. "Still, I'm glad he's here for you. After what happened with your brother..."

Her words lingered, all the louder for being unspoken. Lachlan's absence was like a splinter buried beneath the skin. The more Isla tried to push it from her mind, the deeper it burrowed, until all she felt was its constant, nagging pain, a reminder of a wound still too raw to soothe.

"My brother made his choice," she said stiffly. "I've made mine."

She pushed herself to her feet, tucking the length of the sheepskin blanket behind Eimhir's frail, bony back. "Try to rest. If tides be kind, the dawn will bring a new beginning."

Eimhir's pale eyelids fluttered shut as Isla turned and climbed towards the bridge. The wind whipped her hair loose from her braid and stung her cheeks as she pulled herself up the steep wooden steps of the quarter-deck. Above her, the sails billowed furiously, their emerald tones as dark as the sky behind them.

Nishi stood at the helm, her dusky brown skin worried with creases as she thumbed the wheel. "No surprise there's a squall coming. But there's more than one storm on the horizon, and it's not this one that worries me."

"What do you mean?"

"I have no love for the Admiralty, but I am not so foolish as to seek to make an enemy of them either. We Sea Kith stay out of matters of the land." Nishi released a long sigh as she surveyed the horizon. "Yet for better or worse, we're caught up in this now, and maybe it's right we are. We claim to be of the sea, yet we ignore the Admiralty's violence on the waves as long as it is not aimed at us. We ask spirits of salt and spray to come to our aid and offer no protection in return when the trawlers and hunting boats pillage their waters. I fear if we do nothing, there will soon be little space left for us to exist in peace."

Isla's throat tightened. "I'm sorry for dragging you into this. When we met in Kinraith, I never expected any of this to happen."

"Fickle be the waves. We can only go where they take us." Nishi shrugged. "I gave Eimhir my word that she could count on our help. All you did was ask me to uphold that which should never have been in question." The corner of her mouth pulled into a grudging smile. "You would do anything for your crew. That is the sign of a good captain."

Isla choked out a laugh. "I may be mistaken, but I'm fairly certain a captain needs a ship. The only thing awaiting me at port is a trip to the gallows."

"A ship is only part of it. Finding one's purpose on the open water, one's home on the waves—that is the true calling of a captain. It's something we Sea Kith understand well." Nishi tilted her head. "I know not where the tides will take you, but I can tell this much: the sea is in your blood, Isla Blackwood." She nodded to the horizon. "Now, it's time for you to prove it. Show me our next heading."

Isla pulled a rolled-up sheet of parchment from her cloak and spread it on the small wooden table beside the helm. The makeshift chart was blotched with seawater stains, its edges already curling. Isla had detailed their course from Arburgh in careful lines, marking down each drift, each change in heading. The island lay somewhere in the blank space—still hidden, still unblemished by the ink on the end of her quill. All she had to go on was her memory, the fleeting glimpses of silver-etched lines atop the ebony desk in the Grand Admiral's office. But as long as she was certain of where they were, she would be able to find where they needed to go.

"Another five degrees south," she said, running her finger across the parchment. "From there, we should approach the island from the west."

Nishi grimaced. "That heading will take us into Beira's Passage. I only ever made the crossing once, fighting swells the height of the *Jade Dawn's* main mast. Those are treacherous waters. No ship would dare risk the wrath of those currents without at least one sentinel on board. Are you certain your island lies there?"

"I started plotting a course that night at the garrison. The guards came before I could finish it, but I remember where the island lay." Isla rolled up the parchment and slipped it into her cloak. "The heading is the right one. If the crossing is so treacherous, I'm only more convinced. What better place for the Grand Admiral to keep his most precious trophy than an island protected by swells only a sentinel has a hope of breaching?"

Nishi's lip ring glinted as she smiled. "Well, let it never be said the Sea Kith fear to sail where an Admiralty vessel has already gone." She heaved on the wooden handles of the helm, pulling on the giant wheel with one hand as she consulted her compass in the other. "Five degrees south, as you said. Our course is set. If tides be kind, we'll reach your island by high noon tomorrow."

Isla turned her gaze to the churning waves. "And if they're not?"

"Then we sail into the storm, Blackwood." Nishi flashed her teeth. "And pray the *Jade Dawn* sees us through the other side."

CHAPTER THIRTY

I sla felt the change in the ship the moment they hit Beira's Passage. There was something different about the roll of the deck, the way the hull bucked and swayed. These were more than choppy waters; the waves were hungry for timber and sail, throwing themselves high into the wind like rising walls.

"The currents here run wild and deep," Nishi had warned her. "If Beira wants to feed on our hull tonight, I fear even Kerr won't be enough to save us."

It was only now Isla understood what she meant. Salt and spray stung her eyes as she fumbled across the deck, hands wound around the guide rope to keep herself from slipping on the slick surface. Her boots squelched, the chill of the water biting through the sodden wool of her stockings. She barely had time to gather her breath before the ship crashed down again and another huge wave swept over the prow, engulfing the entire deck.

Isla squeezed her eyes shut as the water crashed over her, doing its best to rip her away. When it subsided, she spluttered helplessly from her nose and throat, the salt sharp on her tongue as she coughed out seawater.

"If you think it's bad now, wait until we hit that squall." Nishi stood staunchly at the helm, grappling with the handles as the *Jade Dawn* leapt and crashed against the waves. Her tricorne hat had been swept away, and her hair clung to her cheeks, coiling at the ends. She spat a mouthful of seawater onto the deck and shouted, "I want everyone at their posts! And those sails better be stowed proper this time. The fathoms aren't likely to let us escape twice."

Isla hurried towards the rigging and met Darce rushing across the deck, his footsteps clumsy on the slippery surface. "Isla, you need to—"

"If you're about to tell me to take shelter below, save your breath. We can't afford to lose our heading. Nishi needs me on deck."

"Give me a chance to speak, will you?" Darce grasped her shoulder. "It's Eimhir. She's taken on some kind of fever, but it's nothing like I've seen before. Her sweat is thick with salt, and all it does is burrow deeper into her skin. She scratched herself bloody before exhaustion took her. She's sleeping now, but I don't think her suffering has eased any for it. I'm not sure she'll make it until morning."

A sickening touch of dread crept into Isla's heart. "She must. There's no other choice. If she doesn't claim the pelt, the gun-anam—"

A distant rumble resounded through the air, smothering the rest of her words. It was like the storm heard her. As if it too knew what was at stake and had crawled across the waves to stop her.

She fixed her eyes on the bleak horizon. A roiling wall of black clouds crawled across the water, stretching like terrible wings. It carried with it the haze of rain—silent at first, then filling her ears with the distant whisper of a roar that grew and grew until it unleashed its fury on the deck.

Isla flinched as the droplets hammered off the wood and lashed at her cheeks, rattling her skull. The squall had caught them. Their only way out now was through the other side.

"Eimhir will hold on," she said, raising her voice against the wind. "She must. And I need to help Nishi keep our heading. If we lose our course now, we lose everything."

Darce didn't answer. His eyes were fixed on something far on the horizon. "Look."

Isla followed his gaze. A flash of lightning illuminated the storm clouds and the shadows within.

Her blood froze. She knew those shadows.

"The gun-anam." Darce's voice was a breath at her ear, half swallowed by the wind. "I can feel them from here. It's stronger than last time, like they're singing in my blood." He shuddered, shaking the rain from the ends of his hair. "You know I never wanted this. Would never have chosen it. But if this magic in me might help ward them off..."

"Forget it," Isla said sharply. "I already told you, I want no part of your sentinel oath. Keep your blood in your body where it belongs."

"If you would just *listen*—"

She pushed past him and clambered towards the stern. Already the deck was streaming with water, rippling along the timber like a river as the ship rolled from one side to the other. Through the blur of rain, she could make out the hazy figure of Nishi in the distance, teeth gnashing as she heaved the huge helm around in her hands.

"Captain!" Isla yelled, fighting against the roar of the wind. "Prepare for—"

Her lungs filled with icy seawater as a monstrous wave crashed across the deck. It swept her from her feet, engulfing her in its watery jaws before it spat her out against the gunwale. She hit the wooden hull with a sickening thud. Pain shot through her shoulder, turning her vision black. Her lungs seized as she tried to breathe, choking on the water she'd gulped down.

She managed to roll onto her hands and knees and retched across the wood, salt burning her throat on the way out. When she lifted her head, all she could see through the rain were blurry shapes charging across deck, their frantic footsteps pounding against the timber.

Darce rushed to her side, his arms firm around her waist as he carefully helped her to her feet. A nasty gash had opened on his temple, blood mingling with rainwater as it trickled down his cheek.

"They're coming," Isla said, her voice rasping. "I have to warn Nishi."

"She'll realise soon enough." Darce shrugged the leather straps of his claymore from his back and drew the huge sword from its wrappings. Isla remembered the silvery blood-like substance dripping from its edge the night Darce burst into her room at Blackwood Estate all those months ago. She hadn't known what the gun-anam were back then. All she'd felt was the icy fear from their presence, a fear that settled bone deep.

Now, it was different. Now, she knew exactly what she was afraid of.

"They're here," she whispered. "The mist..."

She pointed towards the bow, fingers white. Overhead, the shroud of black storm clouds still clung to the tips of the masts, rumbling with thunder and flashing with sheets of lightning. But around them, the salty air was dense and pale. The mist drifted in slowly, unaffected by the violent gusting of the wind as it crept across the deck.

The chill turned her lungs to ice. Already the puddles across the deck glistened silver as they became glassy and brittle. The mist clung to her, trailing its cruel touch across her skin, colder than the lashing rain. Frost formed on her cheeks, her lips. Her fingers turned from white to blue. Every hair on the back of her neck stiffened.

That was when the first shadow emerged.

Before Isla had time to raise a scream, the gun-anam drifted forward, its wraithlike form little more than a drizzly haze. It slowly lifted one of its shapeless arms, then plunged a sword of mist and spray through the throat of one of the deckhands.

Isla clapped a numb hand over her mouth as the deckhand fell. The woman hit the timber with nothing more than a gurgle, a river of red spilling from her throat. The blood seeped into the wood and dripped through the cracks into the ship's hold below. Its rusting iron stench churned Isla's stomach. She remembered that smell: the rot and flayed flesh scattering Blackwood Estate. The bloated bodies washed up on the blood-soaked shore of Caolaig. She'd seen this before. She knew how it ended.

Darce charged, swinging with both hands as he leapt towards the gun-anam. Isla braced herself for the harsh clang of steel on steel as the wraith brought its sword up to parry Darce's furious blow. Instead, the blades met with the roar of the sea. They crashed into each other like waves, echoing with the scatter of spray on the wind.

Isla fumbled at her belt, wrapping her hand around the hilt of her cutlass and drawing it loose. This wasn't Blackwood Estate. There was nowhere to run. If she was to survive, she had to fight.

The gun-anam swirled towards her, trailing mist across the deck. She lunged desperately, sweeping the blade in a low arc to drive the wraith back.

It was a sloppy blow. Too frenzied, too rash. Her sword met thin air, the momentum of her swing sending her stumbling into the gun-anam's path.

Isla froze.

Darce didn't.

It was over in a single stroke. Darce's claymore swung through the rain, cleaving through where the wraith's neck might have been. The wisps scattered and spilled across the deck in silver droplets, streaming along the timber to return to the sea.

Isla stared at the puddle. The creature was gone. Not killed—not any more than rain and mist and memory could be killed—but the chill of its presence dissipated amongst the drizzle, releasing the tightness in her lungs.

"Your swordplay still leaves much to be desired," Darce said, steadying her with an outstretched arm. "It's clear to me now why you prefer pistols."

Isla snorted. "And here I was, too polite to mention how stiff you looked swinging that claymore of yours. Are you certain your shoulder has fully healed?"

"As well as can be expected." Darce winced, rubbing a hand across the place the selkie's axe caught him during the attack on the docks. "Your concern is touching."

"Don't flatter—" Isla broke off at a shrill shriek overhead. Shearwing circled above, flapping its giant wings like it was trying to chase away the mists. Over the howling wind, the clash of swords filled her ears.

Darce met her eyes. "More of them. I fear they'll only keep coming."

"Then we'll have to keep stopping them."

Isla staggered towards the stern, fighting to keep her balance as water surged over the deck. The mist was closing in thicker. She could barely see the riggings of the mast or the far edge of the gunwale. Even the thunder was muffled beyond the dense shroud settling around the ship.

Nishi fought by the helm, grappling with the handles with one hand and brandishing a rapier in the other. The needle-like blade glinted as she danced around a gun-anam, silvery droplets flying from the sword's pointed tip. Kerr stood beside her, white hair plastered to his cheeks as he cast wards and traps across the deck. A gun-anam drifting towards him hit a protective enchantment like it had run into an invisible wall, dissolving into a silver puddle at Kerr's feet. Another sank down into the deck until it became a swirl of agitated wisps. Isla imagined the *Jade Dawn's* sea spirits furiously dragging the wraith through the ship's belly, returning it to the water it came from.

"Blackwood, watch out!"

She spun around at Nishi's warning, raising her cutlass in time to meet a fearsome blow from another gun-anam. The wraith towered over her, its faceless breath reeking of rot and salt. Her arm went numb as she pushed back against its blade. Tendrils of mist snaked across her skin, seeping into her muscles.

"Tides...take you," she spat.

The wraith gave a watery roar and reached for her with its other hand. Isla gritted her teeth, swinging her blade desperately towards the place that might have once contained a heart.

The cutlass slipped from her grasp and clattered against the deck. Isla stumbled against the rigging. The gun-anam was nowhere to be seen. Perhaps she'd scattered it into mist. Perhaps she'd managed to...

Her eyes fell to the silvery droplets on the deck. Already they were rising, swirling into the mist sweeping across the length of the *Jade Dawn*. It was all she could see now, white and dense, so thick with water she felt like she was drowning with every breath. Her heart slowed, blood chilling in her veins.

In the distance, someone screamed. Isla couldn't see who it was. She couldn't see anything.

She dropped to her knees, sliding her hands across the slippery wooden surface as she crawled towards the sound. Muffled cries and agonised screams echoed through the mist from every direction. A pair of boots appeared in front of her, then disappeared as they were dragged backwards, leaving a bloody smear across the timber. Bile rose in the back of her throat at the stench of piss and blood and brackish salt water.

Her hands fell upon something soft, and she recoiled as she recognised the touch of cold, wet flesh. One of the Sea Kith lay bloated and crumpled on the deck, eyes distant and glassy. Seafoam spilled from their still lips. Their skin glistened translucent blue.

They couldn't win, not against this kind of enemy.

Isla crawled into the small alcove under the stairs leading to the quarterdeck, squeezing her legs to her chest. Her teeth chattered until she could barely feel her jaw. Each breath came shallower than the last. Tides, she was so *cold*. It was too much to bear, too much to—

"Isla? Isla!"

Through the numbness, she felt a strong pair of arms wrap themselves around her. Holding her. Keeping her from drifting apart, from losing herself in the mists threatening to suffocate them all.

"Darce?" His name tore from her lips, leaving her throat aching. She looked up to see his dark eyes staring back at her, filled with calm acceptance.

"Please," he said. "You have to let me do this while we still have time."

There was no movement in the mist. Perhaps the gun-anam had taken their fill. Perhaps they were the only ones left.

She shook her head violently. "I won't let you bind your life to mine just so you can keep your promise to my father. You deserve more than those kinds of chains."

"Is that what you think this is about?" Darce choked out a laugh. "Isla, you're a bloody fool."

"Isn't it?" She wrenched herself from his grip and pushed herself to her feet. "You got us out of Blackwood Estate because it was what he wanted. You stayed with us because he asked you to protect us. Now you want to offer your tides-gifted soul? I couldn't bear being the one to take your freedom from you, Darce."

"And I couldn't bloody bear it being anyone else." He stared at her as the rain hammered down between them. Droplets clung to the ends of his hair and dripped down his cheekbones. His dark brown gaze held her in place, sending a shiver through her that had nothing to do with the wet or cold.

"Darce…" His name brushed her lips, sending a painful ache through her chest. Something deep and dark and full of want pooled inside her, begging to be let free. This was what she'd wanted. *He* was what she wanted. But not like this, not from desperation or duty or—

"It's not about my promise to your father," Darce said, breaking through her thoughts. "It hasn't been for a long time. Maybe it was easier to lie to myself, to tell myself that's why I couldn't leave your side. It gave me something to hide behind, something to keep away the truth." He shook his head, sending water flying from his hair. "It's not about him. It's about you."

His sword thumped against the deck. Then his hands were on her cheeks, his grip tender and unrelenting all at once. He held her, gaze sharp and questioning, until he seemed to read something in the flash of her eyes or the hitch in her breath or the way she leaned in and—*tides*, his lips were on hers.

The taste of him was all salt and rain, but Isla didn't care. She'd drown if it meant she could feel the press of his mouth against hers for even a moment longer. His lips were soft and wanting as they parted, and Isla met them with a need she'd never known before. The rain streamed down between them, but all she felt was the firmness of his hands on her face, the gentle insistence of his tongue as he kissed her deeper. She forgot the cold, consumed instead by urgent longing. Tides, she forgot how to *breathe*. Nothing else existed but the way he was holding her like she might drift apart in his hands, the way he was tasting her like there was nothing else he wanted on his lips.

Too soon, he broke away, eyes dark as they trailed over her. Something warm and wanting pooled in Isla's chest, sending a tremor through her entire body. She didn't want him to stop. She *never* wanted him to stop. Even now—*especially* now, if this was the end.

Isla wound her fingers around his as she removed his hands from her cheeks. "You have an odd sense of timing. But if we're for the fathoms tonight, I can think of worse things to take with me."

"That won't happen," he said hoarsely. "There's still a way I can get us out of this, if you'll only let me."

"Darce, I told you I—"

The rest of her words died in the gasp of breath she drew into her lungs. Another wave leapt across the deck, its waters black and churning. But this one didn't wash across the timber and crash against the masts. Instead, out of its crest grew a creature. It rose from the foam, striding from the water in a silent equine gait.

The gun-anam's dread mount. The kelpie.

Isla staggered back, dragging Darce with her as she stumbled across the rain-soaked deck. The kelpie tossed its watery head, standing on rippling muscles of sea and spray. Isla could smell its brackish reek, thick with salt and rot and death. She couldn't move. Her legs froze solid, fixing her to the deck as the beast stared at her with empty eyes half obscured behind a mane of mist.

Trembling, she lifted her eyes to its rider. There, she saw the snarling jaws of the seal skull that had haunted her dreams since the night at Blackwood Estate. The empty eye sockets turned on her with their dead, fathomless glare. Whatever manner of spirit this gun-anam was, it could see her. It had always been able to see her.

The wraith slipped off the kelpie's rippling back, drifting to the deck in a cloud of mist. Its armour of blackened bone dripped seawater in a silvery trail at its shifting feet. All Isla felt as it stalked towards her was the chill in her throat. Her skin turned brittle as the wind bit into her with cruel, cold teeth.

The gun-anam reached towards her with a watery hand. Isla tried to scramble back, but the numbness had burrowed through her flesh. She couldn't move. She couldn't do anything but wait for the wraith's icy touch to freeze the air in her lungs and drown her in her own body.

"Isla, no!" Darce's breath clouded in front of him as he grabbed his claymore from the deck. His fearsome blade flashed as he swung the sword in a cleaving arc aimed at the gun-anam's seal-skull head. It was a blow full of fury, full of desperation. Isla could see the weight of it as the claymore drove through the air, edge sharp and hungry.

The gun-anam reached out its hand and caught the blade.

Isla froze. There was no splatter of silver, no scattering of mist. Instead, watery tendrils crept across the steel. The droplets circled and chased each other, winding together until the length of the sword was wrapped in drizzle and wisping vapour.

The blade shattered.

Darce stumbled, his face ashen as he clutched the broken, jagged hilt in both hands. He stared at it in disbelief as the gun-anam advanced upon him, his mouth pale and gaping.

Do something, Isla begged silently, her lips too numb to speak. *Don't let it end like this.*

It was too late. The gun-anam reached out its wisping arm, encircling Darce in its grasp. Darce's face turned the colour of bone, all the colour leached out under the gun-anam's deathly touch. His throat quavered, releasing a gurgling sound. Seafoam spilled from his blue lips.

The gun-anam reached its arm to the sky and drew a dagger from the mist. Isla could only watch in horror as the blade swirled in the air, shimmering with rain.

Darce threw her a wistful look filled with pain and regret. Then the dagger fell.

"No!" The scream ripped from Isla's throat, shattering the ice in her breath. Something loosened in her chest, and then she was running, running for the blade on its way to Darce's heart.

She crashed into him, knocking him out of the way in a tangle of limbs. She might have followed him to the deck, but something was holding her upright, pinning her in place.

It didn't hurt, not at first. She was too numb for that. Then the cold seeped in. It entered somewhere between her ribs, biting like a shard of ice with its teeth in her gut. The chill crept to her sternum. She was drowning and freezing all at once. She was drifting away like the mists.

Isla trailed a hand to her stomach. Something warm and wet gushed around her fingers, the heat from it burning her palm. She brought her hand to her face, staring at it through blurred, hazy eyes. A red, sticky substance slid between her fingers. Blood. Her blood.

The gun-anam reared back, a bloodcurdling shriek resounding from behind its seal-skull mask as it pulled its blade from her stomach. The keening filled Isla's ears. It sounded like the bottom of the sea racing to meet her, dragging her to its crushing depths.

The creature hesitated, its wisping form drifting between her and Darce. Then Eimhir struck.

She appeared from nowhere, barefoot and shivering under layers of thick fur. Isla barely had time to register the glint of the axe in her hand before she leapt, swinging the flat blade towards the gun-anam with a desperate ferocity. The gun-anam slunk back and Eimhir leapt again, charging with a snarl on her salt-scarred face. The furs slid over her shoulders as she brought her arm back and swung the axe again, the blow hacking and wild.

A low, watery hiss escaped from the jaws of the gun-anam's seal skull. A deep gash split it down the middle, cracking it open so the silvery vapour seeped out. The wraith stilled, turning its ghastly head between them. Then it swept back, rising in a column of water as it mounted the kelpie.

Eimhir roared and leapt after it, but the dread mount reared its rotten, brackish head, sending spray flying across the deck as it charged to the edge of the ship. A moment later it was gone, leaping over the gunwale to plunge into the roiling waves.

Eimhir turned, her face drained of colour. "Caraid, what did you do?"

Darkness seeped in at the corners of Isla's vision as she fell. She was vaguely aware of something firm latching around her waist, holding her together, pressing against the bloody gash in her stomach. Hazy figures surrounded her, barely more than shadows. It all seemed so distant, so out of reach.

Someone leaned over her, flaxen hair falling about his cheeks. Kerr, she remembered. The sentinel. He cast a worried look over her, then gestured to someone behind her. "Your blood, Sergeant. She needs it now."

"It's too late," Darce said, his voice hoarse.

"Did you think we sentinels were the only ones who had to make a sacrifice for the blood oath?" Kerr said. "Both captain and sentinel must spill their blood for the bond to forge. She's done her part. Now it's time to do yours."

Isla craned her neck to find Darce by her side. His face was gaunt and pale as he clutched the broken hilt of his claymore in both hands, knuckles white.

"Don't," she gasped, the effort burning her lungs. "I can't accept it, Darce."

Nishi knelt beside her and took her hand. "You already have." She pulled down the collar of her shirt, exposing a deep scar down the centre of her chest. It was an old wound, faded, mingling with the ochre-coloured tattoos swirling around her collarbone. "You made your choice, like I did. Now, your sergeant will make his."

Her words hung in the air, clinging to Isla's skin like the mist. She lifted her chin, heart aching as she met Darce's gaze. There was no doubt there, no hesitation.

He drew the broken blade across his palm. The jagged edge sliced open the skin cleanly, and Darce's blood spilled out.

"I was already yours," he said quietly, and pressed his hand to her side.

Isla screamed. A white-hot pain ripped through her as Darce held his bloodied fingers against her wound. Her back arched as it coursed through her body, chasing away the ice in her blood, boiling her veins.

As suddenly as it came, the pain subsided. It drained from her body, leaving her hollow and numb. Isla gasped for breath, but tasted no air. She was drowning again. This time, she did not fight it. She let herself float away in the arms of the sea, cradled by the waves. When she blinked, everything faded. The blurred figures disappeared, their voices drifting off with the wind.

Yet through it all came the comfort of carrying something with her, something she never had before. And when she allowed the darkness to take her, she felt a piece of Darce follow.

CHAPTER
THIRTY-ONE

W hen Isla awoke, the storm had passed.

She knew it before she opened her eyes. She felt it in the languid motion of the hull, swaying gently. No water dripped from the cabin roof. No tired groan came from the wooden walls. The swells that had battered the *Jade Dawn* had subsided. They'd made it through Beira's Passage.

Isla pushed herself up on her elbows, wincing as the wound in her gut twinged in protest. The pain rippled through her abdomen, but its bite was not as sharp as the previous night. It was as though the worst had already passed, like she'd awoken to find herself already half healed.

Then she remembered.

Darce.

She bolted upright, finding his slumped, sleeping form on the other side of the cabin. His crop of black hair fell across his forehead, covering the deep gash along his temple. There was a deathly pallor to his face, his eyelids still as he slept. The lips she'd kissed only hours ago were bruised and cracked, parting with the strained rhythm of his breathing.

"I never understood how a sentinel's magic worked, but I suppose now it makes sense." Eimhir sat on the edge of the bed, voice weak and rasping as she surveyed Darce. "After all, do we selkies not do the same? To pass on a pelt means spilling blood for another. Perhaps we are more alike than I ever realised."

"Is he..." The question caught in Isla's throat, raw and aching.

"Kerr says he'll recover, but it will take time," Eimhir said. "After all, he gave up part of himself to save you."

Darce's breaths were shallow, the rise and fall of his chest ragged. Something in Isla seized, though whether it was guilt or yearning or regret, she couldn't be sure. All she knew was that she'd done this to him. He'd made a bond in blood to keep her alive. It was everything she'd ever wanted, and everything she'd ever feared.

Tides, what had he *done?*

"If you're feeling up to it, we should head above deck," Eimhir said. "The captain told me to bring you to her once you woke. She'll explain it to you better than I can."

Isla swung her legs off the side of the bed and slipped her feet into her boots. The leather squeaked from the water, the woollen lining still damp around her stockings. She pulled on a fresh linen shirt and cloak, then followed Eimhir through the *Jade Dawn's* musty corridors to the main deck.

The sky was free of storm clouds now, instead streaked in orange and pink as the sun pushed over the glittering line of the horizon. Isla spotted Kerr at the gunwale, face tired but determined as he moved his hands in shifting patterns, muttering under his breath.

"Keeping the waves calm," he said, by way of explanation. "I expect it to be easier now there's two of us on board with the auld blood in our veins. The tides favour us this morning."

Isla flushed, unable to speak. The reminder of what Darce had done for her—what he'd given up for her—sat heavy in her heart, weighing her down like an anchor. Every time she thought of him, something pulled tight in her chest.

She lifted her head, searching the deck for the captain. Nishi stood by the helm, her lip ring glinting in the morning light.

When she caught sight of Isla, she beckoned her with a blunt hand. "Glad to see you made it through the night, Blackwood. It's never certain that the blood oath will take. That's what makes it so much of a sacrifice."

Isla pursed her lips. "I still don't understand what happened, or why Darce did what he did. I told him—"

"What you told him doesn't matter. Your actions spoke truer than any words possibly could." Nishi sent her a knowing smile. "I showed you my scar last night, didn't I? It happened a long time ago, back on my previous ship when I was but one of the crew. We were boarded by pirates. Brutish, violent thugs who wanted to kill more than they wanted to steal. One of them tried to run Kerr through with a sabre. I put myself in front of him, like you did with Darce last night."

Isla's eyes drifted to the collar of Nishi's shirt. The faded edge of the scar was still visible on her tattooed chest. "You were willing to give your life for his."

"Aye, and *that's* the nature of a blood oath. It is not something that can be forced unwillingly. You have to want it. You have to mean it. I took a fatal blow for Kerr, and in return he spilled his blood for me. Auld blood knows what it means to sacrifice. It creates a promise between captain and sentinel, a bond not easily broken. It was that bond that saved me all those years ago. The same bond that saved you last night."

"But now Darce is bound to me."

"And you to him." Nishi gave her a pointed look. "It is not as terrible a fate as you fear. You're alive, aren't you? As is the sergeant. I only wish I could say the same for all my crew." She drew her dark brows into a frown, face falling. "We lost too many to the fathoms and more still to those tides-damned creatures that came out of the mist. Had I known what my word would cost me, I might not have given it so freely."

"And I would not have asked you to keep it," Eimhir said. "It was never my intention to see you suffer."

Nishi closed her eyes and let out a long breath. "Forgive me, selkie. My heart is heavy this morning and my words sharp for it. My people know better than most how the tides provide for us as much as they punish us. There is a balance to the sea, one which must be kept. That is the nature of the auld ways and the promise I made you. I cannot regret keeping to it." She lifted her chin. "But those creatures that attacked us... Two decades I've sailed for, and never have I seen anything like them."

Eimhir stared at the waves. "We selkies call them gun-anam—the soul-less. They are what happens when one of us loses our pelt. We surrender ourselves to the sea and become one with the spray, haunted by what was taken from us. Perhaps they know my time is near. Perhaps they came for me."

Isla turned to Nishi, fear pulling tight. "We have to find that island. If Eimhir can't claim her aunt's pelt, she'll die. She'll become one of them."

Nishi gestured to the open waters. "We drifted too far off course, Blackwood. Lost our bearings during the attack. I have little idea of where we are, much less where this island is. The best we can hope for now is to head south and make berth in Bréchon."

"Bréchon?" Isla's heart stilled. "But Eimhir..."

Eimhir drew her lips into a crooked smile. The pink skin was cracked and peeling, the corners crusted with salt. "You tried, caraid. That is what I will take with me when I go."

"We can't give up. We've come too far for that. We've lost too much." Isla's voice cracked, tears welling in her throat. "I won't let all this be for nothing. I can't."

She walked over to the edge of the ship, pressing her hands against the gunwale as she leaned over and looked at the waves below. The sea had quietened, rolling in languid swells that yawned and sighed as they crashed against the hull. The morning sunrise settled into a pale yellow-grey with patches of blue sky. All she could see in the distance was the far-off line of the horizon. No island. No land at all.

Perhaps it *was* over. Perhaps this was how it was to end, regardless of how unfair it felt. The tides didn't care what she'd given up to get here.

They were fickle. They had a will of their own, one she couldn't match, no matter what Eimhir said.

Something cold pressed against her stomach, and she opened her cloak to find Muir's compass dangling from her coat pocket. Its brass casing was covered in blood, staining the already-tarnished metal a dark red. She wiped it off as best she could and flicked the seam open with her thumb, watching as the needle swept around in her palm.

Isla frowned. The needle wasn't moving like it had before in Muir's house. There it had been listless, sliding whichever way she'd tilted the compass. Now, it strained against the angle she held it at, pulling around to a determinate point no matter how she moved it. It was working. It had found something.

She flipped the compass over, fingers trembling as she wiped off more of the blood. It smeared across the dull golden casing, settling into thin, intricate grooves carved into the brass.

Isla stilled. Etched before her eyes was the same sea serpent she'd seen on the map carved into the Grand Admiral's desk. There, it had looked like nothing more than a decorative flourish, a cartographer's imagining of a mythical guardian around the island. Now, she realised what it truly was. The Cirein-cròin of legend. Muir's namesake from his time in the Admiralty.

Tides, she was right. Her uncle was involved in this somehow. He'd left this for her.

She snapped the compass shut and raced over the deck, boots sliding on the wood as she hurried to the helm. The wound in her stomach twinged furiously, sending pain across her ribs, but she pushed it from her mind as she came to a skittering halt in front of Nishi.

"I have it," she said breathlessly. "I have our heading."

She flicked the compass open, heart racing as the needle jittered and swung, coming to rest in the same place it had before.

Nishi pulled her own compass from the pocket of her long, two-tailed captain's coat to consult it. A frown fell across her face. "That trinket of yours has seen better days. It's pointing us due east, not north."

"No." Isla locked eyes with Eimhir. "It's pointing us to her aunt's pelt."

The spit of land appeared on the horizon later that morning, a shadow between sky and sea. At first, Isla thought she was imagining it. Perhaps it was nothing more than a trick of the sunlight as it broke on the sea's blue surface. She held her breath as the *Jade Dawn* sailed closer, fearing the speckle in the distance might disappear if she did as much as blink.

It wasn't until they dropped anchor that Isla allowed herself to believe she was right. A formation of craggy sea stacks rose from the waves, their rocks stained yellow with lichen. Behind them lay an inlet with white sands and brilliant turquoise shallows, a shoreline far too peaceful for the wild waters surrounding it. They'd done it. They'd found the island.

Unfortunately, the Admiralty had got there first.

A shiver prickled Isla's skin as she peered through the spyglass to the far side of the island. There was no mistaking those black sails and snarling figurehead. The massive hull barely moved with the waves. Its masts stretched to the clouds like wooden pikes. It was a ship like no other, a ship that could chase away even the gun-anam.

The *Vanguard of the Firth*.

"More trouble," Nishi said. "I may not like the Admiralty, but facing down the pride of their fleet in uncharted waters isn't something I'm prepared to do."

"Nobody will have to face down anything." Eimhir appeared beside them, her face drawn. "You delivered me to where my aunt's pelt is being kept. As far as I'm concerned, whatever favour you owed me has been fulfilled. The rest is for me to do alone."

Isla flinched. "You can't do this by yourself. The Grand Admiral will be waiting for you."

"I am not afraid of him, weak as I am. He owes me a reckoning for what he stole, and I will see it through." She drew her lips into a ragged smile and placed a hand on Isla's shoulder. "You are my caraid, Isla Blackwood. You showed me a human can be worthy of friendship, worthy of trust. You made me believe in something that should have been impossible. But this is not your fight."

"I made it my fight when I chose to help you. I don't regret that. The only thing I'd regret is letting you face this alone."

"I won't be alone for long." Eimhir turned her gaze towards the island, the wind ruffling her crop of dark blonde hair. "My ancestors are waiting for me. It's past time I find them."

"Eimhir, wait!"

It was too late. By the time the words left Isla's mouth, Eimhir was already on the gunwale. Her bare feet were streaked with salt and grime, curling around the wooden lip as she bent her knees. The furs slipped from her shoulders as she threw back her arms, leaving her shivering in a light linen tunic. Scars of salt mingled with the gooseflesh across her marred skin as she balanced there, wavering for only a moment before bending her knees and leaping into the waves below.

Isla rushed over to the gunwale, only for a strong hand to pull her back. She wheeled around to find Nishi holding a fistful of her cloak.

"We might be through the worst of Beira's Passage, but the currents around these waters are still too strong," she said. "If you go in after her, you'll be dragged to the fathoms. I don't want to be the one to tell your sentinel we lost you while he slept."

"Then help me get onto that beach."

Nishi fixed Isla with a sombre gaze. "Take the tender. I'll give you as long as I can, but if that ship begins to move, we'll be gone. I am no friend of the Admiralty, but I cannot give up more than I already have to help you."

"I understand." Isla hesitated. "Tell Darce..."

"He'll know. And if we've left this place by the time he wakes, he'll find his way back to you. He is your sentinel, after all." Nishi extended her hand. The ochre and terracotta swirls of her tattoos peeked out from under her sleeve, dancing across the dusky brown of her skin. "Remember what I said, Blackwood. The sea is in your blood. If ever the time comes you decide to make a life for yourself on the waves, the Sea Kith would welcome you among our people."

Isla's shook Nishi's rough, callused hand. "Thank you. For everything."

Minutes later she was in the tender, knuckles white as she clutched the oars and waited for the boat to hit the water. This close to the waterline, Isla saw how tired the *Jade Dawn* looked; its proud hull was cracked and splintered under the green paint, its keel besieged by kelp and barnacles. She'd asked more of the ship and its crew than she ever deserved. If it wasn't here waiting for her when she returned, she couldn't blame the Sea Kith for it. Not after what they'd already done.

Once the ropes were loosed, Isla began to row for the island. The waves were stronger than she expected—her arms burned with every heave, and a painful trickling from her stomach told her she'd re-opened her wound with the force she was putting into each stroke. She still felt the ghost of Darce's touch against her skin, the way he'd poured part of himself into her.

Something strained at her heart, as if the distance she'd put between them was already too great.

He'll find his way back to you, Nishi had said.

Isla could only hope she was right.

She pushed on, forcing the pain and doubt from her mind as she neared the island and slid the tender into the sand with a crunch. The water shimmered under the sun, so crystal-clear that Isla could see scatterings of shells and delicate strands of seaweed under the surface.

It wasn't at all what she imagined. She thought the island would be a grim and foreboding place, with crumbling ruins shrouded by mist.

She expected to find her surroundings leached of colour—sand like ash beneath her feet, thickets of gorse and bracken dead and spindly. Instead, its breathless beauty tugged at her. Of all the places the Grand Admiral could have chosen to hide his trophy, he'd picked here. Not a fortified vault buried under the capital, but an unprotected haven under the open sky.

Why? Isla thought. *What is this place to you?*

She followed Eimhir's footprints over a gentle knoll, the yellow-green fronds of brittle beachgrass rustling in her ears with the wind as she picked between the sand and stems. Over the wash of the waves she heard the call of the island's birds: an oystercatcher's whistling chirps, the throaty caw of a circling skua, the rattling rasp of tiny corncrakes in the grass. Nothing else disturbed the air but the shifting of sand beneath her feet and the ragged breaths tearing from her lungs.

She clutched Muir's compass in her hand, following the needle as it twitched. Every step tightened the squeeze of her heart against her ribs. It wasn't just Eimhir's trail she was following—it was her uncle's. His compass had led her here. The map bore his legendary namesake. Isla wasn't sure she wanted to consider how he might have been involved. She didn't have time to dwell on those kinds of fears, not when Eimhir was walking straight into—

The crack of a gunshot ripped through the air, scattering the silence. Isla jumped as a flock of nesting gannet took flight in a jumble of caws and cries, white wings clapping as they fled from the rocky shore.

She quickened her pace, sliding over the top of the next dune and trampling through dry fronds of beachgrass as she followed the sound of the gunshot. Further ahead stretched a brilliant green machair, the flat grassy plain teeming with orchids and wildflowers. At first, Isla couldn't see anything. Then she caught sight of a flat white slab nestled amongst the grass. As she crept closer, she saw it was made of marble, covering a set of stairs leading underground.

Her eyes fell across the small cairn of pebbles beside the entrance. The stones had been placed carefully, each one gleaming and polished. It was the kind of reverence one might reserve for a grave or a crypt, not a vault for hiding stolen trophies.

Something wasn't right here.

A low groan came from the bottom of the stairs, and Isla crept into the darkness, hand on her pistol. The air was dry against her cheeks as she slipped down each step, praying her boots made no sound against the shifting soil.

When she reached the bottom, she lowered herself to the ground and peered around the corner. Eimhir was leaning against a limestone block in the middle of the small chamber, blood pouring from her shoulder.

On the other side stood the Grand Admiral.

Isla sucked in a breath. She'd only caught a glimpse of Alasdair Cunningham at the garrison, his face half hidden behind a mask. Now she saw the man the rest of Silveckan referred to only by his title. He had the same blue-grey eyes as his nephew, the same soft curls framing his cheekbones. But the circles around his eyes spoke of something darker, a weight that showed itself in every shadow, every crease of his skin.

Eimhir pressed a hand against her bleeding shoulder, baring her teeth in a feral grin. "You think a wee bit of blood will stop me from claiming what is mine?" She spat on the ground. "I came here willing to spill far more than this. You'll have to do better than that."

The Grand Admiral made no reply. Instead, he drew a small lead ball from the pouch at his waist and slipped the shot into the chamber of his pistol. The gun was a long, sleek thing, beautiful and dangerous. Isla caught a glint of black pearl set amongst the polished ebony stock. That pistol knew violence. She could tell from the way it nestled against his palm, waiting coldly for his command.

The Grand Admiral raised his arm, pointing the barrel at Eimhir's head. "Spill all the blood you want, lass. It won't change anything. You are not the only creatures who know of the auld ways. My sentinel sealed this chest using my blood, and only my blood can open it. You've come all this way for nothing."

It was the first time Isla had heard him speak. She'd expected his voice to sound cruel, but instead it brushed against her ears in a soft burr.

Eimhir clenched her jaw. "The way I see it, you've just given me another reason to kill you."

"I'm sure you'd like to try." The Grand Admiral drew his mouth into a thin smile. "But this is the end for you, selkie. Tides take you, like they should have long ago."

The barrel of the pistol was a pinprick in the darkness. In a heartbeat, it would be over.

Isla burst from the bottom of the stairway, hand steady as she pointed her own pistol squarely between the Grand Admiral's eyes. The wooden stock sat patiently in her hand as she cocked the hammer. "If the tides take her today, I swear they'll take you too," she said. "I suggest you choose your next move wisely, Grand Admiral."

He swung around, bringing his pistol to bear on her. But he did not pull the trigger. Instead, the gun trembled in his hand and a deathly pallor drained all the colour from his face.

"Mara."

The sound of it was profound on his lips, uttered in a single breath as he stared at her with stricken, unblinking eyes. It hung in the air, its weight echoing through the silence. The word brushed against Isla's ears, begging to be heard.

She tightened her grip on the pistol, her heart turning to ice. "What did you call me?"

"Mara," Eimhir echoed, her voice half a whisper. "But... No, he couldn't have. It is a name he cannot know. One he has no right to speak."

"I don't understand."

"Neither do I." Eimhir looked dazed, her words muttered half to herself. "Mara is the name of the selkie we lost to his greed. The name of the selkie whose pelt he stole all those years ago."

Isla turned to her, unable to stop the shiver across her skin. "But that would mean..."

"Aye." Eimhir swallowed, face paling. "Mara was the name of my aunt."

CHAPTER THIRTY-TWO

A cold fist curled in Isla's stomach. Her body felt weak and dizzy, like it had somehow betrayed her. She was acutely aware of the sweat beading across her forehead, the dread churning in her gut. Something was *wrong*.

"How is this possible?" The Grand Admiral was still staring at her, pale and transfixed. "Your hair, your eyes... You look just like her."

A hard lump lodged in Isla's throat. She swallowed, wrapping her fingers tighter around the pistol. "Whoever you think I am, you're mistaken. My name is Isla Blackwood. We've never met until now, but I believe you're familiar with my uncle." She drew Muir's compass from her coat pocket, dangling the chair between her fingers. "It's thanks to him I found this place, after all."

The Grand Admiral lowered his arm, his hand shaking as he brought the pistol to his side. Something in his expression changed. His eyes held a haunted shadow, his face white as he stared at her, aghast. "The compass led you here? No, I would have known. I would have..." He trailed off, his mouth closing around the rest of his words. "It can't be. Muir, what did you do?"

"He left me a way to find this place." Isla clutched the compass in her fist, the brass casing sticking to her palm. "I always wondered what he did to get himself exiled from the Admiralty. Now it's all becoming clear. He discovered this island for you, didn't he? He was a great navigator. He found the perfect place for you to hide your precious trophies. But you couldn't bear someone else knowing how to get here. It was too much of a risk. That's why you cast him out. You wanted to make sure Muir never stepped foot on a ship again."

"You don't know how wrong you are." The Grand Admiral said, voice hoarse. "Muir...your uncle...was my most trusted sentinel."

Isla stilled. "That can't be true. He wasn't—"

"He was. The auld blood ran strong in him. He was more powerful, more loyal, than any of my other admirals. A seafarer with no match, save perhaps for the Cirein-cròin itself." A tight smile strained the Grand Admiral's lips. "You're right about one thing—he did find this island for me. He helped me build this place and used his sentinel wards to protect it. He hid its location behind a means only blood could unlock. A means you now possess."

Isla's eyes drifted to the tarnished golden chain the compass hung from. Flecks of red still covered it, dry and flaking. The needle hadn't worked when she'd first held it back in Arburgh. It was only after the storm it began to swing. Only after she'd smudged her bloody fingers over its dull casing.

"But that doesn't make sense," she whispered. "I'm not of Muir's blood."

"The compass wasn't bound to Muir's blood." The Grand Admiral met her eyes with an unflinching gaze. "It was bound to mine."

Isla's cheeks turned numb. She felt the colour drain from her face. All she wanted to do was scream her lungs dry or double over and retch.

The compass wasn't bound to Muir's blood. It was bound to mine.

It wasn't true. It *couldn't* be true.

"A daughter." The Grand Admiral looked at her, eyes shining in disbelief. "*My* daughter. After all this time..."

331

"Don't listen to him, caraid." Eimhir buckled against the stone block in the middle of her room, her voice no less fierce for how weak it was. "Your uncle's compass must work in some other way, by some other magic. You cannot trust a word he says. He killed my aunt, our last dreamwalker. He stole her pelt."

"Killed Mara?" A flicker of emotion darkened the Grand Admiral's face, though whether it was anger or grief, Isla couldn't be sure. "You don't understand a thing, do you? I didn't kill her. I... I loved her."

A ghostly silence hung from his words, broken only by the snarl ripping from Eimhir's throat. "Liar," she hissed. "What would a human know about loving a selkie? You wanted her pelt, nothing more."

The Grand Admiral drew his lips into a thin line, his face taking on a haunted pallor. He looked at Isla, fixing her with a stare that turned her heart to stone. "I will not hurt you, child. Just as I would never hurt Mara. She saved my life."

Isla's fingers trembled around the pistol as she lowered it a fraction of an inch.

The Grand Admiral's eyes darted to the pistol, then back to her. "It was nearly thirty years ago, during a bad summer storm out in the Strait," he said. "I was younger then, more reckless. In trying to secure one of our lines, I was thrown from the ship. I knew the moment the waves crashed over my head that I was going to drown. The fathoms were waiting for me. I had accepted my fate. Then *she* came." He swallowed, his eyes glazed and distant. "She carried me to safety. She watched over me until I woke. And when I saw her for the first time, I knew I'd find no greater beauty in this world, no greater love."

"Love?" Eimhir's voice rattled. "You took what you wanted from her and left her to die."

"I loved her," the Grand Admiral said. "And she loved me. When the Admiralty's search party finally found me on that ragged scrap of rock, she returned with me to Arburgh. We began a life together, in secret. I never cared about what she was. She was enough."

A low growl rumbled from Eimhir's throat. "More lies. The sea is everything to my people. She would never have left it willingly, not for anyone. Especially not a human."

"And yet, she did. I understood better than anyone what kind of sacrifice that was." The Grand Admiral lowered his head. "I'd have given up the sea and everything it offered for the chance to keep her with me. In the end, that was my mistake."

A shudder ran through Isla's body. She parted her lips, trying to find the strength in her voice to speak. "You took her pelt."

"She left me no choice." The Grand Admiral's expression hardened. "At first, I was content to let her return to the sea. She always came back. But as the years passed, she stayed away for longer each time. I feared that one day, she'd leave for good."

Eimhir barked out a harsh laugh. "So instead, you stole her soul from her. You claimed you loved her, yet you were content to let her wither and die in front of you?"

"No," the Grand Admiral said. "I could never bear to see her suffer. Every month, I brought her to this island. I returned her pelt and let her bathe in one of the tidal inlets. It was not what she wanted, but it was enough. It wasn't what I wanted either, but it was the price I had to pay for keeping her with me, keeping her safe."

"The price *you* had to pay? What about her?" Eimhir shot Isla a desperate look. "You've already heard enough. Kill him now, and let us be done with this."

Isla shook her head. She couldn't push away the coldness seeping into her at each word the Grand Admiral uttered. She didn't want to hear any more, but she *had* to. This was the truth she'd been searching for, the answers always just out of reach.

"Muir," she whispered, his name sticking in her throat. "What part did my uncle play in all this?"

"He was my finest sentinel. I trusted him with my life, with Mara's life. He didn't like me taking her pelt for safekeeping, but he went along with it because I asked him to. He was a loyal dog, until he wasn't." The Grand Admiral's voice took on a dangerous edge. "Muir lost her. I could never forgive him for that."

"She ran away, didn't she?" Something hot and fierce swelled in Isla's chest. "She chose to die rather than stay with you."

The steel disappeared from the Grand Admiral's expression, easing the bitter lines on his face. Even in the darkness of the crypt, Isla could see the glistening of his blue-grey eyes, wet with tears. "I never believed Mara would flee without her pelt. She told me what would happen to her, how much she would suffer. I couldn't understand why she would do that to herself. Now I see you, and the truth is obvious."

Cold sweat trickled down Isla's temple, and her fingers slipped around the pistol. "What is the truth?" she managed, voice shaking. "I want to hear you say it."

"Mara was your mother. She left...for you." He bowed his head, salty trails streaking his cheeks. "All these years I thought Muir was merely careless in letting her escape. But he must have known she was with child—with *my* child. He must have helped her. How else could you have ended up where you did?" He let out a short, bruised laugh. "Isla Blackwood, you said? Of course, he sent Mara to his sister. You look just like her, just like them both. Perhaps that was why Muir risked everything to help Mara. She always did remind him of Cat."

Tides, but it all made sense now. The shock on Muir's face when she'd knocked on the faded paint of his door, like he'd seen a ghost come back to life. The fear in his voice when he'd told her to stay away from the Grand Admiral. The way his fingers had fumbled to the compass he kept in his pocket, aged and tarnished as it was.

I promised her, he'd said. *I promised them both I'd do whatever it took to keep you safe.*

Now, finally, Isla understood. "He tried to protect me. They all did."

"Muir took from me that which was most precious. Not only once, but twice. And the second time, I didn't even know." The Grand Admiral lifted his chin, meeting her gaze. "You need no protection from me, child. If you believe nothing else I have told you today, you must believe that. You are all that is left of her. You are mine."

Isla didn't want to believe it. She wanted to unhear every word he'd spoken, to scratch at her ears until they bled. But the truth was there in front of her. No matter how much she wanted to push it away, it could not be ignored.

There is something I must tell you, something I should have told you long ago, and it requires words a quill cannot do justice to.

There it was—the memory of desperate words scratched on parchment, the ink black and guilty. The tattered scraps of her mother's letter were gone, lost to the depths of the river, but the echo of them still remained. Every word was like a whisper against her ear, the ghost of Lady Catriona's voice strained and pleading.

Come home, my child. Allow me to give you the gift I have kept from you for too long, before it is too late for us both.

The weight of the truth settled around Isla's heart, filling it with lead. Her mother knew. Her father knew. It was why they'd tried to keep her from the sea ever since she was a bairn. They understood what they were protecting her from, even when she didn't.

Grief pulled tight in her chest. This wasn't what was supposed to happen. There should have been something *more*—an understanding that seeped into all the cracks that had splintered and widened over the years, filling in the spaces that had been missing. Instead, she only felt numb. An aching chill curled inwards, eating through her bones, leaving her hollow inside.

Eimhir stared at her, face sallow and marred. Gone were the rage and doubt clouding her eyes. The only trace of emotion left on her salt-crusted skin was the crease in the middle of her brow. "Could it be true?"

"There's only one way to know for certain." Isla slowly lowered her pistol, returning it to her belt with one hand as she reached for her cutlass with the other. The Grand Admiral didn't move. He watched with shining eyes as she drew the blade back and sliced the edge along her palm.

She winced as the blood welled up, hot and stinging against her skin. The red droplets oozing from the gash felt like they belonged to someone else, someone she'd never known. If what the Grand Admiral said was true, this was his blood. But it was also her mother's blood.

Selkie blood.

The stone chest stood in front of her. Isla held her breath as the blood trickled across her white skin and dripped onto the rough limestone block below.

Each drop hit the lid with a faint *tip*. They quavered, thick and glistening. Then they sank into the stone, slowly spreading in dull, fading splotches of red.

Isla froze. Nothing happened. The stone chest stared back at her, grey and unyielding. Maybe Eimhir was right. Maybe the words the Grand Admiral had spoken were all lies.

Then came the crunch of stone, and a crack appeared in the middle of the chest. Isla watched in horror as the lid parted in the middle, the huge slab splitting in two as the stone slid back into the walls of the chest with a gravelly rumble.

Her mouth turned dry. There, lying in the musty shadows, was the pelt they'd been searching for.

A stolen soul.

The pelt was a grey bundle of rags, dull with dust. It didn't have the familiar sheen Eimhir's had before it was stolen from her. How long had it been locked here in the darkness? How long had it waited in this tomb, separated from the bones and blood that once gave it life?

Part of her wanted to reach out her hand and bury her fingers in the fur, lifeless and grimy though it was. But Isla couldn't move her arm. Something had taken root, paralysing her, crushing her heart and lungs until she could hardly breathe.

She glanced at Eimhir, her throat raw with anguish. "It's yours. She was your blood too. It belongs to you."

"No." The Grand Admiral's words rang out harsh and brittle. Isla dropped her cutlass, hand flying to the pistol on her belt, but it was too late. He had already levelled his at Eimhir, his expression hard and unrelenting.

"Wait." Isla scrambled forward, juddering to a halt when the click of the hammer rang in her ears. Her hand trembled around her own pistol as she held it outstretched, finger poised on the trigger. "Please, if anything you've said is true, you won't hurt her. She is Mara's family, like I am." Grief rose in her chest, constricting her throat. "I don't understand. All these years, you've hunted selkies. Stripping them of their pelts. Killing them. *Why?* If you loved her, why do this to her people?"

"Because she *chose* them." The Grand Admiral rasped out each word, eyes glittering. "I loved her, and she left me for them. For nearly thirty years, I blamed them for that. But now I see she didn't choose them—she chose you." A tremor danced through his jaw. "If I had only known, I might have been able to forgive her, forgive them. Now, it's too late."

"It's not too late. Eimhir is her niece. She's *dying*." Desperation seeped into Isla's voice. "Mara would want her to have it. She'd want you to save her."

A strange expression fell over the Grand Admiral's face. A shadow dark with hope, or maybe the death of it. It twisted his features, bringing to the fore all the grief and bitterness and betrayal written across the years. It gave her a glimpse of the man he was. Worse than that, it showed her the monster he'd become.

There was no hope for him. There never had been.

"You will not take what is left of her from me," he whispered.

A heartbeat of silence lingered. Then Isla squeezed the trigger.

The crack of two shots echoed around the crypt. One lodged in the dry, earthy wall behind Eimhir, whistling past her head. The other bit into the Grand Admiral's chest with a soft thump.

Isla stilled. Her pistol was warm against her palm; she felt the beat of her pulse in her finger as she loosened it from around the trigger and lowered the gun to her side.

The Grand Admiral stared at her, his blue-grey eyes sharp with pain. His mouth closed around a name that might have been hers. Then his gaze clouded and dimmed as he folded in on himself and slumped to the ground. Blood seeped in a wine-coloured stain across his white shirt. His head hung low and limp.

Isla's grip shook around the pistol. She gulped down a breath hot with the remnants of burnt black powder. The last living part of her was gone. Killed by her own hand.

No, she realised. Not the last living part. Not anymore.

She thrust the gun into her belt and grabbed the cutlass from the ground. The pelt still lay in the darkness of the stone chest. Isla grabbed it with one hand and threaded her other arm around Eimhir's shoulder, helping her towards the stairs. The fur felt dead, devoid of any lustre or comfort. It scratched at her palms, rough and brittle. Perhaps that was for the best. The pelt wasn't hers, not truly. Not when taking it would come at the cost of Eimhir's life.

Pale autumn sunlight streamed down as they struggled across the machair, wading through the long grass and colourful bursts of wildflowers towards the shore. When they reached the sand and beachgrass of the dunes, Isla half dragged Eimhir up and over the shifting summit, stumbling down the other side to the beach.

The turquoise shallows lapped against the sand as Isla laid Eimhir down by the water. Eimhir parted her salt-scarred lips, sucking in rasping breaths. Isla heard the struggle in her lungs, the wheeze at the back of her throat. She was out of time.

Isla tore her cutlass from her belt. The blade was still smeared from where she'd sliced it across her palm. "Your blood," she said. "I need your blood. Forgive me."

Eimhir's eyes clouded. The parts of her face that weren't scratched bloody were caked in salt. Her cheeks were sunken, lips cracked. This was the only way to save her. Why, then, was she staring at Isla with grey sorrow? Why did she look as though she'd already given up?

"I cannot take it." Eimhir choked out the words. "I thought I was the last hope for my people, but it's not me. It's you. You are Mara's child. You have the best chance of inheriting her dreamwalking gifts. It has to be you."

Isla took her hand. Her palm was callused and bloody, rough with salt. She brought Eimhir's knuckles to her lips. "I won't do it. Not if it means losing you, my friend. My caraid. My cousin." Her voice cracked, sending a painful ache through her heart. "Please. I don't want you to—"

A rattling caw broke cut her off, and she leapt back as Shearwing flitted past and landed on the shore with a heavy splash. The bird cocked its head, watching her with beady eyes as the waves lapped against its huge webbed feet. It opened its fearsome beak, exposing its yellow gullet as it released another throaty caw.

"What do you think it's doing here?" Isla asked.

Eimhir gave no answer. A pale shadow settled over her eyelids, and only the faintest of breaths escaped her bloodied lips.

Shearwing spread its huge feathers, white belly flashing in the dying sunlight as it took off, skirting the leaping waves towards a ship on the horizon.

The *Vanguard of the Firth*.

The ship sat still and imposing on the distant waves, its black sails hanging like shrouds from its masts. She didn't want to go anywhere near it. Why was Shearwing...

Kerr's voice filled her ears. *He is our scout, our guidebird.*

Tides, it was *here*. Quinn had given Eimhir's pelt to the Grand Admiral. And the Grand Admiral had brought it with him.

The turquoise water glittered in the sunlight. She could see down to its crystal depths, where swaying fronds of seaweed and scattered periwinkle shells nestled against the white sand. The hush of the foam against the shore was like a whisper calling her. It knew as well as she did where she belonged.

Eimhir lay in the sand, pallid as the grave.

"I'll come back for you, cousin," Isla said softly.

She removed her boots first. The waves lapped around her ankles, numbing her toes as she spread them against the sand. Then she slid off her breeches and pulled her linen shirt over her head, letting the garments sink beneath the waves. The wind nipped at the bare skin of her collarbone and snatched at her hair. Its cold teeth worried her waist, brushed across the tender gooseflesh of her breasts. There was nothing left between her skin and the sea.

The pelt lay in a heap near her feet. Isla stooped low and gathered it in her arms, brushing her fingers across the fur. It felt weightless, absent of the burden it should have contained after all she'd gone through to get it. The fur slid easily over her skin as she pulled it into place around her shoulders.

Her cutlass lay in the sand, half submerged by the retreating tide. She picked it up and rested the blade against her wounded palm. This was it. If she did this, there was no turning back. She'd be making a choice she couldn't regret, couldn't run from.

Shearwing was a speck against the clouds, retreating further and further every second. If she was to follow, she had to do this now.

The blade trembled in her hand. Isla took a breath, then drew the edge across her palm, widening the gash already carved into her skin. Blood poured out anew, silky red in the fading orange light. She smeared her palm across the fur, leaving ugly stains against the grey.

It wasn't enough.

Isla grimaced, then flipped the cutlass and turned it inwards on her stomach. The half-healed wound burst open again, spilling blood across her bare skin. It spread across her belly and down her naked thighs, seeping into the pelt hanging loosely around her body.

Something changed. The pelt stirred against her skin, shifting against her prickled flesh. A strange sensation bled from the fur, sinking in through her pores and dissolving somewhere inside her.

She looked down at the pelt spilling across her shoulders and legs. It wasn't drab and lifeless anymore. The grey fur had so many tones it seemed as if it was in motion, ebbing back and forth like the sea from the shore. There were dappled patches of blue, almost black, like the darkest depths of water, and flecks of white like sunlight fracturing the surface.

It was beautiful. It was hers.

The pelt melted into her skin, cascading across her flesh. It was itchy at first, but not painful. Fur spread over her, a blubbery layer forming over what was once human skin. The inside of her lips ground, and she felt the odd sensation of her jaw elongating, her bones becoming denser. Her teeth grew longer and sharper, forcing her mouth into a new shape. Her tongue turned thick and coarse.

She was changing.

The flesh of her legs fused together, and she fell headfirst into the water. At first, she panicked, forgetting how to breathe. Everything was blurry as salt stung her eyes. She squeezed them shut and winced at the crunch of her bones as they twisted into new shapes: her spinal cord stretching into a streamlined arch, her arms retreating into her torso as webbed rubber grew at the nubs, ending in bony claws that were once digits. She lost all sensation in what had been her feet; instead, a thick hide grew beneath her, splaying into twin flippers. She felt her organs compress and expand, shifting position in the hollow of her chest.

When she opened her eyes again, the sea had changed. The water was no longer blurry but sharp and glittering, drawn in outlines from the refracted sunlight streaming down from the surface. The colour had disappeared, blues and greens leached from her vision, but the mottle of shifting greys and blacks somehow seemed more beautiful than the vibrant hues she'd been able to perceive with her human eyes.

She turned towards the open water. There, little more than a shadow in the distance, was the submerged keel of the *Vanguard of the Firth*. She saw the seaweed and barnacles clinging to the timber. She saw the rusting anchor holding the ship in place.

It was waiting for her.

Isla flicked her hind flippers, something fierce and wild rising inside her. The sound of the ship echoed in the chamber of her ears. The currents brushed against her whiskers. Down here, she had no need for stars or sextants.

For the first time she could remember, she knew exactly where she needed to go.

CHAPTER
THIRTY-THREE

S wimming through the water in selkie form was like returning to a place Isla never knew existed. There was something *right* about the way the sea felt around her, the way the water slid over the arch of her back and the webbing of her flippers. Her new body moved in ways she hadn't known it was capable of. Her senses shifted, detecting movement and sound and sensation where her human form couldn't. Invisible currents brushed against her wiry whiskers, sending signals to her brain. Her rubbery nostrils closed against the water without her realising it.

Ahead, Shearwing plunged through the surface, wings pinned against its long body as it hurtled through the water. It circled around her, then shot forward, flapping hard. The angles of its wings looked more like fins as it pierced through the currents, leaving a trail of bubbles in its wake.

Have you never seen a razorbill dive? Kerr asked her once. *They are creatures of the sea as much as we are.*

As Shearwing swam beside her, Isla sensed a whisper of consciousness in the bird, a presence to it she hadn't felt before. Kerr was right. The razorbill was of the sea, like she was.

She followed the bird as it slipped through the water. Her streamlined body glided with ease, filling her with a giddy rush that might have made her laugh had she been able to. It was so effortless, so natural. Part of her never wanted to resurface at all, unless it was to fill her lungs with salty air before diving down again.

Then she saw the looming hull of the Grand Admiral's ship and remembered exactly why she was here.

Quinn's taunting words rang in her ears. *He knows what she's after. Now, he has a means of bargaining with her.*

A ripple of grim satisfaction ran through her. It was too late for Alasdair Cunningham to bargain with anyone. The Grand Admiral was dead.

She only hoped it wasn't too late for Eimhir.

The *Vanguard of the Firth* was as foreboding below the waves as it was above, its keel like a shadow blocking out the sun. The selkie part of her knew it was a place she should stay far away from. The human part understood that too, but understood even better that she had no choice.

The iron-wrought chain of the ship's anchor hung steady in the gloom, stretching from where its crown nestled in the seabed to the glittering fractals of the surface above. Isla swam up to it, circling cautiously as she rose higher. It would be difficult to climb, but there was no other way. If Eimhir's pelt was on board, she had to find it.

Slowly, she let herself float to the surface. Once her head broke through the choppy waves, she focused on allowing her pelt to peel back from her body. The sensation of bones grinding and organs shifting was as unsettling as before, but the transformation seemed quicker this time. Her sealskin shrank back until it was nothing more than heavy, sodden fur clinging to her skin. It had been shapeless before, but now it curved across her bare shoulders and across her chest, falling in long folds around her thighs like a tunic-dress.

Isla filled her lungs as she fought to keep her chin above the waves. The water was colder than when she was in selkie form, already numbing her fingers and toes. The spray tasted sharp and brackish as it splashed her face. Her soft flesh and flailing limbs were strangers in this place. She had to find her way to the *Vanguard's* deck, to put groaning timber beneath her feet once more.

She hauled herself out of the water, wrapping her hands around the huge links of the chain and pulling herself up one arm after another. Her muscles felt stronger than they ever had. Each movement was coiled and powerful as she dragged her weight higher. She clasped her feet around the dangling chain, soles scratching painfully on the rust.

Isla climbed higher, fingers numb and arms burning. She'd left the leaping spray far below. The water was so distant she didn't dare look down. All she could do now was find a way from the chain onto the ship.

Isla gritted her teeth. It was only too likely the Grand Admiral had kept Eimhir's pelt close, and the captain's quarters would be at the stern. To get there without being caught would be impossible if she continued to the top of the chain and crawled onto the *Vanguard's* deck. Her only choice was to cling to the hull and go around.

She twisted her neck to glance at the tackles attached to the lower shrouds. The coiled loops of rope hung from wooden blocks above a series of long platforms set along the side of the ship. If she was quiet in her movements and kept herself below the level of the gunwale, she'd be able to traverse to the stern.

"Tides, if I could ever count on you for anything, let it be this," she muttered.

It was a small swing from the anchor's chain to the first platform. Isla braced herself, then leapt towards the wooden shelf. Her arms sprawled over the slippery surface and she pulled herself up, huddling against the ropes in case anybody on deck heard.

The platform creaked as she slid between the taut lengths of rope looping from the tackles. There was barely room to keep her balance as she edged towards the end of the platform. The slightest slip would send her tumbling to the waves below, likely with a nasty knock or two against the formidable hull.

Another creak came from the timber as Isla stretched to the next platform. It was like the *Vanguard of the Firth* was keenly aware of her presence and wanted to do all it could to betray her. The wood scratched against her as she shuffled along, its splinters like teeth. The half-open gunports watched as she crept over them, their cannons waiting in the shadows. She was riding the back of a sleeping beast, and if it woke, it would surely devour her.

Eventually, she clambered onto the last platform. Shearwing hovered above her, flitting back and forth on its huge wings. Then it let out a squawk and swooped onto the edge of a balcony around the corner.

The Grand Admiral's quarters. It had to be.

Isla steadied herself on the edge of the platform and leapt. She sailed over the wooden railings and landed on the other side of the balcony with a painful thud, the air rushing from her lungs as she hit the deck.

A triumphant caw spilled from Shearwing's beak as she pushed herself to her feet. The balcony overlooked the *Vanguard's* stern, offering Isla a dizzying view of how high she'd climbed. Behind her stood two tall windows, diamond panes glittering in the sunset. In the middle of them was a set of reinforced double doors, their wooden frames thick and unyielding.

Isla pulled the handles, but nothing gave. "I suppose it was too much to hope he'd leave them unlocked." She turned instead to the windows and sent Shearwing a sidelong glance. "I've seen how sharp your beak is. Can you break through that glass for me?"

She didn't expect the bird to understand her, but all the same a knowing gleam danced in Shearwing's beady eyes. The razorbill fluttered from the balcony railing onto the wooden floor, its great webbed feet splayed as it hopped to the window. It drew back its curved neck, then jabbed with its white-striped beak.

Isla winced as the glass shattered. There would be others on board who'd heard it too. She didn't have much time.

She slipped through the hole, tucking her arms to avoid catching her skin on the broken shards still hanging from the frame. The setting sun cast the walls in a muted orange glow as she darted her head around the room, looking for where Eimhir's pelt might be hidden. The Grand Admiral's quarters brought the same strange sense of familiarity she'd felt back at the Admiralty Garrison. She'd recognised him in the sparse walls, the plain furnishings, the need to have sight over the waves. Now, she understood why. He was part of her. Somehow, on a level she couldn't bear to think about, she knew him.

Her eyes found a sturdy lockbox at the foot of the bed. The wood had been polished until it shone, and the iron hinges gleamed smugly at her in the fading light. No doubt this was locked too. And if the Grand Admiral had taken the key with him...

Isla remembered how his body snapped back under the force of the shot. How his blood spread across his chest, soaking his white shirt as he sank to the ground. Was it guilt she felt? Regret for the man she'd never known, the monster she'd never known was part of her?

She turned to the weapons stand near the Grand Admiral's desk. A double-barrelled musket. Twin pistols. The curved blade of a cutlass. And there, almost an afterthought, a small, spiked boarding axe.

Isla grabbed the axe from the rack and twirled it in her hand. It was not a weapon she was used to wielding. She didn't have Eimhir's wiry arms or brute strength. But she was no longer the human she'd thought she was. Her body could give her more now. She only hoped it would be enough.

She hurried to the lockbox and drove the axe into its lid with a wild swing. The spike crunched against the wood, biting deep. Isla tugged on the haft until it came free, then brought the axe back over her shoulder. Her muscles were still tight from the climb, but there was a reserve in them she'd never had before, a grit that urged her to keep going. She didn't need a key, not when she had brute force and desperation on her side.

The next time she brought the axe down, the wood around the hinges began to splinter. She was nearly through. A couple more hefty blows and—

"Put it down, Isla."

She stilled, hardly trusting herself to breathe. Out of the corner of her eye, she saw Lachlan edge into the room, bracing himself on his rosewood crutch with one hand.

He drew his mouth into a wry smile. "I suppose I shouldn't be surprised to find you here. It's just the kind of thing you would do. But how did you get in here without..." Isla watched the change in his expression as his eyes trailed over the folds of her pelt, the puddle of water forming at her feet. A sudden paleness drained his cheeks of colour. His gaze clouded in confusion, like he was seeing her for the first time.

"What is this?" he said, face ashen. "I don't understand."

"Perhaps it's better if you ask your friend Blair about that. Let him tell you the story of his uncle's rise to Grand Admiral, and all the rotten details along the way." Isla choked out a laugh. "Believe me, it makes for quite a tale."

He swallowed, eyes fixed on her pelt. "You're one of them. A selkie."

"I didn't know, Lachlan. Don't you think I would have..." She broke off, tasting bitterness on her tongue. "Strange, isn't it? It seems you're the true firstborn heir of Blackwood Estate after all. As for me, well..." She gestured to the fur around her shoulders. "Now I know why it never felt like home."

The silence between them hung thin and fragile, like it might shatter with the quietest breath. Lachlan's brow pulled into a frown as he stared at her, and *tides* did it hurt that she could still read so much of him in the small tells of his expressions. The pain and grief in the pinch of his mouth. The exhaustion paling his cheeks. The flicker in his eyes that almost looked like relief.

"It makes sense now," he said. "I never understood why you chose Eimhir over me, why you were willing to give up all we were fighting for. She was a stranger, and I was your brother, your blood." He shook his head, forcing a strained smile. "But I was never really your family, was I? No wonder you found it so easy to walk away."

His words rocked her like a blow. "You can't be so foolish as to believe that."

"No?" He glared at her, accusation flashing in his eyes. "From where I'm standing, it all seems clear. You're one of those things that killed our father. You always were."

A cold wave of grief stole the colour from Isla's cheeks. "What happened to our father was not my fault. I never wanted that. I never wanted any of this. If you think for a moment I could possibly hurt—"

"I don't know what you're capable of. Not anymore." He tightened one hand around the handle of his crutch. In the other, he lifted the shining barrel of a pistol.

Isla lowered the axe. "Are you going to shoot me, brother?"

"Are you going to make me?" He stepped closer, pistol trembling in his grip. "I don't want to do this, but I have my orders. I have a place here now. I can't let you take that pelt. It belongs to the Grand Admiral."

"It belongs to my *family*," Isla shot back.

Too late, she realised her mistake. She felt Lachlan flinch, saw the pallor settle across his scrunched, pained features.

"Leave, Isla," he whispered. "Before it's too late for both of us."

Isla glanced at the wooden lockbox. Through the hole she'd hacked in the lid, she caught a glimpse of speckled fawn fur. "You know I can't do that."

The click of the hammer echoed in her ears as Lachlan cocked the pistol.

"Then I'm sorry," he said.

Isla leapt forward, grabbing his arm and wrenching it into the air. The shot cracked off the ceiling and sent a shower of splinters down on them. Lachlan struggled, but she was on him too quickly, knocking him off balance as he fumbled with his crutch.

She wrapped her fingers around his and prised them away from the pistol. His skin was warm and dry to the touch as she fought him, the sensation odd and unfamiliar. As he pushed against her, she caught the heightened smell of damp wool and wax and soap from his clothes. The grunt from his throat sounded different to her ears. Had he always been this much of a stranger? Or had her selkie senses only widened the distance that had opened between them after all these years?

Isla tore the pistol from Lachlan's hand and threw it across the room. The gun hit the floor with a *thunk*, skittering along the timber. Without hesitating, Isla sent an elbow into her brother's stomach and watched as he stumbled on his crutch, crashing to the floor. The flash of anger and betrayal on his face sent a twinge through her chest. She'd hurt him enough already. This was nothing more than the sting of salt pressed into a raw wound.

She pushed aside the guilt and turned to the wooden lockbox. Eimhir's pelt lay nestled inside, its sandy tones bright against the shadows. Isla reached through the hole she'd smashed with the boarding axe and grabbed the fur. The soft folds seemed to beat within her hands as she pulled it free. She'd found it.

A bite of steel pressed against her neck, and she froze.

Lachlan had hauled himself upright, knuckles white as he grasped the handle of his crutch with one hand. In the other was the blade of his sgian dubh. Isla couldn't see its decorative hilt or pointed tip. She only felt its pressure against her throat.

"Do it then," she said, her voice laced with regret. "If I've hurt you so much, you'll be glad to be rid of me."

Lachlan said nothing, but the blade in his hand trembled against her neck. The slightest flinch from either of them would see blood spilling from her throat, covering the wooden floorboards in red. Maybe it was how this was always going to end. Maybe it was what she deserved after all she'd done to him.

"You saved my life twice with that sgian dubh," she said. "Would you really use it to kill me now?"

"You're a selkie." A strangled sound tore from Lachlan's throat. "Why shouldn't I?"

"Muir told me that blade belonged to my mother. He said it was meant to protect me, that he was glad it ended up in your hands."

A bitter smile twisted Lachlan's lips. "Whose mother? Mine, or yours?"

"Does it truly matter?"

All Isla heard was the echo of her unanswered question. It rang around the room, sharp and jarring. Then it faded, leaving behind only the hurt and regret that existed in the insurmountable waters separating her from Lachlan.

"I don't care whether or not you share my blood," she said. "You're my brother. Nothing could ever have changed that, apart from you."

The tension pulled taut between them, ready to snap and leave them both drifting. Then Lachlan buckled, tawny eyes shining as he pushed her away. "Go. Before I change my mind."

"Lachlan..."

"I said go." He let his arm drop, the sgian dubh's shining blade gleaming between his fingers. His face contorted as he adjusted the crutch under his arm. "If I kill you, I'll never be free of your shadow. All I can do now is let you go, like I should have done long ago."

Isla held the bundle of furs close, fighting the ache in her chest. If she didn't leave now, she never would. Perhaps it was too late to save her brother. But she could still save Eimhir.

She ducked through the broken window, gulping down the salt in the air, blinking away tears as the wind bit at her lungs. Over the other side of the balcony, the sea beckoned.

She glanced back at Lachlan through the crooked shards of glass. He was already beyond her reach, a ghost of her own making.

"All this time I thought I was the one who was lost," Isla said softly. "But it was never me, it was you. They were so concerned about giving me shelter that they left you out in the storm. I'm sorry for that. I'm sorry for everything."

If he answered, she didn't hear it. Instead, she filled her lungs with the wind and threw herself off the balcony to the leaping arms of the waves below, leaving her brother behind for the last time.

CHAPTER THIRTY-FOUR

Eimhir's pelt hung heavy between Isla's jaws, its fur dragging through the water as she pushed her hind flippers as hard as she could. The seabed dimmed under the setting sun, but her selkie eyes still spotted towering yellow ribbons of kelp, the angled wings of a skate skimming across the sand, the jagged spines of a sea urchin nestled among the rocks.

When Isla at last reached the shallows, she shed her pelt, skin tingling as the fur melted from her pores into its loose gathering of folds. She released Eimhir's pelt as her mouth shrank and became human again. Above her head, the glittering surface beckoned her to rise, and she filled her lungs with fresh air as she broke through.

Eimhir was lying where she'd left her, grey and unmoving on the pale sand. But she wasn't alone. Someone was kneeling over her, a water skin between their hands, splashing the liquid over Eimhir's face.

Darce.

He hadn't seen her yet. Isla watched him, her now-human heart hammering against ribs that seemed too fragile to contain it. His tousled hair spilled across his forehead as he leaned over Eimhir. His brow was deep and worried, his mouth set in a hard line. The sight of him tugged something deep beneath Isla's flesh and blood and bone, something she hadn't known existed until now. It thrummed like a second heartbeat under her skin. He had part of her soul now, or she had his. She could feel it as surely as she could feel the part of herself contained in the dappled pelt hanging around her shoulders.

Isla rose from the water, conscious of the way her soaking fur clung to her skin. A ripple of fear chased down her spine as she slowly waded onto the white shore.

Darce looked up, his face pallid. His eyes were dark and unblinking as he stared at her, betraying nothing. Then his gaze fell to the pelt.

"I can explain," Isla said breathlessly. "Let me—"

She didn't have time to finish. Darce closed the distance between them, crashing through the waves to pull her into a rough, desperate embrace. His warmth surrounded her, bringing heat to her cheeks, making her feel like she could melt into him. Tucked into the hollow of his chest, she could feel every breath from his lungs, every beat of the blood between his heart and hers.

"I didn't believe it was you," he said, pulling away. "Isla, I thought you were…"

She wrapped her hands around his leather vambraces, fingers white as she squeezed. "Eimhir was out of time. I had to help her. I had to…"

The fawn-coloured fur of Eimhir's pelt lay washed up on the sand, the waves lapping around it. Isla gathered it in her arms and hurried over to her, separating the folds as she ran. When she reached Eimhir's side, she fell to her knees, skin scratching against the sand as she pulled the pelt around Eimhir's salt-scarred shoulders.

"Tides, let it not be too late," she murmured. "Let her live."

She dug her arms under Eimhir's back and pulled her to the water. The waves washed over her, purple-blue and crystalline in the encroaching dusk. They sank into the speckled fur of her pelt, lapped at the bleeding scars across her skin. Was it a trick of the fading light, or was some of the salt falling away?

Isla waited. All she could hear was the hush of the waves, the whistle of the breeze nipping at her ears. Then came the slow yawn of a wave larger than the others, one that rose from the depths and washed over Eimhir's pale closed lids.

Her eyes opened. At first, Isla could only see their whites, wide and frantic under the water. Then they turned black, growing and bulging from Eimhir's face like glittering bubbles of ink.

Isla snatched her arms away from under Eimhir's spine and stepped back as she began to change. Her pelt spread over her arms, melting into her pallid skin and sprouting thick fur as it cascaded over her body. She rolled over and slipped deeper into the water, becoming a shadow below the surface.

After a moment, she re-emerged, her seal head bobbing through the waves. Isla met her eyes—not grey but a beady, shining black. She recognised Eimhir in those eyes, her selkie eyes.

"Where is she going?" Darce frowned as Eimhir disappeared under the water again. "Isn't she hurt?"

"More than either of us can imagine," Isla said. "But she needs to be out there. It's the only way she'll be able to start healing."

They stood with nothing between them but the tug of wind and the darkening sky. The waves brushed against Isla's bare shins as she buried her toes in the sand. Part of her yearned to go after Eimhir, to follow her into the sea and swim with her. But for the first time she could remember, the water was not the only thing calling to her.

Darce waded to her side, slipping his fingers under her chin to tilt her head towards his. Only a breath existed between them, begging to be closed. His gaze trailed over her lips, dark and desperate. Then he leaned in and pressed his mouth to hers, kissing her with a kind of hunger, a kind of need she'd never known. His tongue moved against hers, wanting and urgent. His shaking breaths brushed her skin every time they broke apart, filling her ears with their longing. Every touch sent a new kind of shiver racing across her skin, a new kind of warmth pooling in the pit of her stomach. She wanted to dissolve like the salty spray on the wind. She wanted to drown in him, and tides take anyone who tried to stop her.

Darce drew back, chest heaving. His pale cheeks had a flush to them, his brown eyes glittering with the same need that rose in Isla. "I thought I'd lost you. When I got here, I found Eimhir alone, half dead in the sand. Your cutlass and pistol lay scattered at her side, but you were nowhere to be seen. Then I saw the blood, and I lost all hope."

"The blood?"

"I found a trail across the sand." Darce gestured to the dunes, scattered with small puddles of red from Eimhir's wound. "I followed it to a crypt in the middle of the machair, but nobody was there. After that, I feared the worst."

Isla froze. "Nobody was there?" she repeated, her voice so thin she thought it might break. "You didn't find the Grand Admiral's body?"

"There was no body, only another bloody trail leading in the opposite direction. Leading towards the side of the island where the *Vanguard of the Firth* is docked." Darce rubbed his forehead. "I thought he took you. I thought he hurt you."

Memories flooded Isla's mind. The red stain across the Grand Admiral's chest. The way he'd crumpled to the floor. The pistol quaking in her grip. The remorse she couldn't make sense of.

"I hurt him," Isla said. "Or at least, I tried. That shot went clean through his ribs. How could he have possibly…" Her words disappeared in a rattling breath, their taste acrid on her tongue. He was still out there. The man who claimed to be her father. The monster who'd ripped a pelt from the selkie he loved, who'd hunted her kin to punish her for running from him.

"I thought I killed him," she said, voice cracking. "Now, he'll never stop. He'll come after me, Darce. He won't give up until he has me, not after what I took from him. Not after realising what I am, what I *truly* am."

"A selkie."

She met his eyes, fearful of what she might find there. But Darce's gaze held no revulsion. Only a calm, measured understanding. "You knew."

"I had my suspicions." He glanced at the waves. "When we first met Eimhir, she said she followed a trail of spilled blood to track us through the wilds. Auld blood. But I never suffered a scratch that night. All the blood covering me belonged to somebody else. But you..."

Isla's hand drifted to the back of her head. She remembered the selkie knocking her down, her skull cracking against the cobbles. "I was not the only one wounded that night. Lachlan bled worse than I."

"Lachlan wasn't clutching a letter from Lady Catriona telling him of a secret she needed to share," Darce said. "At first, I thought she meant to tell you that you were a sentinel. I hated that you wanted it to be true. You were desperate for some kind of purpose, and all I wanted to do was shield you from the fate it would bring you."

"It was a foolish hope," Isla said. "A bairn's hope. Pretending I had that kind of magic, wishing for it my whole life... I thought it would give me some kind of meaning."

"It might have." Darce took her hand, wrapping her icy fingers in his. "You said it yourself—all I wanted was to be your anchor. That's what it means to be a sentinel. But you needed more than that, more than I could give you. I knew there was something deeper in you than I could touch, something that called you to the water. That was when I realised you weren't a sentinel at all. You were a selkie."

"Yet you made the blood oath anyway."

"How could I not?" Darce said. "I never felt the call of the oath until you came back to Silveckan. You woke something inside me I could not run from, no matter how hard I tried."

He ran his hands up her arms, and her bare skin prickled under his touch. When he reached the place where her pelt fell across her shoulders, he hesitated, then buried his fingers into the fur.

Isla leaned in against the heat of his chest. Every part of her was shivering. Not from the chill of the water or the bite of the breeze, but from being this close to him. She could almost taste the warmth of his lips across the sliver of distance between them.

"Maybe you are made for waters I cannot follow you to," Darce murmured. "But that doesn't mean I'll give anything less than my life to keep you safe for as long as I can. You are the piece of my soul I was waiting for, Isla Blackwood. And now, it's yours. My soul, my heart, my life. If you had no need of an anchor, I would have been that wild wind you asked for. I would have been whatever you needed me to be."

He pressed his lips against hers. The kiss was soft, the deftest brush against her mouth. He tasted warm and sweet, and Isla knew the memory would linger on her lips long after he'd pulled away, long after they'd parted.

"Would have?" she said, throat thick with tears.

A surging wave crashed onto shore and Eimhir staggered out of the water, her dark blonde hair wet and bedraggled. Even with her pelt back around her, she still cut a wretched figure—her cheeks sallow and sunken, the angles of her bones protruding from her shoulders.

"More Admiralty ships on the horizon, approaching fast," she said, breathless. "We don't want to be here when they drop anchor, much as I'd like to see their shock when they realise their Grand Admiral is dead."

"He's not dead." Isla fought to keep the tremor from her voice. "Darce didn't find his body, only a trail of blood leading away from the crypt."

"But how..." Eimhir paled. "If he's alive... Isla, you know what he'll do. He won't let you or your pelt slip his net. He'll turn all the seas red to get you back. If you thought his slaughter of my people was bad enough already, it's nothing compared to what's coming."

"Then we run. We return to the *Jade Dawn* before it's too late and—"

"The *Jade Dawn* is gone," Darce said. "Nishi spotted the Admiralty ships through her spyglass shortly before I left. She allowed Kerr to bring me here on their second tender, but told me she couldn't wait for me to come back." He let out a long breath, his eyes dark as they surveyed the waves. "I cannot blame her. She's already lost too much in helping us."

"Gone?" Isla repeated, her voice hollow. "Then what are we to do?"

Something was wrong in the way Darce was looking at her. His gaze brimmed with regret, with a sorrow Isla felt like a shard of ice plunged into the depths of her chest.

"You run," he murmured. "Just like you said."

The stillness that followed his words seemed to halt time itself. All Isla felt was the pain behind her ribs, the burning of each breath. The echo of his voice muffled the crash of the waves and whistle of the wind. It didn't make sense. She didn't *want* it to make sense.

"We still have the tender I came across in," she said, pushing defiance into each word. "We could make south for Breçhon."

Darce let out a dry chuckle. "You might yet be a captain one day, but you cannot hope to sail a tender across these waters, much less outrun a convoy of the Admiralty's finest brigantines. If you are to escape, it must be in the water, not on it."

"And leave you here to die?" Isla retorted. "No, I won't do it."

"They won't kill me. I'm a sentinel, remember?" Darce grimaced. "My life still has value to the Admiralty. They'll want to take me alive. But you're a selkie. If you're still here when the Grand Admiral's reinforcements arrive—"

"It's worse than that, auld blood," Eimhir said. "She's not just a selkie. She's his *daughter*. That brute hunted my people for decades because my aunt chose to surrender herself to the sea rather than sacrifice her child to his grasp." She turned to Isla. "We must run. Now he knows who you are, he'll stop at nothing to get you back. To get your pelt back."

Isla scrunched her hand into the damp fur of her sealskin—her mother's sealskin. "You should have taken it. It should have been yours."

"It was never mine to take," Eimhir said. "You must be the one to bring it to our clan. We need you, caraid. You can't let him win, not after all Mara did to save you."

Darce glanced between them, face ashen. "She's right. Everything you've done these last few weeks was to retrieve that pelt from the Grand

Admiral's clutches. If you stay here, it will all be for nothing. You have to go."

"Not if it means leaving here without you."

Darce sighed. "Stubborn to the last, wolf cub. I should have known you'd give me no choice."

He moved his arm to his belt, wrapping his fingers around a pistol that was all too familiar to Isla.

Without thinking, her hand drifted to her waist and closed around empty air. She had no belt, only the grey lengths of fur that hung over her body. She'd left her pistol on the shore when she'd gone into the water.

Now, it was in Darce's hand.

Isla's stomach turned cold. The wood of the polished stock gleamed in the dying light. The mother-of-pearl casing winked at her from his side like there was some kind of jest at play.

Darce gave a pained smile. "You always did say you preferred pistols."

The words spilled from his mouth, a half-murmured apology lingering in the breath of them. For a moment, Isla couldn't speak. Her voice dried up, turning her tongue to ash.

"What are you doing?" she whispered.

"Helping you choose." He lifted the pistol into the air, barrel glinting as he pointed it at the orange-streaked sky. "Dozens of Admiralty soldiers will have already started scouring this island. When they hear the shot, they'll come for us. If you want to save Eimhir, if you want to save your people, you better be gone before they get here."

Anger rose in Isla's chest. "You expect me to leave you so easily? What about the blood oath?"

"It's only because of the blood oath that I have the strength to let you go." Darce's eyes glittered. "You have my soul, Isla. No matter where you go, there is no stretch of water vast enough to keep me from you. If tides be kind, we'll find our way back to each other."

"Don't say that," Isla snapped, desperation cutting through each word. "I am through with letting the fucking tides decide the course of my life. I'm *choosing* to stay. I'm choosing you."

Darce looked like he might break. Something wretched flashed across his face, twisting his expression into a wound that clawed at Isla's heart. Then it was gone, and all she saw was the resolve in his gaze.

He pulled back the hammer, and the pistol cocked with the sound of betrayal. "Forgive me."

The shot cracked through the air. Its sting echoed through Isla's ears, irrevocable. Somewhere in the distance, she heard the clamour of voices raised in alarm.

"We have to go." Eimhir slipped her hand into Isla's, her palm rough from the salt scars. "Please, caraid. Mara's pelt—your pelt—is our only chance of one day stopping the gun-anam. We can't lose you. *I* can't lose you."

Isla glanced back at Darce. His hand trembled around the pistol—around *her* pistol, which was hers no more. She couldn't take it where she was going. She couldn't take him either. That was a truth he'd come to terms with before she did. A truth that stung all the more now she understood it.

"I would have stayed with you, if you'd let me," she whispered.

As she turned away, the wind whistled, drowning out anything he might have said in reply. Perhaps that was for the best. Anything he said now would only drive the blade deeper. She had bled enough already.

The sea stretched out in front of her, waiting. Isla took a breath, then squeezed the callused hand beneath hers and allowed Eimhir to lead her home.

EPILOGUE

They swam through the night, pausing only for fleeting bouts of sleep. It was a wonder to Isla that her new body could hover under the surface without sinking as she rested, how her nostrils and ears knew to close against the sea while she slept.

Perhaps it shouldn't have been such a surprise. This was where she belonged.

In the morning, she chased Eimhir through the water as dawn broke. The fragmented glitter of the surface was like a mosaic above her, a veil across a world she wasn't sure she wanted to go back to, even if she could.

Maybe you are made for waters I cannot follow you to. The echo of Darce's words filled her ears, their memory a painful clutching at her heart. Leaving him had left a shadow on her soul, an ache that refused to relent. She hadn't been prepared for how deep the pain sank, how bitterly its edge cut. It dug under her skin like a blade, paring her to the bone as it twisted.

You have my soul, he'd told her.

She had to believe that. She had to trust that whatever bond had been forged between them on the deck of the *Jade Dawn* was more than a broken oath, a promise unfulfilled.

She'd found her way back to him once when the sea separated them. She would do so again.

After a time, Eimhir turned her bulbous black eyes towards her and let out a low-pitched whistle.

Follow me, it seemed to say.

The seabed swept by as they shot through the ever-brightening water. Isla caught glimpses of cod and pollock flitting between ribbons of kelp. She felt their timid movements in her whiskers, and her empty stomach growled at her to give chase. But Eimhir was rising now, propelling herself towards the surface. Isla adjusted the angle of her body to follow, trailing through Eimhir's wake to come crashing through the waves.

A small skerry rose in front of them, its granite face covered in gull shite and molluscs clinging to the rock. Eimhir hauled herself from the water, pelt melting from her skin as she slipped into human form and landed deftly on the overhanging ridge. Isla did so with less grace. Her seal belly thumped over the rock before she shed her pelt, leaving her to pick herself off the wet surface as the soaking fur shrank across her skin.

When she could speak again, she asked, "Why did we stop? There doesn't look like there's anything else out here for miles."

Eimhir lowered herself onto a slab, stretching her bare legs. Her pale skin still bore the traces of salt, the scars red and angry. "We're far enough from the Admiralty that we can afford to rest for a moment. If we go much further, we'll be entering into the territory of my clan. Once we do this, there's no turning back."

Isla brushed her hand over the sodden folds of her pelt. The subtle tones of morning grey and dappled black shifted under the sunlight, the colours rippling against each other. This tug pulling her towards the open water—it was her soul calling to her. This was the part of herself she'd been missing.

"I resented my mother for so long," she said, throat constricting around the words. "She never seemed to understand. Now I see she understood all too well. She took me in knowing what I truly was, and at the end, she tried to make things right."

Eimhir squeezed her hand. "She brought you back to Silveckan with her last words. She helped you find what was lost. The pelt is yours, Isla.

It always was. But now you've claimed it, you are bound to it like any other selkie. Lose your pelt, and the part of you that is human won't be enough to save you."

A sharp gust of wind swirled around the skerry, its teeth trailing across Isla's skin and snarling at her hair. Across the waves, the clouds hung low on the horizon. Another storm coming. One she couldn't escape, even if she wanted to.

"The Grand Admiral will come for it," she said. "I *know* him, tides take me. He won't stop until he takes it back, takes *me* back. And when he does..."

Fear trickled down Isla's spine, bringing with it memories she wished she could forget. Mist turning her skin to ice, the chill bleeding into her bones. The brackish breath of the dead on her cheek. Spray singing in her ears, mingled with the watery clap of hooves on cobbles.

The gun-anam had never terrified her more now that she knew how easily she might become one.

Isla wrapped her furs tighter, seawater trickling down her skin. "What happens now?"

Eimhir rose to her feet, scattering droplets of water as her hair flew in the wind. "I fulfil my promise to my clan. I bring them the pelt they tasked me with finding." She offered Isla her salt-scarred hand, a crooked smile tugging at the corner of her lips. "I bring you home."

Home. The word nestled in Isla's heart, touching a part of her she hadn't realised was so deeply buried. "I think... I think I'd like that."

She joined her palm against Eimhir's. The cold beat of blood pulsed between them, separated only by skin and salt.

"You don't have to do this alone," Eimhir said. "I'll be here to help you, caraid. We're family. We always were."

The last thing Isla saw was the stretch of her smile. Then Eimhir was gone, the sandy tones of her speckled fur spreading across her shoulders as she disappeared beneath the waves once more.

Isla stepped forward. The jagged granite ridge of the skerry fell away, yielding to the open water. She stared through the shimmering surface to a world below she couldn't imagine, one that had been kept from her for so long.

Come, cousin.

The voiceless whisper came from below the waves, like the song of the sea itself.

Isla pulled her pelt around her. Below, the depths waited to welcome her into their arms. She filled her lungs with salt and spray, ready to leap.

The sea called to her, and she answered.

AFTERWORD

Thank you for reading! If you enjoyed Sea of Souls, please help other people discover the book by leaving a review on Amazon or Goodreads. Word of mouth is so important for independent authors and helps more books like this get written!

Want to see what's in store next? Sign up for my author newsletter for exclusive updates, sneak peeks and release news!
https://bit.ly/scrimscribes

You can keep up to date with future releases by visiting ncscrimgeour.com and signing up for my newsletter, or by following me on Facebook, Twitter, Instagram and TikTok at @scrimscribes.

Also By N. C. Scrimgeour

A dying planet. A desperate mission. A crew facing impossible odds. Humanity's last hope lies with them...

Time is running out for the people of New Pallas. Nobody knows that better than Alvera Renata, a tenacious captain determined to scout past the stars with nothing but a handpicked crew and a promise: to find a new home for humanity.

But when a perilous journey across dark space leads to first contact with a galactic civilisation on the brink of war, Alvera soon realises keeping her word might not be as easy as she thought.

Her only hope lies with the secrets of the ancient alien waystations scattered across the galaxy. The mysterious technology could be the key to humanity's survival—or bring unwanted attention from the long-forgotten beings who built them....

<u>The Waystations Trilogy</u>
Those Left Behind
Those Once Forgotten
Those Who Resist

Ingram Content Group UK Ltd.
Milton Keynes UK
UKHW012002130723
425104UK00004B/35